THE CITY BEYOND

THE CITY BEYOND

LUCILLE EMERICK

CUTTING EDGE

ISBN-13: 978-1-962896-69-6

Published by
Cutting Edge Books
PO Box 8212
Calabasas, CA 91372
www.cuttingedgebooks.com

CHAPTER ONE

G rant Monroe had accomplished in the year eighteen hundred and ninety-five nearly all he intended. At the age of thirty-three, he had acquired the stature and independence of considerable wealth, and was accorded the social position that goes with success in market operations. All this was incidental, however, to the singleness of purpose that originally brought him to St. Louis from the Cuban plantation he inherited at the death of his father. The course he then elected to follow deprived him of much he had learned to value, a peace he sought, a happiness, and a way of life to which he could never again aspire. Yet he weighed the loss against probable gain, and was satisfied.

Most men have two sides to their natures. Monroe had three, one which faced the world with equivocal self-possession, that other implacable inner self he held to be the real core of his being, and the dormant shadow of a man unknown to him. It was this unacknowledged identity that finally emerged to betray him and ultimately drove him back to the solitude of the plantation, much as a person gone into another room for a certain article might forget the object of his errand and return to his starting point in the hope of prodding his memory.

He sat on the screened veranda of the plantation house and slowly reread a letter recently arrived in the mail from the States. The plunging rain that whipped into the deserted cane ditches was a fit companion for his tight-lipped mood. But neither the weather nor the seething unrest in nearby Havana occupied his attention. Like others accustomed to the tropical climate, he accepted the heavy rains that laced the island with sodden humidity from April to November as an unavoidable evil. The political uprising was in his opinion a private affair between the Cubans and Spain, long brewing and requiring only the recent economic collapse to flare into violence. Unlike most Americans, he was neutral toward both the insurrectos and the government. Being American, he had escaped the nightly raids of the guerrilla bands which Maximo Gomez employed to harass the loyalists. And being disinterested, it was improbable that he would be drawn into the situation by either side.

With a frown he put the letter aside and reached for a cigarette on the table by his elbow. There had been no logical reason to leave St. Louis at this time, he acknowledged moodily. Juan, the taciturn overseer whose competence was unequaled on the island, conducted the seasonal activities of the estate with reliable thoroughness. The last of the cane had been cut months ago and dragged by oxcart to the *central,* and the blacks who came for harvest labor had returned to Jamaica. The long line of low-slung barracks was empty except for the permanent quarters where the regular hands were housed. The planting was done, and the ratoon crops cultivated.

He stared at the wilted cigarette in his hand, asking himself for the hundredth time why he had returned. He had business in St. Louis, business that had already waited too long. Harlan Jenkins had nibbled the carefully prepared bait, and years of work were about to pay dividends. The fat, heavy-jowled investment broker was eager for a share in the easy money that glittered provocatively in the imminent future. After that it was merely a question of time until the past caught up with him.

And yet Grant Monroe's thoughts were not on Harlan Jenkins. He lit a cigarette and tossed the match, still burning, into a tray littered with broken stubs. St. Louis had soured to his taste, he told himself irritably. The absorbing bitterness had lost its tang. He needed time to think; he had to revive his enervated sensibilities.

A huge gray tomcat sidled across the floor and began to caress his leg with a throaty purr. His frown deepened, and he sent it sprawling with the toe of his boot. He disliked cats, and the estate abounded with them. The tom collected himself indifferently and padded off to the other side of the veranda where he sat watching the man with great, expressionless eyes.

"Nita!" he called impatiently, mashing the cigarette on top of the heaped stubs. "Nita, come here and get this cat!"

The girl appeared at the door almost at once and came onto the veranda with a smile. By virtue of being Juan's daughter and because she desired the post, Nita had for the past several years been accorded the status of housekeeper. If the place was not spotless, it was at least presentable. Grant was aware that Nita was unpopular with the older servants, most of whom mistrusted the swift flow of her interchanging moods and resented the intensity of her dark, young beauty. With the unself-conscious poise of her imperious bearing, she presented a sharp contrast to the others whose large families and menial work had long since robbed them of the spirited buoyancy of youth. Her marriage the previous spring to one of Gomez' lieutenants might have been an excuse to hire an older woman for housekeeping duties, but Grant had been away at the time. And recently, since the young insurrecto had the misfortune to be captured and imprisoned by the Spaniards, life at the plantation went on virtually unchanged.

"*Si*, Señor Grant," she said, going over to the tom and picking him up. "You do not like cats, I know. I try to keep them away when you are home, but they come in out of the rain."

She addressed him in English, though his Spanish was as fluent as her own. She had been nine when he began to teach her his tongue, partly to divert himself from the daily monotony and partly because she was always underfoot and the language lessons kept her occupied. An apt pupil, she had applied herself with passionate intensity, listening in rapt attention as he spoke of life in the States. Her eagerness led him to spend more time with her than he would have otherwise and she, delighted by his slightest word of praise, always spoke to him in the medium of her lessons.

"My father says the cats do much good," she went on, holding the animal, "They kill the field rats that come into the barns."

He watched with an expression of distaste as she fondled the creature. "Toss him outside," he said disagreeably. "He'll not drown."

She continued to smile, and the strong white teeth gleamed against full, red lips. "*Si*, Señor Grant. He will go now and find himself a dry place in the stables." She opened the screen and deposited the cat on the step. "He can take care of himself, that one."

Grant regarded her with detached appraisal as she straightened and stood with her back to the screen. The resemblance to the angular youngster who once dogged his footsteps was gone. Thin as a hungry bird then, her face had been a small, pale oval, the black hair sleek across the top of her head and twisted in two long braids that dangled down the back of her faded cotton dresses. Now her hair was brushed free and caught at the nape of the neck with a yellow ribbon. The bright yellow of her dress was striped with vivid green, and the low bodice clung to the swell of soft, young breasts. The face was cool and pale, but the eyes pulsed with vibrant warmth and the red mouth was soft in the ivory smoothness of her skin. Nita, in her native intelligence and clear beauty, had become a woman.

She moved about the plantation with an instinctive grace, the more flagrantly provocative because it was a natural expression of the fullness of life flowing in her veins. Grant was inadvertently reminded of the time he had come upon her in the embrace of one of the field hands. Though she had torn herself away in a torrent of denunciation against the man, he knew there had been response in the arch of her body and a warm, answering pressure of arms and lips. He had sharply reprimanded the man and had taken her, weeping profusely, back to the house. Later he had suggested to Juan that the girl might be happier away from the plantation, perhaps in the States with an aunt who lived in New York.

"She will not leave," Juan had stated simply. "This is home to her, señor. And she waits for the insurrectos to manage the release of Pedro Ortiz. She would not be content away from the island."

Grant had shrugged. It was, of course, none of his affair. "From now on," he said with unrelieved impatience, "keep those cats out of the house."

Her smile vanished. "You are worried about something," she said soberly, taking a fresh ashtray from another table and exchanging it for the one at his elbow. "You are not like yourself these days. This morning when I straighten your room, I find things here, there, everywhere. You are angry, I think. Always now you throw things, and frown. And smoke all the time."

"How do you know I throw things?" he demanded. "Have you been listening at doors?"

"Oh no, Señor Grant!" she exclaimed quickly. "But one can hear without listening."

He regarded her with an uncompromising stare and her sultry eyes warmed as they met his. They reminded him of another pair of eyes, vivid in their flashing depths, and the muscles of his face stiffened imperceptibly. The recollection was like a sharpened blade, driving him deeper within himself, intensifying the edge of his irritability. A feeling of desperation drove him to his feet.

"I'm going out," he said abruptly. "You needn't stay this afternoon. I'd advise you to leave for the cottage before the roads are worse."

He went bareheaded into the rain, slamming the door behind him. Bright anger flushed her cheeks as she watched him go, his long stride carrying him effortlessly down the road and out of sight. Her body trembled as she thought heatedly how stupid he was, this Grant Monroe. Not stupid, of course, like Pedro, who could think of nothing but leading rebels in their reckless forays against the Spaniards. Pedro, with his visionary dreams of a free Cuba, who left a woman alone in the night to slip out to sea and guide in boats loaded with smuggled arms and gunpowder.

She had missed Pedro at first when he did not return to her at all. She had even cried a little, thinking of the inhumanities of the *reconcentrado* camps if the Spaniards did not execute him at once as a traitor. But this was the fortune of war, was it not?

And Pedro was never the man she knew Grant Monroe to be. As long as she could remember, Grant was the object of her enraptured dreams. For the brief year he attended a seminary in the States, she had reluctantly put away those dreams. Then his father's death, the result of the ravages of fever on a body weakened by years of hard work in a tropical climate, had struck at the invisible core of the man. Grant Monroe turned his back on a life of self-abnegation and religious devotion to return to the practical pursuits of the world, and Nita's secret hopes began to live again.

But not for her had he renounced the sober habiliments of the religious order to which he had been committed. She came to realize this eventually, though she was never quite reconciled. Only at rare intervals did she see him, for he spent most of his time thereafter in St. Louis. Nevertheless her heartbeat quickened and the rich blood flowed warmer in her veins when she was near him. She knew his moods and pleasures, and even as a child she had sensed that he lived within himself for some deep, inscrutable purpose of his own. She knew too with a baffled, angry resentment that the strength in him would drive him to the accomplishment of that purpose, whatever it was.

On his latest arrival at the plantation, she had been quick to detect the change in him, the gnawing restlessness and uncertainty. This was the work of a woman, she thought vehemently with the unerring instinct of her sex.

She turned back to the room and her glance fell on the letter he had been reading. Impulsively she went to the table to examine the thin pages with their long, slanting script. It was not a love note, she discovered. Much was meaningless to her but she went through it assiduously, eager to uncover any scrap of information about his life in the States.

St. Louis, August 2, 1895

My dear Grant,

Your sudden and unexplained departure came as a surprise to me, though I realize now I might have anticipated something of the sort. One who has known you as I have could not fail to observe that recent quick-tempered moodiness, so at variance with your normally controlled character and rigidly disciplined emotions.

The plan you chose to follow in St. Louis was your own, but I can't help feeling a measure of responsibility. Whether or not you could have been dissuaded, I do not know. I've often thought it better had you not chanced to see me that day on the avenue. Even as you called, instinct bade me to hurry away. Then I recognized you and my incredulous delight swept away every other consideration. That bleak year of your father's disappearance and the succeeding years of silence fell away like the ghosts of a bad dream. Yet I think I was prepared for what you were to tell me. Your eyes held the truth even before you spoke of the fever that took his life, the climate and arduous work. My bitterness and yours inevitably joined hands as we remembered what had been lost in the past.

Later I was able to think more clearly. I tried to prevail upon you to return to Cape Girardeau as your father would have wished, but without success. When I saw you would not go back, I lent my support to the design you had in mind, encouraging you with more sincerity, I fear, than wisdom. Because of a sense of guilt which will not be denied and because I could not be more attached to you were you my own son, I am writing now with this unaccustomed frankness.

You were always very dear to your father, and he hoped for your happiness above all things. You will remember as a boy in St. Louis his integrity, his understanding and deep, human sympathy. I cannot believe these qualities changed in the years of his exile. He would not have wanted you to continue at the Seminary if that life was wrong for you, but he must have meant you to find an inner peace and sustaining strength there among those who were dedicated to the service of God. My own Methodist upbringing is a long way off now, and even further removed from the creed to which you have been educated. But I know your father's profound feeling for his church and from him I learned its power to touch the heart and fire the imagination. When you left the retreat at Cape Girardeau, you did not, as you thought, sever yourself completely from the influence of those teachings. You will never be able to do that. The truths you learned from boyhood will always be with you. They will warn you to forget the mistakes and injustices that once touched our lives, to live among men without bitterness and contempt. No one can change what has already been done. There remains only the present and the future, and the opportunity to use them for happiness or for regret. The wisdom of the choice must lie with you. But I beg you to decide where your happiness lies, then follow that course regardless of other considerations.

In closing, I should mention that I met Theodora Jenkins on the street this morning. She told me that she will return to Vienna this fall to continue her music with Tagliev, but perhaps you know this. I am always uncomfortable about these accidental encounters with her, as you can readily understand. Since the peculiar circumstance which brought us together when I was abroad last year, Theodora takes a certain friendship for granted. However, I shall hope that an awkward situation can be avoided.

Trusting that this finds you in good health and that you will see your way clear to return soon, I am devotedly yours,

LILY OLANDT

Nita flung the letter aside. The reference to Grant's precipitate departure dovetailed ominously with the pointed mention of this person who was to return to Vienna. She had been right, she thought furiously. A passionate hatred seized her as she thought of the woman with the long, strange name, hatred for the beauty she must have and for the lovely ways that would ensnare a man like Grant Monroe. She could kill a woman like that, she thought intensely.

Then she drew back, frightened by the violence of her emotions. *Madre de Dios,* what nonsense was that? There were other ways for a woman, surer ways. Grant was here now. He had come home to forget that one in St. Louis, this she knew. And forget her he would.

CHAPTER TWO

Grant walked aimlessly, oblivious to the rain and the mud which sucked at his boots with each step. He went as far as the central, then past the newly planted acres which had been pastured the last few years, fields which had yielded the first crops of cane for his father. Continuing on to the junction, he picked up the last mail, a sheaf of advertisements and circulars from firms in the States. The afternoon was spent when he returned, his clothing soaked through to the skin. And waiting for him at the house, a small apron tied over the spraying yellow of her skirt, was Nita.

"The cook had to leave," she explained quickly, seeing his frown. "Because there was no one to prepare dinner for you, I stayed."

"You should have gone to the cottage," he said impatiently. "The mud is deeper now."

"It is not bad," she demurred. "I am accustomed to it."

After he had shaved and dressed, he sat down to the meal she had waiting for him. Tired muscles relaxed, bringing the belated warmth of physical well-being, but there was no lessening of the mental tension that had been with him since his arrival.

"Where is Juan?" he asked as he finished a second coffee and she hovered nearby, removing dishes and smoothing the table cover.

"He has gone to move the cattle," she told him. "The rain has flooded the ditches in the south pasture."

"When he gets back, I want to see him. I've decided to take the morning boat back to the States."

He did not notice the consternation in her face or the sudden stiffening of her body. "You return so soon?" she asked. "You have been here only a few weeks!"

"Isn't that long enough?" he remarked with a quizzical smile. "My disposition what it is, I should imagine you'd want to be rid of me."

But she was thinking rapidly, He cannot go now. He must stay here until he has forgotten her. Aloud she said, steadying her voice on an impersonal level: "It is not right for you to leave. There are problems here, and my father will need you to advise him. The repairs to the barns, the buying of oxen, the drainage of ditches ..."

"I've been over all that with him," he interrupted. "Juan can manage as well when I'm gone."

"But if there is trouble with the raiders?" she suggested on a note of desperation. "Many cane fields and barns have been burned."

"I doubt there will be trouble here," he said tolerantly, both annoyed and amused by her arguments. "Your father has a knowledge of insurrecto activities, and he is assured that Gomez will do nothing to lose the good will of the Americans. If there were reason to stay, I would. But there isn't."

Her full lips pouted and the expressive eyes darkened. "You are in the States all the time," she said with passionate suddenness. "Why do you not stay here in the home that is yours?"

His face changed curiously as the irony of her words struck his consciousness. Home here where his father had started a new life twenty years ago? No. Nor was it the exclusive club where he resided in St. Louis. Unconsciously his thoughts went to a house on the edge of the city, a quiet dwelling that stood with imposing dignity on a wide, elm-shaded lawn, the clean, tall pillars of its portico gleaming against the dark red of its brick walls.

He stood up abruptly, and his face was hard. "Give Juan my message," he said curtly, "and be sure you leave for the cottage before dark."

Her heart beat wildly as she watched him go into the next room. "*Si,*" she said in a swift, intense undertone. "I shall tell him."

He went into the living room and took one of his father's books from the shelf. There were times when reading occupied a mind that otherwise refused to relinquish its hold on an exhausted body. His eyes followed the printed pages until after he heard Nita go out. Then, unable to carry on the pretense, he flung the book aside and drew his legs up on the sofa. He no longer fought the thing that was a consuming sickness within him. The image of a woman sprang to life in his tired brain, and all the hatred he summoned against Harlan Jenkins, all the bitter contempt and ruthlessness he had nurtured through years of planning and studied effort, could not erase it.

Had he known Theodora Jenkins in those early days when he repudiated the promptings of a dormant inner self, he could have put her aside quietly and with a natural firmness. There was a time at the Seminary when he had almost won the calmness and strength to carry him across the threshold. Now all that was changed.

The shattering effect of his father's death had left him with the unalterable conviction that a job remained to be done. The inner self awoke with throbbing insistence and he knew he would have no rest until he saw the task accomplished. His only obligation now was its completion. But there had been a price exacted. He had become vulnerable, a prey to conflict, imperfections, and doubts. The realization was not new to him, and it brought him small satisfaction. Nor was he comforted by the thought that between his world and Theodora's lay the irreconcilable barrier of his affair with Harlan. Wearily he closed his eyes. The self-discipline and concentrated endeavor of his appointment with the past escaped him then in the one enveloping thought of this woman.

He did not know how long he slept. An odd feeling that he was not alone brought him out of his restless dreaming. The rain was still slashing against the roof and pouring down the gutters. One lamp burned on the table across the room, its dim glow a feeble circle of light against the surrounding darkness. Nita stood in the shadows, her wet hair clinging in ringlets to her face. For the brief span of an instant, her features merged with the image in his brain, and the surge of his blood was swift and warm in his veins. Then he was fully awake, and he sprang up.

"Nita!" he exclaimed angrily. "What are you doing here at this hour?"

Her words came in a breathless rush: "I was afraid. Please do not be so angry with me. My father sent word he is staying the night at the central, and I am alone in the cottage."

"You're alone?" he demanded. "Where are the servants?"

"There's only Maria, and she sleeps so soundly nothing can wake her. I could not bear to be there in the storm. And tonight … tonight I was frightened. I heard a noise and I ran out. You cannot ask me to go back, not now," she finished on a pleading note, coming close to him.

Her cloak fell open and he saw the pale gleam of shoulders and the rising swell of her breasts beneath the transparent film of a night garment. The fever that had burned in his blood for days leaped to life, and he heard the sound of his breathing above the driving rain, harsh and strange in the quiet of the room. She saw the change in his expression, and the beat of her heart quickened.

Now he would forget her, the woman who twisted his thoughts so cruelly. She, Nita, would make him forget. Softly her arms circled his neck and she swayed against him.

"You little fool!" he said roughly, disentangling her arms and pinning them to her sides in a bruising grip. "You don't know what you're doing!"

Pain mingled with ecstasy and her face raised, her lips seeking his. "Grant *querido*," she murmured caressingly, her warm mouth moist against his unyielding lips.

His face was gray in the shadows. The same delusion that had absorbed him before seized his imagination and he was unable to turn away. Not Nita's but another woman's lips touched his in the dim silence of the deserted plantation house, another woman's face lay against his own, another woman's presence filled the room.

CHAPTER THREE

T he dream flashed like a strong white flame and was gone. He thrust her aside with a sudden savage strength, and she sat down abruptly on the sofa. "You can sleep here," he muttered indistinctly. "In the morning I'll take you back to the cottage."

He went out into the darkness and rain, oblivious to her look of speechless anger and humiliation. Driven by his own bitter thoughts, he walked quickly along the familiar black roads. His tireless stride carried him in a wide arc about the estate, but there was no escape from the devils that rode his heels.

The first gray lifting of night brought a respite from the rain. He came within sight of the plantation house again and paused. The wet pillars glistened dimly in the pale light, beckoning with derisive mockery. With an abrupt sense of discovery, he realized that the familiar walls were no longer the haven of retreat he once had known. The customary hospitality of the grounds, of the island itself, had ceased to be a reality for him. He was being shut out, silently, blandly, inexorably. He had alienated himself from this world, and there was no turning back. He thought about the Seminary, but it too was a part of his life that had been cut away when he had walked back into the glittering avenues and obscure bystreets of St. Louis. Cape Girardeau was only a memory now, the almost forgotten ambition of a youth reaching for an ideal with which to blot out the face of an intolerable reality. His father, he remembered with fleeting intensity, had entertained strong hopes for his graduation at the theological institute. But to the restless and troubled young man, the mission school had been a means of escape, an escape which in the end eluded him. The lines about his mouth tightened. He had known then what was to be done and he knew now.

He returned to the house to find Nita asleep on the sofa, her mackintosh drawn up over her shoulders, one arm upflung with a small, limp hand resting on the mass of black hair, the full lips parted slightly in the appealing softness of a child's. The memory of her ardor hardened the anger within him, and his face was uncompromising in the growing light. Nita had always been a strange child, running wild with but little supervision from old Maria, the nurse. He should have known the woman she had become and the recklessness of the unbridled spirit that rode her feelings. She had been aware of what she was about last night. He remembered Juan and Pedro Ortiz, and his expression became austere. Juan must be convinced that this was no place for Nita. The lonely life at the plantation was unsuited for a young woman and, other considerations aside, her safety was threatened if and when the insurrection spread. She would be out of danger in New York with her aunt and would have much to occupy her mind that she lacked here.

Nita lay motionless, pretending sleep and watching him through long, tangled lashes. He had not forgotten the fever that drove him into those dark moods, her heart told her. He could not forget that other woman even with Nita in his arms. The thought of his nearness was still an intoxication to her senses and her hand stirred unconsciously, impelled by a desire to touch the cool cheek and smooth lips that had pressed against his.

Grant saw the incomplete movement and his face became inscrutable. He went to the sofa and shook her gently. "Nita, it's morning."

She opened her eyes and a slow smile curved her mouth. "Grant," she murmured lazily, her lips caressing the word.

"You don't understand, Nita," he said with a slight frown. "I'm taking you back to the cottage now."

She sat up and began rearranging her hair. "But I shall prepare breakfast for you," she demurred with a quiet obstinacy. "Coffee, strips of bacon ..."

"The servants will be all over the place in an hour," he interrupted firmly. "They'll know you spent the night here, and there will be talk."

"Servants and talk do not matter," she replied with a little shrug of annoyance.

"They matter more than you seem to realize," he retorted. "But there is time if we go now."

She stood up and quick tears sprang to her eyes. "You are sorry I came last night," she accused him. "You do not care about Nita."

Her eyes implored him, and in spite of himself he was moved. "Come," he said in a gentler tone, taking her cloak and placing it about her shoulders, "we'll go the short way and reach the cottage before Maria finds you gone." Then, because the trembling mouth and widened eyes were again those of the solitary child who had grown up on the plantation, he bent and kissed her forehead.

"Your trip to the States?" she asked, emboldened by this small concession. "You do not go today?"

"I told you my plans," he said quietly. "I intend to drive to Havana with your father as soon as he returns." He saw the threatening storm that gathered anew in her eyes and added: "It might be wise if you leave too, for a time at least. With conditions as unsettled as they are, I don't think you should remain at the plantation."

"I shall be with you?" she asked, electrified by the overwhelming possibilities of the idea.

"No," he explained quickly. "But you can go to the States. You might visit your aunt in New York, where you will have advantages that you are denied here."

This was so far from what she expected that she was stunned. But he went on to describe in glowing terms the life that awaited her, and she listened with growing calmness. All was not hopeless. He had made plans for her, and for that she was glad. He wanted her to go to her aunt's, perhaps that she might learn to talk and act like the expensively gowned women in the great cities. And her knowledge of geography being what it was, she saw a further advantage in the plan. If Grant insisted upon returning to St. Louis, then she would go to New York where she could be near him!

"I shall go," she agreed with more enthusiasm than he had hoped. "My father will be happy too, I think."

Later that day, as he sat beside Juan in the surrey that took him to Havana, he spoke of sending Nita to the States.

"You talked with her about this?" Juan frowned. "She does not object?"

"She does not object," Grant assured him. "She seemed rather pleased with the idea, I thought."

Juan was silent for a time. She would be safe in New York, this child who was all he had. There were matters about which he had not spoken to Grant, ominous warnings that the island would be torn by a long and bloody war. Great quantities of arms arrived each night with promises of more to come, and many new recruits flowed daily to the army of Maximo Gomez. The insurrectos could not hope to hold a government of their own without a bitter struggle or without help from the Americanos. And with the coming of war, would it not be better for Nita in New York?

"The journey can be arranged," he said finally. "I shall secure passage for her on the boat to New York."

CHAPTER FOUR

G rant Monroe delayed several days in New Orleans, looking after matters pertaining to shipping schedules and trading contracts. When at length he returned to St. Louis, the paralyzing lethargy of the past month was gone. The familiar sight of wharves, warehouses, and crowded waterfront traffic was like an injection of virulent elixir in his veins, and the city again held its old meaning for him. He smiled thinly. He had not changed. The same driving determination that brought him here after his father's death drew him now. Nothing, he thought narrowly, could remain in his way or cause him to alter his course until his purpose was accomplished.

He went directly to his club where he glanced through his accumulated mail, then turned his attention to the afternoon newspaper handed him by the room clerk. A brief item about a petty ward heeler whose body had been taken that morning from the river caught his eye. He did not know the dead man, though he was acquainted with others like him. Johnny Crayle had been no more than a speck on the complex panorama of the hurrying waterfront community, one of those gray, parasitic shadows that cling to the outer skeleton of a city's political structure.

Grant read the item through twice before going to his apartments. After refreshing himself from the journey, he put through several calls on his private telephone, summoned his carriage, and departed.

On a busy street in the downtown district, he instructed his coachman to draw up at the curb. Stepping leisurely to the street, he made his way in the direction of the waterfront, past the thinning stream of men and women whose daily bread-and-butter struggles had raised the sprawling city to the stature of a Midwest metropolis. Office buildings and stores gave way to grime-laden warehouses and utility shops as the street sloped to the river. In the early twilight, the fresh-water smell was all but lost among acrid fumes from endlessly belching factories. The heady fragrance of roasting coffee beans mingled indiscriminately with the rancid odor of lye and tallow. Streets temporarily deserted by retreating laborers and clerks came to new life as the evening's watchers appeared in darkening doorways. Farther back, invisible to the passer-by, the city's shadowy urchins could be heard gathering in anticipation of another night's rendezvous.

No one gave more than a disinterested glance at the meticulously groomed stranger swinging along silently in the falling darkness. He moved effortlessly, blending into the squalid obscurity of the neighborhood with the same unique ease that took him to a board of directors' meeting or the drawing room in one of the mansions on the heights. His stride quickened as he turned into an alley near the waterfront. Half the distance of the block, he stopped in front of a battered, unpainted door at the rear of an old frame building, relic of the days before industry took possession of the wharves. The knob turned easily in his hand and the door swung open, closing behind him.

Inside, the passageway was dim and musty. The only light was a small gas flame in a dirt-encrusted globe at the head of a narrow flight of stairs. He paused momentarily, glancing upward. An expression of sardonic contempt crossed his face as he studied a door at the top of the stairway. The deceptive light lent angularity to the darkly handsome cut of the features, and the hardened lines and planes, sharply drawn in the oblique shadows, were those of a man who walked with a restive bitterness. The eyes were cold. The thin mouth was tight-lipped and immobile.

The flame in the gas jet wavered in the stream of air circulating in the drafty stairwell, and he moved toward the stairs. His step was deliberate in the ascent and he was careful not to touch the dusty handrail or brush against the smudged wall. At the top he rapped briefly on the door, then opened it.

The interior was a small, windowless office, dirty and unpainted like the rest of the building. A man sat at the desk, sorting and counting a quantity of paper money. He looked up at the interruption and motioned toward a chair.

He was a heavily built man, middle-aged and graying. Shrewd, alert eyes told him all he wanted to know in one swift glance, and an agile mind stored away minute details for the time he could find them useful. A manner as sharply dangerous as it was disarming plus an impressive record behind the political scene gave Al Reed the careful respect of his constituents and the unremitting enmity of his opponents. Seldom had a man used his abilities more profitably. Reed had a knack of turning every asset and talent to his own advantage, with the net result that even adversity became a stepping stone to greater gain.

"You're early," he commented, neatly arranging the bills in two separate stacks. "I thought you'd be delayed on other business tonight."

Grant inspected the chair by the desk with a critical eye. "Fortunately no," he said, seating himself. "I like to keep appointments on time."

Reed shoved one stack of bills toward the edge of the desk. "There you are," he said briefly. "I put a third in the campaign fund."

Grant picked up the money, flipped the edges of the bills carelessly, and slipped them intact into an inside pocket. "That fund is a bottomless vat," he said dryly. "I've always found it curious that your method of controlling politics includes flowers and undertakers for the dead, and bushels of potatoes for the living."

"Hell, everything counts," Reed said easily. "A ward is a community in itself and nothing goes unnoticed." He regarded his visitor reflectively, a slow smile spreading across his face. "Besides, I like doing favors for people. I find it an excellent tonic once in a while."

"Oh?" Grant said with an unpleasant inflection. "The favor you did Johnny Crayle must have given you quite an invigorating lift."

Reed's smile vanished and for a moment he said nothing. Instinct warned him to use caution. An admission that he was behind the Crayle job could be dangerous. At the same time he knew that the hard-faced man opposite him wasn't likely to be deceived. Grant Monroe had his own methods of obtaining information, and very possibly he was already in possession of the facts. Well, what of it?

With characteristic arrogance, Reed decided to hit the issue squarely.

"The rotten little rat asked for it," he said bluntly. "Hell, the son of a bitch was trying to cut in on the big money. When he saw he couldn't, he went to Hillson to spill everything he knew, then threatened to go to the State Capital. Damn it, Grant, what could you expect?"

Grant knew that the circuit attorney, Hillson, would contact Reed as soon as he rid himself of his unwelcome visitor. Crayle had to be stopped before he could reach the governor with enough facts to launch a possible state investigation.

"I expect you to conduct your affairs without killing," Grant said coldly, an undisguised threat in his tone. "You're slipping, Reed, when you can't keep the boys in line with your usual techniques."

Reed's face flushed. He prided himself on his ability to handle any eventuality with a wide margin of safety. But the Crayle business had taken him by surprise. There hadn't been time to maneuver the former ward heeler into a position where he'd have to run to save his own skin. Nevertheless, Reed rather liked the way he had managed things. Using Nick Ferrento from Kansas City had been sheer inspiration. There wasn't a chance that Nick could be traced. Even if the impossible did happen and Nick was brought back for questioning, Reed was confident that he could deal with the situation.

His anger subsided and he leaned back comfortably, his broad thumb stroking his chin reflectively. He liked power, and he liked the respect he was accorded wherever the weight of his hand was felt. He never thought of the money he received as bribes. To him they were fees in the same sense that fees for services are paid to men in other professions. If he prospered at the expense of some, he was merely doing what every businessman does to survive, and he considered himself no worse than any man who made a dollar where he could. He picked candidates on both party tickets with indefatigable sagacity, knowing in advance what the election returns would bring. One of his greatest personal triumphs was the coalition group, ostensibly a reform movement but in actuality only another arm of the machine. The seats in the assembly were occupied by his men, and each statute that went on the books felt his influence.

It was curious then that an intangible worry pursued him in his dealings with Grant Monroe. A hunch, he called it, and he attached importance to hunches. Acting on them in the past had been a considerable factor in his spectacular rise and had on more than one occasion saved his life. Usually he had reason for these premonitions. But there was nothing to go on here. Nothing more than an odd sensation of acting by prearrangement, as though he were being slowly drawn into a baited trap. Occasionally he had a feeling that he had known the man in front of him before. That was impossible, of course. Monroe was in his early thirties. Years ago he would have been an unshaven youngster. Nevertheless, the nebulous uneasiness persisted.

"Hell, the thing's done now," he said carelessly. "I don't like violence any more than you do, and I doubt that it will happen again."

"I hope not," Grant said narrowly. "I thought you understood that our arrangement holds only if you can handle matters without trouble."

Reed ignored this. He reached for the remaining bills on the desk, put them in the drawer and turned a key in the lock. "Lily," he stated in a matter-of-fact tone, "gave Steve a cordial reception but dodged the assessment. Know about it?"

Grant's face became expressionless behind its flinty mask. Only his eyes were alive, and they bored steadily into those of the man behind the desk. "Stay away from her, Reed," he said softly. "You collect enough from others."

They looked at each other, Grant implacable in his uncompromising coldness, the older man scowling his impatience.

"Christ damn!" Reed exploded with uncontrollable violence. "She's no better than the rest of the mangy lot. Hell, a whore is the same whether she's on the riverfront or over in the West End!"

Grant's face whitened. "I said stay away from her," he repeated without raising his voice. "I mean it."

Reed was perhaps the only man in St. Louis who knew of the relationship between the uncommunicative man facing him and the woman in her fifties who owned the Belle Arms, plush quarters of a select assortment of female companions who provided relaxation for an exclusive clientele. And Reed's understanding was negative. An alliance between a man like Grant Monroe and the operator of a bordello was beyond his comprehension. Had this been the only particular about the younger man that baffled him, he would have passed over it readily. Reed usually accepted men as he found them, yet that inescapable quality about Monroe troubled him. At the same time he was astute enough to value an association such as theirs. Not only had it proved extremely profitable, but Monroe was the one man who could ease certain matters in places that Reed himself did not dare to go.

He decided not to press the issue. "All right," he said shortly. "If the others are willing to support the machine, I won't argue about the Olandt woman."

Grant Monroe said nothing. To him, Lily Olandt was a symbol. A symbol of his obsession, a reminder of his hatred and a spur to his every calculated move. He had been a boy when he first knew Lily, and his acquaintance with her then had been brief. He could not guess all that happened to her in the intervening years after their lives were torn apart, and he had never asked. Nor was he concerned with what she was now. The thing that mattered to him, that colored his thinking and gave purpose and direction to his life, was the irrevocable past. Lily Olandt was a part of that picture in his mind.

He had recognized her immediately that day she had passed on the street nine years ago. In appearance she was much the same as he remembered. The chestnut hair was fashionably coifed, the figure was still shapely in its trim, firm lines, and the face had not lost the contours and fair coloring of its youth. The eyes, sharper with a seasoned and knowing penetration, were the only evidence of change. He had turned aside her admonishments that he return to Cape Girardeau with a finality that left no doubt regarding his intentions. When she realized the uselessness of argument, she no longer tried to persuade him.

"You want to even the score," she said thoughtfully in her rich, vibrant voice. "I had my own debt to settle in St. Louis and I found a way. I made them pay and pay well."

He had smiled faintly. Her place was well known from Chicago to New Orleans, a lavishly appointed gentlemen's club of gilt rooms and subtly perfumed boudoirs. Nothing was lacking for the comfort of patrons. Waiting guests found at their disposal an extensive and luxuriously furnished library, and were frequently entertained by string concerts.

The girls were clever, poised, and beautiful, well suited to while away the time pleasantly for visitors, profitably for Lily.

"You are Grant Monroe now," she nodded after he had outlined the plan he had in mind. "Nobody would link you with the past. St. Louis is a dirty, brawling city, but you see how it lives." She gestured with graceful, well-manicured hands. "Merchandise comes in, changes hands, goes out. You have a riverboat that carries sugar from your place in Cuba. You'll need a dozen. They say not enough goods is brought in by rail because there's no way to handle it. Get a drayage outfit, get warehouses, and handle it for them. I'll let you have extra funds. In a short time you'll find yourself with more power than Reed. You'll dictate to them all and make them like it."

Her prediction had been accurate. Grant Monroe, plantation owner, became Grant Monroe, commission merchant. In the space of a few years the North River Warehouses, the Atlas Moving and Storage Company, and the Western Packing and Shipping Corporation came into being and settled as central cogs in the city's life. Dummy corporations in effect, they operated under the nominal control of a few directors who rarely met in an administrative capacity. Those whose businesses functioned because of these services and those whose livelihood depended upon them were ignorant of the fact that Grant Monroe was the controlling interest behind their efficiency. Nor did they know his hand directed the coming and going of new riverboats, carrying cargo from the West Indies and South America, and taking on at New Orleans products from British and Dutch freighters bought in far-off trading posts of the world. Since he chose to operate indirectly, there was none to say who was responsible when a continued scarcity in one line brought higher bidding or when the bottom dropped out of the price scale because of a glutted market.

Few in the city knew him, though many knew of him. To most, he was a man from nowhere, a man they first became aware of as a commission merchant with an interest in a plantation in Cuba. All knew he was a man with inexplicable connections and unestimated means. Many said he would go to the legislature, then Congress. Some said he aspired to the presidency. Others thought he was content with wealth and power at home.

In the dingy upstairs room where his business with Al Reed was finished, he stood up and prepared to leave.

"What do you want done about the credit limit aboard the *Crescent?*" Reed asked, referring to the gambling boat anchored several miles down the river and nominally owned by Pete Solloway, retired pilot.

Grant turned, his hand on the door knob. "Who is it this time?" he asked disinterestedly.

"Young Brad Jenkins. The croupier refused to take more notes last night and the boy got nasty about it. He'd been drinking, and Frank figgered he'd had enough for one night."

"Tell Frank to play along," Grant said. "If the boy likes to go for high stakes, why shouldn't he?"

"Hell, he doesn't use any sense," Reed pointed out. "And Harlan might balk at making good. It's possible the old goat couldn't, in any case. An investment house is only worth the paper it holds, and Jenkins has been running on narrow-market, high-yield bonds and inadequately margined securities for years. He might be in a bad way if he had to raise a sizable sum overnight."

"Possibly." Grant shrugged. A bleak smile passed briefly over his face and was gone, leaving his expression as remote and cold as before. "I suppose the campaign is shaping up?" he inquired irrelevantly. "That drive for civic pride, a better St. Louis?"

Reed understood the implication in the question. "Catching on," he said by way of understatement. "The idea of a new transit system to reach the suburbs is getting the big fellows. Most of the greedy devils would like stock in a deal of that kind."

"No doubt. I rather think that's why Jenkins has been trying to reach me, and why he extended a dinner invitation for tonight."

His voice was controlled but it carried a metallic harshness in the narrow confines of the small room. A familiar dull savagery burned in his blood at the thought of the warm, friendly mansion on the tree-shaded avenue where Harlan Jenkins lived, the mansion that had once belonged to Will Patterson. Each casual visit there was a needling goad, reminding him of the past, stirring the throttling hatred within him.

"St. Louis could use another traction company," Reed was saying. "Interurban is getting too damned ambitious. They want expansion rights in a new franchise, but their offer is half what the deal is worth."

"You'll have your new traction company," Grant said, turning to go. "I'll keep you informed during the week."

The door closed behind him and again the politician had the feeling that the interview had balanced on a false note. Perhaps it was the undercurrent of tension that seemed to strike a familiar keynote in the recesses of his mind. He had been aware of the same suggestive undercurrent on his first meeting with Grant Monroe, a feeling heightened by the peculiarly intimate knowledge Monroe seemed to have of certain undisclosed matters that had taken place two decades ago. Only the devil himself knew the real story behind the Patterson affair. The devil, and Grant Monroe.

CHAPTER FIVE

On the sidewalk, Grant drew a watch from his pocket and glanced at it. Less than twenty minutes had gone by since he left the main street. The lamps were lit, but the last reflected glow of the sun still clung to wisps of clouds and cast a pale reflection over the buildings. He walked quickly now to the waiting carriage and directed the coachman to drive to the Jenkins mansion.

Leaning back on the seat, he turned a disinterested glance out the window. For a time the monotony of block upon block of identical houses pushing against the street was unbroken. Then as the thoroughfare left the plebeian atmosphere of toil and sweat, the structures separated, retreating behind luxurious lawns and ancient oaks, achieving the dignity of residences. Some distance from his destination, his attention was caught by a disabled carriage sagging warily on a loosened front wheel. Recognizing Rufus, the old retainer who drove for the Jenkins family, he ordered his carriage to a halt.

"Can you fix it or can't you?" a woman's voice demanded impatiently.

"I'se a-fixin' it, Miss Theodora," Rufus said in a placating tone. "Them no 'count boys at the livery hain't took the trouble to go over it like they should."

"A fine thing!" she exclaimed in exasperation, leaning out the window to see how the repair was progressing. "Brad using the barouche, and this rig falling apart!"

Grant regarded her silently. He had been acquainted with Theodora less than six months, for Harlan's traveling daughter preferred Switzerland and Vienna to the home fireside. They had been sharp months, punctuated by uncertainty and violent, inexplicable moods. He reflected now on the customary cool civility of previous conversations with her, and an ironic smile touched his features. But he was not amused. The two of them found little in common, and he was familiar with the fact that Theodora's views usually manifested themselves in marked disagreement with his own. Moreover, her habit of regarding him with circumspection was considerably irksome. He was impotent against that guarded barrier of formal reserve and baffled by the thinly veiled distrust which was clearly visible through her strict observance of propriety. His smile became quite rigid as he thought of the several occasions when that distrust had threatened to break into open hostility.

Contrary to the accepted precepts for womanly behavior, Theodora Jenkins maintained strong opinions and seldom hesitated to voice them strongly. And contrary to the usual predisposition of unmarried females, her absorbing interest was music, which she pursued with incredible seriousness. A faintly sardonic gleam crept into his expression. In some way she fancied herself a composer. An extraordinary pursuit, he commented mentally, when most ladies were content to perform the compositions of others with passable effect.

Familiar with every detail of the face outlined in the open window, he was nevertheless absorbed. Conceding Felice's audacious loveliness and bewitchingly feminine appeal, and even granting the irresponsible Brad a fair amount of good looks despite a petulant turn of expression, the observer was invariably impressed with Theodora's singular beauty. To a trained and critical eye, there was no fault or defect in those cool, strikingly vivid features. A smooth sweep of rich, black hair framed a clear, high forehead and skin of luminous texture. The narrow, straight nose, descending to a sharply defined tip and nostrils that were somewhat flaring, lent symmetrical beauty to the mold of curving cheekbones and sculptured chin. The mouth, pursed in vexation, was wide and full, a deep moist red in the early evening light.

She saw him and her eyes, arrestingly dark and passionately alive, flickered in brief surprise. Almost immediately their expression changed and her look was indignant, heavy with suppressed fury. "I suppose," she said testily, "this sort of thing amuses you!"

Grant lifted his hat, and his smile was the essence of courtesy. "Permit me to offer my sympathy and help, Miss Theodora," he said engagingly. "I shall be delighted to drive you the rest of the way."

"If you want to help," she said firmly, "tell your driver to lend a hand fixing this … this confounded rig!"

He sighed regretfully. "I'm afraid Sam wouldn't be very useful. He's never had a flair for repairs. Besides, we'd both be delayed. It would be more to the point and simpler if you accept my invitation …"

"Thank you, no," she interrupted, disappearing into the rear of the carriage.

He grinned broadly at the vacant window. "I'm sorry you decline my offer," he called reproachfully but with a marked finality. "However, since I have a dinner engagement with your father, I have no choice but to proceed on my way. He is not one to be kept waiting. Nor am I, with the immediate prospect of an excellent repast just ahead. Drive on, Sam."

There was an instant of silence from the interior of the disabled carriage. Then she reappeared at the window. "Wait," she said with evident reluctance.

"Yes?" he inquired on a polite note.

"I'll go." She reached for the door of the carriage but he was out almost at once, holding it open for her. "Why didn't you say you were calling on father?" she asked impatiently. "All this foolishness could have been avoided."

He did not reply. Revealed in the light of the street lamp, Theodora Jenkins was a woman of unequaled attractions. She stood tall and straight beside him, her shoulders held with natural poise only a few inches below his own, her eyes nearly on a level with his. A simply designed carriage dress that would have been a conventional garment on another was a superlative foil for her incomparable figure. An exquisitely molded bosom rose to matchless perfection, then tapered to a slim waist. Hip and thigh melted entrancingly in a long, full curve, and below, the witchery was completed by incredibly slender, shapely feet.

An expensive item for old Harlan, this. And money wasn't flowing so readily now. At the thought, Grant enjoyed a perverse glimmer of satisfaction quite apart from the pleasure he derived from contemplating her personal charms.

She waited, regarding him with composure. "I thought you were eager to drive on," she reminded him after a pause. "Shall we go?"

He met her eyes with equanimity. Temperament and pride, he thought wryly, wondering where they could lead if circumstances were different. Lily had had beauty and talent in her youth, he recalled. Her voice had an exceptional quality that might have taken her to professional heights had she desired. She'd had pride, too. But all this meant nothing when the strands of her life were snarled in the machinations of a power beyond her control. He discontinued his musings abruptly, angered that the thought of Lily had come to him now.

Theodora spoke again. "Well?" she said.

He inclined his head slightly. "By all means," he replied with mock gravity. He assisted her to the waiting carriage and entered after her. Waving his driver ahead, he leaned back comfortably and crossed his legs.

Theodora sat stiffly upright on the seat. The presence of the man beside her filled the carriage with an alien disturbance that invariably irritated her, and she met it with the same rigid aloofness that marked all their encounters.

"I understand you plan to return to Vienna," he remarked conversationally.

"Yes," she replied unwillingly.

"I suppose it is difficult to adjust to St. Louis when one has a taste for travel," he commented. "There are more inviting spots, particularly in winter."

She did not exhibit any reaction to this although the soot-laden fogs that rolled up from the river and the bone-chilling rains had always been unbearable for her. Nor was she inclined to elaborate on the purpose of her return to the continent. The Vienna String Ensemble had unbelievably included her group of "American Fantasias" for early winter performance, but this fact would scarcely interest Grant Monroe. Unless, of course, he found himself amused by her determination to be present for the triumph.

She frowned, remembering the scene with her father that followed her announcement of leaving. Her disagreements with Harlan were rare, and for the most part inconsequential. This time, however, she had been adamant. She was aware that family finances had been limited since the depression. But there was the trust fund from her mother, and that she planned to use. Going abroad was perhaps selfish, but it was her only selfishness. After the death of the invalid woman who had been Harlan Jenkins' wife for fifteen years, Theodora had been the one to render decisions for Felice and Brad, to supervise their needs, help with their lessons, and march them off regularly to church. The dying woman's last words wrung a promise from Theodora to look after them. This she had done, conscientiously and rigorously, super-intending her brother and sister with painstaking zeal.

The thought of them brought a twinge of self-reproach. Brad had been no problem in the old days, a gently mannered, trac-table boy with a lovable smile and bright disposition. Of late he had changed. Reticent and moody, he frequently absented him-self the greater part of the night, refusing to say where or with whom he spent his time. Felice's independence and utter lack of judgment were less surprising, for she had always been thought-less and self-seeking. Theodora was reassured by the thought that Felice would soon announce her engagement to Neil Hunter, and thus consummate an attachment that had grown since child-hood. In Theodora's opinion, an early marriage for Felice would be both sensible and desirable.

Conscious of Grant's quiet scrutiny in the carriage, she determined to ignore him. Turning her head, she stared fixedly out the window. Grant lapsed into indifferent silence, his face a mask of polite reserve.

Inwardly he fumed. For a few unguarded moments, his forthcoming interview with Harlan was forgotten in the sharp awareness of the woman beside him. He was nonplused in the face of her strange alertness and withdrawal, and his vexation mounted as the silence lengthened. He reminded himself forcibly that he was a fool to be affronted by the manners of a woman he scarcely knew. Nevertheless his chagrin simmered steadily until the carriage turned in the private drive to the Jenkins residence.

As they drew up in front of the portico of the comfortable old red brick mansion, his mood changed. A familiar bitter resent-ment sent his blood coursing hotly through his veins. The house waited before him in its silent challenge. Lost in himself, he did not move.

Theodora, impatient at the delay, glanced at him. She was about to speak but the look on his face stopped her. A dark scowl of unadulterated viciousness replaced the usual suave reserve and engaging smile. She drew in her breath involuntarily, shrinking from the savage intensity of his profile, white and rigid in the dim interior of the carriage.

The door to the house was thrown open. Warm light streamed across the threshold, and almost instantly Grant was himself. Courteous and smiling, he assisted her from the carriage and escorted her inside. Theodora recovered slowly. Shaken and uncertain, she found herself wondering if she had been the victim of some queer and distorted delusion.

Harlan Jenkins emerged from the drawing room, his hand outstretched in greeting. "Grant," he said heartily, "and Theodora. You arrived together?"

"The carriage lost a wheel," Theodora explained stiffly. "Mr. Monroe was kind enough to bring me the rest of the way."

Jenkins was a short man in the late fifties. There have been men like him in every age. Wherever a community takes root and flourishes, there are those to promote the ventures, manipulate the wealth, and capitalize on man's wishful dream of sudden riches. Jenkins was carefully groomed, his thinning gray hair combed precisely, his coat and waistcoat buttoned over an ample middle. He carried his pudgy frame pompously, his large head at a forward angle on the thick, short neck. In appearance he bore little resemblance to the two daughters and the son whose features were the fortunate inheritance from their mother. The round face with its heavy jowls, wide lips, and broad forehead possessed a curious mobility that frequently took the form of agreeable good humor, occasionally and with equal facility presented a frozen, entirely blank aspect. The eyes, a vague blue, were smiling at Grant.

"We are grateful, sir," he said with the dignity that seldom failed to impress an investment prospect.

"I am always delighted to be of service to Miss Theodora," Grant replied pleasantly. His eyes wandered to the vacant space above the carved mantel of the fireplace where his mother's portrait had once hung. He did not remember her with any sense of reality for she had died within a year after the birth of her one child. But the portrait had been a beautiful thing, and he had loved it passionately. At the recollection, a thin vein in his temple began to throb. He wondered where the canvas was now, whether Jenkins had destroyed it or sold it for its value as an oil painting. Probably the latter.

There was a stir behind them, and he glanced up to see Felice descending the stairs. Smaller than her sister, the nineteen-year-old Felice was a blonde vision of loveliness in blue silk grenadine as she swept down and across the hall. "Mr. Monroe," she said prettily, gazing at him with the full effect of wide, green-flecked eyes. "We were concerned about you. One reads such dreadful stories about conditions in Cuba!"

"I'm afraid the newspapers have been reporting only the lurid side of the controversy, Miss Felice," he said smilingly. "The disorders have been confined to a smaller portion of the island than you might think."

"It would be interesting to hear a firsthand account," Harlan suggested affably. "Shall we go into the drawing room? A drink before dinner will stimulate the appetite."

Felice led the way with her father and Grant stood aside, waiting for Theodora.

"Tell father to excuse me," Theodora said coldly, sweeping her skirts in an imperious arc as she turned toward the stairway. "I shall be down for dinner."

Grant watched her go with eyes that were suddenly brooding and impassive. At Felice's reappearance in the doorway, he bestirred himself. Minutes later in the drawing room, he was again the debonair dinner guest, sipping an excellent whisky and soda and delighting the flirtatious Felice with his most entertaining manners.

"But the raids!" Felice exclaimed, gazing at him wide-eyed over the slender glass of pale wine she held to her lips. "I should be terrified to fall asleep at night, not knowing when the rebels would come with their torches to burn and plunder."

"I doubt that the sleep of one so lovely would be interrupted," Grant said readily. "Gomez would hang and quarter any insurrecto foolish enough to think of such a deed. Besides," he added with a whimsical touch of realism, "you are an American."

Felice was enchanted. She blushed prettily and tasted her wine. "Just the same," she murmured demurely, "I am thankful there are no barbed wire camps or murdering bands of soldiers in the state of Missouri."

Harlan regarded his younger daughter with an approving eye. "You must remember, my dear," said he, "that wars are fought realistically. When the stakes are high, any means justifies the end."

Grant elevated an eyebrow. "You favor the Machiavellian school of thought, I see," he said wryly. "I've often wondered," he added in a more serious vein, "why the nineteenth century regards him as an evil genius when we support his doctrine in fact, if not in theory."

"Machiavelli merely put down in words what he knew about human nature," Jenkins said. "He was practical enough to realize that man will go to any extreme to win his goal and will justify his actions accordingly."

"A point of view not always supported by history," Grant observed reflectively. "Certainly not in the case of the loser, whose cause goes down to defeat."

"History, sir, is made by the victor," Jenkins asserted vigorously. He was amused to discover that Grant Monroe was something of an idealist. So much the better, he thought with an inward chuckle. He had use for Grant in the furtherance of his scheme to monopolize the new traction development. But he had been wary at first. He knew little about Monroe's business affairs, less about his personal background. The better he came to know his man, however, the less doubt he had concerning the success of his plan.

"The vanquished are neither pitied nor remembered," he added, draining his glass with verve.

There was a sound in the doorway. Theodora stood there, waiting in an attitude that was clearly definitive. The men rose to their feet at once.

"Dinner is ready," Jenkins said affably. "The nature of man and war will wait until we are fed."

Felice, who had suffered the latter part of the conversation with constraint, bounced to her feet. Harlan led the way to the dining room with Theodora, and Felice, her color heightened and her smiles once more demurely coquettish, followed with Grant.

CHAPTER SIX

Theodora Jenkins drank her coffee black. She drained the cup with subdued violence and replaced it on the saucer with an angry little clink. On the other side of the low, flowering centerpiece, Felice toyed daintily with hers, devoting herself to Grant who was thoroughly at home in Brad's customary place opposite Harlan.

Felice was behaving ridiculously, Theodora thought grimly, casting a chilly eye on her sister. She was a delightful picture of attentive femininity, helplessness, and delicious appeal; her laughter rippled at some entertaining remark of Grant's or the rosebud mouth pouted coquettishly when he teased. The soft, taffy-gold hair gleamed like ripe wheat in the candlelight, and the gray eyes were entrancing with their momentary flashes of startling green. Her small bosom with its high, pointed breasts was intimately revealed beneath the cleverly designed bodice of her dress as she leaned forward, listening in an attitude of rapt interest while Grant discussed the current market.

Theodora noted with an inward expression of disgust that Felice was flirting shamelessly. It was insupportable. Neil Hunter, who was earnestly devoted to her, intended to make Felice his wife the moment she gave her consent. Or he had so intended, Theodora amended sourly. More of this and Neil would be off with another. Her expression set determinedly. Neil had family and prestige. He had already been given large responsibilities at the bank and in the not too distant future, upon his father's official retirement, he would succeed as president of the Commercial Exchange. And Neil, who would become one of the wealthiest and most influential men in the city, adored Felice. Theodora perceived a duty here. A duty that could not be ignored, she observed severely, mentally planning to have a talk with Felice at the earliest opportunity.

She stared frigidly at Grant. All this doubtless afforded him a kind of warped enjoyment. The man would have to be blind not to interpret Felice aright. Despite his disarming air of friendliness, Theodora told herself vehemently, she at least would not be deluded. There was too much assurance and outrageous independence about him, she thought with stubborn insistence. She had been incensed at her enforced ride with him earlier that evening and her ill humor was not lessened now by seeing him in Brad's chair, usurping the conversation, impressing her father as well as Felice with his facile remarks.

But her present mood did not spring entirely from superficial antagonism. She could not forget the look on his face as they sat in the carriage, surely not just a trick of the shadows and one's imagination. There was a hooded threat beneath these surface pleasantries, a violence behind these smooth, affable mannerisms. A strong uneasiness quite different from her open resentment took possession of her. Father ought to be warned, but against what?

Involuntarily she sighed. Harlan had carried the weight of too many responsibilities these past years. She glanced at him affectionately, not liking the shadows beneath his eyes or that quick, nervous habit of moistening his lips when he spoke. He was aging, she discovered with a start. The receding gray hair was thinning noticeably, and an unreadable pale restlessness in his eyes puzzled and disturbed her. These were recent changes, of course, brought on by concern for the family.

But she was not reassured. Several times lately the thought occurred to her that he was absorbed in something beyond the scope of present difficulties, but she had dismissed the idea as fantastic. In a rush of loyalty she told herself that he was tired these days. His problems since the depression had taken a greater toll because of his advancing years. "There has been considerable talk about a new traction development," he was saying now to Grant. "I've been interested in the possibilities."

Grant appeared to consider. "It could develop into an extensive project," he conceded. "One that would pay off handsomely if it weren't for the complications."

When he didn't go on, Jenkins said confidently, "I've thought of the angles. The necessary capital would have to be created, but that's a simple matter. Once on the market, shares wouldn't go begging."

Grant shrugged indifferently. "That part would be comparatively easy," he acknowledged. "I had in mind the problem of obtaining a franchise. There might be strong competition from Interurban."

Jenkins leaned forward, unable to conceal his eagerness. This was one of the openings he sought. Grant had certain connections and could undoubtedly give him correct answers on franchise difficulties. "Interurban has the business district and East St. Louis rights," he argued shrewdly. "Why shouldn't another corporation serve the new suburbs out this way?"

Grant smiled inwardly. He knew that Jenkins was angling for information, and the thought gave him a certain amount of pleasurable satisfaction. "No reason, I suppose," he said agreeably, "if you can persuade the assembly to see it your way."

Jenkins frowned slightly. "The assembly takes orders from Al Reed," he said, watching Grant closely. "If Reed favors a franchise, they grant one. And Reed is on record for the expansion of transit facilities."

Jenkins had avoided any dealings with the politician in recent years but he was familiar with the way Reed worked. Initial profits would be cut substantially, for Reed took a large fee for himself and dealt handsomely with the assemblymen whose votes he sought. Jenkins disliked the idea of parting with the needed sum, but he knew there was no alternative.

"In that case I should imagine you'd have little difficulty," Grant remarked carelessly. "Reed would probably give you the necessary cooperation."

He became aware of the new anxiety in Theodora's face, and his eye caught the small, restless movement of her hand. Without warning, the elation left him and a curious impatience took its place. It had been a mistake to discuss the traction venture at dinner, he decided almost angrily. His business with Harlan should be transacted between the two of them, unhampered by the distractions of social amenities.

"You aren't going to do business with Al Reed?" Theodora asked incredulously, both annoyed that he was discussing such plans with Grant Monroe and alarmed by the implied procedure itself.

Harlan Jenkins looked at his daughter with eyes that were for a moment altogether blank. He was a man who liked to have things turn out according to plan, and Theodora was not what he had intended. He had consented to her travel and study abroad with the purpose of demonstrating the folly of her ambition to write music and, equally important, to do away with her unconsciously domineering attitude and air of duteous self-sacrifice at home. He gathered from her actions since she was back that neither objective had been realized.

He suspected that he had been partly at fault in giving her too much latitude years ago. But he had found that the easiest way to deal with her, and a convenient excuse to avoid coping with the younger children. When he discovered his mistake, the pattern had been formed and there appeared no way to break it.

He stared at her now, aware that she could not only be difficult but dangerous with that devotedly dictatorial spirit and uncompromising will. Remembering Grant, his chilled eyes warmed somewhat and his attitude became conciliatory. "We are merely discussing possibilities, my dear," he said with the mildness of paternal tolerance.

"I see no objection to approaching Mr. Reed," Felice said animatedly. "Everything is done through politics these days, isn't it, Mr. Monroe?"

"A great many things are, Miss Felice," Grant conceded with a smile.

Theodora was still bewildered by that thin space of a second when her father had looked at her with his strangely empty, colorless stare. Unexpectedly, she had sustained the disagreeable sensation of seeing inside him for the first time and finding an unknown hostility in place of the familiar fond indulgence. But her practical nature asserted itself immediately and she dismissed the feeling as part of her edgy mood this evening. Now she glared at Grant with undisguised antagonism.

"And what of the risk involved?" she demanded. "What about father's position if the franchise doesn't materialize?"

Grant's eyes narrowed as he met that direct, challenging look. For the first time he glimpsed what it might mean to Theodora if Harlan were brought to ruin. Not in a material sense, nor even in the abasement of pride or loss of prestige, for Theodora had her hidden reserves of strength. But an awakening from this blind, mistaken devotion to the man who was her father could destroy her if it came without warning. If, he added grimly, it found her with no other source of strength to sustain her.

He scarcely heard Harlan's bland voice saying: "You needn't worry, Theodora. I shall employ every possible safeguard, and no investment will be jeopardized."

Theodora flashed him one of her rare smiles, warm and understanding. Grant saw it and was careful to control his rising anger. Familiar as he was with Jenkins' pretensions, he nevertheless experienced a feeling of revulsion. "I'm certain that Grant won't miss an opportunity like this," Jenkins continued smoothly. "You're buying in, aren't you, Grant?"

Grant felt rather than saw Theodora's sharp, penetrating glance. "By all means," he acquiesced with a slight nod. He had not intended to become involved in the traction maneuver, but he saw upon reflection that his participation would not necessarily change the course of events.

Jenkins, apparently satisfied, did not pursue the subject. The dinner finished, he led the way back to the drawing room with an expansive sense of well-being.

"Theodora, my dear," he said, pausing at the door.

"Yes, father?"

"Shall we go to the music room instead? I should like to hear you play tonight."

She hesitated perceptibly out of long years of habit. But deny him she would, for she was determined not to afford further diversion to this man whose dark, mocking eyes were regarding her intently. "No, father," she declined swiftly. "I am tired, and I'm sure Mr. Monroe will understand if I leave you now."

Grant's eyes met hers, and a faint smile played upon the lines of his mouth. "But of course, Miss Theodora. May I look forward to the pleasure another time?"

He held out his hand in a conventional gesture and she hesitated again, nonplused. Perhaps she would have rejected the formality had not Felice stirred just then. Belatedly Theodora extended a frozen hand. His strong fingers closed momentarily over hers, then departed.

"Another time," she murmured automatically, conscious of the palpable glow that touched each nerve in her fingertips. "Good night, Mr. Monroe."

CHAPTER SEVEN

T he tower clock in a nearby church struck eleven as Grant left the Jenkins residence. The night was warm, teeming with the fullness of spring. He walked quickly, driven by the restless animation that had been with him all evening. Well acquainted with his moods in their various phases, he recognized the overtones of tonight's humor and he was bent on escape.

"Where to, Mist' Grant?" Sam asked, fortified by the substantial dinner he had consumed with the domestics and enlivened by the social discourse that accompanied it.

Grant hesitated. Ordinarily he would have returned to his club to read, then retire. Tonight the prospect irritated him. "The *Crescent*," he decided suddenly and for no apparent reason.

On the way his restlessness and impatience deepened. He had to be on guard, he thought darkly, before he was again betrayed into a corroding discontent and white-livered uncertainty. He could not afford to lose perspective now. He had charted his course in St. Louis, and he had come a long way on it. Nothing remained but to sit back and wait for the inevitable operation of the forces of human nature. He had already waited years. Another few months would pass quickly enough.

He stared at the deserted streets, letting his mind drink in the bitterness stored since boyhood. The deadly inaction of waiting raised doubts and drained a man's self-respect, he thought with vehemence. The tiresome monotony of entertaining Felice and her kind led to this unsettling ennui, this destructive uselessness and disquieting fear of his own being. In his present mood, the thought of Felice brought an expression of sardonic mirth to his darkened features. Eager women amused him, but at the same time he found them irritating. He could not resist comparing Felice and that inviting, vibrant expectancy to the enticing promise of a ripe plum, tempting in its succulent sweetness but cold and unsatisfying to the aftertaste.

He would be better pleased, he thought wryly, if she were inclined toward greater restraint. Several times at the table when she fluttered her eyes and posed with the shamelessness of an experienced coquette, he had been seized with the desire to swing her across his knee and administer a vigorous spanking. He was convinced that Theodora had entertained the same urge, and the recollection of her tight expression of disapproval brought him the only actual enjoyment of the evening.

"Can't you get the horses to move faster, Sam?" he asked, leaning forward impatiently.

"Yassuh, Mist' Grant," Sam drawled. "Git along, you Bess! Git, Queenie!"

The twinkling lights of the riverboat made a bold splash against the black expanse of water, and the rhythms of dance music contrasted strangely with the warm stillness of the night. Grant instructed his driver to remain nearby with the carriage and made his way across the movable bridge that served as a gangplank.

The regular house crowd must be in, he observed, seeing the check girl perched with careless indifference at the back of her booth. She looked up, and the bored, downward cast of her expression brightened with animation as she came toward him.

"Good evening, Mr. Monroe," she said, rearranging her skirt with a hasty movement and giving a quick tug to her blouse, drawing it tightly across her small, pointed breasts.

He gave her his hat and gloves. "A slow night, Susie?" he inquired conversationally, returning her smile with a good-natured grin.

"Oh, you know, Mr. Monroe," she said with a shrug. "It's always the same. Things slow down around this time every night."

"You should be out having a good time, Susie," he told her lightly. "Why do you stay with a job like this?"

She flushed with pleasure. "A girl's got to work for a living. And anyway, I have my nights off."

The big frame of Pete Solloway moved into sight behind Grant and she retreated, busying herself among coat hangers and cubbyholes.

"Glad to see you on board, Mr. Monroe," the burly ex-pilot said, extending a huge, calloused hand in greeting. "Been quite a spell, hasn't it?"

Grant shook the proffered hand. "Quite," he assented.

Solloway took orders from Al Reed. But with the subtle understanding of others who worked through the politician, he entertained a deep respect for Grant Monroe and paid him the deference accorded Reed himself. "Let me know if you want anything," he said genially as they parted. "I'll be around."

Grant nodded pleasantly, but his practiced eye was critical as he entered the main salon. The *Crescent* ceased being a riverboat when guests passed inside. The dim lighting and intimate atmosphere were in the urban tradition, and the excellent quality of food and liquor drew many whose object was dining and dancing. Grant walked past the tables and let himself through a door at the rear. Going below deck, he was admitted to the gaming room. The air was heavily tainted with stale tobacco smoke and a strong blend of perfumes and scented powder. The usual card games were in progress, but the big roulette table at the rear had drawn the largest following. He moved nearer to watch, nodding to Frank Lewis, the lean, slow-moving croupier whose steady, disinterested voice called bets in an automatic monotone.

Conspicuous among the players seated at the table was Brad Jenkins, leaning forward with the intensity of the habitué. A dull flush colored his good-looking features, and the light blue eyes burned with concentrated fervor. "Seventeen on black," he said, his voice tipped with eagerness.

"Seventeen on black," Frank Lewis repeated mechanically.

A handful of onlookers stood behind Jenkins, sharing vicariously in the thrill. Other bets were placed and the wheel was spun, coming to rest with its customary maddening slowness.

"Seventeen on black it is," the croupier said unemotionally, and a released sigh stirred through the watchers with a reawakened murmur of conversation.

The slight figure of a girl edged through the group and touched Brad on the shoulder. The youth, busy drawing in his winnings, gave no sign that he was aware of her presence.

Grant frowned as he tried to place her. A slim girl of about twenty, she was wearing a dark green frock of unobtrusive lines. Her hair, the color of burnished copper, was drawn back in a simple coif and fastened in a soft coil at the nape of her neck. Her eyes, too wide and large for the small, pointed face, were uneasy, and there was a hint of nervousness about the pale lips. She leaned down and said a few words in young Jenkins' ear that brought a scowl to his face. His lips moved in a quick retort and he returned his attention to the table. Those nearby threw her amused glances and she withdrew in some embarrassment.

Grant circled the table and joined her where she stood uncertainly. Looking down at the bent head, he recalled where he had seen her. She was Ann, the girl who worked in the Arcade Flower

Shop, and she had on frequent occasions selected and arranged orders for him.

"How do you like the pastime of the gambling set, Ann?" he asked with quiet friendliness.

She glanced up quickly, her eyes suspiciously bright Ann's singular charm was a straightforward honesty and unaffected manner. Her quiet reserve and spontaneous warmth were her only defense against the vulnerability of an oversensitive nature. "Mr. Monroe!" she greeted him, managing a faint smile. "I'm afraid I just don't fit in. I shouldn't have come, I suppose."

"Nonsense," he said lightly. "You haven't been initiated into the mysteries, that's all. Come along with me. Let's find out if there's such a thing as beginner's hick."

She drew back, protesting, but he insisted. The dice table was idle, and he summoned one of the house men. Placing a twenty-dollar bill on the table, he picked up the dice. "Now," he said with a broad grin. "Watch an expert."

He rolled a four and three, and turned to Ann with an expression of triumph. "There!" he exclaimed. "Nothing to it."

She was unable to speak. The bill on the table represented nearly a month's wages to her and she was thoroughly prepared to see it vanish in the twinkling of an eye.

Grant saw her dismay and held out the dice. "See what you can do with them," he encouraged.

"Oh, no," she protested with a breathless laugh. "I can't!" She held up both hands and he saw that two fingers on each were tightly crossed.

"Then this one is for you," he said, rolling a pair of fives.

The house covered the twenty and Grant rolled again. The forty became eighty, and Grant winked at the girl.

"Eleven," he announced, cuddling the cubes in the palm of his hand. The house man nodded. Grant rolled the dice gently and eleven came to rest on the felt tableboard.

The house man broke open a small box and shook out another pair. Grant laughed. "What do you say, Ann? Shall we have another go at it?"

She shook her head negatively, but her face was aglow. "I don't think I'm equal to it," she confessed.

Grant picked up the money. "Sorry," he told the man behind the table. "The lady has had enough." As they turned away, he placed the bills in Ann's hand, closing the slender fingers over them before she had time to protest. "It's yours, you know," he said. "If you hadn't had those fingers crossed, I'd have lost."

"I couldn't take it, Mr. Monroe," she said, aghast. "I just … simply couldn't."

"I always give the lady my winnings," he lied gravely. "And we'll say no more about it. If you like, we can go above and listen to the music. It's pleasanter in the salon, and we might have dinner while you wait for your escort."

She hesitated, casting a worried glance in the direction of the roulette table. Then, at the memory of Brad's abrupt manner and curt words of dismissal, she assented. They left the gaming room unobtrusively and went to the main dining room. A waiter led them to a table in a discreet corner, and Grant ordered dinner.

Her manner relaxed under his friendliness and as she ate, she talked—of the flower shop and the inconsequential happenings of the day, of the house on Elm Street where her mother took in boarders. Her voice, enthusiastic, warmly emotional, and earnest in turn, was low as she spoke of Brad, and her eyes softened.

She's in love with him, Grant thought in amazement and anger. The irresponsible young fool probably didn't know it, but his stupidity would end in unpleasantness for both of them. "You seem to know him quite well," he commented after she finished a glowing account of Brad's qualities.

"He's been a customer at the flower shop a long time," she confided. "In a place like that, you get to know people and what they are like. That isn't the real Brad Jenkins you saw tonight." she finished, a faint color warming the transparent pallor of her cheeks.

"It isn't, eh?" he remarked skeptically.

Her laughter was clear and unrestrained, then she became serious again. "I mean it isn't the true person inside himself," she insisted. "I think he gambles because of the excitement, and because he feels important."

"Perhaps you're right," he said gently, wondering at her curious mixture of naïveté and wisdom. Without quite knowing why, he was impelled to warn her against this hopeless attachment before it was too late. "But in any case, does it matter?" he asked, leaning forward in his earnestness. "Brad isn't for you, Ann. He comes from a different world, a small, tight world of arrogant prestige and polite cruelties. You could never take root there, believe me. They wouldn't allow it."

A hurt, incredulous look came into her eyes, and she flushed deeply. "I can take care of myself, Mr. Monroe," she said with a quick defensive lift of her chin.

Mentally he upbraided himself for blundering like an idiot. He reached across the table and took her hand in both of his. "Forgive me, Ann," he said. "I had no right to interfere."

"There's nothing to forgive," she responded in a low tone. "You tried to be kind, and I understand." Quietly she disengaged her hand from his. "But let's go back now, if you don't mind. Brad will be ready to leave."

Grant assented, but with certain dubious mental reservations of his own. Below in the gaming room, they found Brad still seated at the roulette table, his coat off and shirt sleeves rolled to the elbows, a tall glass in front of him. Grant saw that he had been drinking freely, and gathered that Brad was in the midst of a streak of bad luck. He hesitated, reading the story of the youth's extremity in his eyes. But Ann went immediately to his side. She spoke to him, and Grant was as astonished as the others in the room when Brad turned on her in an open display of ugly temper and frayed nerves.

"I'll leave when I please," he said in a voice that no one could fail to hear. "Go on without me, if you insist!"

The girl stood ashen and trembling in the sudden silence. Every head turned to watch as Frank Lewis came around the table. "You've had enough, Jenkins," the croupier said. "Call it a night and come back another time."

Brad swung around, livid with fury. "Don't tell me what to do," he said, leaping from his chair. "I'll not go until I prove that you've got that wheel fixed!"

Grant was between them, then, dismissing the croupier with an abrupt nod. "Apologize, if you please, to this young lady for your abominable behavior," he said flatly but with unmistakable intent.

Brad glowered at him, unable to check the mounting violence of his emotions. "Grant Monroe," he sneered. "You're probably in on the fix, you cheap, blood-sucking middleman!" He struck out with his fist, but Grant caught the arm and held it in a vise of steel. Frank Lewis moved through the crowd, dispesring it, and the three were left to themselves. Brad, thwarted, stood his ground uncertainly.

Grant dropped his hand. "Sorry I had to do that," he said evenly. "Now apologize to Miss Ann, and I shall see her home."

Brad hesitated, struggling through the alcoholic haze that enveloped his brain. His eyes focused uncertainly on Grant and the girl, and he bowed with short, derisive formality. "My apologies, Ann," he said curtly. "And may you enjoy your ride home!"

"I'll wait, Brad," she said in a voice so low it could scarcely be heard.

Brad looked at her a moment. "No thanks," he said finally with an unpleasant smile "Mr. Monroe will make an excellent escort and will doubtless be a more congenial companion than I."

He turned on his heel and walked away. Grant seethed inwardly at the wretched suffering in Ann's eyes as she watched him go. He touched her arm and she moved forward, permitting him to guide her up the stairs and through the exit.

In the carriage, Grant asked her address and repeated it to Sam. Then he sank back on the seat, respecting her silence. When they drove up in front of a weather-worn frame house with leaning shutters and sagging front steps, he spoke. "The evening was a pleasure for me, Ann. And I hope you won't mind too much if it didn't turn out quite as you anticipated."

She turned, full of gratitude. "Thank you for everything," she said swiftly. "And good night, Mr. Monroe."

She was out of the carriage before he had time to assist her, but he followed as she hurried up the walk. "This is not a neighborhood I would recommend for aftermid-night strolls," he remarked, keeping pace with her.

"You needn't come to the door," she said in some confusion. "I'm perfectly safe."

They stopped before the steps, and he saw the dim, yellow flare of light in the basement. A thin shadow moved back and forth behind the drawn shade. She followed his glance, then spoke slowly. "Ma," she said, "is ironing."

He was touched by the contrition in her eyes and cast about for a way to lighten the moment. "Ann," he said reflectively. "I never learned your other name."

Her head lifted with a curious touch of pride. "Lynch," she said. "My father was Tom Lynch."

He stiffened involuntarily. He had forgotten Tom Lynch, who paid a higher price for knowing Harlan Jenkins than did Will Patterson. Lynch paid with his reputation, and in the end with his life. Ann could have been no more than an infant in those days, he mused. The girl's pride blended with his hatred as old memories rushed over him, and he was lost in venomous contemplation of the past.

Then he recovered himself. He glanced down at the lonely figure at his side, thinking of her attachment for Brad. He drew her to him and tipped her face up toward his. "I won't try to interfere again, Ann," he said gently. "But I'll always be here if you need me. Do you understand?"

She nodded. Her features softened, and her eyes were dark and luminous in the moonlight. "I'll remember," she whispered. She turned quickly and ran up the porch steps.

When she had gone, he walked away slowly. Re-entering the carriage, he settled back on the seat, his hatred again a living, burning compulsion within him.

CHAPTER EIGHT

Theodora awoke after a night of troubled dreams and uneasy tossing. Her first thought was of the previous evening, and she lay back against the pillows, thoroughly unsettled. She ought to have anticipated Felice's foolish infatuation with Grant Monroe, she accused herself belatedly. But who would think to look for such an incredible turn of events? Grant's calls at the house on Harlan's invitation had been rather frequent before his last abrupt departure to Cuba. His manner, however, had always been irreproachably courteous and deliberately, almost indifferently, cool. Furthermore, she thought in perplexity, he was a good deal older than Felice. They simply weren't suited at all.

She would have to take action, of course. She could not stand idly by while Felice became involved with an adventurer. The thought brought her out of bed with renewed energy. Refreshed after she had bathed and dressed, she went down the corridor to Felice's room.

Felice was propped up on the pillows, a breakfast tray in front of her. A pink lace nightcap framed the heart-shaped face and a quilted bed jacket was draped over the princesse nightdress. Felice, Theodora noted with fresh alarm, looked very young and inexperienced and appealing.

"Felice," Theodora murmured with sisterly concern. "Aren't you coming down for breakfast this morning?"

"No," Felice admitted readily, sinking her small white teeth into a buttered muffin. "I am not. I felt like starting the day with breakfast in bed."

Theodora refrained from expressing her natural disapproval at this new evidence of Felice's growing indolence. She wondered briefly if there was a touch of defiance in her sister's tone, but she cast the thought aside as irrelevant. The way to handle Felice was to preserve amiable relations, then tactfully and gently begin to guide her into the desired course of action.

She seated herself near the bed. "It's a beautiful day," she said, forcing the enthusiasm in her voice. "I thought we might go shopping together."

Felice looked at her out of the corner of her eye. "I have an appointment for a fitting with Sophie," she said tentatively. "I suppose we could visit the stores."

She sipped her coffee reflectively, speculating on the possibilities. The day might prove interesting if they stopped for lunch at the hotel near Grant's office. He frequently dined there, and if today was no exception, she could look forward to another meeting with him. "I think it rather a good idea, Theodora," she added in a more animated tone. "We'll lunch at the Weston."

"Wherever you like," Theodora agreed, heartened by Felice's sudden compliance. "We'll enjoy ourselves, and have a fine opportunity to talk."

Felice's alert ear caught the implication in her sister's voice, and her expression became wary. She had never been inclined to indulge in an exchange of confidences with Theodora, and she was on guard not to begin now.

But Theodora continued, disregarding her lack of response. "I know you've been thinking about arrangements for the wedding.

I do want to help, you know, and I'm eager to hear about your plans."

"Wedding?" Felice asked with an air of surprised innocence. "My wedding?"

Theodora was silent a moment. Were matters worse than she suspected? It was unthinkable that Felice was already discarding Neil because of this stupid blind spot for Grant Monroe. At the memory of Grant's smiling complacence last night, her resentment flared anew. With unsurpassed insolence he had succeeded in thrusting himself upon the family, turning Felice's head like the unscrupulous deceiver he was and squirming into her father's esteem to the point where father asked for and gave serious consideration to his advice on investment policy! She was suddenly filled with a passionate hatred against him, and her anger fired the strength of her determination to thrust him out of their lives, back to the nondescript identity from which he had emerged.

But the violence of her emotions did not mask a curiously aching sensation of emptiness. She, alone in the household, recognized this evil influence, and the thought left her with a feeling of desolate isolation altogether new. Several times since she had returned to this house where she had always been a pillar of influence, she had caught herself with doubts and wavering convictions, deeply disturbing in their threat to her accustomed confidence and sense of security. She reminded herself sternly that she could not expect her task to be pleasant. The results, however, she concluded with firmness, would far outweigh the unpleasantness. Nothing was too disagreeable if she could return to Europe in October, secure in the knowledge that the family had settled once more into the normal run of their lives, free of the unprincipled influence of Grant Monroe.

"We shall discuss it later, dear," she said, rising. "Can you be ready to leave at ten?"

Felice's green eyes narrowed at her sister's air of authority, but she was careful not to let Theodora see the old animosity that stirred watchfully. "Make it eleven," she said lazily. "We'll have time to shop all afternoon."

"Eleven then," Theodora said, trying to keep the annoyance out of her voice. "I'm going down to breakfast now with father and Brad."

"Brad?" Felice said with a faintly wicked gleam. "I don't think you'll see him at this hour, Theodora. I heard him come in last night. This morning, to be exact. And I imagine he'll do well to put in an appearance by noon."

Theodora took this information in formidable silence and walked out of the room. Brad, on whom she had lavished all possible affectionate care and whose amenable disposition and lovable traits had fostered her high hopes for him, had been out again all night, heaven only knew where! Something surely must be done to return this household to its former staid respectability. Determined to confront Harlan with the seriousness of the situation, she went directly to the dining room where he, at least, was breakfasting in the conventional fashion.

He glanced up as she entered the door, and knew immediately that Theodora was in one of her purposeful moods. "Good morning, Theodora," he said mildly as she went to the sideboard and poured a cup of coffee. "You look very solemn this morning."

"I'm sorry, father," she said tersely, taking the cup and saucer in hand and sipping it where she stood. "But I feel it my duty to discuss certain matters with you at once."

He sighed inwardly as he stared at the daughter who had always been an enigma to him. How like her mother she was in that arresting beauty and strongly emotional nature. A man looking for a wife could do worse, much worse. But he was not pleased. It was increasingly evident that nothing had transpired during her sojourn abroad to arouse her dormant sensibilities. There was no indication that Theodora, at the undeniable age of twenty-two, was anything but her usual tightly controlled, firmly objective self. Or ever would be. "I can spare a few minutes," he agreed. "Sit down and eat breakfast. An empty stomach is an irritant to the emotions and a hindrance to clear thinking, particularly the first thing in the morning."

"The time has come, I think, to take a firm stand with Brad and Felice," she asserted, continuing to stand. "The situation has reached alarming proportions."

She began to pace the floor, lifting the cup with one hand to emphasize a point, returning it to the saucer as she went on to a new statement. "I don't mean that you are entirely to blame, father. I too am at fault. Poor mama entrusted me with their care, and I promised to carry out her wishes. When I went abroad, I was thinking only of myself. But now while I am home, I shall do what I can to compensate for my neglect of duty."

Harlan Jenkins listened in silence, following his daughter with eyes that were obscurely amused, impatient, and circumspect by turn. His disappointment that Theodora had not as yet found herself a husband achieved a state of active annoyance. Most men, he thought with acute clarity, were strong enough to resist the appetite of the passions if they suspected they might open their eyes after the wedding night to the cold companionship of a willful and accomplished virago. It was considerably safer to take unto one's self a more docile mate and, if inclined, indulge the gratification of the senses more abundantly in extraneous ventures.

The difference, he observed tartly, between Theodora and her mother was Theodora's self-willed and forthright approach. Her mother had been trained by an older generation, one which taught the concealment of unmaidenly characteristics and disciplined a wife to subordinate her will to that of her husband.

"You are referring to what?" he asked in a voice that was strangely disaffected and remote.

"Felice's utter lack of propriety, for one thing," she said, surprised that he asked. "You must be aware of her flagrant disregard of the simple rules of womanly decorum. At dinner last night, her manner toward that ... man was most indelicate! And Brad ..." She stopped pacing and deposited the cup and saucer on the sideboard. "Do you know he was out again all night? Have you any idea where he went or what he was doing?"

"I don't know where he goes or what he does when he's attending the university," he pointed out. "I confess it's startling to discover that he is no longer a child to be ordered to bed at certain times. But that is nevertheless the incontrovertible truth and we must accept it. As for Felice," he continued, unmoved by the incredulous consternation on her face, "I'll admit that I would like to see her married to Neil. My wish has been to see both daughters happily and prosperously married. But I have to acknowledge that Felice as well as you, my dear, is an individual in her own right and will have something to say in such matters."

She stared at him. "Surely, father, you haven't been concerned on my account? I have my music, and you know that's all I want."

He rose from the table as though suddenly remembering that there were other demands on his time. "I thought you might be happier in many ways had you found a suitable husband," he said with unaccustomed honesty. "If you had a home to manage and children of your own, I believe you would find less cause for alarm in the behavior of your brother and sister."

Too stunned to speak, she stared woodenly after him as he left the room, her cheeks slowly coloring with mortification and dismay.

CHAPTER NINE

G rant left his club and walked the short distance to the office where his brokerage business was conducted. Entering the suite by his private door, he went directly to the massive desk near the windows. He sorted the mail quickly, opening a few envelopes and leaving others to the discretion of his secretary. There was a letter from Juan Montevo, reminding him of a shipment of sugar due in St. Louis on the *Southern Star* and informing him that Nita would sail on the twentieth for New York where she would visit her aunt, the Señora Rueda. Grant's expression relaxed in a dim smile. Nita's aunt would see that she was occupied with the newness of the city and its many diversions. He put the letter aside with a sense of satisfaction and called his secretary.

Romaine Withers answered the summons with brisk efficiency. Trained to recognize her employer's moods after five years as secretary and office supervisor, she sensed that the day promised to exact more than its usual toll in work and adroit management. But she was a practical woman as well as a capable one, and she reasoned philosophically that there had been difficult days before and undoubtedly there would be a great many more in the future, all to be taken in stride.

"Good morning, Mr. Monroe," she said crisply, placing a list of price quotations on his desk. "I hope you enjoyed your vacation?"

"Yes, thank you," he responded absently. He gave his attention to the price sheet and she sat down by the desk to wait. The list was a comparative one, showing variations over a period of weeks. He scanned the quotations on sugar and frowned, noting the steady drop in the rate of exchange. Sugar was a commodity that should offer consistent trading even with the recent tariff restrictions. He did not intend to dispose of the new shipment at anything less than a high margin of profit. Since a lag in supply was a reliable remedy for skidding prices, his next step was routine.

"The *Star* will dock today or tomorrow," he said briefly. "Check the time and have the regular warehouse consignment made out to cover the entire shipment."

She responded automatically: "Yes sir," and scribbled a notation on her pad.

The only other item to interest him was coffee, showing an increase over the preceding week's high. "Notify your list of coffee buyers that we have a limited supply on hand for a five per cent increase over the market rate," he concluded. "That's all, except for this mail which you can dispose of as you see fit."

"Yes sir," she repeated, mentally calculating the best manner in which to apportion the morning's work among the staff. She took the envelopes from the desk and consulted her notes. "Mr. Barkley from the Loan and Investment Company is waiting to see you, and Mark Stevens from the Bankers' Exchange."

The flicker of a smile crossed his face. Stevens was after information about the proposed traction deal, he surmised with shrewd accuracy. Barkley, of course, had the same thing in mind with the object of insinuating himself into a directorship. They would have their opportunity, he thought grimly, warming to a curious feeling of elation. Harlan Jenkins would see to that.

He saw Barkley first and was sufficiently noncommittal to whet the man's greed. Barkley left under the impression that the new company awaited only the initiative of a few farsighted individuals like himself.

His interview with Stevens was less reserved. "You're right, Mark," he nodded as Stevens led into the projected traction venture. "The city ought to have a new line. The need for more transportation is immediate, and competition with Interurban would undoubtedly result in better service all around."

"That was my thought," Stevens admitted. "There is only one question in my mind. Jenkins, I understand, is raising the funds. I've never liked him personally. But if you have confidence in him, that's good enough."

Grant said nothing for a moment. He had come to know Stevens since his return to St. Louis. He had seen instances where Stevens failed to foreclose on properties, delaying on one pretext or another until the borrower was in a position to make small token payments against his indebtedness. Stevens enjoyed a comfortable income, but he might have amassed a tidy fortune had he been inclined to take advantage of his position at the Exchange. And Grant knew Annette Stevens, a woman of few pretensions, wholly devoted to her family of four boys and two saucy, pink-cheeked little girls.

"I can't tell you what to do, Mark," he temporized. "Perhaps you are right about Jenkins. Who knows? But it's never a good policy to go overboard even on a sure bet, is it?"

Stevens looked at him thoughtfully. "No," he said after a pause. "I suppose not." He stood up and held out his hand. "This visit was unofficial, you know. I have nothing to do with our clients' investments unless they default in payments or go into bankruptcy."

Grant shook the proffered hand. A sardonic smile crossed his features as he wondered fleetingly if he was losing his sense of perspective. "You can afford to wait," he said in parting.

"The stock will be higher later on, but the risk will be considerably less."

Stevens thanked him and left, and Grant dismissed the matter with a shrug. He signed the letters Miss Withers brought in, then left for lunch.

He stopped at the florist shop to exchange a few words with Ann, but she was not in. After ordering a dozen yellow roses sent to Felice with his compliments, he proceeded across the street to the hotel dining room.

He had given his order to the waiter when Theodora arrived alone to wait for Felice. Her patience exhausted, Theodora had left Felice in the midst of a mountainous array of hats to attend to several errands of her own. She spoke to the waiter who nodded and seated her at the table near the windows.

Grant checked the impulse to engage in the customary civilities of a greeting and settled back to indulge in the not unpleasant diversion of watching her unobserved. But he was not pleasurably diverted. His feelings were compounded of perplexity and exasperation, and something stronger that quickened his blood and plunged him again into a brooding restlessness. Theodora, completely oblivious to the appreciative stares of the male diners in her vicinity, glanced indifferently at the menu.

A veritable island of glacial inaccessibility, he thought with dark irony. It was incredible. Strong-willed and intellectually forceful females should be homely, ungainly, and sexless, not exactly the opposite, with the face and figure of this one. A pity, he told himself irritably, she hadn't the awareness to realize her possibilities instead of expending her energies on a fantastic ambition for a musical career. But his mood was unrelieved. He signaled the waiter and ordered another place at his table, then crossed the room and greeted her with punctilious courtesy.

"Miss Theodora," he said, bowing slightly. "Will you consent to join me at my table?"

She looked up in surprise, then her eyes stared him down. "Thank you," she declined, "but I am waiting for my sister."

"Excellent!" he exclaimed immediately. "You shall both dine with me. Waiter," he said as the man hovered near, "a third place at my table. Another lady will be with us directly."

Theodora hesitated between the urge to humiliate him publicly and her instinctive aversion to scenes. Aware that other eyes observed them with interest, she permitted the latter consideration to prevail. Picking up her gloves in silence, she rose and followed him to his table.

"This is an unexpected pleasure," he continued, seating her. "I detest eating alone, but it is rare that I have the good fortune to share such attractive and stimulating company."

Her manner did not unbend. She said: "Felice and I are shopping. I am afraid our lunch will be a rather hurried affair."

"Long enough, I hope, to allow us to become better acquainted," he smiled.

She returned his look coldly. "In what way, Mr. Monroe?" she asked flatly.

He was not disconcerted by the question or by the tone in which it was asked. But his antagonism was stirred by her contemptuous manner and the unmistakable air of superiority, and his emotional state was responding most unpleasantly. The weakness in her armor was music, was it? Very well, he would explore the subject and see where it led.

"I have been intrigued with your success as a professional musician," he said with forced equanimity. "Since your return, the newspapers have commented quite favorably on your accomplishments. Deservedly, I am sure."

"I did not know you were interested in the arts," she said with an imperceptible smile, tantalizing in its mockery.

He flushed slightly but otherwise his face did not change. "I assure you that I am," he responded blandly. "Quite interested, though only from a layman's point of view."

There was a stir at the door and Felice entered, her eyes searching the room. Grant excused himself and went to her side. Seeing him, Felice was all animation and glowing radiance. "Grant!" she exclaimed. "How perfectly wonderful! I was to meet Theodora here …"

"She's waiting at my table," he told her.

"Oh." A hint of annoyance in her voice bespoke disappointment that her sister had preceded her; but her composure was unruffled. She flashed him an intimate glance, warm and startling in its frankness, and he was in time to catch Theodora's smoldering gaze before she lowered her eyes. Smiling inwardly, he took Felice's arm with immense courtesy and guided her to the table where Theodora waited in stony silence.

"I completely forgot the time," Felice said, sinking into her chair with a pretty show of exhaustion. "You should have tried on a few hats, Theodora. Such blues and lavenders, with all sorts of feathers and gee-gaws for trim!"

"Perhaps we should order," Theodora reminded her dryly. "We don't want to delay Mr. Monroe."

"Of course," Felice said sweetly, turning to Grant with a particularly dazzling smile. "I'll have the salad and coffee." Theodora ordered the same, and Grant sent the waiter away, then returned his attention to the sisters. "Miss Theodora was on the point of enlightening me about the arduous life of a composer," he remarked. "Won't you continue?"

Theodora threw him a withering look. "I doubt if the arduous life would interest you, Mr. Monroe," she said icily.

Felice was instantly alert. Her expression took on a new sharpness as she glanced from Grant to her sister. "Do tell us about the things you write, Theodora," she urged faintly. This was a dull subject and Theodora's discussion would be even duller. If Grant insisted, however, let him find out for himself.

"Another time," Theodora said shortly. "I am sure Mr. Monroe will have a more enjoyable lunch without a discourse on music."

"You do me an injustice," he told her with an unfathomable expression in his eyes. "As chairman for the charity dance this fall, it occurred to me that St. Louis should honor its own instead of featuring the performance of imported talent for the intermission entertainment. You do have compositions that would be suitable?"

"Theodora?" Felice exclaimed incredulously. The suggestion appeared slightly ludicrous to her at first. She thought it over rapidly, then began to take a more serious view of the idea. Such a project would require time and would keep Theodora occupied for a while, conveniently out of the way. Also there was more than an even chance that Theodora's work would show up unfavorably, and Felice was of the opinion that it would be rather good for Theodora to be brought down a few degrees.

Theodora was as startled as Felice. She wrestled with herself inwardly, unable to deny the mighty pull of temptation. She had no excuse at hand since the dance was to be held in September, long before she planned to leave for Europe. There was the possibility that Grant offered her this opportunity to see her decline or, if she chose to accept, to enjoy the spectacle of her humbled pride at a wretched performance. She made her decision suddenly. More in a spirit of defiance than gracious acceptance she said: "I do have a few that are suitable, Mr. Monroe. If the committee wishes, I shall be happy to discuss the matter in detail with them."

Grant, to whom the idea had occurred without the slight-est premeditation, made a mental note to contact the individual members of the committee at once and inform them of this new and interesting development. He observed with dry irony that Theodora's manner had become less guarded. Indeed, she became almost amiable as the meal progressed.

The thought struck him that perhaps he had been too hasty in his proposal. Suppose the perfomance was a fiasco? For all he knew, her compositions might be horribly imitative and ama-teurish. The group that patronized the charity dance had been politely intolerant of accomplished artists in the past. Their man-ner of dealing with a nonprofessional would probably be swift and pitiless.

The situation should have given him a certain amount of perverse pleasure. Instead, he discovered that he was afflicted with an alarming anxiety.

"I imagine that a composer would like his music presented under the most favorable conditions," he remarked reflectively. "Unfortunately, the charity affair is held in an oversized hall. If you think this would be a disadvantage, please don't hesitate to refuse."

"You surprise me, Mr. Monroe," she said. "I would not have consented in the first place had I not been willing to risk the undertaking."

Nonplused, he decided to say no more about the matter. After all, perhaps no one would listen.

On leaving the hotel, he felt inspired to say: "An afternoon like this shouldn't be wasted. I'll send for the carriage, and we can enjoy a drive through the countryside."

"That's quite impossible," Theodora said, reverting to her aloof formality. "Felice and I have an appointment with the dressmaker."

"Bother the dressmaker," Felice exclaimed. "I can have a fitting another time." Theodora's eyes flashed a warning but Felice went on, slipping a small, determined hand beneath Grant's arm: "Sophie won't be able to finish both of us today. You go on, Theodora. Tell her I'll be in tomorrow."

Theodora regarded her sister with a fixed stare. Then, impotent and furious with herself for minding in the least what Felice did, she drew a deep breath and said quietly: "Very well, Felice, I shall leave you here. Good-day, Mr. Monroe, and thank you for an enjoyable lunch."

Grant nodded smilingly. His attention was caught by the sight of a familiar figure on the corner, and his eyes narrowed. Theodora turned automatically. "Lily Olandt," she murmured in pleased recognition, hurrying away to greet the other woman.

Grant watched in deepening perplexity as Theodora, intent on following up the chance encounter, overtook Lily and greeted her with a rare display of affectionate warmth.

"Olandt," Felice remarked thoughtfully, eying Grant sharply. "A strange name. I didn't know Theodora was acquainted with a Lily Olandt."

Grant turned to her, and a faint glimmer of amusement crowded out the brooding restlessness. "I daresay it's not important," said he. "Shall we go?"

CHAPTER TEN

G rant left Felice at her home shortly after three. The hour spent in her company had taxed his endurance to the utmost and he was barely able to conceal his annoyance as he bade her good-by. Alone in the carriage, his debonair smile vanished in the tight lines of unrestrained impatience.

Doubtless his accidental meeting with Theodora at lunch had as much to do with his present mood as the forced pleasantries of his drive with Felice. He could not view Harlan's older daughter in the same cold, dispassionate light with which he regarded others in the family. Nor could he forget her. She continued to stand between him and the plans he had nurtured for years, the unwitting cause of his restless ferment and indecision. He knew with certainty that Harlan's ruin would be the end of Theodora's world, the humbling of her pride, the disillusionment of her ideals and her ultimate degradation in shame and poverty. This should have caused him little concern, he reminded himself savagely. Schooled to the most ruthless consideration of Jenkins and everyone associated with him, Grant had never regarded either Felice or Brad as more than a means to an end. Yet he had only to think of Theodora to be thrown into the wildest confusion.

He stared moodily out the window as the carriage moved at a leisurely pace. The streets ticked off familiarly in his mind, bringing up a succession of half-forgotten memories. Suddenly acting on impulse, he leaned forward and directed his driver to turn at the next crossing. The road they took led away from the city, past the residential district to Kenrick Drive. He rarely visited the Seminary of the Vincentian Fathers, formerly located at Cape Girardeau where once he had been immersed in a life apart from the crosscurrents of hatred and retaliation. His attachment for the school had never diminished, though in recent years he had come to see it through the dimly subjective eyes of the layman. He had been present at the dedication ceremony, a pleasant occasion for him but one which subtly demonstrated the distance he had traveled from those early days. Yet he had departed with a renewed sense of wholeness, that phenomenon of borrowed quietude which follows even the most casual visitor to the grounds or the chapel. Perhaps today he could lose this present mood with its frantic restlessness. At least he would be free of it for an hour, he thought bleakly.

He encountered no one on entering the gate. Without hesitation he made his way along the shaded walk to the chapel. At the entrance, he paused as one of the novices emerged. The student noted his presence, nodded absently in passing, and continued on down the steps. Grant watched the younger man until he disappeared into another building. Something about the set of the shoulders and long stride reminded him acutely of his own youth and the year he had spent at Cape Girardeau.

Vivid recollections burned into his memory, and unexpectedly he was engulfed by a feeling of isolation. The haunting insecurity pressed closer upon him, undermining the visible strength that drove him incessantly. He realized fully and with a sharp sense of pain the space that separated him from these men of clear purpose and complete selflessness. He reminded himself quickly that he, too, had a purpose, a fixed and unalterable purpose. But one irreconcilable with the principles of simple faith as they were lived by the Vincentians. The ghost of a smile crossed his features. Only naïveté could have brought him here, hoping to find moral courage in the working out of a plan of calculated retribution. Years ago the vague stirring of that plan had drawn him away. Today he was irrevocably bound by it. He turned and slowly retraced his steps.

"Grant, my dear boy!" a familiar voice broke into his thoughts. "I recognized you from my window in the study."

Grant stopped as the tall figure of Father Morelle overtook him, hand outstretched in greeting. The priest's eyes reflected genuine pleasure and strong affection. In his late sixties, Father Morelle had lost none of the vigor, the initiative, and the unflagging zeal of his younger days. His strong features and quiet, penetrating eyes were evidence of the scholarly mind and tranquil philosophy that illumined every phase of his life. But Grant readily recalled the wide range of that keenly attuned mind. As acting rector at Cape Girardeau, Father Morelle had energetically and capably discharged the numerous and exacting duties of that post. He met and solved problems decisively and with a piercing directness often startling to colleagues and students alike. Yet he was never stern without kindliness, and he had the rare faculty to judge without condemnation. Spiritually he was close to the broad, human understanding of Saint Vincent de Paul, and in many ways he reflected the practical, farsighted, and uncompromising intelligence of that founder of the Congregation of the Mission.

The two shook hands. "Come," the priest said, indicating a bench in the shade. "Sit down and tell me about yourself. Only this morning I thought about you, wondering how you were employing your talents and how you were getting on."

"There isn't much to tell, Father," Grant said with a disparaging shrug. "In a world where success is measured by the accumulation of money and prestige, I have done well. That is all."

Father Morelle's eyes held a friendly gleam as they sat down together. "Acquiring money is not a disgrace," he said, studying the man beside him. "There are good among the rich, and good among the poor. But tell me about yourself. Are you still at the club, or have you settled down to the responsibilities of marriage and a home of your own?"

"I am at the club," Grant acknowledged.

"A mistake," the priest said firmly. "Years that are lost can never be retrieved. You know this, yet you allow life to slip through your hands." He shook his head slowly. "When you first told me of your desire to leave the Seminary, I did not try to influence you either way. A man must come to his own decision in such matters and only a very few are endowed by nature or disposition to take the final vows. He who does must give of himself without reservation. From the beginning I sensed that something was holding you back, something that in the end would prove stronger than the spiritual compensation to be found in a life of religious service."

"You knew me better than I suspected," Grant said with a reticence that was not lost on the older man.

Father Morelle's eyes searched his face gravely. "Whatever troubled you in those days is still with you," he said sadly. "When you made your retreat at Cape Girardeau, I hoped that self-examination and reflection would give you the understanding to see life in perspective and deal with it accordingly. We all have our demon with which we must do battle. I fear you will have to overcome yours before you find the inner satisfaction that is true happiness."

"You may be right, Father," Grant said. "But the greed, the cruelty, the wrong, which man does to man in the course of a single day are factors you might not be able to appreciate."

"I appreciate a great deal, my son," the priest said with a reflective smile. "I was your age when I first came to the Mission, and I then knew enough of the world to grasp some of the meaning behind the spiritual ills afflicting mankind. My answer was to serve here in the capacity for which I considered myself best fitted. But for you there is another charge. Much remains to be accomplished on the outside."

He was silent for several minutes and Grant waited, wondering what new avenues of thought had been opened by this digression into the past. Knowing Father Morelle as he did, he was nevertheless unprepared for the impact of his next words.

"A splendid city is being eaten by political corruption, graft, and prostitution," the priest continued with a frown. "The excesses committed are responsible for an untold number of broken lives and disrupted homes. We are fortunate in having established the Seminary in a site of beauty and permanence, but it is inconceivable that we permit such conditions to go on around us. The Congregation of the Mission was actuated in a spirit of justice and social equity. Our Vincent de Paul was as relentless in his fight against the political evils of society as he was in his drive to relieve the miseries of the galley slaves on French prison ships. One cannot contemplate the purpose for which the Order was founded and at the same time imagine that it can exist side by side with the very crimes it is pledged to eradicate. Only the other day my attention was called to the fact that a place called the Belle Arms flourishes openly in one of the city's better residential areas. Its ill fame is apparently a matter of commen knowledge everywhere. Ulcers like that must be eradicated before we can build for the future with pride and confidence."

Grant stared steadily at a tiny insect fluttering about the rose bushes that lined the path. For a time he was too disconcerted to reply. The attack had come without warning, and from an unexpected quarter. How could a woman who trafficked elegantly in vice be defended to this priest of the Vincentians? At the same time his loyalty to Lily Olandt was too strongly identified with his own intent in St. Louis to permit him to remain silent.

"I am acquainted with Lily Olandt," he said slowly, weighing his words carefully. "Her background is an example of what the vicious and powerful can do with the defenseless. She took this means of striking back."

"There are no mitigating circumstances," Father Morelle returned without hesitating. "No wrong, however great, warrants taking such measures against an entire community. Justice is an instrument for man, but not vengeance. Unfortunately, many do not believe this until it is too late."

Their eyes met, and Grant felt the priest's clear, direct gaze and deeply intuitive insight probe mind and soul. "And yet justice fails," he said, unable to keep the bitterness out of his voice.

"That is so because the city has long been at the mercy of vultures," Father Morelle said gravely. "Somewhere there must be a man strong enough and with the courage and determination to drive them off. I have often thought such a man might be you, Grant Monroe."

Again Grant was at a loss for words. His preoccupation until now had been mainly with Harlan Jenkins. Only incidentally did his anger touch upon the political leader who dictated the policies of St. Louis. He tolerated Reed insofar as such a course was useful to him, with the mental provision that their association would terminate once his goal was accomplished. Now his pattern of thought underwent a sharp change. Reed was admittedly the reason men like Jenkins existed. Reed created the necessary conditions of graft, lawlessness, and crime. Slowly Grant considered the possibility of eliminating the political boss along with the underlings that carried out his orders, and the idea had distinct appeal. The picture of himself in the role of crusader caused him to smile wryly. Then his amusement faded. He intended to get Jenkins; why not the whole rotten system that bred his kind?

"Possibly some of the innocent would suffer," Father Morelle was saying thoughtfully. "But they suffer in any case, do they not? Such an instance occurred only recently when a former ward heeler was found dead in the river. The announcement was given so little importance in the newspapers, I might have overlooked it if I hadn't known the family involved."

"Johnny Crayle," Grant nodded.

"He is the one," the priest said. "His mother is a hardworking woman of the finest character. She is poor, and Johnny was frequently a sorrow to her. There wasn't even money for a decent funeral."

Grant took out his billfold. "See that she gets this, Father," he said. "If you need more, don't hesitate to call me."

"The money will be put to good use, you may depend on it," the priest said heavily. "Most people are inclined to shrug off a case like this with the observation that Crayle got what he deserved. But I am not certain. Perhaps at the end he had a change of heart. I pray that it is so."

"There may be a way to drive off the vultures, Father," Grant said slowly. "I think it would coincide with plans of my own."

"I hoped it might," the priest said with a strangely intent look. "Perhaps a great city will never realize its debt of gratitude. But know that my prayers go with you."

Driving back to the club, Grant felt a curious insurgence of strength. Perhaps there could be a measure of exoneration in vengeance after all, and equity in retribution.

CHAPTER ELEVEN

The committee members were unanimous in their approval of Grant's suggestion regarding the charity ball, and the musical arrangements for the intermission were entrusted to Theodora. She looked forward with characteristic energy to the start of rehearsals, but when they were actually under way, she was distraught. Miss Daly, a singer of considerable reputation, well traveled and familiar with the artistic atmosphere in European capitals, accepted Theodora's manuscripts willingly but declined to audition them more than once. The appointed afternoon, three days before the benefit, found Miss Daly refusing to use more than half voice due to an unfortunate head cold.

The string ensemble was more agreeable in the matter of rehearsals but their efforts were far from encouraging. Matters were further complicated by the attitude of the first violinist who repeatedly complained that several passages were not within the range of possibility. Theodora bit her lip, stifled her inwardly raging ego, and rewrote the passages in question. She suffered unhappily though silently as they took liberties with tempo and style, and was grateful only for their accurate sense of intonation which enabled them to render the suite with some semblance of its intended effect.

Out of it all she emerged distracted and irritable, her nerves jangled, her face harassed, and her appetite gone. There were times when it seemed that all pride and self-esteem hung on the slender thread of this single performance. And at every thought of the mocking laughter in Grant Monroe's eyes, she was overcome with a violent and insupportable anger.

Nor did her disposition improve with Felice's deepening infatuation. She seldom saw her sister these days. Felice was in and out, for the most part out with Grant. When Theodora did manage to confront her, Felice flatly refused to discuss her affairs and perversely turned aside all references to Neil.

These thoughts filled Theodora's mind with bleak resentment as she was being driven home after the final and, she observed grimly, worst rehearsal before the performance. The warm September night was brilliantly lit by a high moon and clusters of winking stars, but she appreciated none of it. She was bitter against herself for agreeing to the proposal, furious at Grant, and sick from the rebellious heaving of a stomach that had not been fed since morning.

Within sight of the house, she saw Grant's carriage leave the drive. Felice was beside him in the rear, her head close to his shoulder. Suddenly Theodora's restraint snapped. She leaned forward, bereft of caution, and spoke sharply to the old servant who had been drowsing along, peacefully occupied with his own thoughts. "Follow that carriage, Rufus. The one just turning down the avenue."

"Follow them, Miss Theodora?" he asked, startled out of his musing.

"Hurry," she ordered in some exasperation. "Do as I say, and don't lose sight of them."

"Yes'm, Miss Theodora," he said in bewilderment, obediently urging the horses to a trot.

She leaned back, trembling now and wondering what had prompted this mad impulse. What would she do when they arrived at their destination and what was there to say if they saw her? "Not too fast, Rufus," she cautioned, striving to compose herself. "It isn't necessary to crowd them."

"No'm," he said patiently. "Looks like they'se headin' for the *Crescent*."

"The *Crescent*?" she demanded, frowning.

"Thet's a boat, Miss Theodora," he chuckled. "Yes'm, a happy boat."

She settled back a second time and her expression was uncompromising. A pleasure boat, indeed! She saw that she had been right in yielding to her impulse. So this was where Felice went with Grant, was it? But what could one expect of such a man? If the girl were not brought to her senses soon, her life would be utterly ruined.

Grant and Felice had disappeared when she ordered Rufus to draw up at the river front near the *Crescent*. She gave them time to find their way inside before she left the carriage and followed.

Al Reed, talking to Solloway near the door, glanced up in time to see her enter, and a peculiar expression came over his face.

"Who's the new one?" Solloway asked, following the direction of Reed's eyes.

"A Miss Theodora Jenkins," Reed said slowly. "And with a problem on her mind, apparently. Tell one of the waiters to inform Monroe of her arrival. Without," he added circumspectly, "his companion hearing."

He moved over to where Theodora stood hesitantly. "Miss Jenkins?" he said respectfully. "Can I be of service?"

"No," she said frigidly, stung by the thought that she had been recognized. "I ... am waiting for a friend."

She did not know the man who accosted her but it was enough that he knew her. She walked away quickly. Seeing the outer door of the foyer open, she went through to the deck. To her relief, the forward aisle was deserted. She stood there in the shadows for some time, grateful for the cooling breeze against her throbbing head.

"I always admire the river at night," a familiar voice said behind her.

She turned and looked into the quietly amused eyes of Grant Monroe. "I didn't hear you come up behind me," she said rather sharply.

"I'm sorry I startled you," he said. "But you should expect to be approached at a place like this. It's not customary for women to wander about unescorted."

"I am perfectly able to take care of myself," she told him angrily.

He studied her from the shadows. "As you may know," he said with an oblique smile, "Felice is waiting inside. I could invite you to join us, but I imagine you would refuse."

"I would."

"And I might ask why you followed us, but I think I know the answer to that, too."

She flushed hotly. "Do you?" she breathed defiantly. "I'm glad, for it will make what I have to say easier. I hoped that I could appeal to your better nature, and persuade you to refrain from seeing Felice. She doesn't realize what her impulsiveness may ..." she paused, then went on determinedly, "cost her. If you hadn't encouraged her, she would still find pleasure in the company of a young man who is very devoted, a gentleman who will offer her security and an honorable marriage."

His smile became derisive. "And Felice?" he inquired mockingly. "How does she feel about your concern?"

"Felice is too young to appreciate certain values in life," she told him stiffly.

"As you do?" he queried with an infuriating inflection. "I fear, my dear Theodora, your own set of values might well undergo a revision."

A succession of strange and unwelcome emotions flooded over her. She felt suddenly faint, and leaned heavily against the rail for support. "Your opinion of me is unimportant," she said in a low tone. "I only ask you to think of Felice."

"Perhaps that's the trouble," he went on, ignoring her last statement. "No one has ever brought you face to face with yourself. Beautiful, yes. But unsympathetic, headstrong, and quite alarmingly self-centered."

"I ..." she gasped in a choked voice, but she was unable to go on. She gripped the rail desperately. The rage she felt was short-lived, burned out in a few instants by its own intensity, and in its place was a tremendous and stifling futility. She scarcely saw him in the shadows as she leaned there, overcome with a baffling, sick misery unlike anything she had ever known before.

His eyes narrowed as he saw her mouth tremble convulsively. The unnatural pallor of her face glimmered in the moonlight, and he thought of reaching out a hand to steady her. Then suddenly his arms were around her and he was holding her to him, kissing her cold lips with a savage and uncontrolled fierceness. Unaware of anything now but this woman, he made no attempt to control his mounting excitement. She was motionless and unresisting, seemingly incapable of feeling. But this only heightened the fire in his brain and he flattened her body against his with a cruel strength, kissing her unresponsive lips again and again.

Realization came over him slowly, and when it did he released her abruptly, moving back into the shadows. She stood where she was, dazed and uncertain. Still in the grip of a devilish urge to inflict some mark upon her, he said sardonically but in a voice none too steady: "That will illustrate what I mean."

"And a very pretty demonstration indeed," Felice's cool voice interrupted. "Please do not stop on my account."

Theodora partly recovered. "Felice," she said in a strained, odd voice. "I'm sorry you had to find him out this way. But perhaps it's better, after all. I'll take you home …"

"Really, Theodora," Felice drawled in a withering tone, "you are incredible! I have no intention of going home with you. Come along, Grant, if school is out. Dinner is on the table."

Theodora did not wait to hear more. She bent her head and fled.

"Theodora!" Grant shouted, striding after her.

But she was far ahead, and he arrived at the entrance only in time to see her disappear into the carriage and drive off.

CHAPTER TWELVE

"Your cook, Lily, is the best in St. Louis," Grant remarked, leaning back from the table and lighting a cigarette.

The tapering flames of the tall candles suffused the room with a warm light, casting an amber glow on the two glasses of cognac and reflecting highlights on the red mahogany of the table which was visible through the spiraling coils of the lace cover. In its quiet taste and elegantly appointed furnishings, this could have been a dining room in any of the exclusive mansions on the heights. Lily, gowned in soft dove gray, her only ornament a necklace of perfectly matched pearls, might have been the poised mistress of the most respected and dignified home in the city.

"I make a point of having the best," she retorted, nevertheless pleased at the well-deserved compliment.

Grant's visits were infrequent, and she never failed to make occasions of them, taking extra care with the dinner and going to great lengths to make certain it was served in an atmosphere of discreet, comfortable enjoyment. In reality, tonight was little different from other nights when she dined alone except for the cognac and the lace cloth she had brought back from abroad. The table was always set with the best silver and Limoges china, and the candles were always burning in their gleaming holders. Though she sat down to a solitary meal each evening, Lily never compromised with the niceties of life.

"Mabelle," she addressed the light-skinned Negress who had served the meal, "tell Wilma I want her in the reception room. And when you finish in the kitchen, you may go."

"Yes'm, Miss Lily. I'se done soon's I take a tray up to Miss Trudy."

Lily's eyes questioned Mabelle. "Trudy?" she repeated, frowning.

"She ain't feelin' so good," Mabelle shrugged vaguely. "Might be she's homesick."

"Trouble, Lily?" Grant inquired as the maid disappeared through the door to the kitchen.

"Often in a business like this," she acknowledged. "But not what you'd expect. For one thing, I pick my girls well and pay them well. If they use common sense, they'll be all right when they quit. If they get careless, it's the devil to pay!"

"Trudy?" he asked with a cynical lift of an eyebrow.

She dismissed this with a smile, then her expression grew more serious. "Trudy will get along. She was in trouble with a boy back home, and ran off. The baby did something to her, I suppose. Born dead, in spite of all the doctor could do."

"Poor little Trudy," he murmured.

"You're not as hard as you'd like to be, Grant Monroe," she said laughingly.

"And I've an idea you like these tramps," he returned with a good-natured grin.

"I don't mind when they do all right," she admitted. "My favorite was a little French girl from New Orleans. She stayed long enough to polish off the rough edges, then ran away with a thoroughly respected senator. He established her in an apartment in Washington, and contrived to 'meet' her at a diplomatic reception. When they married, everybody wanted to be presented to his 'countess.'"

He laughed heartily. "Quite a recommendation for your charm school. But your place is already rather well advertised. Didn't a certain titled Britisher come all the way to St. Louis on a visit to this country, and not in the interests of international diplomacy either?"

They laughed again. Then she said, watching him intently: "But you didn't come here to engage in light talk. What's on your mind?"

His expression clouded and he returned his attention to the cigarette in his hand. "My pleasure in your company is sufficient reason for a visit," he said with a forced attempt to maintain the light tone of conversation.

"I know you better than that," she said firmly. "If it's Jenkins," she went on as he sipped his cognac in silence, "his board of directors is already issuing stock in the new transit company."

Grant whistled softly. "And I thought I was well informed," he remarked on a note of admiration.

"That's what you've been thinking about, isn't it?" she asked as he fell silent again, fingering his cigarette.

"Perhaps," he said slowly.

Her eyes narrowed, and she studied him in perplexity. "You haven't changed your mind, have you? You haven't decided to call it off?"

His face tightened. "No," he assured her unsmilingly. "In any event, it's out of my hands now. If Jenkins runs true to form, the traction venture will be something St. Louis won't soon forget."

She did not reply immediately and they were silent, each following a line of thought that led back across the years. Lily's were poignant memories, mellowed by the satisfying perspective of time. She had gone beyond the sharp resentment and anger of youth to a rational acceptance of the inevitable. Grant's thoughts were coldly inflexible, congealed in his implacable determination to measure out a merciless justice of his own.

"I don't see you often," Lily remarked after a time. "Perhaps that's why I notice things. You've been different these past months. Moody, short-tempered, not as sure of yourself as you were nine years ago. Is it Jenkins' older daughter?"

The question caught him off guard, but his composure did not desert him. He regarded her out of the corner of his eye, his expression deliberately amused. "Why do you ask?" he said in an elaborately casual tone.

"Because only a woman could make a man hesitate about doing the thing he's wanted to do all his life," she informed him shrewdly.

"Sorry to disappoint you, Lily," he said easily. "Believe me, there is no woman in my life."

But she was not to be turned aside. "I'll be frank with you, Grant. I understand your fixed hatred for Jenkins and all he represents but not to the point where it embitters your own life. There is a price to pay for everything, and I'm wondering if this won't come rather high."

He grinned wryly. "Your interest in Miss Theodora is extraordinary. Is that why you wrote when I was away?"

"You didn't lose much time getting back to the city," she countered.

"If you knew Theodora better," he returned lightly, "you'd see that even an idle flirtation in her direction is an impossibility. As far as she's concerned, the difference between the sexes is mainly one of costume."

"Nonsense," she retorted. "She probably has an intuition about you. After all, your motives toward her father are not exactly amicable." She waited, but be said nothing. "I met her again today," she informed him slowly. "These accidental encounters are awkward. You saw how it was when we met in front of the Weston. I wish I hadn't run into her when I was abroad last year. Theodora assumed because I was talking to Tagliev after one of the concerts that I was just another American like herself, interested in the arts."

A faint smile played around the corners of his mouth. "Well, aren't you?"

"You know what I mean," she said impatiently. "Sooner or later, she will learn the truth."

"Theodora's pride is strong enough to sustain a few shocks," he responded shortly.

"I'm not so sure. Pride isn't the protection you might think. Often the greater it is, the more staggering the blow. Incidentally, she told me about the arrangements for the charity dance."

"Oh?" he said noncommittally.

"You are on the committee this year, aren't you?" she asked. "Why did you let them get her into that?"

He regarded her with some impatience. "As a matter of fact," he said, an increasing edge to his tone, "I was the one who suggested the idea. I thought it an excellent opportunity for her compositions to get a hearing."

"You know better," she scolded. "The crowd that goes to those affairs will take her work like a dose of bitters."

"Not necessarily," he disagreed, crushing his cigarette in the tray with a subdued violence that did not escape her. "If her music is good, they'll listen."

She shook her head slowly. "You've been in love with her for some time, haven't you?" she asked quietly.

His face became rigid. One of the candles sputtered with a sharp, angry hiss. There was silence between them, heavy and disquieting, oddly out of harmony with the external pleasantness of the room. He knew that Lily had not been deceived by his evasions. The tacit understanding between them left much unsaid, but there are things that do not need to be put into words.

"What can I do?" he asked in a changed voice, smothered in its intensity. "She is Harlan's daughter."

Lily drew a deep breath. Tonight she had sensed a bewildering obscurity about Grant, a dissimulation that alarmed her. She was relieved now to see him drop his guard, if only for a few moments. "Forget Harlan," she said simply. "Why go on torturing yourself with the past?"

He looked at her a long moment, measuring all she had meant to him during the past nine years. The purpose of this visit returned to him with acute clarity, and instinctively he recoiled. "Don't worry, Lily," he said in a strangely gentle tone. "It will work out."

He stood up and held her chair. Again she was aware of a subtle alienation between them. Together they walked to the door, a private entrance shielded from the front by great shade trees and thick shrubs. Grant hesitated on the threshold, his expression clouded with indecision. She saw the remorse, the self-recrimination in his eyes, and the grim line of his mouth. She waited, searching for some word that would reach him through this new constraint, but she could think of none.

"This sort of life is wrong for you, Lily," he said finally, measuring his words with painful deliberation. "Why don't you leave St. Louis? You have years of living ahead, and the money to do with them what you please. You can travel, own a chateau in France and a villa on the Mediterranean. You can be with people who will respect you for what you are."

For an imperceptible moment she studied his expression anxiously and her heart constricted in a dull, heavy pain. She realized the bitterness of the inward struggle he had attempted to conceal from her. This was bound to happen sooner or later, she reminded herself rigorously. She should have been prepared. The pang in her heart sharpened, then gradually subsided. When she spoke, her voice was light, almost careless. "You've been reading my mind," she said in a bantering tone. "Frankly, I've been bored with St. Louis, and you are right about making the most of the years ahead. I've always intended to spend my money while I could enjoy it. I meant to tell you that I might wind up my affairs here soon after the first of the year."

She read the answer she sought in his look of apparent relief. She did not need to know why. Whatever his reason, it was enough that he wanted her to go away. She would have done more, much more, for this inaccessible man who was all she had left from her memories of the past. A warm affection swept over her, dwarfing the loneliness ahead, and she smiled. "I suppose I could leave earlier," she considered. "If I put the property up for sale now, I might get a good offer."

The wretchedness in his eyes grew, and he could not shake the feeling that this was all a distorted shadow of reality. "You'll get a better price after the first of the year," he said automatically. "If I were you, I'd sell the latter part of February."

He held her hand briefly in parting, then walked quickly to the curb where his carriage waited. Engrossed in his own thoughts, he was unaware that the Jenkins carriage had just turned the corner a block away.

But Theodora saw him and she leaned forward to question her driver. "What house is that, Rufus? The big place with all the trees and shrubbery?"

The old man's grin widened into a chuckle. "The Belle Arms?" he said in huge merriment. "Thet there's a house of ladies, yes ma'am. A fancy house!"

CHAPTER THIRTEEN

The annual charity dance far surpassed the gala frolics held in previous years. The great ballroom of the Hotel Weston was aglitter with sparkling festivity. A brilliant flood of light streamed down from the crystal chandeliers overhead, enhancing the colorful display of lavish gowns and scintillating on a dazzling assortment of costly gems.

Theodora, dancing with Neil Hunter, had the first moment of the evening in which to contemplate the imminent musical recital that was to highlight the event. The single gentlemen and indeed many of the married had pursued her persistently, claiming one dance after another until she had scant time for reflection. She realized with a start that the hour for the intermission was almost at hand, and she was suddenly preoccupied and cheerless as she glanced about. The assembled throng gave little promise of becoming an appreciative group of listeners, she thought realistically. Doubtless they would strive to maintain a certain degree of attentiveness with that air of polite suffrance people assume when the demands of propriety are particularly exacting. And what could one expect? The intermediate recital was a senseless practice, designed to fill in an otherwise dull interlude. After the lively pleasure of dancing, people were not in a receptive mood for the presentation of serious music.

"What's wrong with me?" Neil asked, breaking in on her thoughts.

"Wrong?" she repeated, startled. "Nothing. Not a thing."

Nothing except a lack of courage, she amended privately, surveying him with a critical frown. His was a pleasant face with clean-cut, agreeable features. Perhaps the closely cropped light brown hair and the candid sincerity of the blue eyes prevented him from presenting a more dashingly romantic appearance. But Neil was twenty-seven and already the nominal executive of his father's bank. Moreover, what he lacked in verve and fascinating charm was counterbalanced by his unquestionable sense of honor and integrity, his manners and breeding, and his unfailing kindness to and consideration for Felice.

He was looking unhappily over his shoulder and she turned to see Felice in Grant's arms, her face radiant and flushed, the dancing eyes alight with her triumph.

"You've let her walk over you since she was in rompers," Theodora scolded. "That's not the way to manage a girl like Felice. You should be more assertive. Go up to her and claim the next dance," she advised firmly as the music came to an end. "She won't refuse if you show her you don't intend to be put off."

"You don't know Felice," he said pessimistically. "My attempts to be masterful leave her unimpressed."

Her retort died on the tip of her tongue however as she saw that there was not to be another dance at the moment. Chairs were being brought in and guests were leaving the floor to stand in informal groups at the side. Filled with misgivings as she was, the friendly murmurs of conversation and rustling of gowns fell with a horrid effect on her ears. She sent Neil off in pursuit of Felice, and retreated unseen behind the heavy crimson portières at the rear.

Georgia Daly's appearance was greeted by a refined shower of hand-clapping and whispered comment, and the recital began. Fortunately Miss Daly, having recovered from the head cold, was in good voice and gave a most commendable rendition of the songs, though the interpretation at times was subordinated to an exhibition of the really remarkable Daly high tones. Theodora relaxed, but not entirely. The call for encores left her with the disagreeable suspicion that the effect on the listeners had been created by Georgia Daly, not Theodora Jenkins. She then subsided into a numb and involuntary state of resignation.

The string ensemble opened with bravado and color, but it was apparent from the start that salon music was futile and incongruous in the vast hall. For the first few minutes utter silence fell upon the assembled group. Then the inevitable rustling of programs was audible, and the gentle, apologetic shifting of feet and conversational whispers rose in an avalanche of muted accompaniment to the nicely constructed cadences of the "American Fantasias." Several women drifted out to the powder room while others wandered off with their escorts to the adjoining hall where the great banquet table was laden with platters of food and huge bowls of cracked ice, champagne, and sparkling soda.

Impaled by an enormous sense of failure and frustration, Theodora stood rigidly erect, staring straight ahead as the music went on and on. At its conclusion she heard the scattered and negligible applause with no visible emotion. A number of the admiring gentlemen whose interest was not in the least connected with the musical offerings of the evening discovered her and crowded about with extravagant compliments. She accepted their flattery with a dignified but unsmiling: "Thank you. Thank you very much."

"May I offer my congratulations too?" Grant asked, skillfully insinuating himself through the group and taking her arm. "In my humble opinion your ability is a promising contribution to the music of this country."

She looked at him sharply, seeking to detect the hidden mockery beneath his words. But his face was grave, and his eyes held only the assurance of sincerity.

"Thank you, Mr. Monroe," she forced herself to say stiffly. "Such a compliment from you is praise indeed."

He led her aside with a brief nod to the others who glared after them with undisguised resentment. When they were comparatively alone, Theodora drew away and stood regarding him in silence. "I don't blame you for being angry with me," he said quietly. "I can only beg your forgiveness for the other night, and hope that you will find the kindness in your heart to forget my inconsiderate lack of manners. Believe me, I am very sorry."

She wondered momentarily if there was, then, a sense of decency in him. But no, she would not be misled by another pose from one so skilled in the art of dissimulation.

"I am sure you are not in the habit of saying what you don't mean," she retorted with a shade of sarcasm. "However, you may be certain that I forgot the entire incident as quickly as possible."

"Then I assume we can be friends as before?" he said engagingly.

"As before, Mr. Monroe?" she repeated with a thin smile.

He flushed, and his smile became less agreeable. "You are aware, I see, that our encounters in the past have been marred by an element of strain," he remarked unpleasantly. "The thought surprises me, for I had not known a lady of excellent breeding would be intentionally remiss."

"Oh?" she said coolly. "And I did not realize that your contact with ladies of breeding was so extensive."

The flush burned deeper in his face, and a slow anger displaced the smiling air of polite detachment. The dancing was resumed and several couples, passing on their way to the floor, glanced at them curiously.

With an effort, he recovered his control. "Shall we dance, Miss Theodora? Perhaps the activity will improve the quality of our conversation."

She was about to refuse when she caught sight of Neil earnestly talking to Felice. She read the hesitation in Felice's attitude as the green-flecked eyes scanned the room, searching impatiently for Grant.

"By all means," Theodora agreed, her frosty manner slightly modified by her decision to divert him.

Grant, who had followed her glance across the room, was not deceived by her acquiescence. He directed her onto the floor without comment. As they danced, her body flexed and turned with supple grace to the lilting rhythms of the waltz but she reflected none of the festive mood that enlivened the other dancers on the crowded floor. Her hand in his was chill and limp, and her face again wore that air of polite condescension that infuriated him. His hatred for Harlan Jenkins began to drum with brutal savagery in his blood, and his anger at Theodora's contemptuous bearing became almost uncontrollable in its blinding violence. Tightening his arm about her, he moved in a series of intricate steps and unexpected turns. She followed perfectly and with ease, her only reaction being an indifferent glance of scorn.

"That third song," he said presently. "What was the title?"

She flashed him a sudden look, charged with suspicion. Reluctantly, somewhat grimly, she answered: " 'You Are Mine, Love.' "

"Ah yes," he nodded reminiscently. " 'You Are Mine, Love.' It was my favorite in the group. Such warmth, such tenderness! You will forgive me, I know, if I say that I was amazed."

Her eyes smoldered dangerously. "Why should you be amazed, Mr. Monroe?" she asked, visibly breathing disdain.

"The beauty of the setting so perfectly portrayed the maid's yearning for her lover," he explained with conscienceless frankness. "The sympathetic and passionately moving music harmonized so ardently with the words that I found it rather difficult to associate the workmanship with you."

"I see," she said, her voice crackling with suppressed fury.

"Don't misunderstand me," he went on guilelessly. "I was merely wondering how a lady of superior virtue can project her imaginative self intimately into the thoughts and feelings of one of her less conventional sisters. The untutored layman," he explained without regard for her growing anger, "is prone to believe that an artist cannot recreate the subtler nuances of passion until he has lived through or at least experienced some similar emotional upheaval. Apparently this is not true in every case?"

She forgot her intention to divert him from Felice. Oblivious to everything but the odious mockery of his smile, she pushed away from him violently. "Your manners are unpardonable," she exclaimed, her cheeks flaming. "And now, please find another on whom you can practice your vulgar witticisms. I've had quite enough for one evening."

She turned and made her way swiftly along the fringes of dancers near the wall. He stared after her, making no attempt to follow. The odd, inscrutable look deepened on his face as the swirling skirts of her gown disappeared through the exit. Not until he was jostled by nearby couples on the floor did he move.

When Felice was free to look for him, he was gone, and she spent the remainder of the evening in Neil's company.

CHAPTER FOURTEEN

Harlan faced Theodora in the quiet dignity of the well-ordered study. "Very well," he said with a hint of weariness in his voice. "I shall talk to Felice. But I warn you she will probably be only the more determined to do as she pleases."

He had found the discussion about Felice's future irksome. Actually he cared little whether she married Neil or Grant Monroe. On the other hand, as Theodora pointed out, there was no indication that Grant's attentions would lead to matrimony. If Felice's security were to be affected, he thought with equity, perhaps he should try to bring some influence to bear.

A maid was sent to summon Felice. While they waited, Theodora marshaled her dignity and scattered composure. Her father's incomprehensible defense of Grant Monroe had nearly led to a disagreeable scene. Father, she thought with asperity, was never able to see that another man might be less honorable and straightforward than he. For the first time within her recollection, an issue had been raised on which neither was willing or able to compromise and which seriously threatened to disrupt the peace of the household.

Felice entered the study with an untroubled air, and after a quizzical glance at her father and Theodora, seated herself decorously and folded her hands. "How solemn you both look," she said with mock gravity. "Is this the start of a weighty family conference?"

Theodora remained standing, waiting for her father to speak. Harlan cleared his throat.

"The matter is of some importance, yes," he said with marked disinclination. "Since your interests are most deeply involved, it deserves your consideration."

Felice was not misled by his careful choice of words nor by Theodora's solicitous attitude. However she said with proper respect and docility: "Yes, father? I hope I have done nothing to warrant your displeasure?"

"No, no," he said. "Nothing like that."

"Felice," Theodora began as he hesitated again. "Father and I think the time has come to announce your engagement to Neil. You cannot postpone it indefinitely."

Felice's eyes danced and the lovely mouth dimpled as she prepared to enjoy herself. "Surely, Theodora, you don't suggest that I marry now? Wouldn't it be highly improper for me to be the first bride in the family? People are certain to point you out as an old maid."

Theodora stiffened but she did not allow her feelings to get out of control. "Perhaps," she replied evenly. "But such talk is unimportant, and scarcely an excuse for you to put off your marriage."

Felice preened and plucked composedly at a ruffle on her skirt. "That's one side of you I've always admired, Theodora," she said sweetly. "You're so independent and so unselfish."

Harlan's ear detected the beginning of an unpleasant exchange and he interposed hastily: "Theodora's main interest is her music. But you, Felice, have a different future. One, we hope, full of ease and security. That is why we feel there should be no further delay about Neil."

"I don't want to marry Neil now," Felice said in a sharper tone. "I'm not sure I ever want to marry him."

"Don't talk nonsense," Theodora said, suppressing a frown with difficulty. "Of course you are going to marry Neil."

"Really, Theodora, your concern amuses me. Why are you so insistent that I marry Neil? It couldn't be because of Grant Monroe, could it?"

Harlan interceded before Theodora could reply. "Mr. Monroe is excellent and charming company, my dear. But you should look to your future with a more objective eye."

"I am glad you agree, father, that Mr. Monroe is a gentleman," Felice said. "Because I intend to see as much of him as I like. As for my future, please do not worry. It is not as black and hopeless as you seem to think."

Theodora, nettled, saw the interview going badly with no help from her father to keep it pointed in the right direction. Tightening her grip on herself, she threw in the final argument which she had hoped desperately would not be needed. "I regret to disillusion you, Felice. And you, father," she added grimly. "And I regret the necessity for bringing up so vile a subject. But it is my duty to speak frankly. Do you know where your Grant Monroe was the night before last? No, of course you wouldn't. Nor would I, except that I happened to be driving past as he was leaving."

They looked at her, Felice smugly amused at what she considered a rather amateurish performance on Theodora's part, and Harlan with closer attention than before, but still wearily tolerant.

"He went to an unspeakable place called the Belle Arms," Theodora went on quickly, unable to control the flush that rose to her cheeks. "No self-respecting, honorable man would dream of visiting such a house. It's all quite dreadful, and I absolutely forbid my sister to be seen in his company again."

Harlan, stunned at hearing this accusation from Theodora and even more discomfited by her mention of the Belle Arms, a name with which he was quite familiar, took immediate refuge in righteous anger. "Theodora, you must have been mistaken," he said sharply. "This is a serious charge, and I insist that you think twice before you accuse anyone."

"There is no mistake, father," she said relentlessly. "I saw him."

Felice, astute enough to guess the kind of house to which Theodora referred, was taken by surprise, resentment, and defiance in turn. "You've been following him again, have you?" she asked indignantly. "Honestly, father, it's humiliating the way Theodora runs after him!"

"I?" Theodora demanded, blazing. "Run after him? That's a wicked, ungrateful remark. I've only been thinking of you, trying to protect you ..."

"You've been infatuated with him since you returned from Europe," Felice asserted maliciously. "You want him for yourself, and you've tried to come between us every way you could manage, even to leading him on the night I saw you in his arms!"

"Felice!" Harlan said abruptly. "I must remind you not to speak in this manner to your sister."

"I'm sorry, father," she said unrepentantly. "She compels me to speak plainly. I'm tired of the way she has tried to influence you against Mr. Monroe, and tired of having her dictate to me. If I am to be allowed to express an opinion, I might suggest that Theodora devote her entire attention to music, as important as she pretends it is. And now that we've said all, I shall go to my room."

She flounced out in angry defiance, leaving them wordless. After a long moment Harlan spoke.

"You might have expected something like that, Theodora," he said sternly, the strong tension of the last few minutes still on him. "Your attack was unpardonable." His defense of Monroe was becoming repetitious enough to be galling. In reality he knew himself to be not particularly fond of Grant Monroe. Harlan was not, to be exact, particularly fond of anyone. But Monroe, with his money and influence, could be useful to him and as such was not to be impugned.

Theodora scarcely heard him. Aghast at the suggestion that she was infatuated with Grant, she had not recovered. She sank into the chair vacated by Felice and stared blankly at her father, wondering whether he too believed such an impossible absurdity.

"Perhaps I was wrong to interfere," she said finally in a remote, still voice. "I've done nothing but alienate myself from both of you."

"That's not true," he said, somewhat relieved at the subdued change in her and strengthened by her sudden preoccupation. "Felice has a volatile disposition, and she strikes out like an angry kitten when she's aroused. You shouldn't take her tempers too seriously."

"Just the same, it will be better for all of us when I go back to Vienna," she went on drearily. "Thanks to the money mama left, I won't need to burden you with my expenses. The interest on the trust fund will be ample with what I can earn tutoring."

He frowned and plucked at his thick underlip. He had not intended to inform Theodora about his recent disposition of the fund. But if she persisted in this notion to return to Europe, she would certainly have to know. And perhaps this was an opportune time. In her present passivity, she would be less inclined to take issue with him over the matter. He did not like the extreme pallor of her face or the hint of hidden panic in her widened eyes, but he counted on her unquestioning faith in his judgment to carry the moment.

"I'm afraid that's out of the question just now," he said with deliberation. "For a while at least, there won't be any interest on the fund."

In her distraction, this information penetrated slowly. Then it was her turn to frown and she did so, with doubt and dismay. "What do you mean, father?" she asked incredulously. "The money is safe, isn't it?"

"I have reinvested it for you," he said in an appeal to the practical side of her nature. "The money will more than double itself in time, and the interest alone will provide you with an enviable income."

"In the new traction company, father?" she demanded, her voice rising on a hysterical note at the appalling thought. "Without consulting me?"

"As you recall," he reminded her with the impelling dignity that had always stirred her prideful and affectionate regard, "your mother designated me trustee of the fund. Had you married, the money would have been yours outright. I daresay she expected you to have it long before this. But according to the terms of her will, I have continued my duty of administering it to the best of my ability."

"Mama left it to me, but she meant it for Felice and Brad as well," she said, trying to think clearly. "She asked me to look after them, and the money was to be a sort of emergency fund for all of us."

"She created the fund when you were born," he told her. "I don't know whether she ever intended to change her will in any way or not. You were always her favorite, and I think she was content to leave it in your name. As for Brad, the tuition for his last year at law school has been set aside. But your scheduled trip abroad, I fear, will have to be postponed."

Mama had not meant him to use the money, she thought painfully. Yet even as her mind rebelled, she chided herself for her lack of filial respect and devotion. Father was astute about investments. If at times he drew upon every available source of revenue to launch a new undertaking, no one could blame him. The management of wide-spread and diversified investments was a precarious and exacting business, and she quite understood the fluctuating nature of most holdings since the depression.

"You needn't fear," Harlan continued after several minutes. "When the traction company starts paying dividends, you'll realize a splendid profit."

"Of course, father," she murmured dimly.

Dazed and baffled, she rose slowly and left the room. Disturbed after the scene with Felice and disconcerted by this final blow to her plans, she went outside for a walk. She was several blocks away when Pete Solloway stepped from a shining new buggy in the drive, walked briskly to the door, and lifted the knocker.

CHAPTER FIFTEEN

Solloway's visit to Harlan Jenkins was brief, and the gambling concessionaire was agreeably apologetic as he mentioned the matter of Brad's debts. "I understand the boy is going back to college soon," he said with a genial smile, holding the notes with Brad's signatures so that Jenkins could inspect them. "I knew you'd want to make good on these before he leaves."

Jenkins stared, and his customary aplomb deserted him. Had Brad become involved in any other escapade, however reckless, he would have understood. But the indebtedness represented by the slips of paper in Solloway's hand was a heavy blow. His face convulsed, and the dim eyes sharpened to venomous pinpoints. "You're lower than I thought, Solloway. "What do you mean by allowing the boy to play your crooked games?"

"I wish you wouldn't take it like that, Mr. Jenkins," Solloway said, unruffled. "This is only a friendly little visit, and there's no reason for hard feelings. I was under the impression you knew about Brad's visits to the *Crescent*. He and that nice young girl of his spent several evenings on board and naturally everything was done to see that they had a good time."

"What girl?" Jenkins demanded with fresh suspicion. He was not of a mind to censor Brad for trifling affairs with women, the kind he shrewdly supposed the young man indulged in during the summer. Harlan had always been persuaded that Brad had a right to engage in a normal amount of dalliance before he was to assume the responsibilities for which he was being prepared.

When the proper time arrived, Brad would marry one of the eligible girls of his own set. Harlan was as certain of this as he was that Brad, with the legal training he had received at the university, would in time operate the brokerage offices on a profitable scale. Harlan did not anticipate the possibility that Brad would fall into a serious involvement prematurely. But there was something in Solloway's remark that put him on guard.

Solloway hesitated. The old man's anger was nearly out of control. Maybe he shouldn't have mentioned the girl. Then he shrugged. After all, what difference did it make? "Ann Lynch," he said, meeting Jenkins' eye easily. "A nice little girl, works in the Arcade Flower Shop. You probably remember her father, Tom Lynch."

Jenkins' face purpled and he almost leaped from his chair. "What's your game, Solloway?" he demanded. "If you intend to use my son to get money from me, you won't succeed!"

"Now, Mr. Jenkins, nobody is trying to get money that isn't due," Solloway said quickly. "This is just a matter of a little business, and I'm sure you aren't going to let your son back down on a gambling debt." Not liking the baleful gleam in old Harlan's eyes, he decided to terminate the discussion. "I'll not press you for the amount today," he said, rising. "But the boys want to close the books by the end of the month. Two weeks will do it, I imagine?"

Jenkins stared murderously at him. He knew that behind Solloway's activities was Al Reed's unseen protective arm. How close the association ran, he could not be sure. In any case, he could ill afford to antagonize Reed. He was shaken more than he cared to admit by the reference to Tom Lynch and wild with fury that Brad was seeing this girl. His headlong fear that Solloway was in a plot against him brought his thoughts back again to Reed. Then he checked himself. Reed had no hold over him because of the past, nor did Solloway. If they had, they would have used it long ago. There was nothing to be gained by allowing suspicion to run away with him. He would handle this as he had handled threats to his security in the past, with deliberation and finality.

"You'll have your money, Solloway," he said at length in a more controlled tone. "But by God, you'd better see that this is the last time my son gets involved in your rotten games."

CHAPTER SIXTEEN

Theodora returned to the house, her flagging spirits rigidly disciplined, her features pale but severely composed. Her nerves, though quieter, were still ragged and when she heard the voices of Brad and her father raised in bitter dispute, her step quickened in fresh alarm. Hurrying to the study, she threw open the door.

"Keep Ann's name out of this, father," Brad was saying heatedly. "She had nothing to do with it."

"Brad! Father!" Theodora exclaimed. "Your voices can be heard in the street."

"Come in, Theodora," Brad said sarcastically. "Come in. This is right in your department."

She glanced from one to the other, utterly bewildered. Her father's face was heavily flushed and damp. The knuckles showed white in the clenched hand on the arm of his chair, and the severity in the cold, pale eyes was unrelenting. It was not like him to quarrel with Brad, she thought confusedly. He had never before reproached any of them in this manner. "What in heaven's name is the matter?" she demanded.

"I think, Theodora, you had better leave us," Harlan said, steadying his voice with an effort.

"Why?" Brad asked in a contemptuous tone. "Don't you think Theodora's high moral sense can cope with the knowledge that her brother has been gambling?"

Theodora sat down slowly. "Gambling?" she repeated faintly.

Her eyes fixed on her brother in a shocked, disbelieving stare. In this new calamity, her mind refused to accept the truth of what she heard. Dimly she thought of Brad as she had once known him, mild-mannered and submissive, never hateful or rebellious or dishonorable. What had happened to him? What had changed him into this thin, hard, defiant youth? Where had she failed, she who had conscientiously guided him in his formative years, striving to inculcate the principles of right and wrong with consistent and impressive earnestness? "But why?" she asked numbly. "Why, Brad?"

Harlan thrust out his jaw. "I find that easier to understand than his preoccupation with a cheap little shopgirl," he stated unpleasantly. "His losses at gambling are one thing; but I'll not tolerate this involvement with Ann Lynch. If Brad continues to see her over my objections, he can consider himself finished at the university. I intended to give him the kind of education others in his class receive at Eastern schools, but if he is going to lower himself to the gutter, I wash my hands of him entirely."

"Father!" Theodora protested in mounting agitation.

Brad stared at his father grimly, saying nothing. He had never felt any close bond of filial devotion for this short, thickset man with glaring eyes and clenched fist. Harlan's negligent indifference through the years had prevented any such attachment. Nor had his sojourn at the university done anything to improve the relationship between them. On the contrary, his schooling had given him the insight to view his father without any of the illusions that bemused Theodora's vision.

His feelings toward his sister were scarcely warmer. He had outgrown her uncompromising discipline at an early age, but he had never found a satisfactory way to rebel. Now as he met their combined accusations, the anxiety that had hounded him for days lifted and he experienced a certain malicious pleasure. Let them absorb the shock the best they could.

His father's ultimatum about Ann was a different matter. He thought of her quiet forgiveness after the scene on the *Crescent;* he remembered her sincerity, her honesty, her faith in him, and his anger mounted furiously. Unable to speak, he turned abruptly on his heel and strode from the room.

"I might see the girl," Jenkins mused, partly to himself, "and buy her off. It wouldn't take much, I imagine."

Theodora's impulse to comfort him was mingled with a deep but uncertain anxiety. The tension in the room seemed to increase with Brad's departure. She had the uncomfortable feeling that something stronger than any of them had taken hold of their lives and, with its tightening grip, was unwilling to release them. Whatever it was, she thought uneasily, had already begun to pull them apart, and all her instincts warned that this was only a beginning.

Nevertheless, in the midst of her uncertainties and misgivings, she was able to take austere comfort from the fact that Harlan agreed at last about the necessity for adopting a sterner parental attitude. Possibly now he would realize that she had been right about Felice too. "Brad will come to his senses, father," she tried to reassure him. "I think we should concern ourselves about the money. How much is the gambling debt?"

"I'll take care of it, Theodora," he said vaguely.

She sensed that he did not want to talk. His disappointment in Brad was a heavy blow and she knew he wanted to be alone. "Whatever you say, father," she said, rising. She paused momentarily, as though forcibly held back by the invisible atmosphere of strain in the room, then slowly made her way to the door.

CHAPTER SEVENTEEN

Ann sat across the table from Brad in a small coffee shop near the flower store. He had not spoken for some time and she sipped her coffee slowly, not interrupting his thoughts. A curious unfamiliarity crept into the waiting silence. His thin, hard face was older, set in lines that would one day deepen into permanence. Strong lines, she saw with an unaccountable touch of sadness, lines that would lose their bitterness through the years in a calm, settled maturity. There was a new quiet in his manner, not the swift moodiness she knew so well, or the passing cloud of despondency which could be erased with a smile and a light word. She sensed a finality and a fixity of purpose about him that brought a queer catch of fear to her throat.

She leaned forward slightly. "You've something to tell me," she said, studying him with troubled eyes.

"I'm not going back to the university this fall," he announced without preliminary.

"Not going back?" she repeated, startled. "Why?"

"It's father," he said darkly. "There's been a row."

"He is angry about the money you lost," she said quietly. "But to keep you from finishing at the university isn't fair. You must go back, Brad. The degree is all you've wanted, your whole future!"

"I'll finish eventually," he said grimly. "If I stay here this winter and work, I'll have the money for tuition. The rest can be managed with an off-campus job. But we'll have to wait to get married, how long I don't know."

She knew what it meant for him to complete his studies and be independent. The delay would be hard to endure, and it carried the lengthening risk that he might not go back for years, if ever.

"How much money is needed?" she asked. "I have a little over a hundred dollars in the bank. I know it isn't much, but if it would help, I want you to have it."

He looked at her strangely, and for a moment he could not find words to answer her. "No thanks, Ann," he said finally in a constrained voice. "Lord knows I've made mistakes, but I have enough self-respect to manage without taking money from you."

She saw the stubborn set of his jaw and knew that he would not change his mind. "Can't you soften his feelings?" she suggested. "If he knows you've quit gambling, perhaps he would see things differently."

"I thought it was the money at first," he said with deepening resentment. "Solloway went to see him. But the gambling wasn't what father found unforgivable."

The small fear began to pulse at the back of her brain. "What then?" she asked with an effort.

His eyes were embittered in their anger. "Solloway told him about you," he said. "Evidently father finds you more objectionable than roulette. It doesn't make sense. He's never questioned anything before. I never thought he cared much what any of us did. Now he emerges from his indifference with fist-shaking ultimatums. He doesn't even know you."

Her color deepened. "He wants you to marry one of the girls in your own class," she said in a low tone. "Someone with money and social position. And he's right. I wouldn't be anything but a hindrance to you."

"I'm the judge of that," he said impatiently. "Father thinks he can force me to do what he wants by cutting off my allowance, but he's wrong. In a way, I suppose, he's done me a favor. I might not have had the sense otherwise to break away from him and live my own life."

"Don't say that," she protested quickly. "You can't give up everything this way. You would regret it eventually, and then you'd begin to hate me. I couldn't bear that."

"I know what I intend to do," he said shortly. "There's no use discussing it any further."

An enormous tiredness crept like a slow poison through her body, and her eyes dimmed. But she knew the only course open to her and, knowing it, drew upon an unsuspected steadiness and courage. "I won't let you do it, Brad," she said in a still voice. "We were wrong for each other from the beginning. I've always known it, but I just didn't admit it to myself."

"You're talking nonsense," he said with quick anger. "I didn't expect to find you arguing on father's side."

"He is right," she persisted stubbornly. "We shouldn't see each other again."

He stared at her with hard eyes. "Look, Ann. I'm not perfect. I've made mistakes, but that's all over now. I'm going to do what I set out to do. I'll get through the university one way or another, and then we'll be married."

She took a deep breath. "No, Brad," she said with queer finality.

His eyes met hers with increasing bitterness. "Then you don't care after all," he said bluntly. "You haven't any confidence in me, either. You think I can't finish school without father's help, and you want no part of me if I haven't a future that's all wrapped up with security and success. All right, we'll not see each other again. I'll keep out of your way, since that's what you want."

He pushed back his chair and stood up. "If you change your mind, you know where to reach me." He paused, but she said nothing. When he saw that she would not speak, he strode away. He stopped at the door to pay the cashier, then left.

CHAPTER EIGHTEEN

Theodora did not know what lay behind Brad's changed manner the following day, nor did she inquire into the matter. To her it was natural that he settle his differences with Harlan and entirely reasonable that he forsake an interest in a girl of whom father disapproved. His departure to the university meant one less anxiety in the accumulating mass of problems that rose on every side.

Foremost among them was the payment of the debt to Solloway, contrived through a private arrangement with Grant Monroe. Theodora's persistent questioning finally drew the startling facts from Harlan. The necessity for such an adjustment was insupportable to her, but she sustained a greater shock on learning the details. Harlan, whose traction enterprise was still without assets, negotiated a sizable loan to take care of certain other obligations as well as the debt to Solloway, and in return gave Monroe a lien on the property. Theodora was filled with a futile rage. Never had she been so helpless, so lost. Accustomed to assurance and purposeful direction, she had always found integrity and serene confidence in her determinations. But that was before Grant Monroe entered their lives, before their security and happiness was undermined by a series of intangible but relentless circumstances.

She spent hour upon long hour in the music room. Felice's suggestion that she confine her activities to music held her between the brink of despair and a numb determination. If anything was to be saved from her shattered pride, perhaps it was to be found in a return to the work she knew. Perhaps the cataclysm of rebellious self-doubts and traitorous, unsuspected emotions which had shaken her courage to its foundations could find expression in the familiar media of tonal modes and chordal combinations. She filled pages of manuscript paper and sent them, crumpled, into the wastebasket. Or she sat motionless before the silent piano, waiting for the inspiration that did not come. She searched for lyrics, and found none that suited. A familiar, amused voice commented silently in her ear: "Too deeply passionate, Theodora. You can't do it justice. And this one is too broadly philosophical, my dear girl. You haven't lived enough to undertake this sort of thing. One must experience life to translate it for others."

The room itself had lost its intimacy for her and mocked her with its placid, undisturbed inertia. Yet she knew it was not only the music room but the entire house which had become alien to her. Remembering Felice's stinging accusation, the desperation of terror would seize her. It was not true, she cried silently. She resented and distrusted Grant Monroe, yes, despised him! In a wave of hopelessness and misery, his cool scorn on the deck of the *Crescent* swept back into the clamoring confusion of her thoughts, and her cheeks burned afresh. She became quite rigid as she thought of those long minutes in his arms when nothing else seemed to exist but the two of them.

There were times when he did not come to the house for days, long periods when even Felice did not hear from him. Felice, however, was not given to brooding. Piqued when there was no word from him, she invariably showed a renewed interest in Neil and for a while it would seem that they had returned to the former uneventful run of their lives.

Perhaps, Theodora would tell herself in the midst of her wretchedness, he would stay away forever. She was thinking of this and of Felice one interminably dull Sunday afternoon when she put aside her manuscript paper and rose to go to her room. The usual Sunday evening meal was a haphazard affair, buffet style. Tonight, she remembered, they would dine in a more conventional manner and it would be appropriate to dress. Felice had gone driving with Neil, and as usual when they spent the afternoon together Neil was to join them in a light supper. Theodora permitted herself to dwell on the hope that they were talking over plans for their future. This time the announcement of a wedding date might be forthcoming.

As she opened the door to the hall, she heard Felice's voice, gayer than it had been for some time, her laughter bright with animation. Then she started back, for the voice that responded was Grant Monroe's.

"I should be angry with you," Felice was scolding lightly. "We haven't seen you in nearly a month."

"I can only ask your forgiveness, Miss Felice," he said. "I have been extremely busy, and I'm deeply sorry that I had no opportunity to call sooner."

At the sound of his voice, Theodora stood frozen, her flesh rigid and cold despite the comfortable warmth of the room. There were only the two of them in the hall. What had Felice done with Neil? What dreadful hypocrisy had she employed to get rid of her fiance when she encountered Grant?

"You can wait in the study," Felice said from the stairs. "I'll be down as soon as I change for dinner."

Her steps were swift and light on the stairway, then there was silence in the hall. Grant's footsteps after a few minutes came toward the study, stopped, and continued on toward the music room. Theodora fell back, waiting. He appeared in the doorway, and they looked at each other a long moment.

"Theodora," he said quietly. "May I come in?"

She did not trust herself to speak at once. When she could manage her voice, she asked: "Where is Neil?"

Something went out of his face then. "I believe Neil had another engagement," he said mockingly. "He did not explain when we parted."

He came inside, and his presence filled the room. The afternoon stillness that pervaded this haven of retreat for her fled, and her heart beat suffocatingly in the charging tension that gripped her. Suddenly the gathering intensity of her taut nerves snapped the thin strands of control. "You are altogether unscrupulous," she said in a low, shaken voice, forgetful of every consideration but the dark, smiling man before her. "I did not think you could be so cruel. It amuses you to trifle with the emotions of others, to trample their lives and ruin their hopes. Is there no decency in you?"

Her voice became more manageable as she denounced him, and he closed the door behind him. Making no attempt to stop the flow of her words, he leaned back, his arms folded, his eyes half shut. As she continued to berate him in a frenzy of accusation, the muscles of his face hardened and his mouth became a thin line. He did not speak until she sank on the bench in front of the piano, trembling and exhausted.

"Have you finished?" he asked evenly.

She covered her face with her hands. "Why did you come back?" she asked, her voice catching on a dry sob. "Why can't you stay away and let us live our lives in peace?"

"Since you ask, I'll tell you," he said in a hard voice. "Last summer I went to Cuba, knowing I had to get as far away from here as possible, wanting to stay away. I came back for two reasons, one of them you, Theodora. As a matter of fact," he added with unhurried emphasis, "you are the reason I'm here now."

She raised her head and started to speak, but no sound came. An involuntary shock ran through her body and she could only stare at him incredulously, her face white in the growing dusk.

"Listen carefully, for I'm going to say this only once," he went on, speaking slowly and deliberately. "I love you, and I want you. Underneath that frozen exterior is a woman, the kind of woman a man wants for a wife. But it's entirely up to you. Think it over, Theodora. When you reach your decision, it will be final."

He went out, closing the door behind him, and she heard his steps quickly retreat. Above the throbbing in her eardrums and the wild pounding of her heart, she tried to grasp the incongruous fact that he had asked her to marry him. Clinging tenaciously to the shattered remnants of her pride, she tried to summon the old bitterness toward him. Even his offer of marriage was done in that overbearing manner, his words an implication of humiliating contempt. In an agony of conflicting emotions, she fled the room and rushed blindly up the stairs.

In the corridor above, she collided with Felice who was on her way down to entertain Grant.

"Of all things!" Felice exclaimed, recovering her balance and shaking out the ruffles of her bodice. "I suppose you have discovered that Grant is here, and you are indulging in a bit of hysterics on my account?"

Theodora stared at her, and suddenly she was angry. Without a word, she turned and went on to her room. Felice shrugged, and went down to the study where she found Grant waiting.

CHAPTER NINETEEN

Theodora was steadfastly silent during dinner, unresponsive to her father's efforts to bring her into the conversation, unaware of Felice's wickedly penetrating glances in her direction, sensing only Grant's presence and conscious of nothing but a frenzied discomfiture as his eyes rested on her momentarily before he returned his attention to Felice and Harlan. She struggled to keep her hand from trembling lest he see, and kept her eyes lowered so that he could not read in them what she herself denied. Her inability to control her disordered emotions dismayed her, and her confusion mounted. To marry him was unthinkable. She could not even remotely imagine herself united in wedlock to this man whose every gesture aroused in her such frantic disquiet, who humbled her and treated her like a difficult child.

"We'll have coffee in the music room," Harlan said, rising from the table. "I'd like to hear Theodora play tonight."

"I ..." she began to protest.

"Don't refuse, Theodora," he interrupted. "It's a small favor, considering your admirable technique and years of training" He turned to Grant. "I haven't heard her play for weeks though she spends a great deal of time in the music room. Perhaps if you ask, she will not decline this time."

"I am sure Miss Theodora will oblige us," Grant said with an obscure smile. "I recall her promise, and I know she does not go back on her word."

He is mocking again, she thought hotly. Well, let him amuse himself if he likes. At least she would not give him the satisfaction of knowing he had destroyed her composure. "Very well," she said. "If you like Brahms, you shall be entertained."

Harlan took the chair by the fireplace, and Grant sat with Felice on the sofa. They were served coffee, and Grant and Harlan enjoyed theirs with cigarettes.

Theodora's fingers moved automatically at first, then she was caught in the sweep of the music. The intellectual, reflective Brahms had long been a favorite with her, and now the deeply moving, passionately expressive Brahms came to life as her inner turmoil sought an outlet in rich harmonies and poignant melody.

She finished and looked up, her eyes brilliant in their depths, a flush on her cheeks. She saw the unqualified admiration in Grant's steady gaze, and the flush deepened. Their eyes caught and held. His quiet look questioned her as clearly as though he had spoken. A sharp, quick fire in her heart answered him, and almost at once she dropped her eyes to her hands.

"I've never heard you do as well," Harlan was saying. "I can't pretend to be a critic, but I would venture to say that your style has matured considerably."

"Thank you, father," she said in a muffled voice. "But you give me too much credit. My style is quite the same, if you discount a few liberties with interpretation."

"Certain liberties give individuality to an artist, do they not?" Grant asked conversationally. "If each performance were stereotyped, art would lose its flavor and become boring repetition of unbearably trite passages."

"I agree that Theodora's playing has improved," Felice said, breaking in on the discussion. "There have been times when I didn't take her music seriously, but I was wrong. I see now that she was meant to devote her life to her art. I suppose that's why she refused the invitation to the Mills hunting lodge next week. Theodora prefers her pads of manuscript paper to the rigors of snow and ice in the mountains."

"I forgot that the Mills were having a house party," Grant said absently.

"You will come, of course?" Felice prompted. "Fred and Martha want you, I know."

Theodora saw Felice at the lodge with Grant, skating on the lake, tramping through the snow on long walks, lounging before the fireplace, and something inside her burst with the blinding force of an explosion. Before the splintering fragments had cleared away, she found her voice. "I'm afraid he won't be able to accept the invitation," she heard herself say in strangely clear accents. "You see, Mr. Monroe and I are to be married."

Nothing she could have said or done would have produced a more volcanic effect in the room. Harlan stared at her as though he could not have heard right, and Felice looked as though Theodora had gone suddenly mad. The green eyes widened dangerously as she forgot the beguiling sweetness she invariably radiated in Grant's company.

"What?" she cried on a rising note.

Theodora ignored her. She looked searchingly at Grant, but his expression had not changed. He went on quietly smoking as though unaware of the prolonged shock that hung in the peaceful Sabbath stillness.

"Is this true, Grant?" Harlan asked, unable to keep the pleasure entirely from his voice as he contemplated this astounding development with enlivened spirits.

"It is," Grant nodded. "Theodora and I will be married at her earliest convenience."

"Well, congratulations, sir!" he said heartily. "I must admit that it is rather unusual to keep a secret of such an impending occasion, but I wish you every happiness."

"How long," Felice demanded, her narrowed eyes aglitter with angry sparks, "has this been going on?"

"I think I shall retire," Harlan interrupted quickly, suppressing his own avid curiosity in the interests of harmony. "Theodora and Grant undoubtedly have much to talk over. Are you coming, Felice?"

Felice said no more. After a final glance of outraged pride and fury, she picked up her skirts and preceded her father from the room.

Theodora stared at Grant in growing dismay, seeming to realize for the first time what she had done. Her thoughts milled about frantically, seeking any straw in the wind. Harlan's indebtedness, the lien on the property, Felice's foolishness, all were props she summoned to her defense against this man whose very presence filled her with strange and involuntary emotions. She saw him approach and moved back in her consternation. Then she drew herself up, waiting, her head high in a characteristic challenging pose.

He stopped and regarded her quietly. "I do not think that you have had time to consider a date for the wedding," he remarked. "Perhaps it will be better if we discuss arrangements another time."

"You may arrange things as you see fit," she said in a constrained voice.

"You will want a trousseau," he pointed out equably. "Don't hesitate to order what you like. I'll take care of the bills, including those for the reception which you will no doubt have here at home."

"There is no need for a trousseau," she said distractedly. "And there will be no reception."

"There will be a reception," he corrected her with a quizzical half smile. "Ours is to be a wedding in every sense of the word. And you will be attired as a bride. You may exercise your taste in the selection of a bridal costume but I insist that you appear in the traditional dress for the occasion. I think you will want it that way, too, when you've had time for reflection." He paused, then moved toward her.

"Don't touch me," she breathed.

There was a faint glimmer of amusement in his eyes. "As you wish," he said with a grin. "But you are going to be Mrs. Grant Monroe, with the responsibilities and obligations a woman has for her husband. Try to get used to the idea, Theodora."

He left with a conventional goodnight. She waited until she heard him leave the house. Then she went to her room, locked the door behind her, and flung herself across the bed.

CHAPTER TWENTY

The forthcoming wedding was much discussed among the first families of St. Louis, and there was many a damsel who suffered and pouted and fumed. But fleeting whispers were scarcely audible, and expiring hope was assiduously concealed. Congratulations and gifts poured in from every side. Invitations were prized, for it was evident as the elaborate preparations progressed that the Monroe-Jenkins nuptials were to be celebrated in keeping with the best St. Louis tradition.

The day following the newspaper announcement of the event, Grant called briefly at his office. In the mail was a letter from Nita. An expression of annoyance darkened his features as he held it tentatively in his hand. With the encouragement of one briefly polite note from him and then no encouragement at all, Nita's letters continued to arrive at regular and frequent intervals. He opened the scented envelope. Glancing over the closely written pages, his eyes narrowed impatiently at her warmly phrased desire to see him, her thoughts of him, her wish to come to St. Louis. She was lonely in New York, unhappy in her aunt's home, and she yearned for the sight of a familiar and understanding face.

He sat down and penned a short, firmly distant note, informing her of his forthcoming marriage and expressing the sincere hope that she would be able to return to the plantation before long. That done, he attended to the other business of the day and left. Stopping at the florist shop, he ordered flowers and potted palms for the reception and directed Ann to supervise the display.

"I'm very happy for you, Mr. Monroe," she said after he had indicated that the entire stock of the store would be none too much. "It will be a fine wedding. People are talking about nothing else."

"Oh?" he asked with the lift of an eyebrow. "And what are they saying?"

"They're looking forward to the occasion," she told him. "Everyone agrees that the wedding and reception will be rather special."

"The wedding list is small," he commented. "But the reception will fill the house, I imagine. You'll receive an invitation, of course."

"That's kind of you," she murmured. "But I'm afraid it will be impossible for me to attend."

He frowned. The girl was unhappy, he observed, glancing at her with closer scrutiny. No doubt her affair with Brad had ended. She was noticeably thinner and there were deep lavender shadows about her eyes. Her face was pale and her lips colorless, and the hand that held the order pad was white and almost bloodless. Only her hair burned with color, as though its gleaming copper strands had drawn the life and vitality from the rest of her body.

"Nonsense," he said with strong insistence. "The reception is for our friends, and I want you to come."

"I'll think it over, Mr. Monroe," she said finally, smiling faintly. As she watched him leave, she knew that she would not accept the invitation. She would willingly have foregone the privilege of arranging the floral decorations but she had promised and there seemed no plausible excuse not to go through with it. That much she would do for the man who had given her his friendship.

After leaving Ann, Grant ordered his coachman to proceed to Kendrick Drive. At the Seminary he waited until Father Morelle concluded conferences with several of his theological students, then accompanied the priest to his study.

"Even if I hadn't read the newspapers," Father Morelle remarked when they were alone, "I could surmise from your expression that something important is about to take place. Permit me to offer my heartfelt congratulations."

"Thank you, Father," Grant smiled. "I came today to ask you to perform the ceremony. I would consider it a particular honor."

"I shall be happy to officiate," the priest, agreed. "Where are the services to be held?"

"I've selected St. Ann's," Grant said. "My father would like that, I think. I went there with him many times when I was a boy."

"Excellent," the priest nodded. "I shall make the necessary arrangements. Let me see, the young woman's name is Theodora Jenkins, is it not? I believe the paper said she is a daughter of Harlan Jenkins."

"Yes," Grant said with a curious abruptness. "She is Harlan's daughter."

"I'm sure you have chosen well, and that you both will enjoy many years of happiness together."

Grant met the sincerity in Father Morelle's eyes with composure. He had a few private reservations about this marriage to Theodora, but they were slight. In time, Theodora's intelligence would bring her to a realization of the truth about Harlan. The readjustment would prove disconcerting, but her straightforward courage would counterbalance any misplaced loyalty of dutiful affection. As for their personal differences, he was able to discount Theodora's behavior as the inexplicable temperament of a sensitive young woman.

"About our last conversation," he said, changing the subject, "I can give you reassurance that Lily Olandt will leave St. Louis soon after the first of the year. The other establishments can be closed too. Lasting reform however, will have to wait until after the next election. It may be possible then to move against the machine."

"I have prayed to hear that news," Father Morelle said, his eyes alight with piercing energy. "The nature of the local situation is appalling. Even in the assembly graft has been reduced to a systematized formula. A powerful combine fixes prices on everything from installing a railroad switch to a contract for lighting."

"I know about the combine. If my plan works out, they will have more to worry about than price fixing."

"Are you acquainted with Ralph Ballard?" the priest asked, referring to the publisher of a crusading daily which had long protested against the Reed machine. "I am sure you can depend on him for support." Grant nodded. "Ballard's paper will be useful when the campaign is under way."

"You have made a good beginning," Father Morelle commented. "Whatever your methods, they appear to be effective."

Grant stood up and prepared to leave. "My methods are rather devious, Father," he said wryly. "I doubt if they would bear close scrutiny."

"Be that as it may," the priest said earnestly. "Our wish is to see St. Louis worthy of the great traditions of her past, and the means by which this is accomplished cannot be wrong. With God's help, you will succeed." After Grant left, the priest stood at the window for a long time, looking across the present, its imperfections and blunders and afflictions, to the city beyond.

CHAPTER TWENTY-ONE

The days preceding the wedding had left Theodora little time for reflection. Enveloped in the rush of preparations which in Grant's hands constituted endless wearying details, she was swept along in the current. At night she sank into bed exhausted only to rise the following morning to another round of ceaseless activity. Grant handled the responsibilities but for some unfathomable reason he insisted that Theodora give her nominal consent to each minute particular. Once she rebelled. "You do as you please anyway," she said with more spirit than she had shown for some time. "Why do you insist that I go through the ritual of agreeing each time a decision must be made?"

"This is your wedding," he reminded her gravely. "You should be consulted. But matters are in order now, including the list of invitations. I think you ought to glance over it to see whether anyone has been omitted."

"I am confident that you've been very thorough," she said out of the infinite tiredness that beset her. "If anybody has been overlooked, I assure you I would not know the difference."

Since that evening in the music room when she had committed herself, Theodora had never consciously considered changing her mind. Each passing day as the preparations unfolded and the wedding itself took on the proportions of a major event, the possibility of such an alternative became more remote. Nor did she dwell upon the future. The briefest thought of Grant in the intimate setting of their new relationship threw her into a chaos of wild uncertainty. She had only to recall the quiet intentness with which he had asked her to marry him to feel a new flame quicken within her. Her cheeks burned at the knowledge that her acceptance had been involuntary, prompted by a physical and emotional storm over which she had no control. At times the fever was so strong that she could not govern the unsteadiness of her hands or hide the tremulous glow in her eyes. She knew that she could not be happy with another man. Yet this only increased her agitation. In desperation she told herself that she could not trust Grant. There was a devious secret behind that smiling, easy composure, a vague threat she sensed but could not identify. Occasionally she had the odd certainty that two men looked out from those inscrutable eyes, the one frankly engaging and warmly companionable, the other brooding, impassive, and remorseless.

These and other thoughts she kept to herself. She was bitterly disappointed that Brad would not be home for the ceremony. In a wave of fondness, she forgave his past indiscretions and promised herself to be more understanding and tolerant toward him in the future. Felice's hostility depressed her though she had expected it. She had been dismayed when Felice left precipitately for the lodge in the company of Neil, for she was acutely conscious of the talk that would circulate if Felice refused to attend the wedding. Consequently she did not attempt to conceal her pleasure when Felice returned at the last minute, indicating that she would not only be present but would act as an attendant if Theodora wished.

"Of course, Felice," Theodora said warmly. "You can wear that last gown Sophie made for you."

Felice failed to point out that she could not very well absent herself since the Mills were returning for the wedding. Nor did she reveal that Neil had shown unsuspected firmness in insisting that she attend in her proper role. While she made her dutiful gesture of sisterliness, she did not intend to give Theodora the impression that all was forgiven or forgotten.

"I suppose the happy bride has her trousseau in readiness?" she asked, going about the bedroom and inspecting the garments draped over chairs and across the bed.

Theodora winced at the hostility in her voice. "I'm sorry you feel the way you do, Felice. But you didn't care deeply about Grant. You scarcely thought about him when he was away, and you were quite reconciled to Neil in his absence."

"Do I detect a faint murmur of conscience?" Felice asked coldly. "Pray do not let it take the edge off your glorious anticipation of honeymooning with Grant. Incidentally, where is he taking his bride?"

"We're going to New Orleans," Theodora said, busying herself at the dressing table.

"Cozy," Felice commented. "And has the gentleman said where he plans to live on your return?"

"He has not," Theodora replied, nettled by the sarcasm in her sister's voice.

"I presume he intends to make this his home," Felice said with a shrug.

"I doubt it," Theodora said quickly, her control beginning to slip away. "I'm tired tonight, Felice. Let's talk another time, shall we?"

"By all means," Felice said in an exaggerated drawl. "I understand. Good night, Theodora, and pleasant dreams."

CHAPTER TWENTY-TWO

Ann felt an uncontrollable impulse to flee as she approached the wide portico of the Jenkins home on the morning of the wedding. Conscious of the ill-fitting coat that had served too many seasons, the cheap fur of the collar, and the worn gloves and purse she carried, she lifted her hand to the knocker hesitantly, fighting the urge to turn and hurry away before she was discovered. But the door opened and she straightened her shoulders, resolved to do the task ahead as Grant wanted it done.

She was admitted by a maid who was quick to recognize her as one of the shop people who had been coming and going all morning. With a cursory nod, the servant left her standing in the hall and went to find one of the family. Ann waited uneasily, glancing around at the shining woodwork and walls, the polished chairs, and the immaculate carpet which gleamed with soft luster after vigorous and repeated sweepings. A pre-excitement hush hung in the air as though the house itself waited in expectant readiness for the afternoon wedding party and the evening's gala festivities.

She began to plan automatically, visualizing tall floor vases on either side of the marble-front fireplace, a table spray here against the wall. But her thoughts kept turning to Brad. She wondered whether he had returned for the wedding, and she hoped fervently that she would not see him if he were home. She had heard nothing from him since their quarrel in the coffee shop, but she was acquainted with the fact that he had returned to the university. The first pain of their separation had subsided into a numb suffering, and even that was easier to bear when she remembered that his life would be as it should, his future secure. Now with a fresh consciousness of the gulf between them, despair swept over her anew. Forgetting all else but her own unhappiness, she was on the point of turning away when Theodora came down the stairs.

"You are the decorator?" Theodora asked in a preoccupied tone.

"Yes," Ann said. "Mr. Monroe asked me to be here this morning."

"The flowers haven't been removed from the boxes," Theodora told her. "They arrived an hour ago with the potted plants. Rufus will bring them in and place them where you wish, and one of the maids will help you with the vases."

Ann stared at her, taking in the strong features, the statuesque grace and erect carriage, and her admiration was wholly unselfish, completely free of the envy another in her place might have felt. She was puzzled by the shadows in the depths of those luminous eyes and by the abstracted manner in which Theodora spoke. But these were things one could understand, Ann thought generously, reminding herself that countless details must be attendant upon an affair such as this.

"Well?" Theodora said as the girl hesitated.

"I thought you might have specific directions," Ann said diffidently. "The order is large, and I want you to be pleased."

"I shall be," Theodora said with an indifference that rebuffed the younger woman. "If Mr. Monroe placed the responsibility in your hands, I'm sure you are competent." She summoned a maid and gave instructions about the plants and vases, then withdrew.

Ann's vague uneasiness sharpened. As she worked, directing Rufus and the maid, rearranging floral bouquets and straightening a bent leaf or stem, she became nervously sensitive to the mid-morning stillness that had fallen over the house. It was not an exciting stillness, vibrant with anticipation for a joyous celebration, but a deep, waiting silence that had settled sluggishly in the stifling warmth of the dim, high-ceilinged rooms, contrasting strangely with the bright sunlight streaming in through the motionless curtains at the window.

She finished and stood alone in the drawing room for a last critical look. The effect was festive, she decided, but not overdone. The potted palms stood like mute sentinels on the gleaming floor, bare of rugs and polished to a glasslike smoothness for dancing. The raised platform for the musicians was banked with flowers, and sprays of green decorated the wall lights.

The door opened behind her and she turned abruptly as Harlan Jenkins came in. For more than a minute he looked about at the decorative arrangement, then he stared unblinkingly at the girl in the center of the room.

"Who are you?" he asked in a tone he reserved for addressing an inferior.

She felt an instinctive aversion for this man with thick features and pale, unemotional eyes. Brad's father, she thought guardedly, returning his level stare with outward composure. "I'm the decorator from the flower store," she said in a controlled voice.

He walked around the sofa and idly flipped the empty box still lying there. "The Arcade, I see," he commented.

"Yes," she said without evasion.

This must be the girl, he thought, inspecting her closely. She was no remarkable beauty, he observed, noting her thinness and pallor, and the wide, candid eyes that were somehow too questioning, too intense. Doubtless that flaming hair would appeal to a young man with romantic inclinations, but there was little else to recommend her. She probably expected Brad to be home and was lingering about, hoping for a meeting with him. Harlan had been rather pleased that Brad had refused to return. To his mind, this was all the proof needed that his son was well over the infatuation.

"I hope everything is satisfactory," Ann said, picking up her gloves and purse.

"Wait, Miss …?" he said as she started toward the door.

She turned and faced him. "… Lynch," she said distinctly.

"Ah yes, I thought so. You are the young woman who is acquainted with my son, I believe."

"I was acquainted with Brad," she said with unmistakable emphasis. "As you know, that is over."

"Hm, yes. So I was told." He thrust his hands into his pockets and regarded her with a familiarity that was offensive. "You are a sensible young woman, Miss Lynch. I feared you might not see the uselessness of continuing your friendship with my son, and I am most gratified by your reasonable attitude. I have nothing against you personally, you understand. But Brad has, shall we say, certain standards to meet?"

"I quite understand," she said, a thin color rising in her cheeks. The heavy fragrance of the flowers hung thickly in the close warmth of the room, and a sickening faintness pressed in upon her, making it difficult to breathe.

"It's only fair to tell you that Brad regretted any unhappiness he may have caused you," he went on. "We talked it over and thought that some, ah, compensation might clear things up in a friendly way. A few hundred dollars, perhaps …"

A wave of nausea caught in her throat and she swayed slightly. "The money … isn't necessary," she said in a muffled voice. "You needn't be afraid I'll trouble Brad, or you, Mr. Jenkins."

His manner dropped its suave air of patronage. The large head jerked forward, and dark color suffused the heavy features. He took a step toward her, then stopped, his face working convulsively. "Don't ever try," he said with soft and deliberate viciousness.

Terrified by the sudden, inexplicable change in him, Ann retreated. Never, she thought frantically, would she enter this house again. There was something evil here, in the furnishings, the polished mirrors, and richly draped windows. She found her way blindly to the front door and went out to the street. Walking swiftly, she inhaled the sharp November air with deep thankfulness, welcoming the clean sunlight that glittered like a thousand diamonds against her blurred eyes.

CHAPTER TWENTY-THREE

When at last Theodora stood beside Grant in the dim tranquility of the church, she was seized with an ungovernable panic. The sun had renounced its earlier promise and now shone with an occasional dull glimmer from behind the clouds, casting a weird, multicolored reflection through the stained-glass windows. The candles burned with an almost motionless flame in the stilled air. A genteel restlessness stirred among the assembled guests. The rustling of silk and an intermittent, polite cough spread through the nave with a curious uneasiness. Theodora's gown felt like sacking, and her flesh was oddly cold despite the warmth within the church.

"Smile, my love," Grant whispered during an interval of choir responses. "Your pallor is a bit too convincing."

She gazed at him with a blank stare. She hardly saw him, nor was she aware of the quiet concern that lay behind the superficial levity of his words. A feeling of unreality had numbed her senses, and she held onto it gratefully, almost desperately. With a kind of frozen determination, she forced herself into a position of remote objectivity, responding automatically to the ritual that made her Grant's wife, extending a slim, lifeless hand for the ring. The face of Father Morelle with its grave, quiet dignity was like a drifting island to her, forever beyond her reach. Only when she left the church, descending the steps on Grant's arm, did she come briefly to life. Then she thought in sheer amazement and consternation: It could not have happened; I have no memory of any part of it.

The drive back to the house with Grant was a further unreality. He sensed her feelings and, to divert her, chatted lightly about amusing trifles, the dress of one, a frivolous hat, a snatch of gossip he may have overheard or simply invented for her entertainment.

When they returned, she declined to join the others in the buffet supper, and Grant ordered a tray sent up to her room. Here she thought to compose herself. But the incessant activity of two maids who helped her undress, then tiptoed in and out on endless errands, packing extra valises for the trip to New Orleans in the morning, laying out her clothes, allowed her no rest. They had scarcely finished when it was time to dress again.

A short interval before she was to go downstairs, Theodora dismissed the servants and dropped wearily on the bed. A paralyzing exhaustion spread through her body like a drug, and her mind refused to function. She could only sit there unmoving, grateful for a respite, however brief.

The door opened and she started up automatically. Then, seeing Felice, she sank back a second time. "What is it, Felice?" she asked.

"I just heard a bit of news that might interest you," Felice said, coming over to the bed and looking down at her sister with eyes narrowed in wicked pleasure. "Martha Mills was telling me the most amusing gossip. Apparently one of Fred's clients is involved in marital difficulties ..."

"At this moment," Theodora interrupted almost angrily, "I haven't the slightest interest in any of Fred's clients."

"Of course if you don't wish to know," Felice shrugged. "Martha mentioned a bawdy house and I merely thought you ought to know what it's all about. You do go out of your way to address that woman on the street."

"What woman?" Theodora asked, frowning.

"The Olandt person. Lily, I believe she is familiarly known to the men who patronize her establishment."

Theodora grew rigid. "What are you saying?" she demanded sharply.

"She's quite a notorious character about town," Felice went on, obviously enjoying this opportunity to needle the impregnable Theodora. "Fred's client seems to be one of the tired businessmen who go there to … relax."

Theodora said nothing. She stared at Felice, trying to assimilate the fantastic meaning of this preposterous news, utterly unable to grasp the sense of what she heard. "You are mad," she said finally with all the indignation she could summon. "I met Miss Olandt abroad last year. She's a charming and cultivated woman." Yet even as she spoke, suspicions clamored in her ears, drowning out the halfhearted assurance of her words. She had frequently wondered why the older woman evaded direct answers to personal questions, why Lily refused to say where she lived or whom she knew in St. Louis. Was it possible to be so wrong in judging character, so terribly mistaken?

"If you doubt my word," Felice continued, "why don't you ask Grant?"

Theodora's head began to throb with an intolerable ache. "Grant?" she repeated mechanically.

"He appears to know the lady. Fred saw him leaving her place one day several weeks ago." She added with malicious satisfaction: "I presume it was Lily's house he was visiting the time you saw him. I recall that you did mention the Belle Arms." She moved toward the door. "I'm sorry, Theodora, if this has upset you," she said pleasantly. "But I felt you'd want to know."

When she had gone, Theodora got slowly to her feet. Painfully her mind went over past encounters with Lily, recalling a dozen harmless little pleasantries, Lily's friendly encouragement and interest in her music. But Theodora had only bitterness now for the woman who had deceived her, and a deep sense of shame and hurt. Lily Olandt had pretended to be a patron of the arts, a wealthy American tourist abroad, and she, Theodora, had been taken in by the outrageous pose.

She shuddered violently as another thought struck her. Only the fact that she had not known where to reach Lily had prevented her from committing the horrible mistake of asking Lily to the wedding. In her mortification, she let her anger vent itself on Grant. He knew of the deception, she told herself indignantly, remembering the day he had watched her greet Lily as an intimate friend. But he preferred to remain silent, undoubtedly enjoying the impossible situation as a huge joke. Her suspicion that the two of them had been amusing themselves at her expense was unbearable. Grant's acquaintance with Lily was dreadful enough without this added ignominy.

She heard the sound of carriages in the drive, the voices of new arrivals in the hall below, and she started up involuntarily. Somehow she would have to summon the strength to face them, she reminded herself uncompromisingly. For the sake of propriety, for her pride and self-respect, she must go down to them with outward equanimity. Hurriedly, she dashed cold water over her hands and wrists, powdered her flushed cheeks, and smoothed her hair. Then, her step quite steady, her features deliberately composed, she went out into the corridor and down the stairs.

CHAPTER TWENTY-FOUR

The drawing room and living room filled early, and the spacious hall saw a continuous stream of well-wishers. Theodora joined Grant near the door, and the formal reception was under way.

"You are superb, my love," Grant complimented her. "That gown was an excellent selection."

But she was not listening. She glanced about with a sense of discovery that was quickly deepening into a new source of dismay. In the hall and through the open doors to the other rooms, she viewed an extraordinary cross section of St. Louis society and business affairs. A general sprinkling of ward bosses and heelers mingled cigar fumes with merchants, bankers, and executives. Considerable restraint hung over the curiously assorted assemblage. The expensively gowned wives of the social set gravitated toward small groups of their own, conversing in well-bred, genteelly modulated tones. Their plebeian sisters, left to their own devices, stood about self-consciously, smiling with wary politeness and remaining uncomfortably close to their husbands.

How had he dared? Theodora thought, burning with furious mortification. Never had she even remotely suspected he would have the audacity to invite this riverfront riffraff. She could restrain herself no longer. "Shameful!" she whispered in an intense undertone. "How could you?"

He raised an eyebrow slightly. "You are not pleased?" he asked. "I am disappointed. I thought I arranged everything to meet with your approval. We are holding open house because I desire everyone to meet the charming and lovely woman who is my wife."

Her retort was swallowed up in the demands of propriety, for coming toward them was Neil's father, the dignified and portly Miles Hunter, bearing on his arm his wife, Elizabeth. Behind them, Theodora saw with chagrin, was the affable and expansive gentleman who had greeted her on the *Crescent*.

"A delightful party, Theodora," Elizabeth Hunter was saying gently. "This reminds me of the time Miles and I were married. We had a lawn reception and everybody in St. Louis came to wish us well."

She's trying in her kindness to smooth it over, Theodora thought grimly. They all knew what an unforgivable breach of good taste it was to fill the house with this unacceptable hodge-podge. She managed a smile for the Hunters, but her expression froze instantly as Grant introduced Al Reed and a rather plain woman, his wife.

"Congratulations, Grant," Reed was saying heartily. "Quite a celebration, eh, Ruby? Grant Monroe always does things in a big way. And this is the bride. But Miss Theodora and I are already acquainted. We met ..."

"Yes," Theodora interrupted in alarm, fearing he would go on in a voice loud enough to attract the attention of the Hunters, who were still nearby. "I am happy that you and Mrs. Reed were able to join us tonight."

She saw Grant's inscrutable smile and flushed hotly. As usual, he was enjoying her discomfiture with his peculiar sense of humor. He knew she was powerless to do other than accept the situation with as much tact as she could command. His self-assurance was preposterous, she thought angrily. In his present role of host, he was conveying the astonishing impression that he was not only groom but master of the house. Father, who ought to be receiving with them, was somewhere inside, relegated to a position of negligible importance.

She thought of the room upstairs adjoining her bedroom where Grant's dressing gown hung in the closet, where his personal effects were already set out on the bureau. He was at home here, moving about with an air of familiarity, giving orders to servants, changing the location of a chair here or a table there as the mood suited him. As though, she thought with sharp clarity despite the curious quickening of her pulse, he had come to stay.

"Most of the guests have arrived," she said to him in a controlled voice. "If you don't mind, I shall leave you with the honors."

"There seems to be one more claim on your attention," he remarked as Felice and Neil came toward them.

In Felice's arms was a bulky package. "This was just delivered, Theodora," Felice said, placing it on a table beside a vase of flowers. "I thought you'd like to open it and put it with the other gifts."

Theodora complied without enthusiasm. Guests crowded around expectantly as she removed the outer wrapping, then layer upon layer of tissue paper. There were appreciative exclamations from Felice and the others as an exquisite coffee urn stood revealed, beautifully wrought in gleaming silver. A small card fluttered from the wrappings and Grant reached for it, recovering it a second before Felice's quick hand would have had it. He glanced at it, then handed it to Theodora.

She read the words written in a bold, slanting hand, and stared in disbelief. "... regret that I cannot be with you this evening. The gift ... a small token ... conveys my sincerest wish for your long and continued happiness ... Lily Olandt."

With a convulsive movement, Theodora crushed the card in her hand. She turned accusingly toward Grant, visibly shaken, her eyes deep and intense, her mouth trembling and starkly vivid in the sudden pallor of her face. In this ultimate humiliation, she forgot the guests nearby whose polite restraint failed to hide the consuming edge of their inquisitiveness.

"Who sent it, Theodora?" Felice prodded, her eyes narrowing vindictively as she observed her sister's odd behavior.

"It's ..." Theodora said with difficulty, "it's from ... a friend."

Grant's expression was an enigma. "Shall we go into the other room?" he suggested easily. "I'm sure our guests are eager for the dancing to begin."

Theodora permitted him to lead her into the drawing room. The disappointment among the others was apparent, and many a sharp, speculative glance followed them as Grant led her to the floor for the first dance.

"That woman!" she breathed in a scorching whisper as soon as she could manage her voice. "That dreadful woman!"

He said nothing. He transferred the crumpled card in her hand to his pocket and swung her into the lively steps of the opening waltz.

"The joke is over," she went on, unable to stem the tide of her indignation. "I realize now what a fool I was to be deceived by her, and I'm only thankful that I found out when I did. You may tell her, and the two of you can have another laugh, if you like."

"I assure you she did not mean to hurt you," he said quietly. "She has the kindliest feelings toward you, and her wish for your welfare is quite sincere."

"How dare you defend her?" she gasped furiously.

His expression closed, and the lines about his mouth tightened perceptibly. "We won't discuss it," he said briefly. "And now shall we smile for the edification of our guests? It's customary, you know."

CHAPTER TWENTY-FIVE

Theodora exhibited a remarkable air of self-control and dignity. She danced with Neil and again with Grant. Then, despite her efforts at discouragement, she was claimed by other of the gentlemen who became less constrained and more convivial as the evening progressed and the liberally provided beverages went to their heads.

She was equally distant with them all. Paul Nixon, whom she knew as a close friend of the Mills couple as well as the elected assemblyman from this district, drew slightly more favor than the rest, but he was accorded only one waltz. Nixon, whose cultivated manner and social acceptance set him apart from his political associates, was persistent in his efforts to claim her again. But she refused, excusing herself with unmistakable firmness.

She observed with strong disapproval that her father, far from taking exception to the presence of so many outsiders, was mingling freely with them in a spirit of uninhibited jollity. Apparently he found much to discuss with Al Reed for the two of them had their heads together in a lengthy and quite serious conversation. Theodora contrived to speak to Harlan alone in an interval between dances, but their exchange of words did little to relieve her state of mind.

"I suppose I am responsible, father," she began in a strained voice. "I should have inspected the list of invitations before they were mailed."

"What are you talking about?" he asked, eyeing her with unconcealed impatience.

"You mean you are pleased?" she demanded incredulously.

"Why not? Grant has gone to great lengths to provide a suitable reception. You haven't forgotten that we are indebted to him for all this, as well as certain other favors?"

"I haven't forgotten," she said grimly. "But does that give him the right to fill the house with his coarse friends? Can't you see what he is doing? He considers this his home now, and everything in it. We're only here because he is pleased not to turn us out!"

He frowned. Theodora was working up to something unpleasant and he wanted no part of it. Yet there was a curious incident the other day. A small thing, the hall table moved to a place nearer the door, but he had noticed it immediately. He had been vaguely disconcerted. A maid explained that Mr. Monroe thought it more appropriate in its new location, and Harlan had shrugged. But several times later as he passed the hall, he found himself glancing at it in growing annoyance.

"You are overwrought, Theodora," he said in a sharper tone. "When I am financially able, I shall return his money, and the debt will be wiped out."

"He'll never let you pay him back," she said with an odd certainty. "This is what he's been planning. I knew it the night he came back from Cuba. Before he got out of the carriage, I saw him stare at the house, hating, wanting it. I think he had forgotten me. There was an inhuman look on his face, a look of ugliness and cruelty."

Harlan had never felt alarm for her before but his apprehension mounted now. She had been acting peculiarly, he remembered uneasily, since she announced her intention to marry Grant. This afternoon during the ceremony, she had moved and spoken like a person in a trance. He had heard that women often reacted in unaccountable ways as the wedding night approached, but he had never associated hysterics with Theodora.

"Why don't you go to your room awhile?" he suggested in a placating tone. "Rejoin the party later."

She said nothing more, knowing it was useless. At eleven, no longer able to endure the meaningless conversation and tiring round of dancing, she withdrew. Retiring to her room, she closed the door and turned the key in the lock. She went immediately to the other door which connected with the adjoining room. That key was gone, she discovered. A deep flush spread across her face. He thought of everything, of course.

She undressed and lay on the bed. Out of sheer exhaustion, she slept for a time. When she awoke, the house was quiet. A steady rain thrummed against the roof and splashed against the windows. Looking about, she saw that the room was undisturbed. Both doors were closed, and the one lamp burning dimly on the dressing table cast a subdued glow on the familiar pattern of the carpet. The guests had gone, and the musicians. The painful pleasantries of the evening had ended. She lay unmoving, staring at the ceiling and fighting off the flood of recollection that surged in upon her.

She ought to put out the lamp, she thought remotely. Forcing herself to rise, she started across the floor. A draught of cool air streamed into the closed warmth of the room and she stopped abruptly. The door to the other room had opened and Grant stood in the shadows, watching her. The sight of him threw her nerves into an uncontrollable frenzy, and her body began to tremble violently. "Go away," she said in a low, shaken voice. "Go away and leave me alone."

His eyes narrowed at the apprehension in her attitude. He saw her sudden fright, the marble whiteness of her profile, and the convulsive movement of her hand as she drew her dressing gown closer about her shoulders. This was Theodora Jenkins, he reminded himself then. Harlan's daughter. He had been deceived into thinking that she could love him. He had been betrayed by the fever in his blood, the dream he could not escape. For another minute he stood regarding her with inscrutable eyes, then he reached her side and carried her, rigidly, unprotesting, to the bed.

CHAPTER TWENTY-SIX

A deep and pervading quiet settled over the house after Grant and Theodora left for their extended sojourn in New Orleans. Harlan Jenkins found the unaccustomed silence oddly constrained after the recent feverish activity of the wedding preparations and final celebration. He had always taken a conscious pride in this house which he had possessed from its original owner, and he was acutely sensitive to its moods.

The mere sight of the wide portico and tall colonnades, the tacit hospitality of the spreading structure set well back amid its green lawn and old elms, never failed to fill him with a sense of clever accomplishment. He had only to cross its threshold to know an expanding and gratifying self-esteem. The beautifully finished interior was a tribute to his ability to get what he wanted, to get all he wanted, and to pay little or nothing in return. Even the furnishings, some of which he had acquired when the house became his, had their meaning for him as reminders of the ingenious resources and adroit manipulation which were cornerstones in his success.

Now the house rested, and in the silence its individuality affected him in a curiously personal way. He began to notice details he had never seen before, the carved pattern encircling the newel post at the foot of the stairway, the dark mahogany finish of the woodwork and floors, the flowing grain in the smooth marble of the hall fireplace. The house seemed to be inviting his inspection, calling attention to its fine points and excellent construction. In this new awareness, all his faculties were sharpened. Each particular brought to mind the care with which the house had been designed and built, recalling at the same time the man who had made it what it was.

At first he thought of Will Patterson with humor and satisfaction. Patterson had been stupid. He let himself be destroyed. If he hadn't been a fool, he would have seen that Lynch was tracking down irregularities in the funds. He could have prevented the examination of the books until certain adjustments were made, and none of the drastic measures that followed would have been necessary.

As these mental excursions into the past increased in frequency, Jenkins grew impatient, then annoyed. His complacency became strained, his vanity was uneasy. Once he went so far as to wonder if it were true that something of the builder remained with a house as long as it survived. He was amused at the thought, and irritated. But the idea took hold and he could not shake it. When Felice announced her immediate intent to marry Neil without fanfare or elaborate preliminary arrangements, he was relieved at the diversion. Remembering his sporadic role of father, he offered token resistance. Felice would be considerate to wait until Theodora and Grant returned, he pointed out. Felice laughed unpleasantly and assured him that she was not in any way concerned with such proprieties.

The quiet wedding was followed by an informal dinner to which only a few friends were invited. The pair established residence at the Hunter mansion, postponing the traditional wedding trip to a date in February when they planned to leave for a Mediterranean cruise. The house, which had been quiet before, now was encompassed in a profound and immutable silence. Harlan found himself actually looking forward to Theodora's return. Life would be normal again, he thought wryly, with Theodora back to dominate the household.

CHAPTER TWENTY-SEVEN

A light, whirling snow blanketed St. Louis in the early morning hours but by mid-afternoon when Grant and Theodora returned, the overcast sky was disgorging a torrential rain. The streets and walks had been washed clean by the downpour, and only scattered patches of soot-encrusted snow still lay on the lawns.

Theodora entered the comfortable interior of the house with a grateful sense of homecoming. While servants carried the heavy valises upstairs, she greeted her father in the old affectionate manner. He was obviously pleased. He shook hands heartily with Grant and invited them to join him before the fireplace in the living room.

Grant declined. "You must excuse me," he said. "There are several matters I should attend to this afternoon. You won't mind, Theodora?"

She was removing her hat before the hall mirror. "No," she said, not turning around.

"A glass of whisky will do no harm," Harlan urged. "The weather here is a change from New Orleans, and you'll find it's easy to take a chill."

"I'll have the whisky later," Grant promised. "It will be most agreeable when I return."

He left, and Harlan turned to Theodora. He thought she looked pale but doubtless it was the afternoon gloom that made her seem listless and without color. "You'll feel better when you have tea," he told her cheerfully. "I'll ring."

"Later, father," she demurred. She did not care to sit down with him just now and chat over a cup of tea. There was nothing to say. She was infinitely weary of conversing, weary of responding when she was addressed, weary of pretense. "I'll see about unpacking," she said vaguely, turning away.

He watched her go up the stairs, and his thick lips rolled reflectively. He had expected her to come back in high spirits, a glow of health on her cheeks and at least a degree of happiness and contentment showing in her demeanor. Instead she was subdued and drab, more unapproachable than before. He would never understand Theodora, he concluded, frowning. Inwardly he was fervently thankful that she was Grant's problem now.

Theodora went directly to her old room and sank down on a chair with relief. Here she would have some measure of that privacy she felt she desperately needed. The hotel suite in New Orleans had been spacious and excellently appointed, but it had been shared with a stranger. A thin color stained her cheeks as she thought about the past three weeks. After that first night in this house, Grant had made few overtures. He accorded her unfailing courtesy and consideration, for the most part maintaining an attitude of unmistakable reserve. She was grateful, of course, she told herself repeatedly. But the situation was awkward when one shared the same suite of rooms, the same bed at night. She had been frantically uncomfortable as she lay stiffly beside him in the darkness, waiting for the steady sound of his breathing that indicated sleep. She would remember their first night together, and only the sting of her nails biting into the flesh of her palms could still the convulsive trembling of her body. Often hours passed before she slipped guardedly into sleep, to dream fitfully and uneasily.

Once she opened her eyes during the night to find her arm outflung across his shoulders, her hand against his face. But he slept soundly and did not awaken. She had remained awake until daybreak, confusedly conscious of the warm sensation that lingered from that brief closeness. Her determination mingled with a treacherous loneliness as she turned from him and stared heavily out the window at the graying sky.

Such complications would not arise here, she told herself firmly. She had her own room, he the adjoining one. Evidently he had intended to make this his residence from the first. When she had put the question to him, he remarked: "It would be rather foolish to do otherwise, wouldn't it?" And with Felice gone, she supposed it would. There were many rooms in the big house. Even had Felice and Neil wanted to live here, there was ample space. She did not dwell on the fact that the house virtually belonged to Grant. Soon after they had left St. Louis, she had asked him to destroy the paper that represented Harlan's indebtedness, and he had refused.

"Father intends to repay you," she explained quickly, seeing the quizzical look on his face. "His word is sufficient guarantee for that. But the property is important to him in a way you wouldn't understand. Father has always regarded the house with particular pride. I think that somehow he looks on it as a milestone in his life. There is an anxiety about him lately that I've never known before. I'm sure if you withdraw your claim, you would do much to relieve his mind."

"I had no idea the arrangement troubled you," he replied with an amused smile. "I think you are imagining your father's reaction, but in any case I'd rather you didn't concern yourself with the matter."

"I am concerned with it," she persisted. "That's why I ask you not to keep the paper father gave you."

His smile faded imperceptibly. "I should like to oblige you, my dear," he told her. "But in business transactions, I must follow the dictates of my own judgment."

When she saw he would not be persuaded, she flushed angrily. "You are doing this deliberately," she said heatedly. "You want the property, and you took this means to get it, hoping father would never be able to redeem the note. You've always wanted to possess it for some inexplicable reason of your own. But you'll not win."

He moved nearer and put his hand over hers in a gesture that may have reached for understanding, or may have been an expression of tenderness.

She drew away, trembling violently. "Don't," she said, her voice shaking in its low intensity.

His face turned to granite. He regarded her steadily, then he said slowly: "Very well, Theodora, we'll do it your way. I can wait."

He did not refer to the incident again. Indeed, he seemed bent on ignoring the estrangement between them. There were times when she was almost persuaded that her conduct meant little to him one way or another.

Not until they were leaving the hotel did he drop that mask of indifference. Their last day had been brimful, a whirl of sightseeing, shopping in the French quarter, lunch, coffee, cocktails, and finally dinner in a succession of gay, colorful restaurants. A sense of intimate companionship had arisen between them, and Theodora found herself talking breathlessly, nodding in quick agreement at a word from Grant, laughing as together they were amused by the idiosyncrasies of the driver who transported them through the maze of streets and narrow cobblestone alleys.

Then the hotel room, the hasty check to see that everything had been packed, and Grant, turning to her with an odd seriousness she had not seen in him before.

"We're leaving, Theodora," he said. "We're going back to St. Louis. I don't know what we'll find there, or how we'll meet it. That's why I want you to remember today, if you can." He drew a small box from his pocket. "I thought, perhaps, you would like this," he said, handing it to her.

She raised the lid and saw a delicate necklace of silver and diamonds glimmering against the white satin lining, an almost perfect mate for the bracelet she had carefully treasured from her mother.

"But how did you know?" she exclaimed, deeply moved. "This is a beautiful match for a bracelet I've never worn."

"You like it?" he asked.

"It's …" her voice trailed off as she looked at him uncertainly. "It's very lovely," she finished, closing the box gently.

"Theodora," he began haltingly. "Perhaps I should tell you …"

"Don't," she said in a low voice. "Not now."

He caught her in his arms, and the devouring hunger in his embrace enveloped the leaping fire within her, dissolving her last measure of self-control.

She flushed, remembering. There was a knock on the door, and she started to her feet abruptly. "Come in," she said unsteadily. It was the maid who had come to help her unpack. Theodora threw herself into the task at hand with an energy that drove other thoughts from her mind.

CHAPTER TWENTY-EIGHT

The new traction development owed its initial success to the number of confirmed speculators on Jenkins' list. There followed the usual manipulated price rise in shares, and the rush of small investors was on. When the drive leveled off, Jenkins opened negotiations with Al Reed. In January he was ready to conclude the pact, and he met Reed by arrangement in the latter's home.

He was relieved when the door to the modest house was answered promptly and he was shown without delay to the study. Jenkins was aware that prominent men from other parts of the state as well as St. Louis found their way to this door. Nevertheless he did not care to be seen calling on the politician. In many instances representatives did business for their superiors, but in cases where the use of an intermediary was not feasible, obscurity was often desirable. This was such an instance.

Reed's punctuality flattered his conceit. He smiled at the rapacity with which the politician evidently wanted to consummate the deal. Small wonder. Two hundred and fifty thousand was not a negligible sum. Jenkins had no intention of parting with it in entirety, however. He would temporize tonight. A gamble with stockholders' money was risky even if he knew he could cover the loss within hours after the franchise was in his hands.

"Come in," Reed greeted him affably, motioning toward a chair. "Drink?"

Jenkins was tempted, but he thought better of it and refused the offer. He preferred to keep the interview on a purely business basis. Seating himself in the chair Reed indicated, he came directly to the point: "I don't have the news you expected. Certain matters have not as yet turned out in accordance with my hopes."

The expression in Reed's eyes hardened subtly and his manner became more guarded. "You've been selling shares, haven't you?" he inquired.

Jenkins found the truth more useful than fabrication. "Not as many as I expected," he admitted. "The heavy investors want to see the franchise put through before buying into the company. Of course," he added quickly, "they'll all want to get in on it when the matter is settled."

"Hell, you know the boys over town won't move until our negotiations are closed," Reed said bluntly.

Jenkins shifted his position uncomfortably. He knew that time was pressing. The activity of Interurban for renewal of their old franchise plus added suburban privileges made his own position more precarious every day. And he shrewdly suspected that their representatives were responsible for the tentative attitude of bankers and other large investors toward the new company.

As though reading his thoughts, Reed said: "I'm not trying to be unreasonable. But there isn't much time. If you're to get the franchise, you'll have to act damned fast. I'll be frank with you. I promised to contact certain key men tonight and inform them whether the deal is completed."

Reed had not exaggerated. He knew that Interurban was pressuring the assembly. His services in securing a valuable franchise were more than Interurban would pay, but this had not stopped them. Reed was not misled by the present lull. And something he could not put his finger on, a sixth sense perhaps, told him the assembly was not above acting on its own initiative if the price was right. Like many another who ruled, smoothing his way by elevating underlings to power, he knew how easily men could be ambushed by the intoxication of authority.

He was not fond of doing business with Jenkins. He had never liked the fat broker since their paths first crossed years ago, an occasion that had been mutually satisfactory but one which Reed preferred to forget. The traction setup, however, would bring the assembly back into line, and leave a fifty thousand fee for himself. "I can't guarantee that the terms will be open indefinitely," he concluded, "unless I'm in a position to talk business tonight."

Jenkins squirmed inwardly. He had tried to stall, hoping he could swing the deal without being driven to extremities. But he could not afford to let the franchise slip through his fingers. "I'll have to meet the amount out of private funds," he yielded reluctantly. "If we don't get the franchise, I'm ruined."

Reed suppressed a smile. He was fairly certain that the money did not represent Jenkins' private resources if, indeed, he had any such resources at the present. "Don't worry," he reassured the broker. "The franchise will be taken care of as soon as the assembly reconvenes."

On the way home Jenkins fidgeted. He argued that the money was lost in any case, without a franchise. Present commitments would devour it, and there would be no more forthcoming. But his state of mind was in no way improved. He wondered unpleasantly what would transpire if the shareholders discovered that their investments had vanished. His manipulations in the past, with one exception, had been legal, at least insofar as the vague laws on investment operations were concerned.

He did not care to think about that exception. In his present mood, the satisfaction he derived from contemplating that noteworthy example of cleverness and dispatch was absent. But against his will, his mind kept turning back, recalling images and scenes that were all but forgotten. His lips felt dry, and he moistened them nervously. He knew that it would always be with him, a hulking shadow in the back of his mind. That was the way with things that were never quite finished. Loose ends dangled hopelessly, and one was never free of them. Patterson's luck held in the end, he acknowledged grimly. Nothing had been heard of him since that day over twenty years ago when he disappeared. Where he went would probably never be known, but he was certain to avoid St. Louis.

Jenkins cursed under his breath. He was like an old woman these days, jumpy and irritable. If he were to see this traction deal through, he would have to keep himself in hand.

The hour was late when the carriage drove up in front of the darkened house. Jenkins dismounted, the uneasiness strong within him. Hurrying inside, he went directly to the study, turned up the one dimly burning lamp and poured a brandy. He had raised the glass to his lips when he stopped, frozen into immobility. The room with its long rows of bookshelves, its heavy oak chairs, the writing table, and the comfortable divan beneath the windows was the same in every detail but one. An old leather armchair had been brought in and placed before the fireplace. It had been refinished now and polished, but he recognized it as the same chair that had been here years ago, part of the estate that had been Patterson's.

A man's hand rested motionlessly on the arm, the rest of his body hidden from view by the back of the chair. Jenkins stared hypnotically at that hand, transfixed by the idea that Patterson himself sat there waiting, staring silently into the dying coals in the fireplace. The drink fell from his nerveless hand, the glass splintering on the edge of the writing table, liquid and particles of broken glass scattering on the rug.

Almost immediately the man in the chair sprang up, and Jenkins came out of his delusion to face Grant Monroe.

"What …?" Grant said, his brows lifted in surprise. "You gave me a start. I must have fallen asleep. Nasty accident," he commented, glancing at the broken glass and stain on the carpet. "Did you cut yourself?"

"No, fortunately," Jenkins replied, trying to regain his composure.

Grant took two more glasses from the liquor cabinet and filled them. "Here, you can use this. You look as though you'd seen a ghost."

Jenkins smothered a curse at the thought of the discarded furniture in the attic. He had forgotten it was there. "That chair," he said, accepting the drink with a hand that was steadier now. "I suppose you found it upstairs?"

"I hope you don't mind," Grant acknowledged. "You've a number of sound items in the attic, and old furniture is a hobby of mine. I discovered this chair several weeks ago and had it refinished. Attractive, isn't it?"

Jenkins drained his glass. "Yes," he said. "Yes, I suppose it is. But I can't say I care for it in here." He moved away and sat in another chair.

"You ought to use some of the pieces you have stored away," Grant continued, ignoring the mild protest in Jenkins' voice. "The paintings, for instance …"

"They aren't mine," Harlan said abruptly. "They belonged to the former owner of the house, and I never felt I wanted to use them. As a matter of fact, I'm not sure what is up there. I haven't looked in the attic in years."

"You should," Grant said carelessly. "You'd find some excellent items. You don't object to my prowling?"

"No," Jenkins shrugged. "No, certainly not."

"Fine. And now I think I'll leave you. Are you sure you're all right?"

"Don't worry about an old man who fumbles once in a while," Jenkins replied. "I'll be around a good many more years if I do nothing worse than break a glass."

Grant said nothing. He went out, leaving Jenkins to stare reflectively at the empty chair by the fireplace.

CHAPTER TWENTY-NINE

In the Jenkins dining room, the labored dinner conversation faltered and was heavily resumed. Harlan thrust out his jaw and frowned. An occasional family gathering was obligatory, he conceded reluctantly, but an infernal nuisance. He scarcely heard what was said in his mounting impatience for the meal to end. Tonight he planned to broach the traction project to Miles Hunter, but he preferred to wait until the two of them were alone. If he could interest the retired banker in the venture, he would be able to replace a large part of the deficit he incurred to pay Reed.

His eyes swept the table briefly, and he was not entirely displeased with what he saw. Felice was established now in her life with Neil, her manner assured and possessive, the large stones of her rings glittering imperiously on her left hand. Neil had little to say tonight. But he had always been reserved, and his devotion to Felice was as apparent as ever. In Harlan's opinion, Felice was exactly the right wife for him. Her quick fire and ambition would never allow him to settle into the sterility that marked his father's career as a banker.

Miles Hunter was conservative and deliberate in all things. Harlan grudgingly admitted that Hunter had weathered the depression when the best of his colleagues had gone down to ruin, largely because of his foresight in maintaining the bank's huge reserves. Today, retired and secure, he was not a promising investment target, but Jenkins was determined.

His wife, Elizabeth, still retained a pale reflection of the beauty she had possessed in younger days. Her gentleness and soft, fragile manner were a decorative and charming background for her husband's ponderous thoroughness. She smiled affectionately at him now as he addressed Grant.

"Tell me, Monroe," he asked good-humoredly, "am I a smug, selfish old man to enjoy my retirement as I do? Elizabeth thinks I'm becoming as useless as a worm in a cocoon because I prefer my books and a glass of brandy to an evening of gallivanting about the city."

"I didn't say that, Miles," Elizabeth protested calmly. "I only remarked that you should take more interest in civic affairs."

"I place considerable value on books and a glass of brandy myself," Grant observed pleasantly. "However, I daresay Miles still maintains his active interest in matters of public concern."

Harlan noted that Grant presided at the other end of the long table with his usual effortless charm. With an odd sense of discovery, Harlan turned the thought over slowly in his mind. In a peculiar fashion, the table seemed suddenly reversed. Harlan as always occupied his accustomed chair, but it was no longer the host's traditional seat of honor at the head of the table. That distinction had subtly passed to Grant Monroe through some invisible chemistry of human relationships which Jenkins was at a loss to analyze. Harlan's eyes narrowed and the wide nostrils flared with the intake of his breath as the realization scraped the core of his conceit.

But the moment passed, and he leaned back in his chair. One was never wise to indulge in emotions. He had learned control the hard way, through years of prudence when a slip would have meant ruin. He did not intend to blunder now.

Grant's money, of course, was an undisputed advantage. Lately Jenkins had become increasingly sensitive to Grant's proprietary status within the household, and this awareness had already begun to vex him. He suspected that he was allowing himself to be influenced by Theodora's unwarranted attitude, a circumstance that increased his annoyance. There were times when her view of the temporary property arrangement was incomprehensible. She seemed, he thought bluntly, to be totally unaware that Grant was her husband. He noted in some surprise that Theodora was unusually pleasant tonight, graciously and smilingly self-possessed. "Grant is right," she said, leaning toward Elizabeth Hunter. "We all know Miles's generosity to charities, to say nothing of the other fundraising campaigns to which he contributes."

"Miles is a darling," Felice put in deftly. "I've heard him say he would like to finance some philanthropic undertaking for the city, one that would benefit everyone."

"Perhaps park improvements would qualify," Grant suggested readily. He saw in amusement that Harlan was now drumming on the tablecloth in active annoyance. "Paved walks instead of gravel paths," he went on with lively enthusiasm, blandly ignoring Harlan's baleful glance, "recreational facilities for children, displays of tulips in season and other attractions. There's no end to what can be accomplished."

Harlan found himself on the point of interrupting, and for a second time had to take himself in hand. He observed that he was growing careless, a flaw that did not frighten him as it would have years ago but which disturbed him nevertheless. The urbane manner was becoming an increasing effort. Patience, he reminded himself sharply, was the sole instrument of self-preservation for the wise.

There was a lull in the conversation and he seized the advantage. "Shall we return to the drawing room?" he suggested, rising.

"After-dinner conversations are more enlivening if one relaxes in the comfort of an easy chair."

He assisted Elizabeth Hunter with her chair and, as she went ahead with the others, he fell back with the elderly banker. "Cigar?" he suggested, reaching for the silver-embossed humidor that held his special brand.

The movement was arrested, however. He drew his hand back abruptly and stared unpleasantly. The humidor on the sideboard was an alien one, hand-carved from old teak and embellished with a series of intricate inlays, one he had never seen before. The muscles of his face began to work curiously, and he sucked his lips between his teeth.

Undoubtedly Grant had made the substitution. The original was probably reposing in the drawing room on one of the small tables. Damn it, why hadn't he mentioned the exchange? Didn't he know a man grew accustomed to having things in certain places around the house? The unexpectedness of these discoveries was beginning to get on Harlan's nerves. Since the night he had come upon the Patterson chair in the study, he was hypersensitive to any triviality.

He remembered Hunter, and saw that the banker was watching him with a puzzled expression. "Nothing like a good cigar after dinner," he said with forced heartiness. He lifted the lid of the humidor experimentally and examined the cigars. His, naturally. He offered the humidor to Hunter, who accepted one.

"You know about the new traction line, of course," he continued in an affable tone. "How does the idea appeal to you?"

"The development has merit," Hunter conceded judiciously. "The outlying sections are growing, and there is need for people to have the convenience of easy transportation."

"Exactly. This is an excellent opportunity to invest in a worthy undertaking and at the same time be assured of continuous profits."

"Personally, I favor a new line," Hunter nodded. "I may purchase a block of shares after the franchise is cleared. I understand Interurban is expanding too," he added, lighting the cigar from a match in Jenkins' hand.

Harlan dropped his voice confidentially. "Their bid hasn't a chance. I doubt if they can renew the franchise they now hold."

Hunter was noncommittal. "Let me know when you're set," he said, "and I'll back you for what you may need."

Jenkins was forced to let it go at that. He concealed his displeasure with as much grace as possible and followed his guest into the drawing room.

CHAPTER THIRTY

Theodora sat in her bedroom alone. She had been glad to see the Hunters leave, Neil and Felice to a late party given by an acquaintance, the portly banker and his wife home to retire. The uneventful family gathering had been pleasant enough, she acknowledged, trying to put her finger on the reason for the apprehensions that persisted in the back of her mind.

For one thing, Felice's customary self-assurance had been vaguely irritating. Theodora particularly resented those sharply inquisitive side glances as Felice covertly watched her and Grant in turn, an almost malevolent glitter in the green depths of those eyes. Neil's pleasure in his wife and his obvious attachment were all Theodora could have wished. Certainly no one could find fault with Neil. Yet tonight his very attentiveness provoked in Theodora a further unreasonable impatience.

She had been on edge, too, when the conversation in the drawing room turned to the traction project. Harlan's tedious claims for the new company failed to gain conviction with repetition, and Felice's numerous questions troubled her. There was no reason why Felice shouldn't be apprised of developments, but it was the first time to Theodora's knowledge that her sister had shown an interest in business matters.

Perhaps her feelings were intensified by the arrival that day of a letter from Vienna. Tagliev had thoughtfully forwarded a few newspaper clippings on the performance of the Fantasias with a short note, expressing his hope that she would go on with her work to greater creative expression and technical perfection. The critics had been generous in their praise, and she translated their encouraging remarks with awakened nostalgia.

But her satisfaction was not what she had thought it would be. There was no glow of accomplishment or newly fired ambition as she put the clippings and note aside with the bills and other mail on the top of her dressing table. She glanced indifferently at them now and saw that the papers had been disturbed. Leafing through them, she noted that the bills were missing.

Grant had taken them, possibly when she was downstairs supervising the cook's preparations for dinner. Her expression changed as she thought about him here in the room, looking through the mail, perhaps idly fingering the tinted crystal vials on the dressing table. She stared accusingly at her reflection in the mirror, seeing the faint rise of color in her cheeks, the tremulous, softened lines of her mouth, the sudden vivid darkening of her eyes. It was a slight thing to quicken her pulse and send the warm blood flowing strongly in her veins, she thought angrily, despising herself for this weakness.

Her reflection grew colder, the haunting dissatisfaction hidden under a mask of outward indifference. This was the way she wanted it, the way she had planned. A marriage that was not a marriage, her power to humiliate Grant, to hurt him. The door closed between them.

She heard his step in the corridor outside and turned involuntarily, one hand gripping the edge of the dressing table to quiet the inner turmoil that trembled beneath her flesh. But the footsteps did not pause. She heard him continue on to his room, enter and close the door. She wondered what she would have done if he had come in, and for some minutes she sat there rigidly, incapable of moving.

When she arose, she was pale but controlled. She hesitated, then went to the door between the two rooms and knocked lightly. "Grant?" she called in a low tone, her hand on the knob.

"Come in, Theodora," he said.

As she opened the door, he put aside the book he had been reading and came to his feet. She saw a faint surprise on his face, and something more. Perhaps it was hope, or a kindled warmth that asked for closeness between them. She knew that by a word she could erase what had happened, and the knowledge did nothing to steady her.

"Don't get up," she said, taking the other chair near the reading table. He sat down again, waiting. "I came to ask you about father," she continued, watching his expression slowly change. "After the Hunters left, he called you aside. Is it money?"

"Yes," he admitted after a slight hesitation. "I regret that I'm not able to advance more at this time. The money I have is tied up in merchandise that moves slowly."

"Why does he need it?" she asked, frowning.

He considered, then decided to tell her part of the truth. "For the franchise, I believe," he said. "Usually these matters come rather high."

"A bribe," she said with loathing.

He laughed. "One usually refers to it as a fee. A rather common procedure, I assure you."

She searched his expression. "How much is ... required?"

He shrugged. "You must understand that a franchise is a unique set of privileges, often in force as long as ninety-nine years. Any company who obtains one is extremely fortunate in having the favor of city officials. The continuing profits of public utilities are incalculable. I don't know what is being considered in this case, but I suppose it is a substantial amount."

"You encouraged father at the start," she said bleakly. "If it hadn't been for you, he would never have engaged in this impractical undertaking."

"He scarcely needed encouragement," Grant said dryly. "I believe he will tell you himself that he attempted this venture on his own initiative and out of a sense of expediency. Like many others since the depression, he has had to look for new sources of income."

"You helped him in the beginning," she said accusingly. "Now when he's committed to seeing the project through, you turn him away."

He inclined his head slightly. "I'm sorry," he said evenly.

She rose. "I don't think you are. I think you want to see him ruined. You would have him lose everything, his house, his money, his prestige, and the respect of his friends."

His eyes had become inscrutable, and his face was again cold and inflexible in its hard lines. "In spite of your unflattering opinion of me," he said, unmoved, "I can do nothing."

She flashed him a contemptuous glance, choking back the retort on the tip of her tongue. She started to turn away, but he stopped her.

"Theodora?" he said tentatively.

She waited scornfully.

"I hope you will forgive me for glancing at your newspaper reviews," he said. "I couldn't help seeing them when I took the bills in your room. I'm glad the performance was so excellently received."

"Thank you," she said coldly.

"I'd like to know that you will go on with your music. You have the talent, and I believe the work would be a source of happiness and satisfaction to you."

"I appreciate your interest," she retorted. "Does this mean I can return to Vienna?"

He smiled faintly. "No. I am merely suggesting that you would be happier if you resume your work here."

"I see."

He was watching her intently and she stiffened defensively. But he did not move. "Good night, Theodora," he said quietly.

To her sudden, acute embarrassment, she felt her cheeks burn hotly. Wordlessly, she left the room and closed the door behind her.

CHAPTER THIRTY-ONE

Felice and Neil returned to the Hunter home at a late hour. Despite the gaiety of the party they had just left, Felice was in a sullen mood. Each encounter with Grant and Theodora stirred her discontent and prodded her malicious anger. Neil respected her feelings with a well-meant silence, a technique which unfortunately only served to inflame her ill humor. She was adroit enough to conceal the reason for her peevishness but her irrepressible temper found devious ways of expression.

"Father is certainly working hard for the traction company," she said pettishly, removing her necklace and rings. "I wonder if it will be appreciated."

Neil made no comment, and she frowned at the door to the adjoining dressing room where he was preparing for bed.

"Neil, are you listening?" she demanded sharply.

"Yes, dear," he replied. "Appreciated by whom?"

"Grant and Theodora, of course," she said crossly. Felice had never been greatly concerned with the feelings of any but herself and she wasn't now. Nor was she sympathetically disposed toward Harlan, whose favoritism toward Grant and Theodora rankled incessantly. But she needed an excuse to vent her spleen and Harlan was a convenient subject. "It wouldn't occur to them to be grateful for what father is doing," she said spitefully. "After all, they are the ones to benefit."

"You mean because Grant owns stock in the company?" Neil asked, coming into the room. "I imagine he knows what he's doing. This is probably just another investment to him, and he's willing to gamble on its success or failure."

Felice paused in the act of removing the pins from her hair. "There is a doubt then about whether it will succeed?" she asked carefully.

"There's always a risk in a new undertaking," he said, tossing his dressing gown over a chair. "Particularly where the entire venture depends on obtaining a franchise from the city." He lay down on the bed, thumped his pillow in the ritual that irritated her beyond measure, and leaned back comfortably.

She did not answer immediately. The risk, of course, depended upon Harlan's having sufficient funds to swing the deal against competitors. Investors were scarce. Most people, like Miles Hunter, preferred to wait until the franchise was actually secured before committing themselves. She stared thoughtfully at the pale ovals of her fingernails. A doubt raised, a rumor started, and Grant Monroe's investment would be worthless. Whatever her father had put in would be gone too, but this was a matter of little concern to her. For one thing, she was fairly certain that Harlan had none of his own money invested. He had used Theodora's trust fund for his own ends, but it wasn't like him to venture a dime of his own even if he had it. She had fewer illusions about him than Theodora, and her shrewd appraisal of his self-seeking vanity left her no cause for a troubled conscience.

If anything were to be done, she thought narrowly, now was the time. She and Neil would leave shortly for their Mediterranean trip and there would be no further opportunity. "You hear about these things at the bank, I suppose," she remarked. "You know when depositors draw out money to buy stock, don't you?"

"In some instances," he admitted. "If we purchase shares for them, or approve loans for the purpose."

The green eyes hardened beneath the lowered lids. "You don't act without investigating, do you?"

He looked at the cool beauty of her reflection in the mirror and smiled. He was puzzled by her persistence, but undeniably pleased. Tonight was the first time she had shown any interest in his affairs and he found it reassuring.

"You are developing quite an interest in banking, my dear. But don't worry. I'm sure the traction project is sound."

"Just the same, it would be wrong not to look into it," she suggested. "You have to protect the bank as well as the depositors."

He frowned slightly. The problem had indeed come up, and there were several applications for such loans pending. He knew his father's attitude and knew that the older man's advice would be negative. But Neil had not reached a decision. The question of investigating had several aspects. Jenkins needed the additional capital, yet the status of the company had not been established as altogether sound. On the other hand, refusal to grant the loans might cause unfavorable repercussions among other possible investors, a circumstance that could destroy the undertaking at its inception.

"This is a late hour for a discussion on banking," he reminded her mildly. "Why are you so interested?"

"I'm worried, Neil," she said, her voice coaxing. "I don't want you to be unduly influenced by your regard for father or Grant. You should put yourself first. Look into the situation and if the risk is too great, you can advise the depositors properly."

He was immensely pleased. There had been times since their marriage when he had been tortured by the thought that she was still infatuated with Grant Monroe. He had done his best to reject the notion but it haunted him intermittently. Knowing Felice all her life, he readily acknowledged that he did not understand her. She could be warm and infinitely lovable, and without warning suddenly grow cold and distant, a glittering hardness in those strange eyes that deeply troubled him. Often when he held her in his arms he was aware of her withdrawal and he faltered, feeling uncomfortably loutish and inadequate. Usually he was considerate, and the demands he made on her were few.

Her unmistakable concern now for his welfare proved him wrong about Grant Monroe, he thought with humble gratitude and new hope. "I'm glad you feel that way," he said warmly. "Not many men have wives who put their husbands' interests ahead of every other consideration."

"Then you will be careful?"

"I'll investigate the company," he promised, closing his eyes against the glare of the lamp and relaxing in the comfortable softness of the bed.

She waited until his regular breathing became a quiet snore, then undressed and got into bed beside him.

CHAPTER THIRTY-TWO

Al Reed was fond of saying that after he had received a fee for negotiations of importance and had exerted the needed influence, his custom was to return home and pray. Usually, he added with gravity, his prayers were answered. Grant Monroe smiled with grim humor. He could not quite picture the politician at his prayers but if such indeed was his occupation, Reed might well be arduously employed. The influence he had exerted on the inner circle of the assembly did not guarantee their actions in the face of stronger persuasion.

The time to tighten the net had arrived, and Grant was prepared. His association with the politician had been a calculated necessity, and its termination after Reed had outlived his usefulness was a foregone conclusion. Moreover, Reed had his own debt to settle with the past. The Patterson affair was an early instance of the abbreviated justice of paid juries and corrupt law enforcement officials. It was not the last, but it was one among innumerable others which Reed would have reason to recall.

Grant's mission that morning took him to three banks where he maintained accounts. From each he withdrew sizable amounts in bills of large denominations. At the Commercial Exchange, he nodded a pleasant good-morning to Neil through the open door to the latter's private office. He was ready to depart when Neil left his desk and intercepted him near the entrance.

"Can you spare a few minutes. Grant? I'd appreciate it."

Grant acquiesced readily and the two went into the austere quiet of the dignified and vaultlike room which had been Miles Hunter's hallowed precinct since the bank had been founded.

"Off the record," Neil began as Grant sat down and lit a cigarette, "I think you have some information I need. You can be assured that I'll keep whatever you say in the strictest confidence."

"I'll be happy to be of service if I can," Grant said, blowing a thin stream of smoke into the air.

Neil hesitated. He had acted entirely on impulse, and now it occurred to him that perhaps it was unwise to invite Grant into his confidence. If, as Felice said, his stake in the traction deal was high, Grant wasn't likely to reveal any unfavorable information. But Neil primarily wanted assurance that Jenkins would obtain the needed franchise, and he knew that Grant was apprised on that point.

He respected Grant Monroe's integrity, despite the occasional rumors one heard. There was usually speculation about a successful man, particularly if his affairs were not a matter of public knowledge. And Neil found himself actually liking this tall, puzzling man now that there was no longer rivalry between them. He could understand how Felice had been attracted. That dark, smiling composure and soft manner would inevitably flatter a woman's ego and stir her interest. The thought of his wife and their conversation last night filled him with a deep sense of gratification, and his friendliness visibly warmed.

"We've had several applications for loans recently," he explained, "from depositors wishing to invest in the new rail company. It's our custom to inquire into the financial soundness of the firms involved in such cases. A precautionary measure, you know. Safeguards the bank as well as our depositors. I don't doubt that the company's financial condition is in order, but I've been wondering when the assembly will act on the franchise application."

Grant was aware that Neil's sense of duty would keep him from approving the loans if there was a doubt concerning the franchise. And he knew the effect this action would have on the value of the Jenkins' stock if it were known that a powerful bank such as the Commercial Exchange refused to gamble on the new company. Who had planted this doubt in Neil's mind, he wondered in oblique amusement. Miles? Felice? Grant smiled inwardly as he thought of Felice's ill-concealed antagonism since he and Theodora had returned from New Orleans. Her interest in the traction venture after dinner last night began to take on new meaning. The kitten's vengeful claws were possibly doing him a service, he observed dryly.

Aloud he said: "I am flattered that you ask my opinion, but frankly I haven't the slightest idea when the assembly will act."

"I naturally assumed that you were a principal stockholder," Neil pointed out, "and familiar with the franchise angle."

Grant hesitated. "My investment is not as sizable as you seem to think," he confided with apparent reluctance. "Unfortunately most of my assets are demanded in other channels and I've been unable to give Harlan the backing he wanted. I did what I could, but I'm only a small shareholder along with many others."

Neil frowned. He did not know whether to believe Grant or not. Felice had been certain that Grant's holdings were substantial, but she may have been wrong. After all, what reason would he have for concealing the fact?

"I'd like to take care of all pending business before Felice and I leave next week," he mused aloud. "We plan to be abroad two months, possibly longer."

"I appreciate your position," Grant remarked. "With the strong opposition from Interurban, all stockholders are taking a chance on Harlan's ability to secure a franchise. Do what you think is best. But it appears to me that anyone desiring to invest on a loan would do well to wait a while longer."

Neil was impressed by the singular frankness of this advice, and thanked him in all sincerity. They parted on genial terms and Grant returned to his office, certain that Neil would reject whatever loans were pending for the purchase of stock in the new railway.

Neil would have been astounded had he seen the visitor Grant received in his office a short time later. The president of Interurban nodded briskly and sat down to the business at hand. He extracted some papers from his briefcase and affixed his signature. Grant scrutinized them thoroughly in turn, and was satisfied. Without further delay, he turned over the money he had withdrawn earlier from his accounts, and the transaction was completed.

CHAPTER THIRTY-THREE

The appointment concluded, Grant stared out the windows at the jagged outline of the city's ugly smokestacks. The crowding warehouses, offices, and industrial buildings were gray under the sullen winter sky. Below, the black waters of the Mississippi hurried past the bend as though eager to be gone from the poisonous discharge of the factories and mills clinging tenaciously to its shoulders.

His thoughts held no hostility for the panoramic scene below. St. Louis, concerned more in the past with growing pains than with decent city administration and honesty in its courts, had been an easy prey for the tight political machine that regulated every vein of public life. If not Al Reed, there would have been another like him. The city was at last struggling out of its adolescent indifference to an awareness of its bigness and strength, slowly awakening to a realization of its weaknesses and mistakes. The Patterson affair had brought Grant Monroe back to exact payment for the past, but there was more to be done. It would be accomplished, he thought with surety, remembering the promise he had given Father Morelle.

He was surprised that he felt no elation. His only feeling now was impatience to be done with the job. How was it, he thought morosely, that a man worked and planned for years in the conquest of a supreme goal only to find himself empty of satisfaction when that goal was attained? Perhaps this was the clever irony of existence, the hidden leveler to crown achievement with dissatisfaction, bringing with each success a larger sense of incompletion and uselessness.

His thoughts went to Theodora as they invariably did in one of his bleak moods. His wife, he thought wryly. She showed no inclination to effect a change in their relationship. It was as though the wedding had never been. She was implacably aloof, not with the old spirited antagonism but with a quietly controlled, waiting determination that was impervious to kindness or assault. He wondered with sudden clarity how she would react if confronted now with the truth about her father. He could understand if she simply refused to accept the facts out of blind filial devotion. Rather that than a militant attempt to justify Harlan's actions in her misguided belief that he could do no wrong.

Grant was annoyed that he could not think of her apart from the man who was her father. Mrs. Grant Monroe, not Theodora Jenkins, he reminded himself, though he knew the formality of marriage had changed nothing. Since their return from New Orleans, she had preserved her remote identity as well as the inviolate privacy of her bedroom, withdrawing from him firmly and as frequently as possible without arousing the suspicion of her father or the servants. He saw her at meals and on an occasional evening when they sat with Harlan for a dull hour after dinner. The weather was often inclement, but he had several times suggested a Sunday afternoon drive. She had declined on one pretext or another, and he refrained from any further proposals.

His thoughts were interrupted as the door opened. "A young woman to see you," Romaine Withers announced crisply. "She's waiting outside."

He glanced at her in some surprise. "A woman?" he repeated with a puzzled frown.

"Señora Ortiz," she enunciated carefully. "She said you knew her. Shall I send her in?"

His surprise changed to incredulity and the frown deepened. "Of course send her in," he said, nettled. "What are you waiting for?"

Miss Withers' expression reproved him, but there was a suspicion of humor in her eyes as she turned away. Grant, however, was too preoccupied to mind. What was Nita doing here? Why wasn't she in New York where she belonged?

Nita made her entrance quickly, sweeping across the room in vivid scarlet and black moire, her furs across her arm.

"Nita!" he greeted her sharply. "What the devil brings you to St. Louis?"

"You are not glad to see me?" she asked with a little pout. "You should say, 'Nita, how nice you look,' or 'Nita, how happy I am to see you,' not what devil brings you!"

His impatience mounted. "You're not unattractive, as you know," he admitted grudgingly. "But why aren't you in New York with your aunt?"

"You are angry with me," she said, seating herself and gazing up at him with eyes widened in contrition. "I did not think you cared so little for Nita. I stayed in New York until I could no longer endure it. I was unhappy, very unhappy. And lonely. And so," she concluded with an expressive lift of the shoulders, "I said, I shall go to St. Louis!"

"You received my letter?" he asked.

"*Si*," she replied.

She had received it, the short missive expressing the hope that she was enjoying the city and would be happy there until she could return to the plantation, and telling her that he was to be married to this Theodora Jenkins. The letter had made her quite angry. But there had been a dashing captain of the United States Artillery who eloquently consoled her and devoted himself gallantly to the task of filling the emptiness in her life. The captain, unfortunately, had been recently joined by his wife, and both left precipitately for his new assignment at a base in the Midwest.

"You are married," she went on emotionally, "and you want to forget Nita. You do not care what happens to me now."

"That's nonsense, Nita. I've always been fond of you, and concerned with your welfare. But St. Louis is no place for you. You belong in New York, until conditions improve on the island."

"I won't stay in New York," she said strongly.

"There's nothing for you here," he retorted in exasperation.

Quick tears sprang to her eyes. "You are hard and unfeeling," she lamented. "I am so alone, and so miserable. It is unbearable."

Her tears made him uncomfortable, and he had the disagreeable suspicion that her voice, if not her words, carried beyond the door to the outer office. He remembered in annoyance the lurking amusement in Miss Withers' eyes. Nita's expressive inflection would render her meaning palpably clear even if the flow of her words was unintelligible.

"Don't do that," he said uneasily as a fresh flood of tears spilled forth. He searched his pockets and came up with a clean kerchief. "Here, use this."

She took it obediently and dabbed at her eyes. "Let me stay," she pleaded. "I won't be any trouble to you, I promise."

He frowned. It was doubtful that the situation in Cuba would be settled within the year; in all probability it would grow worse. Nita would have to return to New York. But obviously, he thought rapidly, this was not the time or the place to persuade her.

"Come along," he said as she prepared to weep anew. "You can spend the night with us, and in the morning we'll talk it over."

Intent mainly on getting her outside, he took his coat from a closet and directed her without further delay through the side door to the corridor.

CHAPTER THIRTY-FOUR

Theodora inspected the cook's preparations for dinner and ordered a rich port wine, her father's favorite with roast. Recently Harlan, who as long as she could remember enjoyed his food in ample quantities, was becoming indifferent at the table. He consumed only a third of his usual portions, eating that without relish. She was particularly anxious that he regain his former appetite. If he dined properly, he would be better able to cope with whatever problems preyed on his mind. He was deeply troubled, she knew, by the negotiations for a franchise. He manifested an odd nervousness, glancing behind him at times as though he thought someone in the house were following him, or inclining his head abruptly as if listening to sounds of footsteps or voices beyond a closed door. Slight noises that once would have gone unnoticed now startled him, and often he sat in his accustomed chair in the study for hours, staring moodily into space.

She wondered that he never used the comfortable leather armchair which Grant had reclaimed from disuse in the attic. But he seemed to prefer the straight-backed Windsor. Sometimes she thought the leather chair vexed him. She had noticed when they were alone that he had a curious habit of glancing at it as though expecting to see someone there. Once she had been impelled to turn her head with his, but there was obviously nothing remarkable about the unoccupied chair.

She was secretly alarmed. Father had never before exhibited a lack of control or a capacity for nervous mannerisms, even when mama died. He was no longer young, she thought devotedly, and the strain of this new enterprise was taxing his energies severely. She ardently hoped that his efforts would be successful and that he could comfortably retire from the pressing responsibilities of active life. If he failed, she feared his health would not stand the disappointment.

Satisfied that the roast would be timed to well-browned perfection and the dinner tempting to the most jaded appetite, she left the kitchen. She entered the hall on her way upstairs as Grant and Nita stepped inside the door.

"We have a guest, my dear," Grant said, seeing her. "I may have mentioned Juan's daughter, who has been in New York with an aunt. This is Nita. Nita, Mrs. Monroe."

Theodora inclined her head automatically. Grant once said in passing that the overseer's daughter had been sent to New York to await the outcome of the Cuban revolt. She inspected the younger woman with surprise. This was not the child she had imagined with sympathy and understanding, the forlorn little native girl who fled the dangers of the insurrection. This was a woman, sophisticated in her furs and small modish hat with its scarlet trim. A rather knowing woman, Theodora thought, one who excited anything but pity.

Nita was also inspecting Theodora, but without surprise. Except for hair as dark as her own and eyes strikingly similar, the señora was as she had expected. Coldly beautiful, and unfeeling. She did not love Grant, one could see. This one loved only herself. How, Nita wondered heatedly, can men be so stupid?

Aloud she said prettily: "I am happy to meet you, señora. It was good of Grant to offer me the hospitality of your home."

"Oh?" said Theodora. She leveled an inquiring look at Grant.

"Nita ran away from her aunt," he explained. "She wasn't particularly happy there."

187

"I should think she would be happier among her own people than with strangers," Theodora commented dryly.

"But Grant is no stranger," Nita hastened to assure her. "I have known him all my life."

Grant thought it advisable to terminate the interview. "She'll spend the night with us," he said pleasantly. "In the morning we'll decide what to do. If it's all right with you, Theodora, she can occupy Felice's old room."

"Oh, quite," Theodora said, ringing for the maid. To Nita, she said: "You will be comfortable, I think. If you want anything, let us know. Dinner will be at seven. Felice's room," she added briefly to the maid who answered her summons.

"My luggage, Grant," Nita said, turning to him with a troubled air. "I did not know where to send it, and the man said I could leave it at the station until someone called."

"I'll have Rufus pick it up," Grant assured her.

She thanked him again with profuse gratitude and turned to go with the maid. When she was gone, Grant followed Theodora into the drawing room.

He lit a cigarette and studied her through the smoke. A shaft of late afternoon sunlight fell across her face, and it touched marble. He felt suddenly tired. The activities of the day, added to Nita's unexpected arrival, had depressed him, and he knew with disheartening certainty that he could not turn to Theodora in his loneliness. Had he been wrong about this woman? Perhaps her pinnacle of isolation was indestructible, and it was useless to hope for a change.

"How long have you decided to keep the girl here?" she asked in an expressionless tone.

"Until we can persuade her to return to New York," he told her. "I can't send her back to the plantation without knowing more about the situation. A peaceful settlement may be possible. I don't know. In the morning I'll see what I can find out."

"There's nothing further to say about the matter, I suppose," she said levelly, turning away.

Good Lord, he thought angrily, what is the matter with her? "Theodora," he said sharply as she reached the door.

"Yes?" she said, turning to face him.

She was regarding him steadily, waiting. "Nothing," he said irritably, after a moment. He looked for an ashtray, found one, and crushed out his cigarette. "Perhaps you'd better inform the cook that there will be an extra for dinner."

"Yes," she said unemotionally. "Of course."

When the door closed behind her, he did not move for some minutes. Rousing himself finally, he crossed the room and seated himself near the fireplace. Leaning back, he studied the room through half-closed eyes. In the afternoon gloom, gathering shadows settled on the chairs and sofa, the walls, the curtains, the mantelpiece. The contours softened and shifted, and he saw each piece as it had been years ago, the furnishings of the drawing room he knew as a child.

No, the sofa was wrong. It should be nearer the windows. And that chair, the one his father had used for reading, should be drawn closer to the fireplace and the lamplight. Rising quickly, he made the changes and a keen, bitter pleasure burned through him. Surveying the effect, he recalled another missing detail. The crystal candlesticks that had adorned the mantel. There was still time before dinner to find them. Perhaps he could locate them in that old trunk under the eaves. It was worth trying.

CHAPTER THIRTY-FIVE

Harlan leaned forward, quite taken by the vivacious Nita's flattering smiles and bright chatter. He had apparently thrust his concerns into the background and for the present, at least, was enjoying himself immensely. He finished a satisfactory meal and sipped generously on a second glass of red wine as he exchanged lively remarks with their guest.

"I can't believe such a delightful young woman was lonely in New York," he said roguishly. "Surely the gentlemen in the East have an eye for beauty and charm? In my younger days I would have given them a run for their money."

"But you are not old, Señor Jenkins," Nita rebuked him archly. "You are only in the prime of life."

He winked. "One is never older than one feels and, dammit, I feel thirty again, I do indeed!"

Theodora, who thought the conversation was bordering on the bawdy, suppressed a frown. "You are married, Nita?" she asked, glancing at the wedding band on Nita's slim hand. "I don't believe Grant mentioned your husband."

Nita's expression was suddenly sober. "He was a patriot, señora. Pedro was a man of fine ideals. He dreamed of a free Cuba and gave himself for the cause." A few tears gathered in her eyes and sparkled on the long lashes as she glanced down at the hand that wore the ring.

"I am sorry," Theodora said. "I didn't know."

Grant cleared his throat. "Pedro is alive," he announced in a matter-of-fact tone. "And from last reports, quite well. He had the misfortune to be captured and imprisoned by the Spaniards."

"In the reconcentrado camps, one never knows," Nita said with impassioned insistence. "They torture and starve and beat the prisoners, and many are shot."

"Let's not think the worst, my dear," Harlan advised. "Worry is the betrayer of beauty. Breeds wrinkles and sours the disposition. Your Pedro will probably be released eventually, and you'll find him none the worse for his experience."

She favored him with a sad smile. "You are right, señor, about worry. It is never profitable. I try to be brave. Even when I am unhappy to be so far from home, I tell myself it is not for always."

"I suppose you miss the life you had," Theodora said stiffly.

"I could not help missing the plantation," Nita told her with ardor. "It is home to me. But you are so very kind here, I feel happier than I have since I left. And this house, it is so beautiful!"

"You like the house, Nita?" Grant asked with a tolerant smile.

"Ah yes," she said warmly. "It reminds me in many ways of the plantation house."

"Is that so?" Harlan remarked. "I understood that dwellings in tropical areas were different in construction. Built with an eye for casting off heat, rather than keeping it in."

"They are for the weather, as you say," she agreed. "But Señor Monroe, Grant's father, built it for beauty too. When I drove up this afternoon and saw this lovely place with the high portico, I could not believe my eyes. It is like home, I said. Except for our screened veranda on the north and no upstairs rooms, it is almost exactly the same. And this room, with its big low windows looking out to the garden, is arranged much like our dining room at the plantation."

"I'm sure I would like your plantation house," Harlan said. "Have you any photographs, Grant?"

"No," Grant said easily. "I don't think there have been any made of the place."

"Most houses bear similarities if one looks for them," Theodora said, inexplicably annoyed by Nita's possessive references to the plantation. "This one, I daresay, is not unique."

They rose, Harlan assisting Nita with a courtliness Theodora thought unnecessary. "We retire early," she said with dignity. "But I suppose Nita is tired from her journey?"

"I?" Nita said, expressing surprise. "Oh no, señora. I am almost never tired."

"We can't send our guest to bed immediately after dinner," Harlan said, invigorated. "Come along to the drawing room, Nita. You can tell me more about this remarkable plantation house and your life there."

CHAPTER THIRTY-SIX

If Nita was almost never tired, Theodora thought acidly, she did not demonstrate the fact by early rising. Theodora found Harlan himself up rather late, reading his mail at the dining room table.

"Only coffee, father?" she said with strong disapproval. "You don't expect to do a day's work on coffee and cigars?"

Eh, what's that?" he said, preoccupied with the quarterly statement from the River Savings and Investment Bank, the establishment he entrusted with the proceeds from his various transactions.

"If you waited until later to smoke," she insisted firmly, "you would enjoy a proper breakfast."

"Coffee is sufficient," he said impatiently, turning his attention from the mail and draining the cup. "You, I believe, have found it so upon occasion."

"I had a very substantial breakfast," she replied uncompromisingly. "Several hours ago."

"Hm, yes," he frowned. "You retired early. Rather abruptly, I thought. I hope our guest did not mind."

"I daresay she did not," she retorted. "She appeared to be quite at ease with you and Grant."

He picked up his lighted cigar from a nearby ashtray. "I gather that you are not favorably impressed with her," he said somewhat sternly. "One must be understanding, you know. The girl needs kindness and reassurance until she becomes better adjusted."

"I was under the impression she was to return to New York," she reminded him. "Are you suggesting that we keep her here until she becomes adjusted?"

"I wouldn't turn her out into the streets," he said, puffing irritably on the cigar. "If she's happy here, I see no reason to send her away. After all, she lived at Grant's place in Cuba. She is, in a way, a responsibility."

"She was a housekeeper there," Theodora said tartly. "And as for her readjustment, I am of the opinion that Nita is thoroughly capable of looking after herself."

"You do the girl a considerable injustice," he said shortly, unable to control his rising vexation. "I trust you will not convey your unfriendliness in a way that will distress her." He reached for the pot of coffee at his elbow and started to refill his cup.

"Good morning," Nita interrupted brightly, from the doorway. "Your maid, señora, told me I would find you here."

Harlan glanced up and a generous quantity of misdirected hot coffee scalded his free hand. He uttered a subdued but rather strong exclamation, and replaced the pot hurriedly.

"Oh, Señor Jenkins," Nita said sympathetically, crossing the room quickly. "Your hand, it is burned!" She seized a napkin and gently dabbed at the reddened hand, clucking tenderly as she examined the burn. "This is terrible, terrible! And all my fault for interrupting so suddenly!"

Harlan was undeniably pleased at her concern, but uncomfortably aware of Theodora's eloquent silence. "It's nothing," he said in some embarrassment, drawing his hand away with difficulty. "Clumsy of me, but nothing. Didn't have time for another coffee anyway. I should have been at the office before this. Theodora, you'll see about breakfast for our guest?"

"Certainly," she said in an odd tone.

He withdrew hastily, and Theodora rang for the maid. "The cook will prepare whatever you like," she said to Nita. "She usually does the marketing now, but I'm sure she won't mind the delay."

"You are very kind, señora," Nita smiled. "But I do not wish to be an inconvenience. I shall make fresh coffee myself, and toast. It is all I require."

"That won't be necessary," Theodora told her. "We can manage."

"Poor Señor Jenkins," Nita murmured, sadly shaking her head. "He left his papers."

"Yes, I see," Theodora said, moving to the table and gathering up the letters forgotten by Harlan in his haste. A slip of paper fluttered to the floor and she bent to retrieve it. A canceled check, she noted automatically, placing it with the bank statement. Then she was suddenly motionless, stunned by the amount she saw represented on the face of the withdrawal form. Two hundred and fifty thousand drawn on the account of the traction company must represent nearly the total assets, she thought, chilled by a gathering alarm. A glance at the accompanying statement confirmed this.

"Is anything wrong, señora?" Nita asked, seeing the color gone from her face and the shocked incredulity of her eyes.

"No," she said, steadying herself against the table.

The maid appeared and Theodora looked at her blankly, trying to collect her thoughts. "You rang, Miss Theodora?"

"Will you please see that Miss Nita has breakfast," Theodora managed to say. "I must find father before he leaves the house."

She made her way to the hall and intercepted Harlan at the front door. "Your letters, father," she said, controlling her voice with an effort.

"Oh yes," he said briskly, taking them from her. "Thank you, Theodora."

"And this," she added grimly, holding out the canceled check.

He glanced at it sharply, and at her. "Yes, of course," he said quickly, inserting it with the other papers and stuffing them into his briefcase.

"That's a great deal of money," she pursued doggedly. "Almost as much as the company is worth at present. Has something dreadful happened, father?"

"What are you talking about?" he parried in rising irritation. "Dammit, Theodora, I'm in a hurry. I've several important appointments this morning."

"This is important too," she insisted stubbornly. "I must know. If you don't tell me, I'll find out another way."

He scowled. He couldn't afford to have her meddling now. "Very well," he said unpleasantly. "The check you saw represents the current value of a franchise. The price, if you like, for obtaining such rights of way as are necessary for the operation of a public transportation line. Does that answer your question?"

"You had to give all that ... to Al Reed?" she asked in a choked voice.

"You understand that I would be ruined if a thing like this got out," he advised her sharply. "Favors are bought and sold every day in the week, but one doesn't make conversation of them."

"Mr. Reed must be quite a wealthy man," she said bitterly.

"Reed gets his," he admitted. "But the bulk of the money is parceled out among key men in the assembly. What they receive will, I hope, be sufficient to dispel the temptation offered by Interurban. If the banks hadn't started to refuse loan applications, investors would still be available and there would be nothing to worry about. Now that you are acquainted with the matter, I'd advise you to put it out of your mind."

He went out the door, and presently she heard the grating of wheels on gravel as the carriage drove away. Felice, coming up the walk several minutes later, found her there in the hall, leaning dazedly against a chair.

"You look ragged this morning," Felice commented cheerfully. "What's wrong? Grant not treating you properly?"

"I'm all right," Theodora said numbly.

Her horror upon learning of her father's precarious maneuverings was now equaled by a fear that others would find out. She had known that he paid Reed some stated amount but she had never imagined the figure ran to such a staggering sum. Yet this was not all. If a last-minute change of plan turned the tide in favor of Interurban, Harlan's ruin would be absolute.

In the back of her mind a vague plan took shape, a plan compounded of astounding elements quite foreign to her nature. She was repelled, but desperation bred desperate measures. She did not allow herself to dwell on the possible ramifications of this startling idea. It was enough that a means of helping her father had presented itself. There was the farewell party at the Mills home for Felice and Neil, an affair to which she did not look forward with any particular pleasure. But the situation had changed. Included among the guests would be Paul Nixon, and Theodora's inspiration included the personable assemblyman. Nixon's pleasant addiction to ladies rendered him an ideal subject for the plan she had in mind.

"I suppose you've finished your preparations for the cruise," she said to Felice with a forcible display of outward calm.

"Mostly," Felice said carelessly. "The trunks are going on ahead today. We're leaving on the early morning train after the party." She stripped off her gloves and regarded her reflection in the wall mirror with critical approval. "I saw father driving away just now," she remarked casually. "He looked preoccupied, almost ill. Hasn't he been well lately?"

"I haven't heard him complain," Theodora said noncommittally.

"It's unfortunate that Neil had to refuse loans for the purchase of stock in the transit company," she went on composedly. "I heard other banks followed his example, and investments have dropped. This won't mean the end of the project, I hope, after all father's work and the money Grant put in?"

Theodora looked at her sister sharply. "You can stop worrying on Grant's account," she said tersely. "His investment is negligible."

"Oh? I thought ..."

"I'm afraid I know what you thought," Theodora went on grimly. "But father alone stands to gain or lose in the venture."

Felice shrugged. "Father can take care of himself, I imagine," she said. She did not quite believe Theodora's statement that Grant had nothing to lose in the traction enterprise, but she let it pass. There was another interesting development which she had come to investigate, and she was about to broach the subject when the door to the dining room opened.

She turned to see Nita waiting indecisively on the threshold. "Well, well," Felice said slowly, surveying the newcomer with frank interest.

Nita met the cool, direct appraisal with an artless smile. "I see you have company, señora," she said to Theodora. "I shall go to my room while you entertain your guest."

"I am no guest, little one," Felice assured her. "I am the señora's sister, and I came this morning for the express purpose of meeting you."

"I am happy you have come," Nita murmured. "It gives me pleasure to know all Grant's family and friends in St. Louis."

"Grant, eh?" Felice said, highly diverted.

Nita saw the frozen look on Theodora's face and decided to withdraw. She would not be wise to offend Theodora. Grant might send her away. "You will forgive me, please," she smiled demurely. "I have some letters to write. Perhaps we shall meet again?"

"Oh, I hope so," Felice said. "I do, indeed."

Nita ran lightly up the stairs, and Felice turned to regard her sister with amusement. "My room, I suppose?" she asked with an irritating lift of an eyebrow. When Theodora did not reply, she went on: "I learned about your charming guest by accidentally overhearing the kitchen gossip, and thought I would stop in to see for myself."

"Nita is the daughter of Grant's overseer in Cuba," Theodora explained. "She is … visiting us."

"Really? I never doubted that Grant had a past, but I confess I'm surprised he let it catch up with him."

"Aren't you being rather childish?" Theodora said evenly. "Nita is here because of the unsettled conditions in Cuba, not because of Grant."

"Some day, Theodora, you'll come down from your mountaintop and see that life is very different from what you thought," Felice said. "There are women, you know, who make a specialty of other women's husbands. Single men never attract them. And that one has her claws into Grant," she concluded with malicious satisfaction, "or she wouldn't be here."

"You're getting pleasure out of this, aren't you?" Theodora asked wearily. "It makes you happy to think you are hurting me."

"I'm giving you excellent advice," Felice retorted tartly. "Don't take that kitten into the fold or you'll acquire a few scratches that may not heal."

"I'll decide what to do," Theodora reminded her coldly.

"Still the same old Theodora." She turned away, paused at the door and asked with a significant nod in the direction of the stairs: "Are you taking that to the Mills's tonight?"

Theodora hesitated. The problem of Nita had not occurred to her. Fred and Martha Mills would not mind an extra, she considered briefly. In fact, they probably would expect it under the circumstances. And there might be a definite advantage in having Nita along.

"Yes," she said slowly. "I think possibly she will accompany us."

CHAPTER THIRTY-SEVEN

Grant regarded Theodora from the doorway in silence. The draped rose velvet gown she had chosen to wear to the Mills affair displayed her figure in all its statuesque perfection. The soft, warm color brought a reflected glow to the pallor of her cheeks, and the full lips were a deeper red than he had seen for some time. On her wrist was the circlet of silver and diamonds which had been her mother's, and on her throat sparkled the closely matched necklace he had given her in New Orleans. He stiffened involuntarily at the memory, but he held his mind objectively to his consideration of her. The blue-black hair rose from the face in a high, sophisticated coif, sharpening the classic lines of the features. Perhaps it was the severity of the hairdress that created an illusion of hardness, he thought, studying her profile with a slight frown.

It struck him that the dark eyes staring into the mirror were unnaturally bright, almost feverish, and her manner as she surveyed herself was charged with an undercurrent of tension. Outwardly controlled, there was an uncertainty and obscure defenselessness about her as she scanned the reflection in the glass. He turned uncompromisingly from the suddenly awakened yearning that seized him, and his face again wore that inscrutable look of polite detachment.

He thought fleetingly of Nita waiting in the hall below, dramatically attired in a midnight blue watered silk, its tight bodice fitting like a sheath, a star sapphire pendant winking from the white swell of her bosom. He wondered if Theodora intended to overshadow the younger woman with the thought of keeping Nita in her place. It was hardly like Theodora to stoop to an elementary feminism of that sort, but he could think of no other reason for the elaborate care with which she had dressed or, for that matter, her condescension in accepting the invitation at all.

"The effect is delightful, my dear," he said in a tone that invariably seemed to her to be tinged with hidden mockery. "You will be the attraction of the evening."

She had started violently at the sound of his voice and now she turned self-consciously, her color rising as though she had been caught in the midst of a furtive and shameful train of thought. She had, in fact, been in the act of contemplating several possible outcomes of her projected plan for the evening. A cold rigidity had gripped her flesh as she anticipated the likely lengths to which her actions might lead. She told herself that she was being naive. Men were alike, and a clever woman could accomplish whatever she desired if she willed it. Paul Nixon was not different from others. From Grant, she thought, and she was suddenly very still. A frightening weakness assaulted her so sharply she felt ill. When Grant spoke from the doorway, the sickness spread through every part of her body.

She closed her eyes momentarily to steady herself. This was the man who might have given her comfort and reassurance and love. Under different circumstances, he could have given her the security she longed for, and a happiness too great to imagine. The loneliness of the past months rushed in on her, and she was overwhelmed with misery and helplessness and hunger. Was it too late, she thought erratically? What difference about the house, or if his loan to her father was never repaid? Then she caught herself abruptly. Something deeper than the issue of the house, deeper than the surface misunderstandings of their relationship, held them apart. He was a stranger, incapable of understanding, of kindness or gentleness. There was a veiled threat in him, a waiting violence. He would undermine all of them if he could. He wanted to ruin her father, to possess all they had. She could never know security with him, or even momentary happiness.

"I am ready," she said tonelessly, moving toward the closet for her coat.

He assisted her on with the wrap, and together they went down the stairs to the hall below where Nita waited with ill-concealed impatience.

"It is long after eight," she chided them lightly. "You in St. Louis are as tardy as the islanders."

In the carriage Theodora was silent, content to let Nita carry the burden of conversation with Grant. Nita willingly assumed the responsibility for entertaining him, and kept up a light patter of questions and lively comment throughout the short drive to the Mills home.

CHAPTER THIRTY-EIGHT

The trim, substantial house was ablaze with lights when they arrived. Martha Mills welcomed them with the usual inexhaustible hospitality she had for every arrival. "We're happy you could be here," she said, acknowledging an introduction to Nita. "Grant, you've met Fred's brother, the senator. He's back from Washington for a short visit with us. Introduce Nita, will you? Felice and Neil are already inside with the others."

Fifteen or more couples filled the drawing room to capacity, some dancing to music provided by a small orchestra assembled in the adjoining conservatory. They found the senator, a gruff, dignified, florid gentleman considerably older than Fred, talking to Neil and Paul Nixon.

"A United States senator!" Nita exclaimed as Grant presented her to Barton Mills. "I am honored, señor."

"It is I who am honored," he returned gallantly, "to meet the señorita. We in the United States have the greatest admiration and sympathy for the patriots of Cuba."

"Your country has given us great moral courage, Senator," she said with pretty affectation.

"We'd do more if it were possible," he beamed. "Our own hard-won independence leads us to watch with interest and understanding the rigorous hardships your people are shouldering."

Felice, obviously bored, turned to engage Grant in conversation, and Theodora stirred restlessly.

Paul glanced down at her. "Dance?" he suggested.

She assented, and he led her out among those on the floor. "Before the evening is over," he said with an amused backward glance at the senator and Nita, "they'll be the best of friends. Our distinguished guest was finding the party tedious until your charming Nita appeared. Is she staying with you long?"

"I can't say," Theodora replied. "The arrangement is somewhat temporary. I understand she may return to New York."

"She knew Grant in Cuba, I suppose," he remarked casually.

"Yes," she said lightly.

"You are becoming very broad-minded, Miss Theodora," he said with the lift of an eyebrow.

"Indeed," she said, almost coquettishly, "that is one of my virtues, sir!"

His response was to hold her more tightly and she did not resist. In fact she leaned rather intimately against him. Out of the corner of her eye she saw that Grant was dancing with Felice and apparently finding her company quite absorbing.

She gave Paul a bewitching smile, her face quite close to his. "You dance well, Mr. Nixon," she murmured.

"We do seem to be getting on better than last time," he reminisced, emboldened by this unexpected amiability.

"I do not recall that we had difficulty getting on," she demurred.

"I shouldn't wonder," he commented with a grin. "A bride would have other things on her mind."

She looked away. "I am sorry if I was rude," she said quickly.

"So delightful a lady can be forgiven anything," he assured her readily.

"Anything, Mr. Nixon?" she repeated archly.

He smiled down at her but his eyes were more intent. This was indeed a different Theodora, and he was puzzled. Where was that haughty coldness and reserve? Marriage appeared to have wrought a considerable change in her former demeanor. A certain thought struck him. Theodora's sudden warming might possibly be explained by the much-discussed current wrangle over traction franchises. He observed the rising swell of her breasts under the soft rose velvet, the gleaming curves of her arms and shoulders, and it occurred to him that there would be pleasure in taking advantage of the situation. One would have to be discreet, however. He was not a fool. Grant Monroe would not tolerate another man's advances to his wife. Nor did Paul wish to imperil his aspirations to a Congressional seat in Washington by precipitating a scandal.

"A pity we did not get to know each other better a year ago," he said tentatively, his tone intimate. "It could have been pleasant."

"It's rather pleasant now," she said deliberately, with a provocative smile.

The dance ended and couples wandered back to the groups they had left. Reluctantly he released her and they joined the others. He danced with her several times after that, and each time found her smiles more inviting, her words more delightfully phrased for his ears alone.

"The senator is giving a dinner Monday night at the Weston," he said, the last time they were together. "But I don't suppose Grant is interested in the political crowd?"

"Grant has a board meeting Monday," she said on a faint note of regret.

"Too bad. I thought you might enjoy the affair. Of course, it's not a late evening engagement, if one wants to be punctilious in the matter. You could go if you liked. I daresay the attractive Nita has already promised the senator to attend as his personal guest."

Theodora looked over her shoulder and saw the senator, very flushed, his balding forehead glistening from the exercise of dancing with Nita, still leading her on to the lively measure of the music.

"I think I would enjoy the senator's dinner," she considered. "Perhaps it can be arranged."

If Grant was aware of Theodora's interest in Paul Nixon, he gave no sign. They were driven home alone, having left Nita to the bewitched senator who adamantly insisted upon escorting her himself. Once settled in the carriage, however, Grant's casual reference to Paul's future in public life gave Theodora a start. She faced him defensively, but his expression revealed nothing.

"Paul is quite capable," she said levelly. "A man of his type is rare in politics. One is encouraged to believe that a few public servants are above greed and dishonesty."

His face was unreadable in the darkness. "He could go far," he said noncommittally. "Too bad he never married. A wife can be a decided asset in politics if she provides her husband with a suitable background of home life and children. Voters like that sort of thing. An unattached man is always handicapped by fear of what scandal may do to his career. His opponents can tear his reputation to shreds overnight."

"I'm sure Mr. Nixon is too astute to allow that to happen," she said guardedly.

"Possibly," he agreed. "He seems to know what he wants, and how to get it."

He said no more, and she was satisfied that his thoughts had turned elsewhere. She thought about Monday night, and the senator's dinner at the Weston. If she were to help Harlan, she would have to do it this way. And she would do it without Grant's knowledge.

CHAPTER THIRTY-NINE

Felice and Neil were gone when the full effects of the rejected loans were felt. The would-be speculators soothed their disgruntled feelings in the comforting thought that the new railway would have been a poor investment after all. They grumbled to one, then another, until it was generally understood that the Jenkins Company was a bad risk. Interurban officials were quick to capitalize on this turn of events, and before long, rumor had the new venture verging on bankruptcy.

The original shareholders heard, and panic drove them into a huddle. A committee was formed to take action. The board of directors, which had not assembled since their initial meeting, called on Jenkins. The broker received them cordially, exerting himself to the utmost as he reassured them in strong terms.

"I am dismayed that you have so little confidence in me, gentlemen," he said with dignity. "My association with business in Missouri has been extensive for years, and never have I had any but the greatest concern for the interests of my clients."

"It's not that we doubt your management, Mr. Jenkins," Barkley said, apologetic despite the gravity of his fears. "But rumors are going around. We've been worried, naturally."

"Rumors," Jenkins scoffed. "I know what's going on. Interurban had invented a vicious campaign to cut us out of the franchise, but it won't work. I have definite assurance that our franchise is as good as on the books. You can go home and forget about it."

"No harm will be done if we publish a statement of finances," another argued, pressing their demands. "We feel that such a move would ease the minds of the stockholders and be of considerable benefit to the prestige of the company."

To Jenkins' irritation, they persisted. In the end he was forced to acquiesce. "If a statement is what you want," he said benignly, "you shall have it. I'll see that the accountants start on the records immediately."

They left with this concession, and Jenkins closed his office for the day. Mentally he cursed the circumstances that forced his hand before the franchise was cleared. A few more weeks and he could have had things under control. With the city rights in his pocket, investors would come running. Shares would go at his own price, and with pyramiding profits, there would be ample opportunity for the kind of revenue he had in mind.

Harassed and shaken, he decided to see Al Reed before the night was over and get back part of the money at least. He could stall off the accounting for a few days perhaps, but the clamoring would force him to expose his position before long. And this time there was no scapegoat, he thought grimly, feeling the invisible shadow of a man at his heels as he mounted the steps to the house that had once been Will Patterson's.

He let himself in the front door quietly, hoping to avoid Theodora. Her prying concern was a nagging irritant to the nerves, and he had no wish to be subjected to further questions now. He went to the study, intent on fortifying himself with a brandy. Opening the door, he found Nita comfortably established in the great leather armchair, idly flipping the pages of an outdated novel.

"Señor Jenkins," she said, looking up with a pleased expression. "I have been glancing at your books. I hope you do not mind?"

For a brief second, his eye unconsciously flashed to the corner shelf where an uninviting set of investment treatises concealed his private wall safe. They were undisturbed as usual. Even a chronic dilettante would pass up that ancient and dry set of volumes in favor of more promising fare. Turning to Nita, he surveyed the smooth, lovely lines of her face and throat, the ripe fullness of the high bosom above the seductive curve of a narrow waist, and part of the hunted anxiety faded from his eyes.

"Indeed not, my dear," he said generously. "You are to regard this as your home while you are here. I shall be more than pleased if the books offer you some diversion."

He brought out a bottle of his private stock of brandy, and she put the book aside. "Permit me to pour it for you, señor," she said quickly, rising from the chair. "You look so very tired today. I think you work too hard. Here, sit by the fire where you can relax."

She drew him toward the leather chair and he sat down, forgetting his aversion for it under the intoxicating insistence of her slim, cool hands. He watched as she poured a tumbler of brandy, and the heated stirring of his blood quickened his breath. Delectable, he thought pleasantly, moistening his lips with a furtive tongue.

"This will help you to feel better," she said in her solicitous tone, giving him the drink.

"You have already done that," he told her warmly. "Seeing you, my dear, is tonic enough for anyone. Sit with me a while, and talk to a lonely man."

"You are so kind, señor," she murmured with an enigmatic smile as he drained the tumbler with obvious relish. "It is wonderful to be here among people so good." She replaced the tumbler beside the decanter of brandy and returned, seating herself demurely on the arm of his chair.

Had he looked, Harlan might have seen a dim, smoldering displeasure in her eyes that belied the simple sincerity of her words. But his attention was elsewhere. Actually, Nita was bored, peevish, and alarmingly discontented. Since her arrival, she had contrived only a few passing meetings alone with Grant, in the hall or on the stairs when she happened to meet him on his way in or out. His manner toward her was cool and unmistakably reserved, and she sensed a hidden amusement beneath his polite exterior as he studied her at mealtimes or on occasion when they all sat together in the drawing room. He was avoiding her, of that she was sure. Her anger burned deep within her, and she vowed to hurt him in return. She would find a way.

"You are happy here?" Harlan asked abstractedly, his hand stroking her thigh with experimental hesitation.

"Most happy," she assured him, letting her finger trail the edge of his lapel. "If it were not for the cold weather of your winters, I think I would like St. Louis as well as the island. But I suppose one must be born here, like Señor Grant, to be acclimated. One can always come back to the place one knew as a child."

"I did not know Grant was born in St. Louis," he said idly, engrossed in the intaking line of her waist and the rising curve of one firmly molded breast.

"Yes," she nodded. "He did not say it to me, but there was a letter once. I did not mean to look, of course, but I could not help seeing a part about Señor Grant as a little boy in St. Louis."

She was not finding his advances objectionable. She was, in fact, diverted as she actively considered gratifying the profligate old gentleman's appetite. It would be an amusing joke on Grant and his cold, proud wife. But not in haste, she thought astutely. Not with a willingness that would leave Harlan free of an obligation that might one day be useful.

"Do you know this Lily Olandt who wrote him?" she asked, drawing away slightly.

He was to recall their conversation later, along with other of Nita's remarks which he had passed over from time to time. At the moment, however, Lily's name only served to heighten his already mounting excitement. "Don't go away," he said thickly, pulling her toward him.

"Señor Jenkins!" she said, protesting mildly as he forced her down into the chair with him.

He was undeterred. His huge lips covered her face and throat with warm, moist kisses, and his hands fumbled in their eagerness to undo the modest row of buttons at the bodice of her soft blouse. But he was not entirely without caution. His ears, sharpened recently by their haunting suspicion of the slightest unexplained noise, detected the fall of footsteps beyond the closed door. With an incoherent oath, he released her, helping her to stand with an awkwardness born of the emotional storm which still gripped him.

The door opened and Theodora came in. Her glance went from Nita's disarranged blouse and untidy hair to Harlan, who was refilling the tumbler with hands none too steady, a sullen scowl on his features. The thought of her father and this girl struck her with sickening force, and she was unable to find her voice.

"Yes, Theodora?" Harlan said, trying to keep the irritation from his voice.

"If you wish, Señor Jenkins," Nita said, somewhat breathless in the face of Theodora's stony, accusing stare, "I shall go to my room. It is time, I think, to dress if one is not to be late for the senator's dinner."

She left, and Harlan, fortified by a second brandy, turned to face Theodora.

"Father," she began with difficulty, "that woman ..."

"Yes?" he prompted sharply.

"I know what she is," she forced herself to go on. "You must see it too. We've given her shelter, but does that mean we must sacrifice our principles or lose the dignity we have always upheld?"

"You have no cause to be alarmed, Theodora," he said truculently. "You will oblige me if you concern yourself less with these trivialities."

"What is wrong, father?" she asked in exasperation. "What has happened to change you?"

"Nothing is wrong," he snapped in vexation. "Run along, will you? I've had a hard day, and I don't feel like talking just now."

She hesitated, but she was not to be dismissed. "A newspaper reporter called today," she informed him determinedly. "He said his name was Ed Miller. He inquired about your meeting with the stockholders to discuss the financial status of the company, and asked if you wished to make a statement."

"You told him nothing, I suppose?"

"Naturally. But that won't stop him. He'll continue to look for a story, and if he should find out the truth ..."

"He won't," Harlan interrupted with a scowl. "And let's not discuss it now, if you please."

She bit her lip. The thought of Paul Nixon had been with her all afternoon, and she had hoped vainly that through some miracle her father's involvement would solve itself before nightfall. "Has the assembly considered the franchise yet?" she asked.

"You know as much about it as I do," he retorted inconsiderately. "If there is any news, I shall inform you."

"Very well," she said, turning away. "Dinner will be earlier than usual because the servants have the night off. You won't mind being in the house alone?"

"You are going out?"

"Yes," she said vaguely. "I have an engagement in town. I expect it will take ... all evening."

CHAPTER FORTY

At the Weston there were the usual dull speeches and mutual exchange of congratulatory remarks. The occasion was a purely political move on the part of the senator, a goodwill gesture toward the local constituents who elected him and who would doubtless re-elect him.

Theodora slipped in late and sat at the far end of the dinner hall in a seat partially obscured from the speakers' table. Paul Nixon was concluding a talk on the reform platform of the coalition group and she listened attentively, surprised at his ease in delivery, the lucid logic and strength of appeal in his summation. She felt herself being carried by the convincing flow of oratory to a new respect, even admiration, for the speaker. Yet his very eloquence and voluble sincerity stirred an inexplicable rebellion deep within her. The exigencies of her own position as well as Harlan's had sharpened her perception, and new doubts stirred uneasily. Any charlatan mouthing these same words with an equal degree of persuasion could command the same loyalty and esteem. Fluency and shrewd, intelligent organization were the only requisites. Add to that a few gestures of good faith, and the most unscrupulous imposter could win the unwavering support of millions of voters. Nixon, unlike Reed who blustered, bluffed, and ruthlessly elbowed his way into power, made the injustices of the little man his target. He depended on the fallibility of men and women who follow the charmed star of their self-appointed champion wherever it led. Behind this screen, she knew with intuitive clarity, he could move with even greater assurance than Reed himself.

She observed with pitying contempt Nita's preoccupation with Barton Mills, the gay sparkle in her eyes quickening each time the senator leaned toward her to whisper in her ear. Nita had not seen her, she noted with a faintly ironical smile. Theodora was prepared to answer the girl in any event and she was also prepared to inform Grant where she had spent the evening if necessary. But she was satisfied that there would be no need. Nita was wholly absorbed, though from time to time her gaze wandered speculatively to the tall speaker at the other end of the table.

Paul finished amid enthusiastic hand-clapping. The fact that he was in line for better things than local politics was apparent, and the city men did not want to be forgotten when he moved up. Midway down the hall, Al Reed sat at one of the tables with a few of his underlings, composed and silent, puffing incessantly on a long, black cigar, his broad thumb absently stroking his chin. If he regarded the seating arrangement as a slight or saw the growing popularity of the coalitionists as a threat to his heretofore unchallenged supremacy in the machine, he gave no sign. He was the only one of the diners to take note of Theodora's presence, and as his shrewd eyes studied her covertly, her uneasiness mounted.

One of the waiters approached to serve her and she waved him away. Another speaker was introduced and she stood up, making her way unobtrusively to the exit. Paul, who had been watching her since she came in, saw her disappear through the door and he excused himself from his immediate companions.

"Not leaving?" he asked, overtaking her in the lobby.

"I think so," she said. "My appearance here might be misunderstood in view of father's interest in a franchise."

He laughed. "These people are indifferent to that sort of thing. And I assure you that everyone in the room is after something. However, if you don't care for food on a political platter, let me take you elsewhere to dine."

She agreed after a slight hesitation, and at his suggestion they took a public hack to the *Crescent*. The dining room of the pleasure boat was comfortably warm despite the bitter March wind that whipped downriver. Several musicians played languidly for the benefit of a few diners, and the dimmed lights further enhanced the atmosphere of intimate seclusion. Paul gave their orders to a waiter, and they left the table to dance.

Theodora, who recognized no one among the occupants of the room and observed that the others were not in the least interested in her or her escort, felt some of the stiffness leave her body as she slipped into his arms. "I thought your remarks tonight were excellent," she complimented him. "Unfortunately I did not hear the entire talk, but the concluding points were well taken."

"Politics is a strange game," he said. "One can't predict how the cards will fall. A man on top today may find himself friendless tomorrow."

She thought of Al Reed, half the length of the room from the speakers' table. Had he actually the ability to influence votes in the assembly? The doubt brought her up with a start, and she was appalled that her father had given money to such a man in the hope that he could bribe the franchise through.

"I was surprised that Mr. Reed had so little prominence," she remarked casually. "He is so well entrenched in St. Louis, one naturally expects to see him the center of activity at such an occasion."

"Someone is slipping the rug out from under him," Paul said indifferently. "No one seems to know who, or why. But Reed has been losing ground lately."

"I don't understand," she frowned, feeling an increasing alarm for her father. "His influence is thought to be unlimited."

"Let's say his influence is not what it used to be," he compromised. "But why discuss Reed when we can devote ourselves to the enjoyment of a pleasant evening?"

She felt his arm tighten in an embrace that was hardly customary for dancing partners. Her mind, however, clung to its original purpose with characteristic tenacity, and she suppressed the involuntary impulse to push him away. Unable to abandon the subject of Reed, she went on persistently: "Father considers Mr. Reed infallible. I wonder if he has been misinformed?"

"Is the franchise worrying you?" he asked with an amused grin.

Theodora had never been coy, and she was ill equipped in the art of subterfuge. "Do you think there is a chance for father?" she asked with customary directness. "It means so very much to him."

Paul was finding Theodora's proximity a heady intoxication, and his eyes as they met her intensely searching gaze were preoccupied with the anticipation of further pleasant concessions. As for Harlan Jenkins, he had never found much to recommend the man, either in a personal or business way. Moreover, Interurban had the inexplicable good fortune to lay hands on a quite handsome bonus for the award of new suburban rights with the renewal of their old privileges. Reed's proposition for Jenkins was to be shelved. But Paul had no intention of so informing Theodora. Due to the expected repercussions, the assembly would defer action as long as possible. In the meantime Paul was not one to turn his back on a delightful intrigue which the fates had thrown his way.

"You have influence, Paul," Theodora was saying. "And you don't believe Interurban should control all city transportation rights, do you?"

He stopped dancing and guided her back to the table. "I don't believe I've ever had a lovelier dancing partner," he replied, turning her question aside with an intimate smile.

For the time, at least, she was forced to let the matter rest. Nor did he permit another opportunity for a similar discussion. A gay and diverting conversationalist, he entertained her throughout the meal and the several dances they had before leaving.

In the carriage, the pace of his conversation slackened. He was self-assured, impetuous, and deft. Theodora met his amorous overtures with uncertainty and growing alarm. She had planned how to handle such situations until she had gained her objective, but her anticipation had not taken into account the perseverance of his emboldened passion, his amazing strength and dexterity. In bewilderment and anger she attempted to push him away.

He laughed softly. "That franchise," he said in a low tone. "Would you like me to do what I can?"

Theodora closed her eyes.

CHAPTER FORTY-ONE

Grant was free at nine o'clock, but he did not go directly home. He stopped first at the Hunter residence and was shown into the library where the elderly banker had been enjoying one of his favorite books by the friendly warmth of the fireplace. Miles Hunter greeted him cordially and immediately sent a servant for brandy.

"I hope you will pardon this intrusion," Grant said. "I was delayed at a board meeting longer than I expected."

"Quite all right," Hunter returned heartily. "I was delighted when you phoned. Sit here by the fire and tell me what's on your mind." There was pleasure in the older man's eyes and sincere regard in his manner. He offered Grant a cigar, but Grant declined and lit one of his cigarettes.

"You said you wanted to do something for St. Louis," Grant began as the servant brought the brandy and departed. "Something of lasting benefit that would serve as many people as possible."

Hunter nodded. "The park improvement plan was an excellent suggestion. Has the assembly considered the proposition?"

"The assembly," Grant said dryly, "has considered few matters of civic importance recently. They do not concern themselves with slum clearance, law enforcement, or rising criminal activity, let alone park developments."

Hunter's face was grave. "I had hoped the last election would change all that. I've always believed that a few in the political ring

honestly want good government. With Nixon as their spokes-
man they ought to be able to put through needed legislation."

"Paul Nixon is chiefly interested in promoting himself to a
Washington assignment," Grant stated bluntly. "His leadership
is of a variety that goes with the tide at its crest, not the kind that
does battle to alter the course of events."

"If you're right, there is scant hope for a better administration," Hunter frowned.

Grant leaned forward intently. "There is hope, if you and a
few others are willing to take action. Forget about parks and the
usual philanthropic gestures. Those will materialize if the rat
holes are cleaned out. St. Louis has been strangling in the grip of
the tightest political machine in the country. Reed names candidates on both tickets and elects those best suited for his purpose
and pledged to carry out his plans. Each district is bled dry from
assemblymen down to ward bosses and the lowest heeler. Graft
is so thoroughly systematized that a nucleus in the assembly has
established fixed prices on every conceivable job done for the
city. Key men in this combine regularly receive salaries of five
thousand a year from certain private interests in return for pre-
venting hostile legislation."

"I know the situation is bad," Hunter nodded. "But what can
be done? I'm only a retired banker, too old and rheumatic to take
the stump for reform. Besides, the circuit attorney never pros-
ecutes, juries never indict."

"Reed has approved a number of new candidates on the
ticket this year," Grant informed him, "including a young law-
yer who recently came here from Tennessee. He'll run for circuit
attorney and while he's none too eager for the job, I think we've
picked the right man. But the city must elect him, together with
the entire slate of newcomers. That requires money, more than I
can furnish alone."

Hunter had caught the fire in the younger man's intensity, but he was skeptical. "We'll have the same old story of bribes and intimidation," he warned.

"Possibly," Grant acknowledged. "But a few minor convictions in the beginning will jolt the public and prove that bigger game can be caught. Your old friend, Judge Frisch, will cooperate if we bring the cases before him. And a police captain I know will be happy to arrest a few of Reed's boys if he can make a charge hold. He has already done what he could to stiffen resistance in certain quarters."

"The plan may work," Hunter said, swept along in the compelling enthusiasm of his visitor. "But the charge will have to be good."

"Extortion will suffice. Reed's collectors gouge all they can for protection, and shopkeepers and small businessmen pay rather than fight alone."

"You think you can get them to testify?"

"We only need one," Grant said briefly.

"Another detail," Hunter said after a slight pause. "The campaign will need publicity, strong publicity."

"Ballard will give us the backing of his paper," Grant told him. "He has wanted to put Reed where he belongs for a long time."

There was another pause while Hunter puffed furiously on his cigar. "I like it," he said suddenly. "And I think it can be done. You may count on the money, and I'll see Frisch the first thing in the morning."

CHAPTER FORTY-TWO

J enkins was compelled to wait more than an hour at Reed's home before the politician returned. Each passing minute robbed him of the little assurance he had left and heightened his agitation. He chewed violently on his cigar, then tossed it aside in a nearby ashtray and gnawed his lower lip fiercely as he paced the floor. Reed would have to be decent about the money for his own protection, he reasoned. They were in this together. If the newspapers got the story, Reed's position would be exposed as well as his own. Part of the money, say ten thousand, would be enough. Jenkins had the confidence of long experience that he could fictionalize the necessary entries on the books to account for the remainder.

Harassed to the point of desperation, he wrenched his thought from the imminent dangers of bankruptcy. Better to occupy one's self with the pleasanter matters, such as the agreeable contemplation of the charming Nita. If Theodora had not come upon them, he thought, moistening his lips with a quick, nervous tongue, he would have sampled the provocative delights of that passionately molded young body. Nita had been most compliant, he reminisced. Doubtless she missed that husband in Cuba. Her enjoyment in an older man's companionship was highly gratifying, and he promised himself to arrange a meeting with her that would be secure against interruption. He devoted his attention so thoroughly to the anticipation of the event that he had almost regained his customary blandness when the politician returned. Reed concealed his surprise and irritation at seeing his visitor, and invited Jenkins into the study.

"I'll be frank with you," Jenkins confided quickly. "The delay over the franchise is causing me embarrassment. Certain rumors about the company have been gaining ground with the result that I find myself in an awkward position."

Reed stared at him before answering. He was shrewd enough to know that the assembly's delay in taking up the franchise was an unfavorable indication. Since the old guard had formed their combine to deal with every item of business, he had been edgy. They were not as accessible as they had been formerly. They looked for new channels of revenue and apparently were finding many. Moreover, Reed was still smarting under the sting of his slight at the hotel dinner. Every man there owed him for one favor or another, yet there was a subtle but unmistakable cooling toward him. Someone was slowly and skillfully prying his hand loose from its powerful grip on the machine, countermanding his orders, emasculating his effectiveness in the life of the city. Resistance had been growing on every side. There were numerous grumblings, and occasional refusals to pay off on the part of the storekeepers. He had considered each man in turn at the banquet but had been unable to point the finger of suspicion at any, notwithstanding the fact that many there would repay his generosity with treachery if they thought it profitable. He was aware that he couldn't fight what he couldn't see, and he was obsessed with the determination to unmask his adversary. Time was running out.

"The delay is damned unfortunate," he told Jenkins. "But I've done my part. The rest takes time."

"I haven't got time," Jenkins scowled. "The stockholders are panicky, and they're pressing for an immediate accounting."

Reed shrugged. "Stall them off," he counseled. "That's the best you can do under the circumstances."

"Stall them off?" Jenkins repeated, raising his voice for the first time. "And let them know something is wrong? They'd take matters into their own hands, and the whole deal would be aired."

Reed concealed his impatience. "What do you suggest?" he asked in a fairly reasonable tone.

Jenkins didn't hedge. "I've got to have part of the money back," he said. "Ten thousand will suffice, and the accountants can take over the books with my compliments."

Reed had no intention of giving up any part of the money even if the assembly didn't deliver the franchise. He needed all the money he could lay hands on now. "Hell, I haven't got ten thousand to give you," he informed his visitor bluntly. "The franchise money is in a safety deposit vault downtown, waiting for the assembly to act."

"Get it," Jenkins said. "I'll borrow it temporarily and have it back before anyone is the wiser."

Reed shook his head. "I have a key to the vault; so has a representative from the assembly."

"Isn't that an unorthodox procedure?" Jenkins scowled in irritation.

"Matters like this are always handled with circumspection," Reed explained with a trace of impatience. "No one can move without the other party's consent."

Jenkins' thick lips twitched and his color was gray. "I've got to have the money," he said urgently. "I'm ruined if I can't show a cash balance of at least ten thousand. And there isn't much time. That reporter, Ed Miller, has been asking questions."

"You didn't give out a statement?"

"Of course not."

Reed relaxed. "Don't worry about Eddie Miller," he said easily. "I've known him since he was a grasshopper in knee pants. As for the money, I'm damned sorry I can't help you beyond the arrangement we've made. You'll have to get what you need another way. Try Grant Monroe."

"His money is tied up in other things," Jenkins muttered abstractedly. "He can't advance a cent."

"He can't?" Reed said sharply, eying the broker with acute skepticism.

But Jenkins was too confusedly preoccupied to notice. He rose and fumbled automatically with his coat buttons, took leave of the politician, and found his way out. He had to have the money, he reiterated in a frenzy of determination. Whatever the means, he had to have it.

Arriving home, he found the house dark. He went upstairs to his room, undressed, and lay on the bed. Another hour went by and he could not sleep. He got out of bed and searched among the bottles in the medicine cabinet for his sleeping tablets. He located the vial, but it was empty. Finding his dressing gown, he went downstairs in search of a drink. Out of habit he started toward the study, then stopped. No, not in there with that accursed chair.

He retraced his steps and went into the darkened drawing room. Moonlight streamed through the center window where the maid had neglected to draw the shade, and he did not light the lamps. He discovered a decanter of whisky on the serving table near the sofa. Lifting it to his lips, he drank generously, then sank down heavily on the sofa. The silence of the empty house throbbed about him, and the ticking of the hall clock was a loud, then louder noise.

In the moonlight the room lost its familiarity for him and he sat uneasily, his ears straining against the stillness. He had a curious feeling that he was waiting for something to happen, something he could not prevent. He had not accustomed himself to the new arrangement of the furniture, and as he stared in the gloom at the shadowy shapes, the years he had pushed away pressed back upon him. Strange how clearly one remembered, he thought dimly. He could hear Will Patterson's voice exactly as he heard it that night before the police came, over two decades ago.

"The man who shot Tom Lynch was afraid he'd expose the irregularities in the books," Patterson had said quietly. "I didn't know about those irregularities, Jenkins. You did."

Jenkins had left the house then, but in the hall he paused to glance in fleeting curiosity at the thin lad who had been eavesdropping on the stairs. The fire of intense, steady hatred lit the boy's dark eyes as he returned the man's glance. Jenkins had been about to speak but he thought better of it. He might have done something for the boy afterward, he thought uncomfortably. He had intended to make some sort of gesture, but the boy had disappeared from the orphanage shortly after being committed by the court.

Jenkins' nerves suddenly tightened and he leaned forward, hearing the sound he dreaded. Steps from nowhere, moving through the house. Frantic now, he tried to place them. On the stairs, in the kitchen, the study. Patterson was back. Jenkins could not say how he knew it, but he did. He had known it for a long while. Patterson was back in the house that had once been his. Was even now his, he amended with grim, hysterical accuracy. He opened his mouth to call out, and no sound came. The perspiration stood out heavily on his brow and he mopped at it nervously with a kerchief. The steps were approaching, and he knew they were in the hall. The slow, heavy tread was nearing the drawing room doors. Patterson knew where to find him, of course. Patterson had always known where to find him.

The fear clutched him with a sharp pain, squeezing his chest in iron fingers, dragging him down into a well of blackness. Grant, coming into the room, found him unconscious, slumped over on the sofa.

CHAPTER FORTY-THREE

Harlan Jenkins was confined to his bed for a fortnight. During the first days of his illness his family physician held out small hope for complete recovery. Brad was notified at the university with the understanding that he would be called home if his father's condition became worse, and a cable of similar nature was dispatched to Felice. But complications were avoided and convalescence brought about an amazing restoration of the patient's former health. At the end of two weeks he was able to move about the room, and the special nurse was dismissed.

In one respect, perhaps, the illness could be regarded as fortunate. The stockholders, their panic cooled, hesitated before wrecking their one chance to realize a profitable return on their investment. Talk of investigating the company's finances was forgotten and they now became gravely concerned with the health of the man they recently had been hounding. "We must keep up appearances," they reasoned. "There will be ample time to look into the finances after the assembly grants the franchise." They called at the house to inquire about Harlan's progress, to extend their sympathy and express their confidence.

For Theodora, the period of her father's illness was doubly difficult because of the inner turmoil that assailed her in recurring waves each time she thought about Paul Nixon and her surreptitious meeting with him the night of her father's seizure. Thoroughly shaken after leaving him at the carriage, her heart had filled with fresh anxiety as she saw windows alight upstairs and down. She hastened into the house in time to see Grant descend the stairs with Dr. Macklin.

"Ah, Miss Theodora, good evening," the doctor said, seeing her.

Mutely her eyes questioned him, then Grant.

"Your father has suffered an attack," Grant told her in a steadying voice. "But Dr. Macklin thinks he will be all right."

"Yes," the doctor said. "It's fortunate your husband called me as promptly as he did. Mr. Jenkins is responding to treatment, but he is not entirely out of danger. I'm sending a nurse from the hospital to take charge, and by tomorrow we should know what to expect."

The following hours were difficult ones. Nita appeared eventually, expressed herself in sympathetic terms, and unobtrusively retired. The nurse arrived and took over the care of the patient, banishing the family from the sickroom with the promise that she would notify them of any change.

Theodora could not forgive herself for spending the evening with Paul when she was needed here. Somehow she felt that if she had been home, Harlan might not have suffered this illness. Even Paul's hint that he might be able to do something about the franchise did not justify her neglect or alleviate her feeling of guilt.

"You must sleep," Grant remonstrated. "All of us needn't remain awake. Macklin doesn't look for a change before morning, but if there is any word, I'll let you know at once."

Exhausted in spirit and body, she surrendered submissively. She was inexpressibly grateful for his adequacy and reassurance these past hours. A new awareness of him impinged sharply on the tired, anxious confusion in her mind, and she leaned heavily on his arm as he led her to her room. She submitted passively while he helped her undress. His movements were quiet and unhurried, and he drew the covers over her with a gentleness she had never associated with him in any of his moods. As he turned to leave, she smiled wanly and he touched her forehead with his fingertips.

"Father has been under a strain since he began dealing with Reed," she said slowly. "The amount of the bribe was fantastic. How is it possible that one man can control an entire city?"

"It's been carelessness mainly," he remarked. "And selfishness or cowardice or indifference on the part of those who are in a position to change things. But Reed is playing his last hand. The next election will see a different slate of candidates up for office, and it will be one election Reed can't fix."

"You want that?" she asked wonderingly. "You would support a reform movement?"

"Does that surprise you?" he asked quietly.

"I don't know," she faltered. "For some reason, I always thought you were one of them."

"An impression, I hope, which is shared by certain others," he remarked cryptically. "Try to sleep now. You'll feel better after a rest."

She did sleep then, until long after sunlight sent thin, brilliant streamers across the carpet from beneath the drawn shades.

CHAPTER FORTY-FOUR

Al Reed had a theory that victory rides with the aggressor. His power had begun to slip because he had ceased to assert himself with the dictatorial authority that had elevated him to party leadership in the beginning. He had fallen into the comfortable illusion that his position was supremely secure and beyond challenge. To stay on top, a man must arm himself with untiring vigilance. He must guard his fences if the wolves were to be kept at bay. The recent difficulties with recalcitrant shopkeepers, the new attitude of independence in the assembly, the tendency even in certain quarters of the police department to ignore party dictums could be traced to a laxity throughout the organization. Whiplash techniques were needed, and with a renewed vitality reminiscent of the old days, he set about the task of forcing the heretics into line. As an initial step, he summoned Steve Rego and outlined a new policy to be followed regarding future collections of what he chose to call voluntary assessments.

"Take Frank with you," he directed briefly. "If you run into trouble, let them have a demonstration of what we mean. They'll cooperate if a few windows are smashed and stock is ruined."

He made a mental note to get in touch with Nick Ferrento in Kansas City. If his hunch was right, he would have use for Nick before long. Then he proceeded to the vault downtown and withdrew the Jenkins franchise money. Individually he contacted the assemblymen on his standard list. One by one he sought them out, and one by one he badgered, threatened, cajoled, and propositioned. He referred to past favors and old obligations, and suggested a number of unpleasant results that would ensue if his support were withdrawn. In each case he snapped the lock on his ultimatum with the payment of the usual fee for such services, an amount varying from five to fifty thousand according to his man.

The response was invariably the same. As Paul Nixon put it: "You know we're behind you, Al. The boys never doubted your leadership. Where would any of us be without the machine, without you? You are St. Louis, Al. All of us know it."

Satisfied that the forces set in motion were adequate to clear the air, he was walking homeward one night when he met Ed Miller. The reporter fell into step beside him, interested in sounding out the politician on the recent wave of vandalism and hoping to pick up the loose ends of the traction story which had all but evaporated with Harlan Jenkins' illness.

"Evening, Eddie," Reed greeted him affably. "What's on your mind?"

"Almost anything you care to discuss, Mr. Reed," Miller returned. "You make the news in St. Louis."

"Thanks, Eddie," Reed said expansively. "But you give me more credit than I deserve. Afraid I haven't a statement that would interest you just now."

"I thought there might be something on the Jenkins franchise," Miller suggested.

"No. I expect there might be soon, but don't quote me."

"The old boy's attack came at an opportune time," the reporter commented. "He might have had a difficult time of it if the stockholders continued to press for an accounting."

"Expenditures in launching an undertaking of that sort are incalculable," Reed pointed out. "What's to be gained by tearing a man apart in the newspapers?"

"The public has a right to know what goes on, Mr. Reed. They invest in utilities, and if there is a question of fraud or misuse of funds, they ought to be informed."

"I daresay everyone will be satisfied when the franchise matter is settled," Reed observed with finality.

Miller knew that Reed's confidence about the outcome of the controversy probably meant that the payoff had taken place. And as usual, there would be no way to prove anything. The assembly would do Reed's bidding, casting a few votes against the Jenkins company to throw dust in the public eye but carrying the resolution with a comfortable margin.

"The paper has been trying to get a line on the recent outbreaks of violence apparently aimed at small neighborhood stores," he said casually. "I've talked to several of the victims, but they won't furnish descriptions of the men or any reason for the attacks."

"Is that so?" Reed inquired pleasantly.

"I thought you might have an idea about it," he persisted. "Most of the assaults have occurred in your district."

"You're a nice lad, Eddie," Reed said in a friendly tone. "You can go far in St. Louis, and I'd like to see you make the grade. It's all give and take in this world, and knowing when to sit tight. Take it easy, boy, and forget that ambition to break a big news story. Don't look for trouble." They came to the corner and Reed turned away. "Come in any time to see me, and if there's anything I can do for you, just let me know."

They parted, and Miller continued on the dimly lit street.

Halfway down the block a feeble spot of light glimmered from the rear of Bauer's Bakery. Old Ludwig was busy with his loaves of bread and frosted pastry for tomorrow's customers. As Miller approached the store, his eye caught a movement in the shadows across the street and his step lagged imperceptibly.

Coming abreast of the bakery, he glanced in the windows and saw two men in the rear talking to old Ludwig. He was still watching when the taller of the two leaned carelessly on the nearest show-case, and there was a sharp sound of breaking glass.

As though by prearranged signal, two uniformed police emerged from the shadows across the street and headed for the bakery door. Miller whistled softly as he recognized them. If the bright boys inside were working with Reed as he suspected, this was a front-page story. The fact that Kennedy, a recently pro-moted captain in the precinct, sent out his best men to bring in Reed's emissaries was in itself a revolutionary bit of news. Either Kennedy was showing conspicuously poor judgment, or he was acting on orders from someone with enough behind-the-scenes influence to protect him in a showdown. When the police burst into the shop, Miller was on their heels.

"These men annoying you, Mr. Bauer?" one of the officers asked.

"They break the display case," the baker expostulated. "They tell me I must pay them. Voluntary, hah. I say I will not pay, and they talk about accidents. Then that one breaks the display case."

"We were just having a friendly discussion," the taller man said insolently. "I leaned on the glass, and it was loose. Can I help it if the thing broke?"

"You'll have to come along to the station house," the second officer said. "And you, Mr. Bauer. The captain will want to hear what happened."

"But the bread," he protested. "It comes from the ovens soon. I cannot leave the store now."

"Sorry, Mr. Bauer. Can't your wife look after the bread?"

"She is asleep," he fretted. "Maybe I should wake her. Maybe so." He went nervously to the back stairway and called: "Lena! Lena!"

There were steps overhead and the sound of a door opening and closing. "Yah, Ludwig?" a woman's voice answered.

"Lena, you take care of the bread? I am going out."

"Out, Ludwig?"

"It is all right, Lena," he assured her. "I will tell you about it when I get back."

At the station house, Miller was left to cool his heels in the anteroom. When Bauer came out and headed for the door, he pounced eagerly on the lieutenant who accompanied him.

"No questions," the officer grinned. "Captain's orders."

"At least I can talk to Kennedy," Miller said in exasperation. "Something goes on here, and I intend to find out what it is."

"Help yourself," the officer said, nodding toward the inside door.

He found Kennedy alone at the desk, calmly lighting a fat cigar. "Hello, Ed," the captain greeted him placidly. "They tell me you were in on tonight's affair."

"You know what you've done?" Miller demanded excitedly. "You've just pulled in two of Reed's boys. Steve Rego and Frank Masters are two of the regulars. You've probably earned yourself a quick ride back to a patrolman's badge and night stick!"

"Have I, now?" Kennedy said with an Irish twinkle in his mild, blue eyes.

"Give me the story, Kennedy," Miller pleaded.

"There is no story. These guys were annoying a private citizen, and they're being held for disturbing the peace. That's all."

"Your men were on hand expecting trouble," Miller argued. "What's the angle?"

"No angle, Ed. If there's a story, you'll get it. All right?"

"No harm in writing up the facts, is there?" Miller asked glumly.

"No harm," Kennedy agreed cheerfully. "But stick to the facts."

Miller returned to his office at the newspaper to write his facts which, after all, were enough to warrant this closing paragraph:

"It is hoped that the police have succeeded in ending the recent outbreak of mysterious attacks on storekeepers and businessmen in this district. If Mr. Bauer presses his complaint, an explanation of the motive behind these assaults may be forthcoming."

CHAPTER FORTY-FIVE

During Harlan's illness, Grant's kindness only increased the misery of the secret conflict tormenting Theodora. Could she have been wrong about him? Was he generous and good and warmhearted, without the deviousness and cruelty she suspected? Certainly he had been nothing but considerate, unbelievably patient, and tolerant since that first night, now so very long ago. Her conscience assaulted her bitterly when she remembered each sharp thrust, every harsh word, she had inflicted on him. The defensive hostility she had nurtured these past months melted, and she saw him wholly unaffected in his regard for her father, unjustifiably persecuted through her misunderstanding and self-centered blindness.

In her present state of mind, thoughts of Paul Nixon threw her into a miserable state of self-recrimination and shame. Even her infinite relief over Harlan's rapid recovery and her thankfulness that the stockholders no longer threatened to force his hand were diluted by wretched doubts and misgivings about the unwanted involvement. Indecision held her powerless. She despised herself for the bright artificiality of her voice and the evasions she employed each time she was summoned to the phone by his calls. Yet she could not bring herself to deliver the rebuff that would discontinue those calls before the assembly acted on the traction petition. Harlan's illness afforded her an excuse to postpone another meeting with Paul, but she knew he would not be put off indefinitely.

Her uneasiness mounted until she started guiltily each time the phone rang, hastening to reach it before someone else answered the summons. On one occasion Grant found her there, and she was compelled to terminate the conversation in a slightly altered tone, switching abruptly to a noncommittal report of her father's improving condition. Paul's knowing laugh was furiously humiliating, and she replaced the receiver angrily, hating herself for the deception.

Grant did not appear to notice anything wrong. "I ordered the carriage for us," he told her. "You should go out more. The air will improve your color."

She suddenly felt the tiredness that weighed upon her. The strain of the last few weeks had drained the dauntless energy which had supported her through previous crises, and a dragging weariness of spirit robbed her of the last shred of vitality.

"Yes," she said vaguely, trying to erase the thought of Paul from her mind. "I'll get a coat."

The day was mild as they started out, the clear sunshine and faint breeze promising an early summer. More than a year, she thought involuntarily, since she had returned to St. Louis, since she had met this man at her side. Inexplicable tears sprang to her eyes and she turned her head quickly to the window.

"Any particular place you care to go?" he inquired.

"No," she murmured, staring fixedly at the swimming trees and houses. The weariness brought these senseless tears to her eyes, she thought in perplexity, stripping her of all defenses, leaving her as vulnerable and vapory as a schoolgirl. If only he wouldn't be so thoughtful, so kind. Each act of consideration sharpened the edge of her turmoil, plunging her deeper into a hopeless well of confusion.

He gave directions to Rufus, and they left the paved avenues behind. Meadows and farm lands rolled by pleasantly. She relaxed, inhaling the clean, fresh air which carried the odor of rich, black earth and countless unseen growing things within its bosom. She turned to Grant with a dim smile.

"I want to thank you for all you've done," she said simply. "You've been very good."

He smiled down at her and picked up one of her lax hands, holding it in his. "Was that so unexpected?" he asked with quiet seriousness.

She became aware that her hand in his was trembling. Her consciousness of his strength and nearness dissolved the last ounce of her reserve and she could only gaze at him in speechless anguish. He no longer smiled. His eyes searched hers with a question that brought an unexpected rush of blood to her face and intensified the longing deep within her body. The past slipped away, and she had the isolated sensation of turning back from a wind-swept mountaintop and coming face to face with him for the first time. He was strange, contradictory, and unfathomable, yet as close and as familiar as her heartbeat.

He held her in a strong embrace. She knew then that there was no happiness for her apart from this man. Her arms clung to him as their lips met. Dimly she heard his voice, infinitely tender, comforting, reassuring. She could not speak, but her lips moved silently against his in a wordless passion of expression. When the carriage drew up in front of the house, they went inside together, hand in hand.

"There's a message for you, Mist' Grant," the maid said, opening the door. "This girl, Mabelle, come to the back door and says it's important. A Miz' Olandt tole her to fetch you right along, and I promised you'd know soon's you come in."

Grant's hand momentarily tightened on Theodora's. "I'll have to go," he said as the maid withdrew. "Whatever it is won't take long. I'll be back within the hour."

"You're going to that woman," she said, unable to overcome an involuntary tremor of loathing. "What hold has she over you?"

"You'll have to trust me, Theodora," he said quietly. He kissed her, hesitating briefly as he felt the unresponsive touch of her lips. Then he was gone, leaving her to stare after him in the gathering dusk of the silent house.

CHAPTER FORTY-SIX

Grant quieted his impatience with difficulty. He had been reluctant to go, but the urgency of Lily's message left him no choice. The clouded despair in Theodora's eyes filled him with a sense of failure despite his thought that they would sit down together on his return and talk in the same close understanding they had discovered that afternoon. An hour ago it had seemed impossible that anything could come between them. Yet in the space of moments she had slipped into that remote strangeness that set them apart in different worlds.

A grim weariness weighed heavily upon him as he realized that he was powerless now to change things. This was not the time to tell her about the past. She had turned to him today because she thought his concern for her father was sincere. To explain was to destroy that impression, to alienate her perhaps forever.

The thought of Harlan brought a bitter expression to his face. He remembered the sudden surge of anger he felt those first few instants after he entered the drawing room to find the broker collapsed on the sofa. He had not intended Harlan to escape so easily. But his plans had not been cheated after all. Harlan's faint pulse sent him swiftly to summon the doctor, and the flickering breath of life was fanned back to a strong, steady flame. The end was not yet, Grant thought implacably. The man who had killed one and ruined the lives of others would taste the bitterest dregs himself. More than that, he would know whose hand contrived his undoing.

Lily met him at the door to her private apartment. "I hope this hasn't inconvenienced you," she said, seeing his preoccupation. "I wouldn't have asked you here, but this is a nasty business and I don't like the looks of it."

He shrugged off his coat and followed her into the comfortable sitting room where a bright fire blazed against the early evening coolness. "What is it?" he asked directly.

"Wilma found a girl on the bridge last night," she explained without preliminary. "She was about to throw herself into the river for the usual reason. Wilma talked her out of it and eventually persuaded her to come here."

"Well?" Grant prompted. "You've been rescuing girls like that for years without my assistance."

"She's Tom Lynch's daughter," Lily informed him.

"Ann?" he said incredulously.

She nodded. "You probably know her from the flower shop in the arcade. She has supplied me with orders the past two years. But that's beside the point. Her baby shouldn't be born here. A girl like that deserves better, whoever the man is. I've an idea she is protecting him because he has money or social position, and I thought with your connections you might be able to get to the bottom of it."

"You don't know?" he asked.

Lily frowned. "She refuses to talk, and I haven't pressed her. I thought it best to let her get adjusted. But the man has his responsibility."

"What about her mother?" Grant asked, mentally cursing himself for becoming so involved in his own affairs that he forgot Tom Lynch's widow and Ann.

"Ann said she died a little over a month ago," Lily said quietly. "She had lung fever, and couldn't survive the winter. The girl hasn't anyone now and she doesn't appear to care what happens. She's listless, almost as though her spirit is gone."

"Let me talk to her alone," he suggested. "I think we can untangle the affair."

Lily was relieved. "She's in the next room," she said, going to the door. "I'll send her in."

Grant remembered the change in Ann the last time he saw her, but he was unprepared for the drawn pallor of the thin face, the bloodless lips, and the tragic hopelessness of her large eyes.

He spoke her name reassuringly, and added: "Take this chair by the fire. You don't mind talking to me, do you?"

"There's no use, Mr. Monroe," she said dully. "Nothing matters now."

"You're quite wrong," he contradicted her. "The child matters, whether you admit it or not."

She stared at the glowing coals and nodded slowly. "Last night I wasn't thinking very clearly, I guess. I forgot the baby, and that was wrong I'll take care of it somehow. Maybe I'll go away, but I'll take care of the baby."

"The child is Brad's?"

She could not control the dull flush that colored the pale transparency of her cheeks. "Please, Mr. Monroe," she said in a smothered tone. "I'd rather not talk about Brad."

"Does he know?" Grant persisted in the same quiet tone.

"I ..." she began defensively, then stopped. Her hands made a small, futile gesture and her head dropped with lifeless exhaustion.

"He'll have to be told," he continued, reasoning with her in a steady, reassuring voice. "The child is his obligation too, you know."

She came to life briefly like a recalescent flame on the smoldering embers on the hearth. "No," she protested passionately. "I don't want him to know. I won't take anything from him, or from his family."

"You still love him, don't you?"

She covered her face with her hands and sobbed silently. He wondered what Brad would do when confronted with this new responsibility. If there was any decency in him, he would accept the situation in the only way possible. They could be married quietly, and Ann could await the birth of the child here while he finished at the university.

He went over to her and put an arm about her shoulders.

"Listen to me, Ann," he said gently. "I'm going to send for Brad ..."

She raised her tear-stained face. "No, please!" she pleaded in anguish.

He took her hands in his to quiet their trembling and went on tenderly, compassionately: "It's going to be all right, Ann. Try to believe that. At least give Brad a chance."

The tears sprang to her eyes again. "I couldn't do that to him," she insisted frantically.

"Marriage isn't going to hurt him," he said briefly. "I want you to stop tormenting yourself this way. Leave the worrying to me. Run along now, and get some rest."

She stood up, the haunting question still in her eyes. "Brad," she murmured distractedly.

"You know him better than I do," he remarked, trying to draw her out of that tragic hopelessness.

"I said that, didn't I?" she admitted with a wan smile. Then a pale glimmer of hope struggled through her tears. She started to thank him, but he interrupted.

"Just promise to leave everything in my hands," he said.

"I will," she told him softly. "Good night, Mr. Monroe."

Lily returned, her eyes questioning his impatiently. "Well?" she asked.

"Brad Jenkins," Grant told her.

She moved to the fireplace and sat down. "That's a queer thing," she remarked slowly. "Brad Jenkins and Tom Lynch's daughter. What is he like, the young scalawag?"

He drew a cigarette from his pocket and lit it. "I don't know, exactly," he said, staring at the fire. "Whether or not he deserves a girl like Ann remains to be seen. He's attending an Eastern university now, but I'll get in touch with him."

"You're going to send for him?"

"Tonight. I prefer to explain after he arrives. He can assume that he's being summoned home because of his father's illness."

"How is Harlan?" she asked, studying him shrewdly.

"Doing nicely. He will be quite recovered, no doubt, by the time the assembly gets down to the business of considering traction franchises."

"I understand that Reed is back of Jenkins' fight against Interurban," she commented.

"Interurban was handicapped by a lack of funds," he informed her with deep satisfaction. "That, I believe, has been remedied."

"I see. Reed won't take kindly to the disappointment. Since Kennedy has been holding Steve Rego and Frank Masters, he's been out for blood. Are you prepared to take on the entire machine, or is this just a false start?"

"That depends on Bauer," he said crisply. "Kennedy has a guard on him in case Reed tries to get him to change his story."

"Reed will fight back," she warned a second time.

"Reed is on the way out," he replied with a perfunctory shrug. "He's known it for some time but he hasn't been able to figure out how or why. If he were clever, he'd quit now before he adds to the score against him."

"There will be quite a few changes in town," she observed dryly. "I sold the house yesterday at a fairly good price. The girls have gone, all but Wilma. She intends to go to Seattle to live with a sister. If Ann's problem can be settled, you will find Lily Olandt waving a cheerful farewell to St. Louis."

"You will have the kind of life you might have had here," he said morosely.

"And what about you?" she demanded, watching him intently.

"The next election will finish Reed and most of his friends. The new attorney will have a difficult assignment, but he'll be able to get convictions. The job will be finished."

"When it is," she probed relentlessly, "will you have what you want?"

He did not answer immediately. After a moment he flipped the partially consumed cigarette into the fire and turned to pick up his coat. "Yes," he said, "I think I shall. Keep Ann from worrying if you can. I'll send a wire to Brad on the way home. Then we'll see."

CHAPTER FORTY-SEVEN

Theodora had her dinner on a tray in her room. Her chagrin at Grant's abrupt departure to see Lily slowly receded, leaving her controlled and resolute. He had not wanted to go, she knew instinctively, and the thought calmed her vague misgivings and steadied her composure. There had to be an explanation. On his return he would tell her the reason for this visit, and there would be an end to these misunderstandings.

She heard the carriage drive up, the door opened and close, his steps on the stairs. Then he was in the doorway and she stood up, smiling.

"You are not angry?" he asked, coming into the room.

"Not now," she said. "If I don't understand all I should, the fault is mine. I've refused to listen to you, refused to believe in you."

His expression clouded, but he continued to regard her intently. "You won't like what I am about to tell you," he said in a curiously quiet tone. "If I could spare you, I would. But there is no way to keep the truth from you. A girl tried to throw herself in the river last night. Lily Olandt took her in and is caring for her temporarily."

"But why are you concerned in a sordid affair of this kind?" she asked confusedly.

"The girl is Ann Lynch," he told her. "Does the name mean anything to you?"

The name had a familiar ring, and she searched her memory. "Ann Lynch. That's the girl father forbade Brad to see. Father was right, then. I'm grateful that Brad had nothing further to do with her."

"She is going to have Brad's child," he informed her unemotionally.

Theodora stared at him. "I don't believe you," she said in a queer, flat voice. "This is a trick of hers. She's trying to drag Brad into the affair to make him marry her."

"I imagine Brad will admit his involvement," he said. "I sent for him."

"You ... what?" she gasped.

"I know how difficult this is for you," he said tiredly. "But marriage is the only solution for them now. If Brad has any decency at all, he'll want to marry Ann and provide a home for her."

She was trembling violently. "How can you talk about decency when you propose to drag an innocent boy into an affair with a woman like that?" she demanded angrily. "And father, what of him? This may kill him if he finds out!"

His face hardened. "At the moment I am not interested in your father, nor do I care whether he knows or not. I am concerned with Ann's happiness, Ann's and Brad's."

"I won't permit you to go ahead with it," she said indignantly. "I shall explain to Brad that there's been a horrible mistake."

His voice was weary. "You can't solve his problems for him forever, Theodora. He's a man, with a man's responsibilities. He has had to learn the hard way, I suppose, because he's always been shielded. But this time he'll have to stand on his own feet."

"You haven't the right to interfere in his life," she told him defiantly. "If you do this to him, I'll never forgive you."

He paled slightly, then turned abruptly and left the room. In the corridor he paused, glancing at the turn of the stairs where Nita's skirts were disappearing. Had the girl been listening? he wondered angrily. The problem of Brad and Ann would have to be settled, then he would attend to Nita. If she were still opposed to her aunt's home in New York, she would have to return to the island. He had hoped that Nita would leave voluntarily, out of sheer boredom. At every turn he had demonstrated with painful frankness the pointlessness of this extended visit. Evidently such measures were ineffective. He did not relish the thought of the scene she would most certainly create when faced with his decision. But he was adamant. Nita must go.

CHAPTER FORTY-EIGHT

N ita had sedulously followed the ebb and flow of tension within the household, and in her covert watchfulness she was acutely aware of the silent conflict between Grant and Theodora. Her ear detected the recurring false note in their punctilious courtesy and precise manners. She was quick to catch the brooding restlessness behind Grant's studied composure as he looked at his wife in one of his rare, unguarded moments, and the unvarying degree of coolness in Theodora's scrupulous observance of the proper amenities. Such a state of affairs could not go on forever, of course. Grant was a man to have a warm, living romance, not this unearthly remote woman whose disdainful glance chilled the blood and cast a shadow into the heart. Sooner or later he would recognize the folly of this marriage, and when he did, she, Nita, would be here to hold out her arms to him. Then she would quickly forgive his indifference and cruelties.

She had not been pleased with the recent subtle change in Theodora. Since the old gentleman's illness, Theodora's attitude had softened perceptibly. Her manner had become considerate toward Grant, almost dependent. Often they conversed together in low, intimate tones, and Theodora no longer sat in the early evening alone in her room.

Though Nita observed these indications in tightly suppressed anger, her suffering was not as intense as it might have been. Her mind in its irrepressible versatility had a secondary occupation, one that offered an interesting compensation. With the senator's return to Washington and illness in the house, there were no more invitations. Her pastime became the rather dull diversion of ingratiating herself in Harlan's eyes, and this she did with a double purpose. She was convinced that her welcome in the household would continue as long as the old gentleman wanted her to stay, and she was beginning to view seriously the long-range advantages of endearing herself to him. Months had gone by since there was any word from Pedro, a circumstance that considerably freed her imagination to dwell on what she believed to be Harlan's enormous wealth. One could enjoy spending that money, and the limitless supply that would accrue when this transportation line started to move.

Theodora, at first grimly watchful of the hours Nita spent in the sickroom, eventually relaxed her vigilance when it became apparent that the girl's presence had a salutary effect on Harlan's spirits and seemed, actually, to hasten his recovery. He was, in fact, considerably improved when he had the companionship of anyone. The only times his seizure appeared to strengthen its lingering grip were interludes when he was alone. Nita read to him or talked about the island and the plantation. Sometimes she sat quietly, a peculiarly thoughtful expression on her smooth young features as she stared out the window at the budding trees framed against the bright sky.

Her intuitive perception was irresistibly drawn by the air of continuing watchfulness in the household. Once she had relieved the special nurse for an hour and Harlan, dreaming restlessly, had babbled in his sleep like a being terrified in the clutches of a weird nightmare. She made out little when She turned to see Grant in the doorway. The half smile on his face, relentless and cruel, sent a tiny shiver down her spine. She had gone quickly from the room at his nod, turning only at the door to see him seat himself beside the bed, that inscrutable expression in his eyes as he took up the watch.

He frightened her by the implacable strength of his will, yet she knew there were weaknesses in that strength. Aware that her talk about the place in Cuba annoyed him, she took a certain retaliatory pleasure in pursuing this conversational hobby. She suppressed a vindictive smile the time he came into the room as she was telling Harlan of a certain peculiarity that marked his father. The slight limp which had fascinated her as a child, unnoticed except when Señor Monroe was tired at the end of a long day at the central or in the fields during harvest season, still hung with lingering nostalgia in her memory. She knew Grant was angered by the frown on his face and by the abruptness of his tone as he dismissed her, sending her on a foolish errand to the kitchen. If he was angered, then she was happy, she thought with a deepening sense of personal satisfaction and injured vanity. He angered her, too, with his habit of addressing her as an irritating child, his way of treating her with courteous but intentional finality.

This Brad about whom he and Theodora quarreled was the old gentleman's only son. She overheard enough to know that Grant was arranging a marriage which Harlan strongly opposed. Harlan was better now, almost as vigorous as he had been before the attack. It would not kill him, as Theodora said, to know about his son and this Ann Lynch. Not if he knew in time to prevent this undesirable marriage. And he would be grateful to Nita for telling him.

Humming a little tune, she surveyed her reflection in the hall mirror. The possibilities of being Mrs. Harlan Jenkins floated closer and most appealingly. The red dress was very becoming.

CHAPTER FORTY-NINE

The late afternoon quiet was undisturbed. Harlan, intending to call the following morning at his office, was alone in the study. With Theodora out and Grant not expected for another hour, this was an excellent opportunity to go through the papers he customarily kept in the safe behind his camouflage of investment treatises.

The papers were undisturbed and in order. In the morning he would attend to the traction records. By stretching a point here and there, he might make a favorable representation. Doubtless he could cover the entire disposition of the company's assets well enough to pass a perfunctory appraisal. There had been no demand for an exact accounting since his illness, and he did not look for any further agitation. Reassured, he replaced the file.

He was about to swing the safe shut when he stopped. Reaching into the rear of the compartment, his fingers groped until they found what they were looking for—the chill, round smoothness of a metal bore. A sense of relief invariably swept over him when he satisfied himself that the gun had been undisturbed since he put it there. He withdrew his hand, conscious of a fluttering sensation with each heavy heartbeat. He moistened his lips and wiped the perspiration from his forehead. He hated himself for this weakness, this inarticulate terror of the past. But he was powerless to control it.

His head still hummed faintly, but he reached again into the safe and removed a yellowed sheaf of clippings, neatly pinned together with a rusted clip. He was unable to explain the morbid compulsion that made him preserve this record of the Patterson case through the years, nor did he know why he read and reread it innumerable times. His hands trembled as he scanned the details now, following each step from the discovery of Tom Lynch's body a hundred yards from the Patterson home through the trial to its ultimate conclusion. He had been over the account many times but he was always driven to another glance, fearful that something had escaped him, some detail that would rise up out of the past to destroy the wall of security he had built for himself.

So engrossed was he that he failed to hear the melody at first. Over and over the tune drummed persistently into the recesses of his brain, demanding recognition. Pure terror shone in his eyes as awareness came over him. He had never expected to hear that tune again, that snatch of melody Patterson hummed in the old days. In a frenzy of haste, he closed the door of the safe and clumsily replaced the books on the shelf. He had forgotten to put back the clippings but it was too late now. Stuffing them in his pocket, he turned toward the door. Someone was coming, and above the sound of the steps, the melody. He scarcely heard the lilting timbre of Nita's voice. Only the tune filled his consciousness, and in his frantic state the voice might have been that of Will Patterson.

Nita came in and cried out at the ghastly pallor of his face. Murmuring concernedly, she helped him to the divan where he sat down heavily.

"That song," he muttered. "I heard it. He's back … with that damned song!"

Nita was confused. "I was singing, señor. I sing because I am happy that you are almost well."

He stared at her fixedly. "You?" he asked with an effort.

"That melody I learned as a child," she replied, seating herself beside him and propping cushions at his back. "Señor Grant's father hummed it many times."

The color slowly returned to his face. "I've never been musically inclined myself," he explained awkwardly. "Theodora inherited the talent from her mother. That ..." he interrupted himself as she stroked his brow with soothing pressure, "is very good."

"You feel better?" she asked solicitously. "Nita is sorry she startled you."

His heart was steadier now, and the familiar excitement at her nearness stirred his blood with new and vigorous warmth. They were alone in the house except for the cook preparing dinner and a maid who was doing the upstairs rooms. There could be no intervention this time. The obsession that had been deferred through his illness flamed anew, and his arms went around her in a demanding embrace.

He did not see the unmoved calculation in her expression as she met his absurdly clumsy advances, the contemptuous amusement and tiny glitter of triumph in her eyes. It was worth all this, she thought in sharpening anticipation, to be mistress in this household, to be able to override the arrogant Theodora and laugh at Grant with his indifference and infuriating coldness. There would be many opportunities to retaliate, opportunities to taunt them both.

Through the haze in his brain, Harlan was aware only of obstructing lace and obstinate buttons, the yielding softness of firm young breasts and the cooling haven of slim young thighs. This was different, he thought in a rush of heated excitement. Different from Lily Olandt's girls, different from anything he had ever known.

"You're not going back to Cuba, do you hear?" he said at last, as he lay exhausted, swimming in relaxing drowsiness.

She flexed her limbs, remembering the reason she had sought him out. "I had something to tell you," she said on a faint note of reproach, reaching for the red dress that lay in a crumpled heap on the carpet. "Something very important. Now I think I should change my mind."

"Eh?" he grunted, fighting a shortness of breath that persisted alarmingly. "What's that?"

"You will be angry," she teased softly, slipping into the dress. "So angry you will forget Nita."

"An exaggeration, my dear," he said, rallying slowly. "Let me hear and we shall see."

"Señor Grant has sent for your son," she told him. "I heard him saying this to the señora last night. Perhaps I was not meant to overhear because they did not want you to know, I am sure."

"Brad?" he said with a frown. "You must be mistaken."

"I am not mistaken," she assured him. "He is to return because of a girl he must marry quickly. This would be a great wrong, I think, if the wedding took place without your knowledge."

"What girl?" he demanded harshly.

He was sitting upright now and the change in his expression startled her. Had she been wrong to tell him, she wondered anxiously. Suppose … "It is not too late," she explained hurriedly. "That is why I have told you …"

"The name," he interrupted explosively.

"I think it was … Lynch," she said, frightened by his labored breathing and staring eyes which now bulged from their sockets.

He had known even before she told him. Ann Lynch and Brad, he thought bitterly, the old fear ricocheting through his weakened body. He hadn't got rid of the girl after all. She was too clever. How much did she know? he wondered distractedly, remembering Ann's steady, quiet look of scorn the day she had come to the house. What did she have in mind by this obstinate determination to insinuate herself into the family as Brad's wife? A fine mist closed over his brain and invisible fingers reached for his throat. He had to do something, he thought, dimly aware of the bands of pain tightening over his heart. He had to forbid this marriage. What right had Grant to interfere? Damn the man's overbearing insolence. This time he had gone too far!

He began futilely to grope for his clothing and Nita sprang to assist him. *Madre de Dios,* if he died! She had never seen a man die, she thought in terror. These clothes! If only he would stop struggling, she could manage. His desperate fumbling grew weaker, and after a seemingly interminable period she was able to get him clothed. Leaving him slumped against the cushions, she ran to summon the maid. In the hall she met Theodora returning from her walk.

"Señor Jenkins," she gasped, never so grateful to see Grant's wife as at this moment. "In the study … he is ill again."

Theodora did not waste words with the girl. "Get his medicine," she directed sharply. 'T'hen phone Dr. Macklin."

Nita raced to do as she was told, breathing a silent prayer of deliverance.

CHAPTER FIFTY

In the dimmed light of the bedroom, Harlan fought the shadows and the queer tricks his brain played on him. Dr. Macklin, after ordering him to bed a second time and emphasizing the need for quiet and undisturbed rest, had finally gone, and Harlan was alone with Grant Monroe.

He had known what he wanted to say, but the words kept getting away from him. He was confused. He knew this man; he had often talked to him without the slightest hesitation or difficulty. Yet now there was an elusive quality about the figure near the door which was unmistakably alien in the familiar confines of the room. He thought Grant smiled, but no, when he strained his eyes to see better, the face in the shadows was impassive, cloaked in a polite, waiting expression.

"Nita told me," he said in a thin voice, the words coming with an effort. "About Brad. Have to explain …"

"Yes?" the word was tentative, softly spoken.

A chilling numbness spread over Harlan's limbs and he trembled convulsively. The tune Nita had inadvertently hummed that afternoon had affected his mind, he thought erratically. Grant's voice, even his tall silhouette in the dim light, were coming to him out of the past.

"Don't … stand there," he begged. "I can't see in these damned shadows. That's better," he breathed as Grant moved to the foot of the bed. "Brad can't marry that Lynch girl," he continued laboriously. "I forbid it. You've got to see that it doesn't happen."

Grant's face tightened. The contempt and slow, consuming hatred he had nurtured for years drummed in his veins. The bitter taste of it was on his tongue, and the pinpoints of irrevocable determination glinted in the narrowed eyes. Now, his brain repeated insistently. Finish the job. Watch the fear grow in those staring eyes, watch the twitching fingers cease their aimless plucking at the coverlet and stiffen as his body is gripped in abject terror. Tell him that Patterson is back.

The silence deepened. There were footsteps in the corridor, and the sound of a door opening and closing. He straightened involuntarily and the muscles of his face worked curiously. His voice when he spoke was controlled, and his face again wore that expressionless mask.

"Ann will bear his child, and Brad's responsibility is to see her through. He'll have to determine for himself whether to marry her or not."

"Money," Harlan said in an eager, intense whisper. "She'll take it now. See her, offer what she wants. I'll be able to repay you in a few months. Do this for me, Grant. You won't regret it."

"I'm sorry you feel so strongly about it," Grant said abruptly. "For your own sake, you'll have to try to accept matters. Rest now, and you'll see things in a different light in the morning."

"Dammit, Grant, I won't have it, do you hear?" Harlan said with all the violence he could summon.

"I'm afraid this talk is doing you no good," Grant said, moving toward the door. "Ring if there is anything you want."

He left the door ajar and went down the corridor. At Theodora's room he paused, then knocked lightly. She opened it almost immediately and stood aside as he entered.

"Nita told him about Brad," he said quietly, closing the door behind him.

"You know now how wrong you were to interfere," she said with desperate urgency. "There's not only Brad's happiness but father's health to consider. Tell Brad he was called home because of the uncertainty about father ... he need never know about this girl!"

He saw the sleepless shadows beneath her eyes, the pallor of her cheeks, and the weariness in the droop of her shoulders. "No, Theodora," he said slowly. "This doesn't change the situation for Ann."

She knew that further argument was useless. The set determination in his face would yield to nothing. Nothing? If she were to offer herself, would that be enough? Would his love, his desire for her prove stronger than this granitelike resolve to follow through on his peculiar sense of right and wrong?

"Do I matter so little to you?" she asked in a low tone. Her face softened with a faint tinge of color, and her mouth quivered despite her effort to steady herself. "You said once you loved me. If you said it now, would it mean anything?"

He looked at her a long minute, and the pain of her words whitened the mask of his face. "Not this way, Theodora," he said in a strange voice. "No bargains, no reservations."

She drew in a shuddering breath. The agony of self-abasement flowed through her body like liquid fire. "I think you'd better go," she said, turning away to hide her humiliation and misery. "There is nothing more to say."

CHAPTER FIFTY-ONE

Nita bore Theodora's unforgiving hostility in sullen silence, but she encountered some difficulty in dealing with Grant. She received his stern reprimand with an air of injured innocence until she perceived that he was leading up to a final declaration that she must leave. Then, saturated with tears in an unprecedented display of emotion, she fled to her room where she remained for the evening. For a while at least, it would be better to avoid another such meeting with him, and to keep well out of his sight.

She awaited Brad's arrival with sharp interest, and was the first to observe the hack that delivered the young man to the house the following evening.

His surprise at seeing her was obvious, though he was not unprepared for the encounter. This was the foreign tramp Theodora had mentioned in a letter with stiff, carefully chosen words, and about whom Felice wrote with penetrating, sarcastic wit. Theodora was a fool to let Grant keep her in the household, he thought, glancing at her with a slow, insolent thoroughness that missed no detail. His old resentment against Grant flared at this new evidence of gross effrontery. The disgust he felt upon learning of his sister's marriage to the man for whom he had only unfriendliness and distrust was re-established as he watched Nita preen with a provocative droop of her long lashes.

"Will you inform the family that I am here?" he said coldly. "I would like to see my father as soon as possible."

"You are Brad, the señora's brother," she exclaimed with a flashing smile. "You will be happy to know that your father is improving. Last night he had a slight indisposition, but today he is better again. The doctor is quite pleased with his condition."

He frowned. "You say father is better?" he asked sharply. "I thought his condition was critical."

"Oh no," she assured him. "He has been permitted to leave his room and go about the house. Of course, after last night he will have to rest more, but this is not serious."

She would have enlightened him further but Theodora, hearing their voices, descended the stairs swiftly. "Brad!" she greeted him with almost hysterical abruptness. "It is good to see you looking so ... well. Come into the drawing room where we can talk."

She took his arm and propelled him into the room, closing the doors on a thwarted and ill-humored Nita. Inside, Theodora paused and sank down on a chair to collect her thoughts.

"Father is resting now," she said uncertainly. "But you can see him when he has his dinner tray."

She looked at this brother whose lean jaw and deepset eyes reflected a new seriousness and purposeful direction. How to approach the dreadful subject of Ann Lynch's accusation, she wondered uneasily, with a quiet and reserved stranger who regarded her with an openly direct, almost hostile stare?

"What is it, Theodora?" he asked levelly. "Why was I called home?"

She parried the question.

"Dr. Macklin was here this morning," she said. "He has strongly advised against any undue disturbance or ... unpleasantness."

"Are you afraid I shall disturb him?" he asked with weary impatience. "I assure you, I shall not."

"You don't understand, Brad. Father has been recovering. Until yesterday, we thought he was nearly well. Of course, we knew he'd have to lead a quiet, restful life from now on, but he was doing splendidly until he suffered this relapse."

His frown deepened. "You haven't told me why I've been summoned home."

"Grant sent for you," she said unwillingly. "Not ... because of father. He had a reason of a different sort."

"What reason?" he demanded abruptly.

"A girl ..." she explained with increasing difficulty, "has accused you of fathering the child she expects shortly. When father heard about it, he was quite ill. He has been most difficult since, and I am sure it will relieve his mind to know you won't become involved in the affair."

"Apparently I have already been involved," he said dryly. "Come to the point, Theodora."

"I know there's no truth in the charge," she continued miserably. "We'll find a way to handle it. We must. I refuse to let you be dragged into a sordid mess like this, and I'm convinced it would kill father. You know his reaction when he found out about her last fall. A girl like that ..."

"Are you talking about Ann?" he asked sharply.

She nodded mutely, waiting for his justifiable wrath and denial. But there was no wrath, no denial. His face wore a most peculiar expression. "A baby," he said almost inaudibly. She was at a loss to interpret his reaction. He betrayed no understandable anger, no indignation, no scorn. In the midst of his incredulous surprise, he appeared ... pleased! She stared at him in growing consternation and disbelief.

"Where is she?" he asked.

"That's one of the worst aspects of the entire affair," she informed him grimly. "She's with that dreadful woman,

Lily Olandt. There was some ridiculous story about one of those ... unspeakable creatures finding her on the bridge one night. At any rate, she's there in an environment apparently congenial to her."

His face colored angrily. "You've always been intolerant, Theodora," he said bitterly. "You consider bigotry a virtue. In your narrow concept of right and wrong, there has never been room for compromise. I won't argue, but if Lily Olandt is caring for Ann, I am grateful to her."

She recoiled from his words. "You're what?" she asked in a horrified whisper.

"Strange that a woman like Lily Olandt can show us what kindness and decency are," he went on, ignoring the stricken look on her face. "Human virtues are not just meaningless words to be mouthed with pious inertia. You can learn from her, Theodora, what it is to be generous and understanding."

"Brad!" she said in a choked voice. "You dare compare me with that vile woman! I've done my best for you since you were a child. I've always tried to protect you, and now I'm repaid with humiliation and insult!"

"I'm sorry, Theodora. I believe you did what you thought was right. If mother had lived, perhaps things would have been different.

"I'm not blaming you," he added in a kindlier tone. "All three of us were smug, self-centered little wretches from the ground up. But we're wasting time, and I've some things to say to Ann that should have been said months ago."

"Brad!" her voice implored him. "You're not going to leave without seeing father?"

"You said he was in no danger," he reminded her. "If I return tonight, I'll look in on him."

"You can't know what you're doing," she persisted desperately. "That Lynch girl will force you to bring up her illegitimate child as your own. You'll never be free of her …"

"Get this, Theodora," he interrupted roughly. "Ann's child is mine. What's more, I'm going to marry her if she'll forgive me for being an idiot. I love her, and I'm going now to tell her so."

She knew the futility of trying to dissuade him. An irrevocable sense of loss filled her as she watched him go. It was as though her last pillar of support had collapsed. The phone rang, and she made her way slowly to the hall to answer it. The voice on the other end of the wire was Paul Nixon's.

CHAPTER FIFTY-TWO

Harlan Jenkins dressed slowly with trembling hands. The house had been quiet since he had heard Theodora go out. Nita was probably resting, he thought, drawing on his shoes carefully so that no sound would reach the corridor. He struggled with the laces, then straightened, pausing to catch his breath. Glancing out the windows, he saw that Rufus was still whittling on the bench in the garden where he'd been the past hour.

Jenkins moved more quickly now, his determination giving him strength. The pain was in his chest again, but it was not what it had been. He would be careful not to bend down, that was all. In the corridor, he paused, satisfying himself that no one was about. Then he went down the stairs and out the back entrance to the garden.

"I need the carriage, Rufus," he said with a shade of his old arrogance. "I have a call to make."

"Yassuh, Mist' Jenkins," the old retainer said. "You sure hit's all right for you to be goin' out this way? You look mighty peaked …"

"Never mind that, Rufus," he said impatiently. "Hurry, will you?"

As the carriage turned onto the avenue, he directed Rufus to Lily Olandt's place, then settled back to conserve his energy for the interview ahead. He did not speak again until they were within sight of the big, rambling house when he ordered Rufus to draw up at the side entrance.

He was admitted by the maid, Mabelle, and after a few minutes was shown into the pleasant sitting room. Lily was seated at a small desk near the window, checking and sorting old bills, tax receipts, and canceled checks.

"Where are they?" he demanded immediately. "Where is my son, and that … girl?"

"Sit down," Lily said coldly. "Your son has gone driving with Ann. They planned to stop at a few stores so I presume they will be gone quite a while."

"See here, Miss Olandt," he said, stressing her name with an insulting inflection. "I intend to put a stop to this impossible situation. My son is not going to marry that cheap little adventuress, do you hear?"

She shrugged. "I don't see how you are going to prevent the marriage," she said dryly. "They are both of age, they have secured the necessary papers, and the ceremony will take place at the earliest moment."

"If you think I am going to sit back and see Brad marry one of your strumpets, you are mistaken," he threatened.

"Ann has never been associated with me, as you undoubtedly know," she said scornfully. "The girl is entirely respectable, and comes from an excellent family. You haven't forgotten her father, have you?" she finished on a meaningful tone.

He stared belligerently. "What are you getting at?" he demanded sharply.

"You don't know me, do you, Harlan?" she asked quietly. "Look closely. I haven't changed that much in twenty years, have I?"

For a long moment he continued to stare. Then a look of incredulity came into his eyes and his face blanched. "You? No, it isn't possible. Lily … Patterson …"

"And why not?" she challenged with a wry smile. "I was born Lily Olandt—I married Will Patterson."

He was trapped. Frantic thoughts raced about confusedly in endless corridors of his brain. "Lily," he said again, his voice unctuous now. "I had no idea. I never supposed ... never guessed ..."

"I daresay you didn't," she remarked in a bored tone.

"There was no need for you to get into this," he said, gesturing vaguely. "I would have helped you in any way possible. I had the conspiracy charge dropped, didn't you know? I did all I could that year you were detained ..." He faltered again, unable to cope with the steady directness of her gaze.

"The conspiracy charge, yes," she nodded. "A year in prison for destroying evidence. For burning the books that would have convicted you, not Will Patterson, though I was ignorant of the fact at the time."

"You're wrong," he remonstrated. "As your friend, I advised you to the best of my knowledge. I thought to protect your husband, you, all of us. When that didn't work, I stood by, doing everything I could to make matters easier."

"I thought I would enjoy this," she said slowly and with distaste. "I thought I wanted to see you squirm and sweat and lie. But the sight only sickens me."

He thrust out his fleshy lower jaw and his expression became ugly. "I gather there is no use discussing the past with you. Your prejudices blind you to the truth. Nor does all this have any bearing on what brought me here today. My son is not going to marry the Lynch girl and that is my last word. You have influence with them and the means to stop the marriage, and you're going to do as I say."

"Am I?" she asked mockingly.

"If you don't, I can still have that old charge revived. You'll go back to prison and the publicity will be enough to keep you out of St. Louis the rest of your life."

"You're wasting your breath, Harlan," she said evenly. "You see, I know who murdered Tom Lynch. Ann's mother is dead, but she knew what no one else believed at the time. Will Patterson was framed for embezzlement and defrauding the city, framed by entries in the books which you made in the hope of saving yourself. Lynch was on his way to expose you when he was shot. His wife was ill after her confinement, and her testimony was never taken. But she never forgot."

"You couldn't prove that," he blustered. "No one would take your word against mine."

"Perhaps not. But there is Ann. Would you care to have her sign a statement?"

Lily doubted that Ann would ever lift a hand against Brad's father or any member of his family. And she prayed fervently that Ann would never know the truth. But she had no scruples against pressing Harlan to the wall with whatever weapon was at hand. Looking at him, she saw that she had won.

Jenkins was convinced. The fear that had been with him since he had first heard Ann's name linked with Brad's froze him completely. This was the end, then. The end of everything he had worked for, the plans, the shrewd manipulations, the years of carefully guarded words and actions. "What does she want?" he asked hoarsely.

"I believe she wants nothing more than to marry Brad and live quietly without interference," Lily told him. "And you might say I am guaranteeing her chance for happiness." She stood up. "Now I think you'd better leave."

He got to his feet heavily. He hesitated, the one question that had burned in his mind for years clamoring for expression. He could now know whether she would tell him or not, but he had to ask. "Have you heard from Patterson?" he forced himself to say, driven by the morbid fear he could not control.

"Not directly," she said slowly, an enigmatic smile softening the features that a moment ago had been uncompromising in their bitterness.

He turned then and left without a backward glance.

CHAPTER FIFTY-THREE

Theodora looked up from Felice's letter and glanced unseeingly out the windows of the music room. She was grateful for the fact that Felice and Neil had not been here to witness the happenings of the last few days. Felice would learn about Brad's escapade in time, but for the present Theodora felt only relief that her sister was unaware of what had transpired in her absence. On her return the fifteenth of May, there would be nothing amiss.

The hastily scrawled letter complained strongly of the food and the inconvenience of travel, and was threaded with the weary boredom of an endless search for new scenes and excitement. Some persons are incapable of taking the happiness life offers, Theodora thought heavily. They must continually suffer the pangs of discontent as their restless natures draw them always further from the realization of their desires. The evanescent quality of happiness was forever beyond the reach of restive man. An elementary but startling thought occurred to her. Perhaps the attainment of near-happiness was dependent on discipline of the mind as well as the will. Possibly everyone had the quality of contentment within his grasp if he could turn his mind to the enjoyment of living, instead of away. But the observation did nothing to relieve her own misery. She could not escape the wretched futility and devastating aloneness which was becoming all too familiar these days. An involuntary anguish seized her and she sank down on the bench in front of the piano, crumpling the letter in her hand.

Brad, returning to the house for the first time since his arrival the preceding week, found her there, staring dully at the mute keys. "I came to say good-by, Theodora," he said. "I'm returning to the university this afternoon." He waited for her to speak, but she said nothing. "Ann and I were married yesterday," he continued, watching her with a puzzled expression. "I suppose Grant told you?"

"Yes," she said then in a low tone. "For your sake, I hope you won't regret it. You are my brother, and I'll always be deeply fond of you. If you've done this thing, I shall pray that it is for the best."

"Thank you, Theodora," he said with a slight smile. "Ann is at the boardinghouse. The place belongs to her now that her mother is dead. Two elderly spinsters are the only other occupants, and they do their own cleaning and cooking. They mean well, but they're not particularly companionable, either of them. Or helpful in an emergency." He hesitated, then went on: "I wish you would see that things go all right with Ann. If anything should happen ..."

Theodora winced at the request. "No, Brad. How can I forgive her for what she's done to this family?"

"I suppose it was asking too much," he said grimly. "Your mind will be eased, I know, to learn that I'm taking her to New York after the baby is born. I've been offered a job in a law firm there, beginning this June."

He started to turn away, then paused. "Say good-by to Grant for me, will you? It seems I've misjudged him in the past. He's been damned decent, and I'd like him to know that I appreciate it."

"I'm sure he knows how you feel," she managed to say stiffly. Then: "Are you going to see father?"

His face hardened, and the lean jaw set determinedly. "Father? No."

"You don't realize what this has done to him. At first he was violently angry and abusive. He stormed incessantly, and fought to get out of bed. That passed. Now he just lies there, refusing his food, staring at the wall, turning from all of us. I've never known him like this."

He was unmoved. "Ann told me bow he tried to buy her off," he said. "Not satisfied with that, he implied that the money was my idea."

She stood up in her agitation. "He only did what he thought was best for you. That was his way of protecting you against ... her scheming designs."

"Don't compel me to remind you that Ann is my wife," he said in a hard tone. "From now on you will think of her in that light. As for father, I've never shared your unqualified admiration. At best, he's rapacious, unscrupulous, and evasive. He's had no time for any of us. In his eyes, we're a disagreeable obligation to be endured with as little inconvenience as possible."

"You do him a terrible injustice," she said miserably. "Have you no respect at all?"

"I like to face things as they are," he retorted unfeelingly. "If you want to think of him as a martyred saint, that's your business. Defend him and pamper him if you like, but make sure you don't pay with your soul. Your life is with Grant, and you're a fool if you don't realize it."

She stared frozenly after him as he turned on his heel and left the room.

CHAPTER FIFTY-FOUR

The reform movement advanced slowly. The public was at first indifferent, then cynical. People were mildly intrigued for a day or two by the arrests of Steve Rego and Frank Masters, then talk shifted to other interests. No one expected the men to remain in jail; no one expected Bauer to press charges. Grant Monroe, aware that his effectiveness would be curtailed if the Reed faction learned of his activities, confined himself to hidden operations. Most people knew only that Miles Hunter was financing the Independents with the aid of certain other prominent but unidentified citizens, and that Ballard had thrown the full weight of his paper behind them.

An immediate setback occurred when Reed inevitably got to Ludwig Bauer. Grant was in his office when he received the phone call from Kennedy.

"Our witness was badly beaten last night," Kennedy said curtly. "He's alive, that's about all. He managed to slip out to the alley behind the bakery without being seen. Probably Reed called him on the telephone and was convincing enough. Bauer got it there, and the man I've had on duty interrupted the job. Caught the assailant after a chase and shot him as he was heading for the Frisco railroad—a killer from Kansas City named Nick Ferrento. He staggered to the grounds of Kenrick Seminary and died. All we have now is a damned corpse and a witness who won't talk."

"Bauer has changed his story?" Grant asked sharply.

"He won't say anything except that he was mistaken about Steve and Frank," Kennedy replied, his voice grim in exasperation. "Seems convinced now they were only paying him a friendly visit. His one anxiety is to have the matter dropped. And there goes our case."

In the face of increasing pressure from above, Kennedy knew he could not follow through on the original charge without help from Bauer. Nor could he expect any information from the men who were finishing their short sentences for disturbing the peace. Steve's overbearing self-confidence was unshaken, and Frank's loyalty to the boss would take him unprotestingly to state prison if the need should arise.

"I'll go to the hospital," Grant said.

"See what you can do," Kennedy said, not too hopefully. "Tell Bauer he'll have a double police guard until we're able to go after the big fellow himself."

Grant found a detective on guard in the corridor outside the hospital room to which Bauer was assigned. He nodded and was waved inside. The man on the bed was unrecognizable under the bandages. His eyes were barely visible through openings in the gauze wrappings, the nose was a shapeless mound and as much of the mouth as was exposed was swollen and discolored. The rigid outline of splints on the left leg protruded from beneath the sheet. He was obviously in great pain.

"You'll be all right," Grant sat quietly. "The decent people of this city are going to see that this doesn't happen again, to you or to anyone else."

"I say nothing," Bauer mumbled. "Nothing."

"You've got to help us," Grant reasoned gently. "You want to protect others like yourself, don't you? You want to make the city safe for everyone."

"I say nothing," the voice came doggedly.

Grant sat down, talking in a low voice, telling Bauer what others were trying to do to reform the city administration, stressing the importance of Bauer's testimony and assuring him of adequate police protection for himself and his wife. Only when he mentioned the baker's wife did the man on the bed show a distinct reaction.

"No," he blurted painfully, fear showing in the eyes that stared out from the bandages. "They cannot hurt her!"

"She's all right, Mr. Bauer. Kennedy has two men watching the bakery now, twenty-four hours a day."

"I say nothing," was the monotonous reply. And no appeal to civic duty, no assurance of protection, could change that stubborn response.

Grant was not the only visitor to Bauer's room that morning. Ed Miller came, talked to the injured man, and went back to his routine newspaper assignment with the fatalistic conviction that Reed had won another victory.

Then one of those freak twists of circumstance brought to light a bit of paper that was to change matters entirely. Miller ate a brief lunch in the café on the corner, then decided to look in on the assembly chambers in the dim hope that he could pick up some news item. The lawmakers, stalling on the franchise issue, were holding hearings on public school building improvements and tax adjustments. Miller was convinced despite the futility of past excursions to the building that the key to the franchise story was to be found in the devious manipulations that went on behind the closed doors of the committee rooms.

His approach met the usual response from the staff of indifferent secretaries and receptionists. The assemblyman was out at an undisclosed place for an indeterminate time, or he was in closed session and could not be disturbed. Miller was about to leave when the blonde woman who filed and answered correspondence for Paul Nixon came out of his office with a sheaf of papers.

"Let's go," she said to a girl at a nearby typewriter, tossing the papers into a wire basket on her desk. "It's time for lunch."

Miller waited while she took her purse and hat from a lower drawer in the desk, joined the other girl, and started down the corridor. The top letter in the basket mildly stirred his interest. Written in longhand on a type of paper usually reserved for social correspondence, it seemed out of place with the rest of the official papers. He edged carelessly to a position near the desk where he could read the square, methodical script.

A few lines told him that he had stumbled on a scrap of evidence worth more than anything he could unearth in months of patient probing. With mounting excitement, he glanced at the remaining typists in the room. Those at their desks were transcribing notes or staring out the windows. An office boy moved from desk to desk with a refuse barrel, emptying wastebaskets and cleaning stray bits of paper from the floor. No one apparently was paying the slightest attention to the reporter who customarily haunted the building with almost daily regularity.

The letter, he thought rapidly, obviously had no business here with correspondence of a more innocuous nature. Nixon's girl in her haste to be off for lunch had evidently swept it up by sheer accident with others to be filed. Miller was aware that the assemblyman would discover the mistake at any moment. With a single movement that was as swift as it was casual, he removed the letter from the basket and slipped it into his pocket.

From the corridor he heard the door to Nixon's office open. The assemblyman burst out, smothered an angry oath when he saw the girl's empty chair, then began pawing through the papers in the basket. Miller did not wait to see what would happen. He vanished in the stairway leading to the street and in five minutes was back in the newspaper office.

There he removed the letter from his pocket and reread it slowly, undecided as to what use he would put his find. The note, which was addressed to the president of Interurban, stated briefly that Reed had forced the issue by paying over the Jenkins bribe money. Nixon assured the director of Interurban that his colleagues would refuse to "stay bought," and he urged an immediate transaction with the combine that would be satisfactory to all parties. The assembly, he said, would not then be in doubt as to their course of action, and the way would be cleared for a disposition of the Interurban petition.

Miller glanced at the precise signature of Paul Nixon with unrestrained glee. This was more than enough to blow the Reed machine into oblivion and at the same time capture the fattening parasites in the assembly. But he was not entirely carried away. He reflected that considerable damage might be done by a premature disclosure. On the other hand, if there were no immediate repercussions, Nixon might be induced to think that the letter had been unintentionally destroyed, perhaps carried off by the office boy after it had accidentally blown into the wastebasket. When there was no indication that it had fallen into the wrong hands, Nixon would again contact Interurban and the deal would go through as originally planned. With the final action of the assembly in granting the Interurban franchise, exposure of Nixon's letter would carry the volatile impact needed to stir the city out of its twenty-five-year lethargy.

It was unfortunate that Kennedy had to release Reed's men, but they could be picked up for subsequent questioning at any time. And in a final showdown Steve, at least, might be prevailed upon to furnish added information against his boss if he were convinced that such action would be to his advantage.

Miller carefully folded the letter and fitted it into a compartment of his wallet.

CHAPTER FIFTY-FIVE

Felice brought back to St. Louis the same clear beauty and restlessness that had been hers when she left. Yet there was a subtle difference. Somewhere in her travels she had lost that appealing freshness which had been her greatest charm. The delightful embellishments were fewer and more transparent, and the fixed contours of the mold were sharply visible beneath the thin veneer of sophistication. The petulant droop of the lovely mouth was a familiar characteristic of her expression now, and the gray-green eyes were habitually frosted with cynicism.

Theodora was disheartened by this change, but she no longer had the inclination or the will to counsel or interfere. An inborn discontent had always distorted happiness for Felice. Theodora was aware that her own attitudes in the past had often been in unfortunate conflict with her sister's, but any sense of guilt she might have felt was tempered now with perspective. She might have given more understandingly of love instead of dutifully, but she wondered with an odd detachment whether that would have made any difference. There had always been a thin thread of cruelty behind Felice's pretty ways, strung like a fine steel wire thoughout the intricate pattern of her restive disposition.

They were all strangers to one another now, family in name only. An affinity, if it did exist, lay between Harlan and Felice. Theodora was not surprised at the strangeness of the thought. In the final reversal of all she had once accepted as unchanging truth, this was a comparatively, small detail. Nor had she reason for anxiety on Felice's behalf. Neil would always be devoted to his wife. The two would live in the conventional pattern, summering at resorts, attending the races, the symphonies, and plays, entertaining and being entertained. They would bleed life of each day's distracting amusement, never fully realizing what they had missed.

Theodora would have been more concerned, however, had she known of Felice's movements one afternoon late in May. Felice, returning from tea and a dull half hour with Martha Mills, was commiserating upon the inescapable boredom of her eventless life with Neil. The prostrating heat had wilted her dress, her appearance, and her disposition. It had been senseless to go out, she thought impatiently, fanning herself futilely as she sank back onto the carriage seat. The unseasonable weather had turned spring into a parched nightmare. One ought to have had the good judgment to remain home in a cooling bath on such an afternoon. She glanced irritably at the broiling sky, noting that the clouds were still too high and scattered for rain. She was in the act of settling back a second time when she saw something that brought her up with a start. The oppressive heat and humidity, the boredom and ill-tempered dissatisfaction—all were forgotten.

Down the street a carriage was drawing to the curb and a woman whom she instantly recognized as Theodora stepped from the tree-shaded walk to meet it. Felice's eyes narrowed with sharp interest. The man who left the vehicle momentarily to assist Theodora inside was unmistakably Paul Nixon. There was an air of prearrangement about the brief encounter that held Felice transfixed. It was beyond belief that Theodora was indulging in a secret involvement, yet one could not deny the evidence of one's eyes. This would take a bit of looking into, she decided, instructing her driver to stop at her sister's home. The hour was late, and Grant would probably be there. Felice anticipated the triumph of imparting this information to him, information that would undoubtedly come as a surprise. Here was an unexpected weapon with which to retaliate for the festering resentment she endured each time she thought of that marriage. And an infinitely effective one, deadly enough to appease the scorched embers of a rancorous memory.

Nothing was impossible, she observed wryly. She had thought Martha Mills's expression peculiar when she had mentioned Theodora's lack of interest in social activity since Harlan's illness. Martha's vague remark that Theodora did not seem like herself lately took on new significance. Theodora certainly did not, Felice thought with asperity, her mind darting about with enlivened interest. But then everything was changed these days, with the household disrupted by that foreign woman who doted on father and cast lascivious eyes on Grant.

Entering the house unannounced, Felice found Nita in the comparative coolness of the shaded drawing room.

"Señor Jenkins is resting," Nita told her. "I think he is asleep."

"I won't disturb him. I suppose Grant is home?"

"He will be late," Nita explained. "He phoned that he was delayed and would dine out."

Felice frowned in obvious disappointment. In her anticipation of the scene with Grant, she was ill prepared for delay. Then she reconsidered. Perhaps it was better this way. If Nita bore the news, the results might be even more interesting. "And my sister?" she asked, studying the younger woman with oblique intentness.

"I am sorry," Nita shook her head. "She has gone to dine with a friend, I think."

Felice surveyed her thoughtfully. There was no doubt that Nita had forced herself on this household with the intention of exercising her charms on Grant. So far her plan had not worked according to specifications. Apparently Grant would have none of it, and she had turned as a second-best alternative to Harlan. The picture of Nita as a stepmother did not appeal to Felice.

"You must find life tiresome here," she remarked idly. "Things have been quite trying, I understand, since father's illness."

"No, señora," Nita said carefully. "I have enjoyed reading to your father and sitting with him when he did not wish to be alone."

"Yes," Felice said dryly. "You have been generous with your time, and we all appreciate what you've done."

"Your father is a good man," she said demurely. "I have done little to repay the kindness I found here."

"Since father is resting, I won't stay. I'm sorry Grant is out. I particularly wanted to see him."

"If there is a message," Nita offered, "I shall be most happy to give it to him."

No doubt, Felice thought caustically. Aloud she said: "It's nothing. I've been concerned about Theodora, but perhaps it is unimportant."

"You can trust me, señora, if you wish. I am very fond of your sister."

Felice suppressed a smile at her obvious curiosity. "Theodora has not seemed herself since I've been home," she went on in a doubtful tone. "There may be nothing wrong, but I thought Grant ought to know. It's not like Theodora to go out alone with Paul Nixon. She was always so meticulous about doing the proper thing."

Nita's startled eyes flickered. "Paul Nixon?" she repeated.

"Perhaps I shouldn't have mentioned it," Felice went on with exactly the right degree of worry in her voice. "But I rather thought Grant ought to be informed. If there is a way to help matters, he can find it before the affair goes any further. I am fond of both, and I think it would be quite tragic if anything happened to their marriage."

"I had no idea," Nita murmured.

"On second thought," Felice concluded, "perhaps we'd better forget the whole thing. I'll talk to Theodora tomorrow. There's probably a simple explanation."

She left with the sure knowledge that Nita would make the most of her newly acquired information. Felice was satisfied. Discovering a flaw in Theodora's gleaming armor was a distinct pleasure, and its impact on Grant would be all one could desire.

CHAPTER FIFTY-SIX

Grant saw Lily Olandt on the train which would at last take her away from St. Louis. Her departure was unobtrusive and uneventful. The veiled, trim figure, conservatively attired for travel, resembled that of the retiring headmistress of an exclusive school. "Retirement is a good word," she said as they parted. "From now on I dote on the tepid tea of respectability. I shall join the denizens of quiet elegance and devote the remainder of my life to art galleries and museums."

"Won't you find that somewhat dull?" Grant asked whimsically.

"Not dull, comfortable," she assured him. "And if you want my advice, you'll take Theodora away and enjoy a life of your own. Forget the past. You've done enough to break Jenkins and the Reed faction. Let others finish the job."

"Don't worry," he said quietly with a slight smile. "I'll get along. I've always been able to take care of my own interests."

She hesitated, searching the unfathomable eyes of this man who had been almost as close to her as his father. "I'm going to miss you, Grant," she said. "You've been the only person I could talk to, the only friend I've had in years. Funny, isn't it? Grant Monroe and Lily Olandt."

He stiffened perceptibly. "They did that to you," he said with controlled violence.

"If I could make you see there's nothing to be gained by all this bitterness, I would be satisfied," she said urgently. "Your father wouldn't have wanted you here, driving your energies, your life into the muck of the past."

The passengers were aboard and the train, with a deafening roar of steam, was preparing to move out of the station.

"We haven't time to argue the point," Grant said, his expression softening with affectionate indulgence. "Good-by, Lily, and good luck."

He bent swiftly to kiss her, and her eyes dimmed suddenly with tears. She tried to speak but no words came. They looked at each other a long moment, then he turned and was gone.

The thought of escape became unexpectedly inviting as he walked quickly along the warm pavement in the late afternoon sunlight. Perhaps if Ann and Brad had arranged their lives differently, he could have gone away with Theodora. They might have transcended their barricaded walls to find satisfying love and fulfillment in each other. He remembered the afternoon they drove through the early spring countryside, her surrender and unreserved trust, and his eyes closed in an expression of pain. She had been infinitely desirable to him then and their subsequent estrangement had filled him with a mental and emotional torture beyond any conceivable physical suffering.

His wretchedness eclipsed even his carefully nurtured hatred for Harlan. He had on several occasions been tempted to drive home the last knifing blow to Jenkins' tottering world, but something held him back. Something stronger than the fierce need to mete out a relentless justice of his own. To finish Jenkins was to inflict a jagged scar on Theodora, deeper than life had dealt her before, and this he could not bring himself to do.

He returned to his office, signed the neatly typed letters waiting on the desk, and glanced briefly through the afternoon mail. There was a letter from Juan with news that Pedro had escaped the prison camp where he had been held and was now in Havana.

Juan admitted that these were not settled times. But there was talk about a compromise with Spain, and he strongly favored Nita's return to the island. In this, Grant concurred. A fitting place for Nita was with her aunt in New York, but since she refused that alternative she would have to return to the plantation. Aside from Theodora's constraint and his own defensive diplomacy with the girl, he looked with strong disfavor on Harlan's growing fondness for her. There was no place for Nita in Harlan's diminishing horizon.

He tossed the letter aside, making a mental note to inform Nita that evening of his decision. The phone rang and he glared at it in annoyance. At a second ring, the inner office door opened and Miss Withers peered in. He waved her back, wearily reached for the receiver, and opened the conversation.

"That you, Monroe?" the voice crackled over the wire. When assured that it was, the crisp, assertive tones went on: "This is Ballard, at the newspaper office. I've been trying to get Miles Hunter but can't reach him at home. Something big just came up."

Grant's "Yes?" was tentative, puzzled. He knew through his informant at Interurban that the assembly was scheduled to act today on the long-deferred franchise controversy. Evidently Ballard had heard the outcome. But Grant was at a loss to interpret the undercurrent of electric tension in the publisher's voice.

"You know Ed Miller, the reporter who covers the city hall assignments," Ballard went on. "He's in the office now with Norris, the city editor. Miller has a letter in his possession, one written by Nixon to the Interurban outfit. They never received the communication, but that's beside the point. We've got the damaging evidence we need, Grant."

Grant, listening with greater attention, asked: "The letter is genuine?"

"Of course it's genuine. I know Nixon's handwriting myself. And listen to this: he admits that Reed paid bribes on behalf of Jenkins' petition, then goes on to promise the franchise to Interurban if they top Reed's payment. I'm sorry as hell that Jenkins' name is being dragged into the scandal, Grant. But you said you wanted the Reed machine exposed regardless of who happened to be involved."

Grant ignored this. "What do you intend to do?" he asked abruptly.

"Print the entire letter, for one thing. Miller's been holding it until the assembly acted, and this afternoon they put through the Interurban option. The city attorney worries me, though. He's either afraid of Reed or in his pay. If we turn the letter over to him, it may get lost and we'll be in for a libel suit."

"Hand him a copy before the papers are on the street," Grant said. "He can do as he sees fit. If there's no action, all right. The next election will see a new man in office, one capable of doing the job." He thought rapidly, then added: "Does Kennedy still have Rego and Masters in custody?"

There was a pause while Ballard consulted with Norris and Miller. "They'll be out tomorrow," he said after a moment.

"Kennedy might be able to work on them if he knows we have actual evidence," Grant suggested.

The publisher promised to notify Kennedy, then rang off. Grant replaced the receiver and almost immediately the phone began to ring again. He answered and a glimmer of amusement came into his eyes as he recognized Reed's voice.

"I want to see you," the politician said bluntly. "Can you come down to the old office? This is important."

Grant agreed after a slight pause and replaced the receiver a second time. Within a half hour he was striding along the sweltering pavements toward the waterfront office where Reed was waiting.

CHAPTER FIFTY-SEVEN

Grant turned in the alley half a block from the river, noting the figure of one of Reed's hoodlums who lounged in the shadows against the opposite wall. A flicker of grim humor crossed his features. In this last fight, Reed was employing all the measures he had scorned in the old days. Grant passed the man without further notice and entered the dim hallway. Another of Reed's men leaned against the battered newel post, picking his teeth. The man stirred watchfully but said nothing as Grant brushed past indifferently and started to mount the stairs.

At the top, he pushed open the door of the office and stood regarding the politician with a faintly contemptuous smile.

Reed was alone, hunched over in his chair, one of the usual black cigars clamped between his teeth.

"Why the watchdogs, Reed?" he asked. "Don't you trust the forces of law and order in St. Louis these days?"

"This is no time for humor," Reed growled. "Come in and close the door."

Grant complied but remained standing, ignoring the chair by the desk. "You're jumpy tonight," he said sardonically. "You ought to learn to relax."

"The assembly voted the Interurban franchise today," Reed announced with a scowl.

"Well?"

"Is that all you've got to say?" he demanded testily. "I had the Jenkins deal set to go through, and the bastards pulled a last-minute switch. Do you know what that means?"

"Evidently they're not taking orders," Grant remarked laconically.

"The damned fools didn't know when they were well off," Reed said bitterly. "Hell, they always got substantial fees, but that wasn't enough. They wanted more. Now they think they can handle things alone and clip me into the bargain."

"The money bothers you, doesn't it?" Grant inquired with a cold smile.

"They'll settle with me, don't worry," Reed snorted. "What will happen next is more important. They're too stupid to get away with this sort of thing long. Somebody will slip, and there'll be the devil to pay."

"That's one of your admirable characteristics, Reed. You always look ahead."

"Yeah, I look ahead. I do so damned well I make Kennedy a captain and the son of a bitch turns around and hauls in two of my boys on a routine collection night."

"You're still lucky," Grant said, watching him narrowly. "If Bauer hadn't changed his mind about talking, you would be in for an investigation."

"Bauer is the one who is lucky," Reed snapped. "He showed a little sense before it was too late. Not that I couldn't handle whatever Kennedy started, but I had a few doubts about Steve. If they backed him into a tight place, he'd talk to save his own skin."

"You didn't ask me here to talk about Kennedy," Grant reminded him.

"No," Reed said. "I didn't. I thought when I took your advice about making up a ticket of independents for the next election, we'd have things quiet for a while. What's going on? I want the facts, and by God I want them straight."

"There are people in St. Louis who don't like your methods," Grant told him.

"If they want a, fight, they'll get it," Reed retorted.

"You haven't improved matters by sending for Nick Ferrento to beat up old Bauer. Tactics of that sort only stir up public feeling."

"I'll do more," Reed threatened. "I'll get Kennedy before I'm through and I'll deal with the combine. But don't think that's all. I know this didn't just happen. Somebody is back of it, Grant. Somebody is out to get me. And when I find out who ..." He left the sentence significantly up in the air.

"What then?" Grant prompted.

"I can take care of him," Reed said evenly. "I'm not finished yet."

"You've had things your own way so long you can't believe a change is possible," Grant said in a tone that put the politician on guard for the first time. "You can't win, Reed. We've had frequent dealings in the past, and I know your good points as well as the bad. You are fair-minded at least to the men you work with, and among other considerations, you've been useful to me. You want my advice, and you'll have it. If you decide to stay around, you'll be smarter to keep out of trouble from now on. You'll get off easier that way."

Reed stared at him. "Wait a minute," he said slowly. "Are you trying to say you've a stake in the other end of this deal?"

"Stake?" Grant repeated with a twisted smile. "I came back to St. Louis to even an old score. My stake, as you call it, is in finishing the job."

Incredulity, chagrin, and fear mingled with the fury in Reed's eyes as he returned Grant's level stare. "There was always something about you," he muttered between his teeth. "But why? What has St. Louis done to you?"

"Not St. Louis, Reed. Harlan Jenkins, and the rotten system of jury fixes, hired witnesses, and corrupt police you threw up as a screen when you first took over the city."

"Jenkins?" Reed repeated, stunned. "You've been after Jenkins?"

"Harlan Jenkins should have paid with his life over twenty years ago," Grant continued in the same implacable tone. "But he was able to frame another man, and he did so with your tacit consent and cooperation."

"The Patterson affair," Reed said almost inaudibly.

"I see you remember. You were happy enough to have Tom Lynch out of the way when he found out about Jenkins swindling the city on that construction deal. You probably received a substantial share of the proceeds. But you had to have a scapegoat before the real story was aired. Tell me, how much did Jenkins pay you to fix things?"

But Reed was not listening. "You are Patterson's son," he said indistinctly. "Grant Monroe Patterson. I had forgotten there was a boy …"

There was a sharp silence as his words trailed off. Reed's heavy breathing was the only sound in the close confines of the room. "You think you can rid the city of politics, is that it?" he said finally. "Don't you know there will be others to step into my shoes? The system will go on as long as man governs man. Nothing can change human nature."

"What happens next is a matter for the voters to decide," Grant shrugged. "You and I go our separate ways. The *Crescent* is yours if you want it. Sell it if you wish. The rest of our agreement is, of course, canceled. We can be of no further use to one another."

"Just like that, eh?" Reed sneered. "You don't suppose I'm going to sit back and lose everything without lifting a finger?"

"You won't gain anything by striking back at me," Grant said with a tight smile. "And I don't think you've the guts to try."

He turned on his heel as Reed came to his feet with an oath. Acutely conscious of the politician's baleful glare from the open doorway above, Grant descended the stairs unhurriedly. In the hall below the man on guard threw a quick glance upward for a sign from the boss. When he reached the lowest step, Grant was prepared for the man's lunge. The two locked in a bitter exchange of blows, coming up hard against the stair rail, the door, and the wall. A strange exultation whipped through Grant's blood as he fought. Years of vengeful waiting and controlled violence found release in the unmerciful beating he administered to the unfortunate bodyguard.

The encounter was brief. Reed's hireling collapsed and sank to the floor as the door opened and the man who had been waiting outside stood on the threshold, eying the scene with stupid incredulity. Grant did not wait. With one hand he dragged the newcomer inside, with the other he sent a crushing blow to the man's jaw. Grant caught him as he fell. Lifting him bodily, he hoisted the dead weight to his shoulder and ascended the stairs. Reed was motionless, his mouth slack, his eyes burning with helpless fury. Grant reached the top and catapulted his burden onto the politician, sending Reed reeling back against the desk.

"Any time you feel like it," he said coolly, straightening his coat, "try again." He descended the stairs a second time and let himself out the door.

CHAPTER FIFTY-EIGHT

On the street, his pace quickened. He turned toward the river and walked for a time without purpose or direction. The intense satisfaction of his encounter with Reed eventually burned itself out. He found to his annoyance that he did not savor this hour of triumph as he might have done. The vengeful pleasure was gone, leaving nothing but restless, nervous energy in its place. The same sense of futility that had been with him earlier that afternoon returned, and he was again seized with a nameless desperation. What he had gained was lost, and what he had lost was all he had ever wanted. He continued to walk aimlessly, oblivious to the passage of time, unconsciously delaying his return home and the inevitability of the decision he had to make.

Darkness had fallen when he found himself back at the deserted office building. Rufus was at the curb with the carriage, dozing patiently in the driver's seat. Grant spoke to him briefly and the old retainer roused himself with alacrity, hastening to hold open the door. As they drove off, Grant settled back with complete exhaustion. A sober determination replaced the restive misery of his recent moodiness. Tonight he would tell Theodora about Harlan and Will Patterson. She could hate him if she would. She could refuse to believe him. Or she could turn away in a final, bitter denunciation. But she would hear the truth, all of it. If she chose her freedom, he would not stand in her way. She could have the house now, for he no longer wished to hold onto it. His lips drew back in a spasmodic grimace of pain. This then was the end of the long, driving hours, the completion of all the planning and slow, careful work. He stared at his clenched fist, then slowly opened his fingers as though by that one meaningful gesture he relinquished the last of his dreams.

He remembered that there was one who had reason to be pleased about today's developments. Father Morelle would want to know. The priest had a right to hear that his cherished hopes for civic reform were now assured, that St. Louis would be free of the domination of Al Reed, free of graft, corruption, and all other evils of political mismanagement and uninhibited criminal activity. Grant leaned forward and directed Rufus to continue on to Kenrick Drive. The thought of the undaunted priest quieted him somewhat, easing his sense of personal loss and unhappiness.

At the Seminary he left the carriage and made his way slowly across the grounds. The quiet of evening had settled over the buildings, and in the humid darkness not a leaf or blade of grass moved. He found Father Morelle in his study, deep in meditation. As the priest rose, Grant was struck by the tiredness of the older man's expression. The face was deeply etched with lines of fatigue, and the eyes, despite their friendly welcome, held a look of weary resignation.

"How are you, Father?" he asked. "I hope you have not been unduly affected by the weather?"

"The unseasonable heat has indeed been difficult," the priest admitted. "The lack of rain is odd, almost as though the hand of God is staying the normal course of nature. I find myself strangely disturbed when I look out the window at the parched grass and trees, waiting night after night under clouds that refuse to give up their moisture."

"We'll have rain soon," Grant replied.

"But you, my son," the priest remarked, studying him with concern. "You do not look well. Have you perhaps met with further disappointment and delay?"

"Quite the contrary. The situation has worked out in accord with our best hopes. By sheer accident, a letter fell into our hands, a letter which will undoubtedly convict Reed and all the assemblymen who for years have been strangling city politics and protecting the crime element. This letter will be published tomorrow in Ballard's paper."

The priest's eyes shone with gratitude and fervent faith. "I knew that God would work matters out in His own time," he said earnestly. "I have been troubled these past days, for I was burdened greatly. The man, Nick Ferrento, died here in the sanctuary of the Seminary. I administered the last rites and heard his confession. If he had lived, I believe Captain Kennedy would have had all the evidence he needed."

"Yes," Grant said grimly. "Nick has been useful to Al Reed before."

"You knew about his connection with the Crayle affair?" the priest asked, puzzled and slightly surprised.

Grant nodded. "It would have been difficult to prove at the time. But we have Reed now on enough counts to keep him in prison for the remainder of his natural life."

"You can be justifiably proud, my son," the priest said warmly. "Yet you don't look like a man who has won such a victory. Is there something you haven't told me?"

"The motive, father," Grant said darkly. "What I did was not inspired by noble impulses, I'm afraid, but by a long-remembered bitterness. And the target of that bitterness was not Al Reed but Harlan Jenkins."

Father Morelle was silent for a time. "I sensed your feelings long ago," he said finally, his eyes grave. "And I suspected that you were being driven by memories of an incident far in the past. What I did not know was the man's name." He hesitated, deeply disturbed. "I hope for your sake that this has nothing to do with your marriage," he finished quietly.

"There hasn't been a marriage," Grant said tiredly. "My wife is a stranger, and will remain so as long as this is between us."

"You have not told her what is in your heart?"

"Theodora is completely devoted to her father," he said bitterly. "I could not bring myself to tell her before."

"You have been wise to keep your own counsel," the priest said slowly. "And you will be wiser still to continue your silence."

"Perhaps. But there are reasons why she must know the truth."

"Think the problem over carefully, my son," the priest admonished. "Words can never be recalled. Wait, and you may find the situation will resolve itself."

"I would like to think so," Grant said, rising. "But I seriously doubt that any power on earth can change matters."

"No power on earth," the priest agreed. "But there is a power, and in your heart you know it." He accompanied Grant as far as the chapel. "God bless you and guide you well these next few days," he said as they parted. He watched his visitor disappear into the darkness, then he entered the chapel to pray.

CHAPTER FIFTY-NINE

Grant arrived home a few minutes past nine to find Nita waiting for him. For an instant he stared at her blankly. In his preoccupation he had forgotten the very fact of her existence.

"You are tired," she greeted him in a tone of intimacy that caused him to lift a wary eyebrow. "Wait in the drawing room and I shall bring you an iced drink."

Since Felice's unexpected visit, Nita had been awaiting this moment with quickening impatience. She had brought a supper tray to Harlan, read a seemingly endless interval until he fell asleep, then hastened to her own room to bathe and dress. A cooling cologne and softly scented powder furnished an alluring background for the sheer, flowered gown that draped her slim figure in becoming folds, and an ornamental comb in her hair added an effective touch to the gleaming coiffure.

Grant acquiesced, partly because he welcomed any suggestion that offered a slight relief from the persistent heat but chiefly because he remembered Juan's letter.

She brought a chilled whisky and soda, and drew up a hassock. "This is like the plantation," she said, seating herself at his feet. "Nita always had a cooling drink at hand in weather so hot. Here you do not allow Nita to do these things for you."

"We have servants for the work here," he pointed out rather unnecessarily. "And you have been a guest in our home."

She repressed a frown at his use of the past tense. "I try to be more than a guest," she said earnestly, "and I am happiest when

I feel I am part of this household. I have tried hard to please you and the señora. When I saw that you wanted your life with her to be all that it should, I was resigned. I said, Nita will hide her heart. She must do nothing to hurt this marriage. Even when I saw you unhappy, I would not let myself speak. But I cannot keep silent any longer," she finished ardently, leaning forward in her intensity.

His brows drew together impatiently. "What's the use of all this, Nita?" he asked. "I tried to persuade you to go back to New York, and I've been willing to wait until you realized that it was the thing to do. If you still can't choose between your aunt and the plantation, I shall have to settle the matter for you."

"You are not happy with the señora," she insisted in a low, passionate tone. "That one could not make any man happy. She is cold and proud and selfish. Grant, listen to me. This is no marriage, and where there is no marriage the bonds should be dissolved. You are wrong to waste your life in this empty, futile way."

He stood up abruptly and walked away from her. "I have news that may interest you," he said shortly. "Pedro is free. He is now in Havana, awaiting the return of his bride."

She stared at him in disbelief. "It is not true," she said hotly. "You are only saying this to taunt me!"

"It is true," he affirmed. "I had a letter from Juan today. Your father urges that you return to the island."

"You are trying to trick me," she said furiously. "Only yesterday I received a letter from my father. If this were true, why did he not tell me?"

He shrugged. "The mail isn't always on schedule," he said briefly. "Apparently he wrote you before he knew about Pedro's escape."

Her chagrin mounted. In her vexation she made an irreparable mistake. "I have news too, which is of interest to you," she said in quick anger. "The faultless señora is out this evening, keeping a secret tryst with a man about whom she tells you nothing!"

He turned on her suddenly. "What are you saying?" he asked sharply.

"Her sister was here before dinner," she went on sullenly. "I do not know whom she wished to see, but she was very upset. The señora, she said, was with Paul Nixon."

"Felice!" he said between his teeth.

At the look on his face, a part of Nita's confidence returned and with it, her composure. "It has been a mistake, this marriage of yours," she told him, placing an urgent hand on his arm. "You cannot find love where there is nothing but coldness and distrust. You will admit it now when you see how she betrays you."

He flung her off angrily. "That's enough, Nita," he said levelly. "You'd better start collecting your belongings. Tomorrow I'll see you on the boat for New Orleans, where you'll be able to make connections to the island."

"You cannot send me away," she flared defiantly. "I shall tell Señor Jenkins, and he will stop you. I shall tell him, too, that you are an enemy and he will believe me. You do not want him to know about your father and the plantation. You have some terrible secret in you, which you keep from him and your wife. When I tell him this, he will know there is darkness and cruelty in you, Grant Monroe!"

"Have your luggage packed," he told her grimly, "and be ready to go at noon."

He was gone before she could reply.

CHAPTER SIXTY

Theodora found Paul in a celebrating mood. They visited the *Crescent* where he ordered champagne to be served below in the gaming room. She was not concerned as before by the thought that she would be recognized as Grant's wife. In her dissolving security and shattered sense of permanence, she had left the safety of conventional patterns and familiar inhibitions. Her very identity had become to her a nebulous unreality, and she was bent on escaping this formless monstrosity before she strangled in its overpowering grip. Having glimpsed the capacity for hell that lay in the human soul, she was driven to the desperate extremity of purposeless flight.

The heady wine was an added stimulant to the recklessness of her mood as the evening wore on. She watched Paul lose on the wheel, win, then lose again. She was dimly aware that he was playing with unaccustomed carelessness, and she was amused to see him squander money with such magnificent extravagance.

When he indicated a desire to leave, she demurred. "Once more," she urged. "You'll be lucky this time."

He laughed. "I know my limit," he said, taking her arm. "Let's go."

"But you've lost so much," she exclaimed. "You might start winning if you give it another try."

"I've learned to quit while I can still walk away," he said. "And I think we'd better leave, in any case. The place is filling with the late crowd. If we go now, there will be less chance of meeting someone we don't care to see."

He was on edge, fighting the vague foreboding that had been with him since the disappearance of the letter he had written to the president of Interurban. He had cursed his stupidity innumerable times. The fact that there had been no indication of trouble thus far did not ease his mind. Ed Miller had been hanging around when the letter vanished, and Nixon did not care to think what might ensue if the morning paper came out with the story.

He would be glad to get out of St. Louis to a Washington post, he thought uneasily. The strain of playing both ends against the middle in the local picture was beginning to tell on him. In the carriage, he gave the driver an address and Theodora turned to him inquiringly.

"I've ordered dinner for us at my apartment," he explained with a bland smile. "The landlady, bless her inquisitive soul, is away and there will be only Julius. But I highly recommend his cuisine. He can broil a steak to a delicate rarity that is unsurpassed."

She started to protest, but the words were never spoken. What did it matter? The glowing effect of the champagne was beginning to wear off, and her devastating wretchedness threatened to return with greater pain than before. To go home now where the furniture, the rugs, even the reflection of lamplight on the quiet walls reminded her of confused and hopeless misery was more than she could endure.

"I trust he handles a steak with dispatch," she retorted with an attempt at lightness. "I'm famished."

"I shall personally do what I can to expedite matters," he assured her. "But we won't have long to wait. Julius expects us."

His presumption in arranging the dinner without consulting her was annoying, but she gave no sign. Paul, content that the evening was still young, devoted himself to the art of sustaining a diverting conversation and she allowed herself to be entertained. All things became simple if one refused to think. And she was determined not to think, about later when the dinner was over and Julius had withdrawn, about tomorrow and the next day and the day after that.

But she was totally unprepared for what did happen. "A gentleman to see you, Mist' Paul," Julius said, opening the door for them. "He's in the sitting room."

"Wait in here," Paul told Theodora, indicating a door to her left through which she saw the gleam of silver and crystal on a candle-lit table. "I'll only be a moment."

But the aside was unnecessary. Grant stood in the doorway, watching them with inscrutable eyes. "Am I intruding?" he asked in a cool tone.

In that second, Theodora's world fell apart. Her hand flew to her throat and she stood unmoving, transfixed by an unexpected terror. She could read nothing in Grant's expression, but she knew the full implication of what this would do to him. Finding her here with Paul was an immeasurable blow to his pride. He had been betrayed in a way that was debasing, and she realized instinctively that no words of explanation would bridge the widening chasm of their estrangement now. Dimly she was aware that Paul was speaking.

"That will be all, Julius," he said. "You may go."

Paul looked at Grant, and all the innate shrewdness, all the presence of mind and instinct for self-preservation at his command was directed toward sizing up the man who confronted him. Underneath that layer of civilized equanimity, he knew, was the atavistic brutality of a man outraged. The thought of another man laying hands on his wife was always insupportable, and Paul was aware that Grant Monroe would retaliate with that swift, merciless hatred of which he was capable.

"I know what you're thinking, Grant," he said on a note of forced sincerity. "But you're wrong. Theodora spoke to me about her father, and I suggested that we talk it over at dinner."

Grant's eyes came alive then, flashing his contempt and violent loathing. "Rather noble of you," he said with stinging sarcasm, "to charge my wife with her share in this little affair. I take it you did not enlighten her about today's activities in the assembly?"

Theodora stared at him, then at Paul. In the faces of both, she read the truth. Interurban had been awarded the coveted franchise. Harlan was completely and ignominiously ruined, and the investments of all who had trusted him were wiped out. She understood then Paul's holiday mood and his extravagant amusement on the boat, and a frightful sickness grew in the pit of her stomach.

"You haven't any right to come in here with your accusations," Paul blustered, changing his approach. "If your wife enjoys an evening with someone else, why blame anyone but yourself? I thought it strange she didn't come to you with her problem. No doubt she would have, if your relations were what they ought to be."

Grant very deliberately reached for him. Half lifting him from his feet, he sent his fist crashing into the square, good-looking face. Theodora heard the dull impact of the blow and saw Paul go limp. Grant released him and he sank to the floor, huddled in the corner against the wall.

"You've killed him," she whispered, fighting the terrible nausea that swam about her in increasing waves.

"I think not," he said in a hard voice. "He is very much alive. When he revives, I imagine he'll be effectively reminded of our brief encounter. And I dare say his head will feel considerably worse after he reads tomorrow's papers. Shall we go?"

She went with him numbly into the enveloping darkness of the deserted streets. He did not speak again until he left her at the door of her own room. Then he said only: "Good night, Theodora. We'll talk another time."

CHAPTER SIXTY-ONE

Harlan Jenkins moved restlessly on his pillows. The shades were drawn against the morning heat, but the still air was thick with the humidity that had hung over the city all night. On the elm outside the window, not a leaf stirred. His tired eyes stared unblinkingly at the wall in front of him. He had to keep them open. When they closed, the past rushed back in vivid, ugly pictures, filling his brain with nightmarish flashes of scenes he had thought forgotten, torturing his eardrums with that accursed tune. It was better to remain awake.

The thought of the clippings he had hastily jammed into his coat pocket gnawed incessantly. He was convinced that by taking them out of their secret place he had released the last shackle of the unseen presence that stalked the house. He pushed back the covers and sat up. Thrusting his feet into the slippers on the floor, he made his way to the closet. His hand felt in the pocket of the coat. Yes, they were still there. He found his other clothes and dressed, panting slightly from the exertion.

Without stopping to rest, he went into the corridor and down the stairs. The morning paper lay face up on the stand. He was about to pass it when his eye caught the heading: *Interurban Plans Immediate Expansion.* He seized the paper in shaking hands and read that the rival company had secured the contested franchise rights for suburban development, and would begin laying the new lines at once. Harlan's disordered thoughts mulled about in frenzied incredulity and impotent anger. He started to crush the paper in his trembling fists, then stopped as he saw the second large headline announcing the graft expose in the city assembly. Nixon's incriminating letter revealing the two-way bribe deal in the traction negotiations was printed verbatim. The condition of the municipal government was termed shameful, and a strong demand was voiced for immediate action to clean out the corrupt politics of the city.

The full realization struck Jenkins with staggering force. Reed's downfall was a double blow. Jenkins would not only have to answer for his traction fiasco, but in the inevitable investigation of the city's affairs he would have to explain his dealings with the political boss. He had to get away, he thought disconnectedly. Leave St. Louis for a time. The uproar would die down eventually. Meanwhile he would need money. He cursed Reed's stupidity in taking the money from the vault to pay the combine before they fulfilled their part of the bargain. But no matter. Reed would have to pay up out of his private funds. He wouldn't dare refuse with the noose tightening momentarily about his own neck.

Jenkins didn't expect a generous sum, but whatever he could get he would use. The thought of reimbursing the investors, even in part, never entered his mind. They would have profited had the deal gone through, would they not? Their loss was a circumstance over which he had no control, brought on through no fault of his.

He went to the telephone to call Reed. Reaching for the receiver, he found it off its hook. That explained why there had been no calls, he thought grimly. Someone, Theodora or perhaps Grant, had taken the liberty of breaking the connection. He rang Reed's number, but there was no answer. Dropping the receiver, he made his way automatically to the study and closed the door behind him. It was some moments before he remembered the errand that brought him downstairs. Then he went directly to the row of books camouflaging the safe and flung them aside.

"Señor Jenkins!" Nita called from the other side of the door. "I thought I heard you come down the stairs a few minutes ago. Are you there, Señor Jenkins?"

He knew the girl would investigate whether he answered or not. With a smothered curse, he inserted the clippings in one of the books and replaced it on the shelf.

"Yes?" he said as the door opened and she entered the room. She had been weeping, he saw with curiosity, and he questioned her in spite of his preoccupation. "Is something wrong? You've been crying …"

Her lip began to tremble, and she drew on the emotional virtuosity that was always an effective weapon. She would show Grant, and she would laugh at him yet. She had slept badly during the night, and this morning, worn out by her tempestuous temper and fretful tossing, she had not awakened until late. But a substantial breakfast in bed, a luxury to which she had pleasantly grown accustomed, and a cooling bath had restored her confidence.

"I do not wish to trouble you," she said, her eyes brimming. "But Señor Grant says I must go this morning back to Cuba. I am so unhappy to leave!"

"He had no right to order you out," Jenkins frowned, irritated by this new problem at a time when he was overwhelmed with his own difficulties.

She wept profusely. "Oh, Señor Jenkins, you have been so kind, so very kind!"

"Here, here," he comforted her gruffly. "This won't do at all." He looked at her tear-stained face and a most startling thought occurred to him. "I have an idea, my dear," he said suddenly. "One which will solve your problem and prove eminently agreeable to both of us. I find that I must leave the city for a time on business, and you shall go with me. Together we'll have an incomparable holiday." He started to draw her to him, but she resisted.

"Señor Jenkins!" she protested. Unable to reflect upon this new turn of chance, she was assailed by a very real and practical fear. If this silly old man let his passion flare anew, one could not tell what might happen. The last near-disaster was all too clear in her mind. He might even die in her arms! The thought struck such terror into her imagination that she pushed him away with unnecessary violence.

He was thrown off balance and came up against the book shelves, his arm dislodging the volume which held the clippings. The book fell to the floor, scattering bits of frayed paper. Nita bent instantly, eager to placate him by this small service.

"I am so sorry," she apologized, gathering the clippings. "I was thinking only that you have not been well."

"I'll take those," he stated in vexation.

But she was staring at one of the yellowed slips. The faded likeness reproduced in the column was the last face she expected to see. This was a handsome man, younger than she remembered, his beard trimmed differently, his face strong and unlined. But she knew those features and quiet, intense eyes, and in her amazement she spoke the words on the tip of her tongue. "Why this ..." she began wonderingly. Then: "Yes, this is Señor Monroe. I would know him anywhere. But the name ..." Her words died as she read the dim newsprint beneath the picture. The account dealt briefly with the arrest of Will Patterson, a prominent St. Louis contractor, who was charged with the murder of city investigator Tom Lynch.

Jenkins had not moved. "What did you say?" he asked slowly.

"This man is Señor Monroe," she repeated in bewilderment. "Grant's father. But I do not understand. The name, Will Patterson ..."

The impact of her words finally reached him. Splintering fragments of memory showered his stunned brain with blinding force. Nita's comparison of the house to the place in Cuba, the limp she had described, that melody ... He had been blind not to have seen it before! And Grant. He moistened his lips slowly. He had been right, then, in his instinctive awareness of the threat that was slowly strangling him by its very nearness. He had been right in the conviction that Patterson had returned. He knew now the one detail he had overlooked, that slim, dark-eyed boy on the stairs. Patterson's son. Grant Monroe Patterson. The chair in the study, the changes here and there, the furniture as it had been before, all was calculated to corrode his nerves, to reduce him to imbecilic helplessness.

Nothing is uglier or more violent than animalistic terror in combination with uncontrollable rage. "This has all been a trick from the start, hasn't it?" he rasped, seizing Nita's shoulders with maniacal strength. "He brought you here to spy on me, to trap me!"

Nita was unable to cry out. Paralyzed with fear, she could only stare at him dumbly, a wordless prayer on her lips. The face pressing into hers was contorted with bestial passion and she knew that she might never leave this room alive. This horrible old man with his tattered newspaper clippings was beyond reason. If she were to tell him she was mistaken about the likeness ... But no, she had not been mistaken and they both knew it. Will Monroe had been the Will Patterson of St. Louis, a man accused of murder.

Yet there had been no murder in Will Monroe's past. One knew these things when one knew a good man. Tragedy, yes.

Disillusionment and bitterness perhaps, but not murder. This man, Harlan Jenkins, with his pale, glittering eyes and his carefully preserved record of that old story, did possess the violence and the perverted cruelty to take a life, she knew.

In a frenzy of effort, she managed to free herself from his bruising grip. Her only thought escape, she fled wildly from the study. In the upstairs room she had occupied the past four months, she dragged her luggage from the closets and began to cram clothes inside with helter-skelter abandon.

Theodora, coming from Harlan's empty bedroom, stopped at the doorway and watched in astonishment. The welcomed spectacle of Nita's departure preparations did not affect her as it might have a few weeks or months earlier. Even her curiosity was dulled, and her surprise neutralized by the automatic continuance of old responsibilities and habits.

"Father is not in his room," she said. "Have you seen him?"

Nita whirled at the sound of her voice, and her dilated eyes stared. "I ... I ... I ..." she began uncontrollably.

"What's wrong?" Theodora asked in a sharper tone. "Father was to remain in bed this morning. I hope he has not left the house?"

"He's in the study," Nita said, returning to her packing. "Nothing is wrong. He wants to be alone, I think."

Theodora's brows drew together in perplexity. "I wasn't aware that you intended to leave," she said presently. "Is there anything I can do?"

"No, no, I am almost finished. Señor Grant will call for me, and I shall be ready."

"You seem upset," Theodora said, forgetting Harlan for the moment. "What is it?"

Nita turned a second time. She was about to speak when she stopped. Grant's wife did not know of the unbelievable outburst in the study just now. She knew nothing of Grant's malevolent glitter as he sat at the bedside that strange night of Harlan's delirium, or of the deadly conflict between the two men. She did not guess the hidden strife in this quietly elegant house which would one day surge upward to devour the lives of those who remained here. Nita found herself pitying Theodora, this lofty, unapproachable woman whose marriage was a mockery, whose home was an ulcerating evil of old hatreds and unfinished spite.

"Do not distress yourself, señora," she found herself saying almost gently. "I leave today because it is what I want to do. I only wish now to thank you for the hospitality of your home."

"I'm glad you were at home here," Theodora told her uncertainly. "I shall think of you and hope that you find your happiness wherever you are."

"And I shall pray for you, señora," Nita said with spontaneous warmth. She turned her head. "That is the carriage, I think. Señor Grant will not like to be kept waiting. I shall go down now, and ask the driver to come for my bags."

"Rufus will carry them down," Theodora said, holding out her hand in a gesture of farewell.

Nita pressed it impulsively a brief instant, and was gone. Theodora waited until Rufus came for the luggage, then she moved to the windows overlooking the front drive. Nita was already in the carriage with Grant, and Rufus was installing the suitcases.

Oddly enough, Theodora felt no elation, no satisfaction, no sense of relief as they drove away. It was as though Nita had never been here. The room about her was as it had been when it belonged to Felice, as it was when they were children. Without quite knowing why, her mind returned to those old days as she stared across the sun-scorched lawn. Felice and Brad were small again, reciting their lessons at the small table in the nursery. She heard herself sternly insist upon repetition when Brad stumbled on the spelling lesson, and she saw Felice's dreamy gaze wandering restively to a bright pair of robins on the elm outside the window.

A sigh escaped her as she remembered the security of those days, the comfort of familiar problems and straightforward, easy solutions. But had they been easy? she wondered. Had she failed with their lives as well as her own? It had been simple enough to go by the stated rules. Her strong awareness of responsibility had been heightened by her father's remoteness, and in her aloneness there could be no compromise, no hesitation. In those days she never doubted the unwavering convictions, the strict adherence to moral formulas or the infallibility of sane and acceptable judgments. Only recently had the realization of complete failure and utter frustration swept aside the comfortable cornerstones of her life, leaving her with cruel and vulnerable uncertainties.

She brushed a damp strand of hair back from her forehead with a vague gesture. This was another hot, unbearably humid day. But there was an uneasy tension in the atmosphere unlike the inertia of the past two weeks. An impending sense of the inevitable seemed to come from the air itself. The hovering clouds were charged with an energy generated by the excessive heat, and they massed darkly against a green-tinted sky. Vagrant winds lifted dust from the road in sulphury spirals, but they brought no coolness. There was something she had to remember, she thought, prodding her bemused senses to weary activity. Father was below in the study. She ought to look in on him. She ought to persuade him to return to bed.

CHAPTER SIXTY-TWO

Grant returned to his office after seeing Nita on the New Orleans boat. But he did no work. For a long time he sat fingering a pencil and staring unseeingly out over the river sky-line. Each time he thought of Paul Nixon, a cold, furious outrage possessed him. The suave assemblyman was finished, he told himself violently. Nixon would not emerge from the local political upheaval to go on to further conquests in the nation's capital. That homage to the principles of honesty and party reform was of no use to him now, nor would it protect him in the days to come when his dealings with the combine would be thoroughly scrutinized in a court of law.

But Grant found nothing in the thought to ease his inner torment. Ironically, the accomplishment of his plan was crowned by the loss of the one happiness he had come to desire most in this life. He knew the Reed machine was smashed. Harlan Jenkins was broken in health and spirit, penniless and about to be hunted down by the wolf pack. The debacle would be complete, he thought coldly, when Jenkins learned the last of the truth, the identity of the man who had done this to him.

Yet the bitter futility refused to leave him. He remembered Lily, and her blunt advice to forget the past. He knew what she would say to all that had happened, and he wondered himself if any of it had been worth while. With a sudden movement, he snapped the pencil in his hand and tossed the splintered pieces into the wastebasket. Perhaps he should have allowed Theodora to spend the year abroad as she wished. But he thought he could win her trust and open the door to the kind of understanding and love he had hoped they would find together. He had gambled and lost. Theodora had gone to Paul deliberately, out of an enormous and compelling desperation. She had been willing to sell herself in the wild hope that she could save her father. Grant was not unaware of her efforts to influence Nixon in the past, but he had not remotely imagined that her frantic despair could lead to the destruction of all pride and self-respecting dignity. For the first time he began to comprehend the full extent of her loyalty, the intensity and depth of her affection for the man who was her father.

Abruptly he flung himself out of the chair and left the office. Returning to the street, he walked at random. He came to the church where he and Theodora had been married, and paused. Slowly he mounted the steps and entered.

The dignity and repose of the interior suddenly struck him with its timeless significance. In an architectural setting worthy of its liturgical services, each stained-glass window, each altar and candlestick, expressed the historical continuity of the church itself, the humanity of her teachings. The organist was rehearsing a *Te Deum,* and the poignant notes rose to the vaulted ceiling with unbearable sweetness. In scattered pews a few persons knelt to pray in quiet devotion before returning to office desk or factory bench.

Grant remembered those early, untroubled days when he had come here with his father, and through his mind flashed an almost forgotten thought. "The truths you learned from boyhood will warn you to forget ... to live among men without bitterness and contempt." Lily had written those words at a time when he needed strength and advice. He had not been able to accept them then. Now it was too late.

The organ music resolved in a final, sustained concord, then hushed. A tense and waiting expectancy hung in the air as the last echo faded. The man in the back of the church felt the invisible urgency in the stillness. It was not too late, he thought with suppressed excitement, but there was little time left, not a minute to waste. He remembered Theodora, and all at once he was seized with the need to go to her. He had to convince her that he would make up for what they had lost. He had to prove to her that there was still time, that they could have their happiness together. Roused by an inexplicable fear, he turned swiftly and left the church.

He glanced at the sky, aware suddenly of strange, erratic movements about the clouds overhead. He halted abruptly. While he watched, the darkening forms changed their course westward and swept toward the east across the dim, greenish sky. He was struck by a curious disturbance in the atmosphere. The air scorched and suffocated despite fitful winds that blew in chaotic frenzy. Dust and scraps of paper in the street blew southward; on the tops of buildings blackened smokestacks sent out thin streamers westward, and overhead in the green, sepulchral sky, vagrant clouds drifted to the north.

He returned to the office in less than five minutes and ordered his carriage. Then he picked up the telephone receiver at his desk and put through a call to the house. Almost at once he canceled it, remembering that he had disconnected the phone at home earlier that morning. He had the operator ring the weather office at the newspaper, and he listened intently at the ominous report that crackled over the wire. The barometer had fallen steadily since noon and the wind velocity was rising momentarily. He replaced the receiver and went to the outer office where he advised the others to wait out the storm where they were. Then he returned to the street.

CHAPTER SIXTY-THREE

Theodora made her way slowly down the stairs. In the hall below, she knew suddenly what had been eluding her memory. The newspaper had been left on the console table. She had neglected to hide it, thinking that Harlan would remain upstairs. Seeing it gone, she was galvanized into action.

At the study, she discovered that the door was locked. "Father!" she called in sharpening consternation. "Are you there?"

There was no immediate answer. Then as she continued to call and rap furiously on the door, he shouted angrily: "I'm busy, Theodora. Stop pounding on the door."

She bit her lip. "Are you quite certain you are all right?" she persisted.

"Quite," he roared.

She turned away, faintly reassured by the bellowing anger in his tone. Going to the dining room, she sat down to a tempting luncheon, but she ate only a thin slice of toast and drank part of a glass of chilled tea.

The maid removed the dishes, then returned. "I don't like to leave you this afternoon, ma'am," she worried. "Cook is off, and Reba went home to nurse her mother. You'll have nobody in the house to help care for Mist' Harlan."

"I'll manage," Theodora told her. "I'll take father a tray later when he's hungry. There won't be anything else to do until you return at five."

Theodora left the dining room. At the study she paused, listening. When she heard the shuffling of paper and a momentary scuffing of feet, she walked away. Continuing to the music room, she sat down automatically at the piano. Outside, the greenish sky had turned a deeper hue, and sickly clouds drifted in watery phosphorescence. The aqueous tinge pervaded the room suffusing the walls and the high ceiling with its poisonous glow.

She looked at the piano keys, glimmering dully in the pale light. Had she lost everything, she wondered numbly, even this? Experimentally her fingers sought a few chords, aimlessly found their way through several familiar passages and finally, carried by a volition of their own, plunged into the sweeping passages of moving harmonies and swift, poignant melody. How long she played she did not know. She had lost all sense of time when she became suddenly aware that she was not alone. Dimly she felt an element of subtle antagonism in the room, and the music died of its own accord.

Turning, she saw Harlan seated behind her, his large head thrust forward in its characteristic pose, the bloodshot eyes sunk deeply in their sockets. She was taken back by the ashen color of his face, the hunted look in the red-rimmed eyes. She had not noticed before how much weight he had lost. His clothes hung loosely on his hunched frame, and the hands clutching the arms of his chair were like knotted claws.

"I've fixed the company records," he told her in a rasping voice. "When the stockholders come, let them look and be damned to 'em."

"You know about the franchise," she said quietly. "I'm sorry you had to find out now. But it wasn't your fault. No one could foresee that the assembly would take matters into their own hands the way they did. Let me help you upstairs to your room now, and I'll bring you a tray."

No one could foresee it, eh? He was convinced that Grant had foreseen it. Interurban hadn't the funds to bribe the assembly without substantial help from some outside source. Grant had refused to lend him additional funds, and he could guess to what purpose Grant had put his money.

"Sit still, Theodora," he said abruptly. He was thinking rapidly. A crafty gleam lit his expression as he studied her shrewdly. In Theodora he had his only weapon. Her loyalty was unshakable. "You have been a devoted daughter, Theodora," he went on in an emotional tone. "I always knew that. What I didn't realize was the depth and accuracy of your intuition. You were astute where I was blind. You saw through the man we know as Grant Monroe, and I was wrong to ignore your warnings."

"Grant?" she asked in bewilderment. "Do you blame him for the loss of the franchise?"

An angry snarl contorted his features. "For that, and every other misfortune we've suffered since he came into our lives."

She paled at his vehemence, but said nothing. If words would ease the strain of his disappointment, she would listen as he talked it out.

"It began years ago," he continued, a plaintive note creeping into his voice. "I was threatened with ruin then, as now. A builder, Will Patterson, contracted to put up a new administration building for the city, and I handled the bonds and city funds allocated to the venture. Things went well until one of the city inspectors went over the books and threatened to expose certain shortages. Nothing came of it because he was found dead one night, shot through the heart."

The words came jerkily, in spasmodic haste and awkward pauses. He quivered with hidden excitement as the secret he had guarded so long found expression. Oblivious to the paralyzing shock that drained the color from Theodora's face, he went on, his tumbling, halting words gaining momentum. "In those days Reed was beginning to emerge as a power in St. Louis. He wanted the case closed in a hurry, and it was. Patterson was convicted and sentenced to die. That would have been the end of the story, but Patterson escaped on the way to prison. He fled the country after somehow locating his son, a boy of about twelve. That boy was Grant Monroe ... Patterson."

She had not moved as he spoke, and she scarcely heard the last. Staring at him, she remembered Brad's denunciation ... rapacious, unscrupulous, and evasive. She saw all that and more in the glinting eyes, the slack features and full mouth, twisted now into a cruel, mocking line. She remembered other things, her mother's request that Theodora look after her younger sister and brother, the trust fund she had left in Theodora's name. And she saw Harlan through the years, not as her pride wanted to see him but as he was, unapproachable and curt, warding her off with equivocations and deliberate subterfuge.

Now she said in a dead tone: "Patterson was not guilty?"

He scowled, thrusting his lower lip forward in the expression she knew so well. "He was convicted, wasn't he? Lynch was found a hundred yards from the house. This house, Theodora. Patterson's second wife lost her head and burned the books. I was with her when she did it, when she threw them into the fireplace so they could not be used as evidence. Only recently I learned that she was here in the city, living profitably as Lily Olandt."

There was a sharp silence. He realized then that Theodora had changed. He did now know how or why, but he sensed a difference. Instead of the instant support and unwavering faith he expected, her wildly staring eyes accused him. He saw revulsion and disillusionment in her face and he knew with a start that he could not lie to her again.

"It was one or the other of us," he whined. "What could you expect? I was trying to make things easier for your mother, for Brad and Felice and you. The money was for all of you. And Patterson was a fool. I could have saved him in the beginning, but he wouldn't make a deal. In his stupidity, he accused me of Lynch's murder. But I was too smart for him," he concluded, his voice trembling on an excitable pitch. "I was too smart for all of them."

"Lynch," Theodora said indistinctly, through the numbing confusion in her brain.

"Yes," he nodded, a pale fire leaping wildly in his eyes. "Lynch. Brad's married to that strumpet now, the old man's daughter. My own son turned against me. They've all turned against me. All but you. You'll remember, Theodora. You'll see that Grant pays for what he's done." He paused to let his words find their mark, then continued venomously: "He came back to destroy us. His marriage to you was part of a careful scheme to ruin all of us. He never loved you. Didn't he bring another woman into the house to flaunt in front of your eyes while he was plotting against me?"

She covered her ears with her hands in a frantic effort to stop the insidious flow of his words. Outside the sky had darkened, and the room swam in the weird green glow reflected from the heavens. Harlan's face with its demoniac hatred repelled her, and she averted her eyes. For the first time in her life, she knew the man before her.

"You were right when you said he wanted this place," the malignant recital went on. "This house was his father's, He got it back, but you can still take it away from him. Find out where he keeps his papers ..."

"Stop!" she cried frantically. "Stop! I won't listen!"

He watched her a minute in silence, then lifted himself from the chair. "You'll do as I say," he predicted. "You'll pay him back."

He left her then, and she heard him return to the study. Inside the music room, the stagnant air became intolerable. Each breath she drew seared her lungs with suffocating heat, and her clothing clung to her body in dank folds. She stood up and made her way to the dim hall. It would rain shortly, she thought dully. Clean, cooling, penetrating rain. Passing the study, she saw the door ajar. A lamp was burning, and Harlan was bent over the desk, examining an object she did not see.

She was unable to think clearly, nor did she try. She went on to the front door and outside where she leaned heavily against one of the pillars. A strong wind had risen and it whipped her skirts in a sweeping arc. The coolness was a welcome relief against her face and arms, and she closed her eyes in weary gratitude. She stood there, a minute, perhaps two, while the approaching storm bore down on the city.

Angry black clouds moved in from the west, their outriders of lightning forking earthward amid deafening peals of thunder. Between the reverberating crashes, she heard the single sharp, explosive shot from within the house. She knew instinctively what it was. Stunned by this ultimate horror, she did not move at once. A soundless scream rose in her throat, then a surging sickness, violent and terrifying. Slowly, painfully, she forced her wooden feet back toward the study, where she knew what she was certain to find.

But she never re-entered the house. She had gained the threshold when a shattering bolt of lightning ripped downward with blinding speed from the black clouds overhead, and found its mark in the heart of the mansion. She was thrown backward across the stone flagging where she lay in a heap, mercifully unconscious.

CHAPTER SIXTY-FOUR

Grant reached the street in time to see the gathering storm gain momentum. The clouds had ceased their aimless shifting and now flew swiftly to the west to join the lightning-shot mass forming beyond the fringes of the city. Luminous forks, sheets, and balls of fire flashed in its angry midst. The growing darkness was split for prolonged seconds by a blinding shaft of white light from the north, and the watchers in the street saw the rapidly growing funnel at the heart of the storm dip, reach, then spiral earthward.

Panic instantly broke loose and there was a rush for street-cars, buggies, and wagons. Grant saw his carriage turn the corner and he leaped inside, shouting to Rufus to hurry. The carriage swayed precariously in the increasing wind. Building signs were torn from their moorings, and telegraph and trolley wires crackled with flashing blue balls. The storm moved in on the city with darkness and sheets of rain. Lightning shot downward and blazes sprang up.

"We're not agoin' to make it in this storm, Mist' Grant," Rufus called out, struggling with the frightened horses.

"We've got to," Grant shouted back.

The full force of the wind was on them then, destroying everything in its path. With unexpected swiftness, the carriage was lifted and thrown against a nearby lamp post. The post fell, narrowly missing Rufus, splintering the shafts and wrenching the reins from his hands. The terrified horses reared and plunged, then fled wildly down the debris-strewn street.

Grant was momentarily stunned. When his head began to clear, he forced open the door of the carriage. Rufus was lying on the street, his head bleeding profusely from a bad cut. Clinging to the broken vehicle, Grant half pulled, half lifted the old servant inside. Making him as comfortable as possible on the floor boards, he used a kerchief to staunch the flow of blood, then settled back to wait out the worst of the storm.

"We been lucky, Mist' Grant," Rufus quavered. "God's lookin' out fer us now."

"The light pole has us pinned down," Grant told him. "There's a chance we'll be safe here."

The frame of the carriage swayed and creaked. Farther down the street at an intersection, a row of telegraph poles became flashing pillars of blue flame. In every direction, wires overhead were thin strings of fire, and insulators hissed and blazed. The air was filled with smoking brimstone and flying debris. The rising wail of fire engines added a further eerie note to the panic of the storm-lashed city.

Grant's face tightened as he waited in agonizing frustration. His fear for Theodora was acute. The quarreling, the countless small ways they had hurt each other, seemed incredible now. He thought how alike they were despite their surface differences and conflicting viewpoints. Theodora's reservoir of forthright courage and undaunted resolve was matched by his own capacity for inflexible determination and strength of purpose. They had inevitably been drawn together, and they were meant to be together always. He closed his eyes, seeing her face in its bewilderment and unhappiness, the colorless lips, the lifeless droop of shoulders that were once buoyant with spirited vitality, and the knuckles of his clenched hands showed white.

With headlong decision, he wrenched open the carriage door before the storm had spent itself. Lifting the servant's slight frame in his arms, he made his way to the nearest house. The door was opened immediately and a man led the way to a cot in one of the back rooms. A thin woman with three small children clinging to her skirts stood in the background, her face pale in the yellow glare of the gas jet which had been pressed into emergency service.

Grant satisfied himself that Rufus would be comfortable here until a doctor could be located. He left his name with the couple, and went back into the street.

CHAPTER SIXTY-FIVE

When Theodora recovered consciousness, the wind had quieted and a steady rain was falling. For minutes she was too dazed to move. Then recollection swept over her and she struggled to rise. Her head throbbed painfully and her body ached in every bone. She had to stand, she thought desperately. She had to go into the house, to the study. She gained her footing and leaned weakly against the nearest pillar.

Then she stared at the doorway in disbelief. Yellow flames were eating the casement, and great gusts of billowing smoke filled the gaping arch. She took a step forward and a blast of intense heat scorched her face. To enter the house through the front was impossible. The entire hall was a roaring furnace. From the lawn, she saw that the fire had already crept into the upstairs rooms. The study wing was nearly consumed, its walls and ceiling beginning to buckle. The lightning had found its mark.

She heard her name called, and turned to see Neil running toward her. A small throng of curious watchers had begun to collect on the street despite the heavy downpour.

Neil had Felice's raincoat over his arm, and he put it around Theodora's shoulders.

"We saw the fire," he said. "Is anyone in there?"

"Father," she said in a strangely quiet voice.

The orange glow of the flames played across the shadows, illuminating the lines and planes of her face with startling clarity.

In the weird light, her expression was lifted to the blazing mansion with a peculiarly exalted fervor.

Neil felt a chill of horror. "Good Lord!" he exclaimed. "Where is he? There may be time …"

She put a hand on his arm. "No," she said with finality. "Look."

Her gaze went to the study where the outer wall of bricks and beams hung for another instant, then crashed to the lawn. The luminous depths of her eyes reflected the living fire that filled the aperture and her breath came faster through the parted lips. A last involuntary shudder shook her body, then the ghost of a smile curved the frozen contours of her face.

She turned to Neil who had been watching her with increasing consternation. "I've an errand," she said composedly. "How can I locate a boardinghouse, one formerly operated by a woman named Lynch? Mrs. Tom Lynch."

"Theodora, are you mad?" he demanded in alarm. "You've got to come home with me. Felice will be worried, and we must tell her … what happened. Come along, you need dry clothes and something hot to drink."

"I'm going, Neil," she said with a curious calm, "to the boardinghouse."

"At least wait until you've rested," he said firmly.

"There's no time," she replied. "I may be late now."

"You can't go on foot and alone," he insisted, keeping pace with her. From the distance they heard the clang of fire engines hurrying here and there, and in several directions the reddish hue of the sky told of widely scattered fires. "Telegraph poles and trees are down, and there's no way of knowing how many buildings are afire. The streets are impassable. It was a tornado, Theodora. One of the worst storms of its kind."

"Don't argue with me, Neil," she said imperturbably. "I know what I have to do."

"At least let me look up the location of this place," he said in exasperation. "There's a directory at the house which will have it listed. Then I'll go with you."

"Very well," she said. "But hurry."

They were met at the door by Felice, Miles Hunter, and his wife. "What hapened?" Felice cried at once. "The house is on fire, we can see the flames from here! Where is father?"

"Father is dead," Theodora said unemotionally.

"Dead?" Felice repeated. "You mean he …? Father, poor father," she began to wail. Elizabeth Hunter moved to her side and put an arm around her shoulders.

"The address, Neil," Theodora reminded him tersely.

"I'll have it in a minute," he promised, turning away.

"Address?" Felice asked, raising her head. "What address?"

"I've a call to make," Theodora told her. "The Lynch girl is alone except for two elderly roomers, and she may need help."

Miles Hunter spoke for the first time. "You can't start out now, Theodora," he reasoned with kindly solicitude. "The streets aren't safe, even if you could find your way to this place. Better leave that work to the police and others trained to handle emergencies."

"I'm sorry," she said quietly, "but I must go."

"Theodora," Felice accused her, the green eyes glittering like jagged ice. "You're hiding something! Father has just met a horrible death, and you talk about calling on some girl we don't even know. Have you lost your senses?"

Theodora looked at her sister, and at the grave concern reflected on the faces of the retired banker and his wife. Strange, she thought dimly, that she had ever tortured herself with petty anxieties. It did not matter that Brad married Ann Lynch, the little shopgirl from the flower store in the arcade. Nor did it matter that Harlan had opposed the match or that the marriage had taken place under circumstances that would afford the malicious gossips ample material for scandalized whispers.

"Ann's baby is expected soon," she explained simply. "She is Brad's wife."

"Brad's wife?" Felice shrieked. "What nonsense is this?"

"They did not wish to announce the marriage until Brad finished at the university," Theodora stated calmly. "I scarcely think that makes any difference, however. Particularly at this time." She turned to Neil as he returned. "Do you have the street and number?"

"Yes," Neil frowned. "The place is on the other side of town. The carriage is coming around for us now."

"We'll start at once," she said, moving toward the door.

"Neil!" Felice said with peremptory suddenness. "You aren't going on this wild chase. That girl will have someone with her. If Theodora insists on tearing around at such a time, I won't have you going along!"

"There, there," Elizabeth Hunter soothed her. "You're all wrought up, poor thing."

Neil's face revealed the uncomfortable shock of his wife's words, but he did not hesitate. "Look after her, mother," he said abruptly. "We'll be back as soon as we find the address and check on the girl."

CHAPTER SIXTY-SIX

The way across the city was a twisted path of crumbling, flaming wreckage. The steady, pounding rain continued to fall, smothering countless fires but adding to the misery of rescue workers and victims. Neil and Theodora found their way blocked numerous times by fallen masonry, beams, and broken telegraph poles with their loosely swinging live cables. Once they stopped at an intersection and Neil leaped out to see if he could help the occupants of an overturned trolley. Theodora saw him remove the limp forms of the conductor and motorman, and one other. He covered the bodies with the motorman's torn coat and left them.

"Dead," he said, returning to the carriage. "The one pinned underneath was drowned, poor devil." He glanced at her profile, quiet and unmoved in the falling darkness. "Are you sure you want to go on, Theodora? The streets are dangerous with these split wires, and some of the buildings are still threatening to collapse."

"I'm going on," she said. "Let's try to hurry."

He signaled the driver, and they resumed their circuitous journey along the rubble-strewn, flooded streets. Nearly two hours passed before they reached their destination. The boardinghouse was intact, having escaped the worst of the storm with only a partially damaged roof. Theodora hurried up the walk ahead of Neil, and pounded on the door.

A thin-faced woman in her late sixties answered the summons. "Oh?" the woman said uncertainly. "I thought it was Sarah. She went to fetch the doctor ..."

"Ann?" Theodora asked crisply.

"She'll need a doctor soon," the woman said helplessly. "I don't know why Sarah isn't back ..."

"Take me to her," Theodora commanded. "Neil, see if you can locate a doctor, any doctor!"

"I'll find one," he promised with more assurance than he felt.

If Theodora had any doubts about the possibility of securing the services of a doctor in the crippled city, her face did not betray the fact as she entered the bedroom where Ann lay, flushed and breathing laboriously from the last fiery onslaught of pain. "You're not to worry," Theodora said with unaccustomed gentleness. "We'll have a doctor soon, and everything will go beautifully."

The girl on the bed stared at her first in disbelief, then with new hope. She tried to speak, but no words came. Theodora straightened the bedcovers with practical thoroughness, then drew up a chair and sat down. Ann's eyes were wet with tears of gratitude and incredulous relief. She started to sit up, but her body was again wracked with liquid fire. Her teeth bit into her lower lip as she fought the pain, but this time there was no panic. Theodora's hand, strong and steadying, poured its own vitality into the struggle of her being until she felt it lift her bodily from the depths of the torturing whirlpool.

"Don't try to talk," Theodora advised with quiet competency. "Rest all you can." To the older woman hovering anxiously near the bed, she said: "Bring her some hot tea. And put water on to boil. Kettles of it."

The second woman, Sarah, returned as Ann was sipping the tea. Theodora put aside the cup she had been holding and left the room to speak to her.

"There's no doctor to be had, miss," the woman told her. "They're all out. 'Tisn't likely one could get through in time anyway, with the streets tore up and the trolley lines dead."

"A doctor will be here in time," Theodora stated firmly. "For the present, there is nothing to do. I'll call if I need you."

She went back to Ann and took up the long vigil. For hours she prayed that Neil would return with a doctor, then she prayed only that the ordeal for the girl on the bed would end. Sometime during the night the rain stopped, but the two women in the tiny bedroom were aware of nothing but the slow passage of the heavy, reluctant hours.

Toward daybreak Ann's child was born, and a few minutes later Theodora looked up to see Neil standing in the doorway with a doctor.

CHAPTER SIXTY-SEVEN

Twenty minutes later Theodora rejoined Neil downstairs. "They are all right," she said with a tired smile. "Ann, and her son. The doctor will be down soon and you can drive him back. After that, I think you'd better return to Felice. She'll worry needlessly while you are gone."

"You're coming along, aren't you?" he asked.

"No," she said. "I'll stay a while longer to see that things go as they should."

Nor would she be swayed. Neil left with the doctor after promising to send the carriage back with one of the family servants to look after Ann and the infant. When they had gone, Theodora wandered into the shabby living room and sat down in a faded plush chair. The early morning sun streamed in through the ancient lace curtains onto the threadbare carpet and worn furnishings. A faint smile curved her lips as she leaned back wearily, gazing at the endless array of blue columbine on the soiled wall paper. For the first time in months she knew a warm and deeply satisfying relaxation. Her poignant awareness of Ann and the child asleep in the bedroom upstairs filled her completely, and for a time she was unable to think of anything else.

An almost forgotten melody went through her mind, and she smiled again, recognizing it as her own. Grant had been right, the love song was the best of her work. She had created it out of an understanding she had not known she possessed. At the thought of Grant, she closed her eyes. A host of unendurable memories overwhelmed her, and her anguish mounted as she was seized with new fears for his safety.

She rose abruptly and went to the kitchen where she found the two spinsters preparing breakfast. The pleasant aroma of freshly baked biscuits and steaming coffee was tantalizing. One of the women drew up a chair for her at the table, and she ate the breakfast they placed before her.

When she finished, she carried a tray upstairs. Ann was awake, and she ate hungrily, sipping the hot coffee with deep enjoyment. She asked to see the baby, and Theodora put the sleeping infant in her arms for a few minutes. Ann tried to thank her again, but Theodora brushed her words aside.

"I'll send a message to Brad as soon as possible," she promised. "The lines have been disrupted since the storm, but we may be able to send a wire tonight."

She left after telling Ann that Neil would be back with a woman to do the housework. When she had returned the tray to the kitchen, she got the mackintosh she had worn last night and started for the sitting room to await Neil's return. In the hall she turned, hearing the door open. Grant stood on the threshold, a Grant she had never seen before. He was unshaven, his face streaked with dirt and perspiration, his clothing torn and his hands blackened and swollen.

His relief at seeing her was obvious. "Theodora," he said, when she didn't speak. "The Hunters said you were here. I passed Neil on the way over, and he told me about Ann and the baby. Are you all right, Theodora?" She nodded mutely. "I spent most of the night getting home on foot, and when I saw the house ..."

He stopped, aware that she was not listening. Her eyes were fixed on his face, and he stared at her in growing wonderment, unable to believe what he saw there. Then she was in his arms and he was kissing her trembling mouth, stifling the heartbreaking sobs, and quieting the convulsive shudders with the reassuring pressure of his arms.

He did not tell her the rest until they were driving back in the carriage which the Hunters had lent him. "The house was completely destroyed. Part of it is still smoldering, but I was able to look around. Your father ..."

"He told me everything," she said in a low, controlled tone. "He found out about you. I think Nita finally made him realize the truth. He went back to the study, and I heard ..." Her voice broke, and she was unable to continue.

His arm drew her closer and for a moment he said nothing. He would have spared her this knowledge if she hadn't already known. "Arrangements for the funeral can be managed quietly," he said presently. "We're going away, Theodora, as soon as it's over. Abroad, if you wish. After a time we can forget, because you and I will never look back."

She knew with a deep and moving certainty that it would be as he said.

THE END

www.ingramcontent.com/pod-product-compliance
Lightning Source LLC
Chambersburg PA
CBHW030636020726
47493CB00006B/1747